the
brightonomicon

Also by Robert Rankin

The Brentford Trilogy:
The Antipope
The Brentford Triangle
East of Ealing
The Sprouts of Wrath
The Brentford Chainstore Massacre
Sex and Drugs and Sausage Rolls
Knees Up Mother Earth

The Armageddon Trilogy:
Armageddon: The Musical
They Came and Ate Us
The Suburban Book Of The Dead

Cornelius Murphy Trilogy:
The Book Of Ultimate Truths
Raiders Of The Lost Car Park
The Most Amazing Man Who Ever Lived

There is a secret trilogy in the middle there, composed of:
The Trilogy That Dare Not Speak Its Name Trilogy:
Sprout Mask Replica
The Dance of the Voodoo Handbag
Waiting for Godalming

Plus some fabulous other books:

The Hollow Chocolate Bunnies of the Apocalypse

The Witches of Chiswick

the
brightonomicon

Robert Rankin

Copyright © Robert Rankin 2005

First published in Great Britain in 2005 by
Gollancz

This edition published in Great Britain in 2006 by Gollancz
An imprint of the Orion Publishing Group
Orion House, 5 Upper St Martin's Lane, London WC2H 9EA

1 3 5 7 9 10 8 6 4 2

A CIP catalogue record for this book is available
from the British Library

ISBN 0 57507 773 5
ISBN 9 780 57507 773 7

Typeset at The Spartan Press Ltd,
Lymington, Hants

Printed in Great Britain by
Mackays of Chatham plc, Chatham, Kent

The Orion Publishing Group's policy is to use papers that
are natural, renewable and recyclable products and made
from wood grown in sustainable forests. The logging and
manufacturing processes are expected to conform to the
environmental regulations of the country of origin.

THIS BOOK IS DEDICATED TO
THE PEOPLE OF BRIGHTON
Who are renowned for their
sense of humour

AND ALSO TO DAVE AND DEE
Who suggested that I dedicate
this book to the people of Brighton,
and remind them of their sense of humour,
in the hope that they would not tar and feather me.

Prologue

It was the day before yesterday.

And I was dead.

I confess that I found this circumstance somewhat dispiriting, for I had always been of the opinion that a long and prosperous life lay ahead of me. To be so suddenly deprived of existence, and at such an early age, seemed grossly unfair and I determined to take the matter up with God at the first possible opportunity and register my extreme disapproval.

The opportunity, however, did not arise and I did *not* have words with the Divinity. Perhaps He had business elsewhere, or perhaps, in His infinite wisdom, He had already mapped out my future and was simply sitting back upon His Throne of Glory, observing the situation.

Or perhaps, just perhaps, He does not exist at all.

My death occurred on Saint Valentine's Day in the Sussex town of Brighton. Or more precisely two hundred yards off the coastline, in the chilly waters of the English Channel. I had travelled down from my native Brentford by train with my teenage sweetheart Enid Earles, hoping for a weekend of sexual adventure in a town that is noted for that sort of thing. I had even purchased, from Mr Ratter's jewellery shop in Brentford High Street, an engagement ring set with faceted glass that might well have passed for a diamond in uncertain light, my hope being to offer this to my love should she display any signs of hesitancy when it came to the moment of actually 'doing it'. Sadly, as it turned out, this ring was given up to the waves and my relationship with Enid never went beyond the platonic. Which is not to say that she did not indulge in the carnal pleasures upon that fateful weekend. Simply that she did not indulge in them with *me*.

We had taken, as I now recall so well, a stroll upon the Palace Pier, where I made some attempts to interest Enid in its architectural eccentricities. She yawned somewhat and I, in my innocence, took this to be a sign that she was eager for bed. I suggested that we take a drink or two in the pier-end bar before turning in (I confess to a degree of Dutch courage being required upon my part, for I was young and, though eager, inexperienced). Enid agreed and I ordered a Babycham for her and a large vodka for myself. And, as an afterthought, asked the barman to add a large vodka to Enid's Babycham also.

We were three or four drinks in when the unpleasantness occurred. This day before yesterday being in the nineteen sixties, Brighton was playing unwilling host to a large contingent of Moderns, or Mods as they were then called, and a goodly number of these young hobbledehoys were milling around in The Pier Bar. They wore gang-affiliated patches that announced them to be members of the Canvey Island Mod Squad. And one of their number – their leader, I presumed, by the nature of his arrogant bearing and loquaciousness – took an unhealthy shine to my Enid.

I have never been a man of violence and although I have always been sure that I would be able to 'handle myself' in a sticky situation, I was vastly outnumbered, and possessing not the martial skills of the legendary Count Dante, creator of the deadly art of Dimac, I suggested to Enid that we should take our leave, head for our rented room and get to know each other better.

Enid, however, did not seem too keen. In fact, she performed shameless battings of the eyelids towards the leader of the gang, who approached our table and made suggestions to Enid that were little less than lewd. I took exception to this and made certain suggestions of my own, mostly to the effect that this interloper should take himself elsewhere at once.

More than words were then exchanged, which resulted

in myself being hauled bodily out of the bar by several burly Mods and thrown from the pier into the frigid waters beneath.

It is well recorded that in those final, fleeting moments that precede the onrush of sudden death, one's life is said to flash before one's eyes, much in the manner of a movie of the biopic persuasion. This indeed occurred to me and I found the experience thoroughly disheartening. Whilst I am certain that those who have lived long and active lives receive a biopic of the Cecil B. DeMille persuasion, wide-screen and in Technicolor, I was treated to a brief black-and-white short, apparently shot on standard-eight stock with a handheld camera and directed by some inept film student with no concept of plot. It appeared that I had done nothing whatever of interest or note and that the substance of my life was destined to be filed away upon some high shelf in a dark corner of the Akashic Records Office, there to gather dust for evermore. Which was as dispiriting a prospect as the actual experience itself had been.

My final glimpse of life and the living was of the pier above and Enid looking down from it. The leader of the Canvey Island Mods had his arm about her shoulders. And Enid was laughing.

And then the waters closed above my head.

And I sank beneath them.

And I became dead.

And sought to take issue with God.

I have small remembrance of what happened next. I have vague impressions, but these take more unrecognisable forms than Gary Oldman.

I returned from death to find myself in a curious room, towels about my head and shivering shoulders, a crystal tumbler of Scotch in my trembling hand, a large and awesome figure towering above me.

'Who are you?' I managed to enquire.

'I am your deliverer,' he said.

'Are you God?' I asked. 'Because if you are, I wish to register my extreme disapproval.'

The towering figure laughed. 'I am not God,' said he, 'although in this life I am probably as close to being a God as it is possible to be.'

'Then I am not dead,' I said.

'But you were. I rescued you from the sea and applied certain techniques known only to myself in order that I bring you back to life.'

'The sea,' I said and took to the swallowing of Scotch.

'Gently,' said the towering figure. 'That is a fifty-five-year-old single malt from the cellars of Lord Alan Mulholland of Hove, to be savoured respectfully from the glass, not gulped away like workman's tea from a chipped enamel mug.'

I savoured and shivered and tried to take stock of my situation. My deliverer seated himself and I took stock of him also.

He was a considerable being, big and broad with a great shaven head, upon the crown of which was a tattooed pentagram. The face of him was heavily jowled, with hooded eyes and a hawkish nose of noble ilk. He was all over fleshy with a girthsome belly and colossal hands, upon which twinkled great silver rings engraved with enigmatic symbols. A suit of green Boleskine tweed encased his ample frame. Brown and polished Oxfords clothed his size-twelve feet. The collar of his shirt was starched, a red silk cravat was secured in place by an enamel pin with Masonic entablatures, and watch chains spanned his waistcoat.

There was indeed a 'period' feel to this mighty fellow, as if he had stepped straight from the nineteen thirties, and there was something more to him, also. A certain something. A certain . . . charisma.

'I have not introduced myself,' he said. 'I have been known by many names. The Logos of the Aeon. The Guru's Guru. The Greatest Man Who Ever Lived. The All-Knowing One. The Perfect Master. In my present

4

engagement, I am the Reinventor of the Ocarina. The Mumbo Gumshoe. The Hokus Bloke. The Cosmic Dick. The Lad Himself. So many appellations, and all falling short of the mark. My given name, however, is Hugo Artemis Solon Saturnicus Reginald Arthur Rune. But you may call me "Master".'

I savoured further Scotch and did noddings of my now bewildered head.

'And what might your name be?' he asked.

'My name?' I thought about this – indeed, gave it considerable thought – but my name had gone. I had no recollection of it whatever. I put down my Scotch and patted at my pockets.

'Searching for your wallet?' said Mr Rune. 'Lost to the sea, I suspect.'

'But I—' And I scratched at my towel-enshrouded head. 'I cannot remember my name. I have lost my memory.'

'It will no doubt return presently. More Scotch?'

I nodded bleakly and did rackings of the brain. I *had* lost my memory. I had no recollection of who I was, where I lived or indeed what I had been doing wherever I had just been doing it. Although I remembered something of the sea.

'You are in Brighton,' said Mr Rune, refreshing my glass, 'in my rooms at forty-nine Grand Parade. Our paths have not crossed by accident. We are all subject to the laws of karma. It is therefore certain that you would have found me sooner or later, but it is convenient that you should have done so now, rather than later, as it were.'

'I fail to understand.' I was shivering more than ever now and Mr Rune was coming in and out of focus. I was far from well, which was hardly surprising as I had so recently been dead.

'I do not think I can talk any more,' I said. 'In fact, I think I am going to—'

Pass out.

And I did.

I awoke the next time to discover myself in a cosy room. I lifted the covers of the cosy bed to discover myself naked beneath them. And for a moment I smiled somewhat, because now I did recall that I was in Brighton with a girlfriend whose name momentarily eluded me.

I turned to view this lovely and to make certain suggestions as to how we might begin our day.

But I found myself alone.

And bewildered.

And then the door to the cosy room opened and a great big man walked in. And the terrible circumstances of the previous night (well, some of them, at least) came rushing back.

'Mister Hugo Rune,' said I and took to shivering once again.

'Rizla,' said Mr Rune, 'I have brought you breakfast.'

'Rizla?' I said and I shook my head. 'I do not think that my name is Rizla.'

'So what might it be, then?' Mr Rune placed a tray upon a bedside table, a tray generously burdened with a fry-up of heroic proportions.

'My name is—' And my memory returned to me – not of my name, but of the memory that I could not remember it. So to speak.

'Fear not,' said Mr Rune, 'it will return. But for now Rizla is as good a name as any.'

'It's not,' I protested. 'It's a rubbish name.'

'It will serve for the present. Enjoy your repast.'

And he departed, slamming the door behind him.

I ate and I cogitated. The meal restored my body, but I remained troubled to my very soul. I did not know who I was, where I had been born, whether I had family or not. It was a horrible thing to experience and it brought me nearly to the point of tears. I maintained, however, a stiff upper lip. Of one thing I did feel certain: I was a brave young man, fifteen to sixteen years of age, by my reckoning, and I also felt certain that I would soon clear up the matter of my identity and return to wherever I had come from and into the arms of those who loved me.

Assuming that there *were* those who loved me.

I felt some pangs of sadness and doubt regarding this. Perhaps I was an orphan boy. Perhaps my childhood had been the stuff of horror. Perhaps I had done questionable things.

The door opened and Mr Rune stuck his overlarge head around it. 'Such thoughts will give you a headache,' said he, 'and no practical good will come from them. Finish your breakfast and join me in my study. We have matters to discuss.'

I did as I was bid, wrapped myself up in the bed sheet and joined Hugo Rune, who was sitting in his study. I had taken in certain details of this curious room upon the previous night, but now, with sunlight tumbling in through the casement windows, I was afforded a clearer view of it and absorbed fully its true and wondrous nature.

The room was well furnished with comfortable chairs of the Victorian persuasion and much period knick-knackery in the shape of mysterious curiosities. There were beasts encased by domes of glass that looked like mythical creatures to me, and there were canes and swords and muskets, too. I spied a brass astrolabe and numerous pieces of ancient scientific equipment, all brazen cogs and ball-governors. An ornate oak dining table surrounded by heavily carved Gothic chairs stood near a decorative drinks cabinet, and there were many, many leather-bound books on shelves and in piles and willy-nilly here and there and in sundry other places. One wall was all but covered by a great street map of Brighton, and upon this map were traced a number of figures resembling men and animals, following the lines of various roads, which put me in mind of pictures I had seen of the Nasca Plains. Which cheered me slightly, because it meant that there were some things that I could remember – books I had read, things that I had seen – although as to where and when, these details remained a mystery.

'What an extraordinary room,' I observed. 'You must surely have travelled all over the world to have amassed such an eclectic collection of ephemera.'

Mr Rune clapped his great hands together. 'Excellent,' said he. 'An articulate young man – a rare thing indeed in this benighted age. Sit yourself down next to me.'

I settled myself into the comfortable chair with which I had made my acquaintance the previous night. 'I still feel unwell,' I said. 'And I think I should not be taking up your time. As soon as I am dressed I will be off upon my way. If you saved my life, sir, then I thank you for it, but I must go now and somehow find out who I am.'

'And how do you propose to go about this?' Mr Rune held a schooner of sherry in one hand, and although I felt that it was somewhat early in the morning to be drinking, clearly he did not. He tossed the sherry down his throat and repeated, 'How *do* you propose to go about this?'

'I will call in at the nearest police station and report myself missing,' I declared.

Mr Rune laughed a big laugh deep from his belly regions. 'That should be entertaining,' he said. 'I hope you won't mind if I accompany you to the police station. I have some business there myself.'

'I have no objections whatever,' I said.

'Good,' said he. 'Good. But before we do so, let me suggest to you that we don't.'

'Oh?' said I. 'And why not?'

'Well,' said Mr Rune, 'if, as has already troubled your mind, you have loved ones, they will surely shortly report you missing. Would you not think this probable?'

'I would,' I said.

'Then perhaps you should wait for them to do so. Keep an eye out for articles in the newspapers regarding missing persons. Wait for your photograph and name to turn up.'

I made doubtful sounds.

'Perhaps you need the toilet,' said Mr Rune.

'They were not those kind of doubtful sounds.'

'Pardon me.'

'I still think the police station would be the best option.'

Mr Rune did noddings of the head. 'The policemen might fingerprint you,' he suggested.

'They might,' I said.

'Which could prove calamitous should you turn out to be a criminal on the run from justice.'

'I am no criminal!' said I and rose from my chair, losing both my bed sheet and my modesty in doing so. I hastily retrieved the sheet and took to re-covering myself.

'Are you absolutely certain of your innocence?' Mr Rune arched a hairless eyebrow. 'Perhaps it is fortuitous that you have forgotten who you are. Perhaps you do not wish to remember your name.'

'Nonsense,' I said. 'I am no criminal. I know that I am not. I am honest, me. I would surely know if I was not.'

'You might not be being honest with yourself.'

'I want my clothes,' I said. 'I want to leave.'

Mr Rune set his empty glass aside and took to the filling of the largest smoking pipe that I felt certain I had ever observed.

'You're not *really* certain about anything,' he said, looking up at me between fillings. 'I have an offer that I wish to make to you. As I told you last night, I do not believe that our paths have crossed through chance alone. I do not believe in chance. Fate brought you to me. I saved your life and I did so that your life should receive a purpose that it previously lacked. Throw in your lot with me and I can promise you great things.'

'What manner of great things?' I enquired.

'Great things of a spiritual nature.'

'I do not think that I am a particularly spiritual kind of a fellow,' I said. 'I am a teenager and I do not believe that teenagers are noted for their spirituality.'

'Would a financial incentive alter your opinion?'

'I wonder whether I already have a job,' I wondered aloud, 'or whether I am still at school.'

'All will eventually resolve itself. Of that *I* am certain.'

'Look,' said I, 'I appreciate the offer, but I do not know

9

you and you do not know me. On this basis alone I feel that the throwing in of our lots together might prove detrimental to both of us.'

'One year,' said Mr Rune. 'One year of your life is all I require.'

'*One year?*' I said. 'That is outrageous.'

'One month, then.'

'My memory might return at any moment,' I said.

'Indeed it might,' said Mr Rune, 'but I doubt it.'

'Hold on,' I said. 'You're not a homo, are you?'

Mr Rune now raised both hairless eyebrows simultaneously and then drew them down to make a very fierce face. 'Sir,' said he, 'no man calls Rune a homo and lives to tell the tale.'

'No offence meant,' I said.

'And none taken,' said Mr Rune, calming himself. 'Some of my closest acquaintances have been of that persuasion. Oscar Wilde—'

'Oscar Wilde?' I said.

'One month,' said Mr Rune. 'A month of your time. Should your memory return to you within this period, then, should you choose to do so, you may go upon your way.'

I must have made a doubtful face, although of course I could not actually see it myself. 'I am assuming that you are offering me employment,' I said. 'What *exactly* and *precisely* would the nature of this employment be?'

'Amanuensis,' said Mr Rune. 'Chronicler of my adventures, assistant, acolyte.'

'Acolyte?' I put a doubtful tone into my voice to go with the look I felt certain I was already wearing on my face.

'I am set upon a task,' said Mr Rune, 'a task of the gravest import. The very future of Mankind depends upon the success of its outcome.'

'Oh dear,' I said, softly and slowly, in, I felt, befitting response to such a statement.

'Never doubt me,' said Mr Rune. 'Never doubt my words. During the course of the coming year I will be presented with twelve problems to solve, one problem per month. Should I solve them all, then all will be well. Should I fail, then the fate that awaits Mankind will be terrible in the extreme. Beyond terrible. Unthinkable.'

'Then it is probably best that I do not think about it.' I rose once more to take my leave, clutching the sheet about my person.

'I can promise you excitement,' said Mr Rune. 'Danger and excitement. Thrills and danger and excitement. And an opportunity for you to play your part in saving the world as you know it.'

'I do not yet know it as well as I would like,' I said. 'I think I should be off now to get to know it better.'

'Go,' said Mr Rune. 'Go. I evidently chose poorly. You are clearly timid. You would be of no use to me.'

I was already at the door. But I turned at the word 'timid'. 'I am not timid,' I said. 'Careful, perhaps. Yes, I am certain that I am careful. But certainly not timid.'

'You're a big girlie.' Mr Rune rose, took himself over to the drinks cabinet and decanted more sherry into his glass. 'Be off on your way, girlie boy.'

My hand was almost upon the handle of the door. 'I am not timid,' I reiterated. 'I am not a big girlie boy.'

'I'll pop around to the labour exchange later,' said Mr Rune, returning to his chair and waving me away. 'Put a card up on their help-wanted board: "*Required, brave youth, to earn glory and wealth*", or something similar.'

'I *am* brave,' I protested. 'I know that I am brave.'

'Not brave enough to be my assistant, I'm thinking. Not brave enough to be my *partner* in the fight against crime.'

'Crime?' I said. 'What do you mean by this?'

'Oh, didn't I mention it?' Mr Rune made a breezy gesture, the breeze of which wafted across the room towards me and right up my bed sheet, too. 'I am a detective,' said he, drawing himself to his feet. 'In fact, I am *the* detective. I solve the inexplicable conundrums that baffle the so-called experts at Scotland Yard.'

'You are a policeman?'

'Heavens, no. I am a private individual. I am the world's foremost metaphysical detective.'

'Like Sherlock Holmes?'

'On the contrary. He was a mere *consulting* detective and he would have been nothing without me.'

I raised an eyebrow of my own. A hairy one.

'Go,' said Mr Rune. 'I tire of your conversation.'

'No,' I said. 'I am *not* timid. I *am* brave. And I am *not* going.'

'You wish then that I should employ you?'

I chewed upon my bottom lip. 'I don't know,' I said.

'Timid *and* indecisive,' said Mr Rune.

'Count me in,' I said.

'You will be required to sign a contract.'

'Count me in.'

'In *blood*.'

'Count me *out*.'

1

The Hound of the Hangletons

The Hangleton Hound

PART I

I did sign Mr Rune's contract, *and* I signed it in blood.

I don't know exactly why I did it; somehow it just seemed to be the right thing to do at the time. Ludicrous, I agree; absurd, I also agree; and dangerous, too, I agree once again. And perhaps that was it – the danger.

I did not know who I was.

I did not know who Mr Rune was.

And even now, some one hundred years later as I set pen

to paper and relate the experiences and adventures that I had with Hugo Rune, I cannot truly say that I ever actually knew *whom* or, indeed, *what* he *really* was.

Although——

But that *although* is for later.

For the now, from that day before yesterday to which I had been returned from the dead, I inhabited rooms at forty-nine Grand Parade, Brighton, in the employ of Hugo Artemis Solon Saturnicus Reginald Arthur Rune, Mumbo Gumshoe, Hokus Bloke, Cosmic Dick, Lad Himself and the Reinventor of the Ocarina.

And he and I were bored.

Perhaps the life of ease and idleness had never appealed to me. Perhaps I had never experienced it before and therefore did not know how to appreciate it properly.

Perhaps, perhaps, perhaps.

On the day that I had signed Mr Rune's contract, with blood drawn from my left thumb, he had taken me off to the tailoring outlets of Brighton and had me fitted with several suits of clothes. I recall that no money exchanged hands during these transactions and that there was much talk from Mr Rune about 'putting things on his account'. And much protestation from the managers of the tailoring outlets. But somehow we gained possession of said suits of clothes and I became decently clad and most stylishly clad, also. Which Mr Rune explained was just as one should look when one engaged in regular dining out.

Dining out was evidently one of Mr Rune's favourite occupations. The man consumed food with the kind of gusto with which a *Blue Peter* presenter might consume cocaine.* Mr Rune really knew how to put the tucker away. And he did it, as he did everything else, with considerable style. Although, sadly, he enjoyed the most rotten luck when it came to restaurants. No matter where we dined, and I recall that we never dined in the same restaurant twice

* Allegedly.

14

for reasons that I will now explain, the outcome of each meal was inevitably the same. Mr Rune would fill himself to veritable excess, consuming the costliest viands upon the menu, along with the most expensive wines on offer, and would sing the praises of the chef throughout the consumption of each dish.

And then, calamity.

We would be upon our final course – the Black Forest gâteau or the cheese and the biscuits – when Mr Rune would be consumed with a fit of coughing. I would hasten to his assistance, patting away at his ample back and thereby mercifully sparing him a choking as he coughed up a bone.

A rat bone!

I genuinely felt for the fellow. How unfair it was that it should always be *he* who suffered in this dreadful fashion, *he* who appreciated his food so much, who chose only to dine in the most exclusive restaurants. Our evening would be well and truly spoiled. Words would be exchanged, harsh words on the part of Mr Rune, words which included the phrases 'a report being put in to the Department of Health' and 'imminent closure of this establishment'.

On the bright side, I never saw Mr Rune actually pay for a meal; indeed, on occasion he received a cash sum in compensation for the unfortunate incidents. And, hearty and unfailingly cheerful as the man was, he always wore a smile when he and I walked away from the restaurant in question.

We dined out, and we purchased clothes and sundry other necessities, mostly of an extravagant nature, and always 'on account', but if the solving of crime was Mr Rune's *métier*, then it appeared that either there was no crime at all upon the streets of Brighton to be solved, or that it was all being amply dealt with by the local constabulary. No one, it seemed, required the talents of 'the world's foremost metaphysical detective'.

I had been with Mr Rune for three weeks now and I was

no nearer either to recovering my memory or to aiding him 'to solve the inexplicable conundrums that baffle the so-called experts at Scotland Yard'. Although I had heard him play the ocarina many times.

Upon this particular day, an unseasonably sunny day in March, Mr Rune and I lazed in deckchairs upon Brighton beach enjoying the contents of a hamper that had recently arrived from Fortnum and Mason, for which Rune had failed to pay cash on delivery due to some oversight upon the part of his banker that would be dealt with at the earliest convenience.

'I do not wish to complain,' I said to Mr Rune, 'for I am certainly enjoying my time with you and I am sure that I have never been so well dressed and well fed in my life, but I do recall you saying that you would have cases to solve, the outcome of which would save Mankind as we know it, or some such thing.'

'I will pardon your lapse from articulacy upon this occasion,' said the Logos of the Aeon, adjusting his sunspecs and straightening the hem of the Aloha shirt he was presently sporting, the one with the bare-naked ladies printed upon it. 'I assume it to mean that you are presently piddled.'

'Are you suggesting that I am drunk?' I enquired.

'You have imbibed almost an entire bottle of vintage champagne, one of the finest that salubrious establishment, Mulhollands of Hove held in their reserve stock.'

'You drank the first bottle without offering me any.'

'The thirst was upon me. I abhor inactivity.'

'That is what I am talking about. Where are these exciting cases of which you spoke? What about the danger and adventure?'

'Marshal your energies, for these things will shortly come to pass.'

'But when?'

Rune drew in a mighty breath and sighed a mighty sigh. Bare-naked ladies rose and fell erotically upon his bosom. 'No one knocks,' said he. 'I would confess to perplexity if I did not bow to inevitable consequence and fortuitous circumstance and understand how the transperambulations of pseudo-cosmic anti-matter shape the substance of the universe.'

'I have no idea what you are talking about,' I said. And I did not.

'All right,' sighed Mr Rune. 'Cast your eye over this and give me your considered opinion. Your *considered* opinion only – do we understand each other?'

'Not very often,' I said and snatched at the object that Rune tossed in my direction. It was an envelope.

'I retrieved it from my post-office box this very morning,' said the Cosmic Dick, by way of small explanation.

Rune had previously opened the envelope, so I removed its contents – a letter – and read it aloud:

Dear Mr Rune

I saw your advert in the *Evening Argus*, that you 'offer satisfaction to those cheated of justice by the British legal system, the constabulary in particular' and that you 'specialise in crimes that are above and beyond the ordinary'. Well, I have one for you.

I am a breeder of rare canines; indeed, my family has been so for several generations. We are well known for it in these parts. And famous, too, having won many ribbons at Crufts – two First Places, a Best in Show and a Wettest Nose three years running. My husband Neville didn't want me to contact you. He says that you blokes don't know sh*t from sugar—

'What is "sh*t"?' I asked Mr Rune.
And Mr Rune told me.
'Oh,' I said. 'Well, that is cr*p, in my opinion.'
'Continue reading the letter.'
I did so.

17

But I want this sorted. It's not right, this kind of thing, and someone should do something about it. I hope you can.

Yours sincerely,
Aimee Orion (Missus).

'What do you make of it?' Mr Rune asked, as he acquainted himself with a jar of pickled quails' eggs.

'Seems a bit vague,' I replied. 'It does not actually say what crime has been committed.'

'Oh, come now.' Mr Rune leaned over to me and snatched back the letter. 'It says a great deal more than that.'

'It does?' I asked. 'What does it say?'

'It says, for one thing, that it was not written by a woman.'

'It does not? Or rather, it does? Does it?'

'You *are* piddled,' said Mr Rune. 'This is written in a man's hand.'

'It is *type*written,' I said.

'Exactly.'

'What?'

'Lost dog,' said Mr Rune. 'Or, more accurately, stolen.'

'A lost dog. That is not much of a case.'

Mr Rune tapped his nose. And did so with the quails' egg jar, spilling vinegar all down his front. The bare-naked ladies looked even more appealing when wet.

'You intend to track down a lost dog?' I reacquainted myself with the champagne bottle, or more accurately sought to, as Rune had drawn it beyond my reach and was guzzling freely from its neck.

'Call me a cab,' said Mr Rune.

'You are a cab,' said I, giggling foolishly (I confess it).

'Buffoon,' said Mr Rune. 'What do you know of Hangleton?'

'Hangleton?' I scratched at the knotted hankie that adorned my head to stave off sunstroke.

'Hangleton,' said Mr Rune once more. 'The address at the top of the letter. Hangleton.'

'Sorry,' said I. 'I did not read the address. But I have been to Hangleton. I have wandered all over Brighton during the last three weeks, in the hope that something would stir my memory. Hangleton is a rather nice place, lots of nineteen-thirties-style houses. They even have their own loony bin.'

'Suggestive,' said Mr Rune.

'I am not,' said I.

'Call me a cab.'

'It's not funny twice.'

'Do you have a mobile phone?'

'Obviously not,' I said. 'They have not yet been invented.'

'Details, details.' Mr Rune raised his left hand. Upon the promenade above, a cab slewed to a sudden halt. 'Bring the hamper,' said the Hokus Bloke. 'We are travelling to Hangleton.'

The cab conveyed us to Hangleton. The cabbie, a truculent fellow who rejoiced in the name of Jonie and supported Newcastle United 'no matter what, and the Devil take the man who says otherwise', discoursed upon the nature of cheese throughout our journey, lingering long upon its supposedly medicinal qualities and how his wife's gout had been cured by Gouda.

Mr Rune sat passively throughout both journey and dis-course, occasionally drawing melodic notes from his reinvented ocarina, and only raised the stout stick that he always carried with him and struck down the cabbie when, upon reaching our destination, the surly fellow had the effrontery to protest about Mr Rune's suggestion that the fare be put on his (Mr Rune's) account.

'You knocked him unconscious,' I said, as we strolled along Tudor Close, the midday sunlight prettifying the mock-Tudor houses, clipped box hedges and front-garden ornamentation.

'Gouda for gout, indeed!' said Mr Rune in a mocking tone, 'It's Roquefort for gout and Gouda for goitres. I can't be doing with a cabbie who is ignorant in The Way of the Cheese.'

'I have to agree with you there,' I said. 'I think this must be the house.'

'Why?' Mr Rune asked.

'Because of the big sign in the front garden saying "Dogs R Us".'

Mr Rune nodded approvingly. 'And that sign brings to mind something that I should have mentioned to you earlier – to whit, the Chevalier Effect.'

'And what might that be?' I enquired.

'An effect most pertinent. You will find that when you come to write up your memoirs of our time together – memoirs which, be assured of this, will become an international bestseller – certain details will become subject to the Chevalier Effect.'

I did thoughtful noddings of the head, at which Mr Rune rolled his eyes.

'Allow me to explain, in as few words as are necessary,' said he. 'It will be many years before your book is published, and when it is, some reader will take issue with the accuracy of what you have written. They will feel absolutely certain that there were no establishments called "Something Or Other R Us" in the nineteen sixties.'

'Then they will be wrong,' said I, 'because we are standing before just such an establishment even as we speak.'

'Precisely,' said Mr Rune. 'Such contradictions are due to the Chevalier Effect.'

'Is it like the Greenhouse Effect?' I asked.

'No,' said Mr Rune. 'It is not. But the same reader will also observe that the term "Greenhouse Effect" was not coined until later in the twentieth century either.'

'I hate to contradict this historically inclined future reader,' I said, 'but I think you will find that I have just mentioned the Greenhouse Effect.'

Mr Rune nodded sagely. 'I agree completely, young Rizla,' he said. 'So kindly open your ears and mind to what I have to tell you.'

I did my best to do these things, and partially achieved them.

'The Chevalier Effect is named after the popular entertainer Maurice Chevalier, and the famous song that he sang.'

'"Thank Heavens For Little Girls"?' I enquired. 'I believe it has always been my opinion that there is something not altogether wholesome about the French.'

'I share this opinion,' said Mr Rune. 'But the song I am referring to is "I Remember It Well" from the motion picture *Gigi*, sung by Maurice Chevalier and Hermione Gingold.'

'I know the song,' I said. 'It is about two people recalling the night they first met, but they cannot agree on the details and contradict each other throughout. To somewhat mild comic effect, I have to say. I consider Bernard Cribbins's "Hole In the Ground" far funnier.'

'I share this opinion also,' said Mr Rune. 'The Chevalier Effect is to do with the decay of time. Once an event has occurred and becomes memory, decay sets in and things run together. Folk recall the event differently: some see it this way, some that way.'

'That is because some of them are right and some of them are wrong in their recollections,' I assured the Perfect Master.

'Incorrect,' he replied. 'They are *all* right. It is the decay of time that is to blame, not their faltering memories.'

'They cannot *all* be right,' I protested. 'An event can only occur one way. We are either standing outside an establishment called Dogs R Us, or we are not. Which is it?'

Mr Rune gave his nose a significant tap. 'When you write your memoirs of our time together, there will be many such anomalies. You will be certain that, for example, a certain song existed at the time, or a certain newspaper, or a certain television personality. Or indeed, that a certain establishment was called Dogs R Us.'

'Which it is,' I said.

'Which it is,' Mr Rune agreed. 'But when you hand your manuscript to a publishing editor, that esteemed personage will take issue with the accuracy of your revelations. They will say that such and such a person did not do such and such a thing in the nineteen sixties. They will doubt the authenticity of your account of events, based upon these anachronisms.'

'Then I will leave them out,' I said, 'or let the publishing editor change them.'

'You will *not*!' cried Mr Rune, and he drew himself up to his full and improbable height. 'You will insist that they remain and you will explain about the Chevalier Effect.'

'That sign definitely does say Dogs R Us,' I said.

'Then you will stick to your guns, young Rizla. I have faith in you.' Mr Rune plucked leaves from the hedge and let them fall to the pavement. 'And now I will explain to you *exactly* how the Chevalier Effect works, so that you may set it down in your chronicles to explain all the seeming anomalies and anachronisms.'

And so Mr Rune did. He spoke with erudition, using terms easily understandable by the layman. And I do have to say that when he had reached his conclusion, I, for one, was truly convinced and would number myself amongst the converted. Because, after all, *I* was *there* and that sign *really did* say Dogs R Us!

I *would* set down here all that he told me, but to do so would be to waste precious time. However, the reader may rest assured that everything chronicled within the pages of this international bestseller did indeed occur as written. And that all the seeming anomalies – indeed, anachronisms even – that appear, such as in Chapter Four with the mention of alcopops, gay icons and certain dead rock stars, are not there due to poor editing; rather, they are there because they *were there* at the time. Due to the Chevalier Effect.

Which explains everything.

Obviously.

'So,' said Mr Rune, 'now that we have cleared *that* up, there is one further thing I must warn you about. In this case, as in others, there is bound to be a spaniel involved.'

'I have no fear of spaniels,' I said, and I crossed my heart as I said so, to add weight to my words. 'Spaniels hold no dread for me. Big soppy things, they all are.'

'On that we are both agreed. But I promise you that there will be spaniel involvement, so remain vigilant and always upon your guard.'

'You are surely joking?'

'I never joke,' said Mr Rune. 'I jibe, I mock, I ridicule, but I do these things only to be cruel to be kind. You have a big spot on the back of your neck, by the way. Here, take this and pin it to your shirtfront.'

'What is it?' I asked.

'A badge,' said Mr Rune.

'It has the head of a spaniel upon it,' I observed.

Mr Rune gave his great nose a significant tapping. 'A word to the wise,' said he. 'Wear the badge with pride. And keep both your ears and your eyes wide open.'

I pinned the badge to my shirtfront, avoiding, by sheer luck alone, severe nipple puncturation. 'Shall we go and knock on the door?' I asked.

'To what end, exactly?'

'To summon the woman, or man, who wrote to you.'

'Ah,' said Mr Rune. 'Of course, you do not – as yet – know my methods. We will *not* knock on the door. We will wait for our client to come to us.'

'I am confused,' I said. 'And I feel a bit of a ninny wearing this badge. What are those garden gnomes doing, by the way?' And I pointed to the pair of gnomes that had caught my attention.

'Copulating,' said Mr Hugo Rune. 'Now duck your head.'

'Why?'

'Just duck it.'

I ducked as requested, registered a loud report and felt a searing of my sun-blocking headwear.

'Ouch,' was what I had to say.

'Keep your head down,' said Mr Rune. 'We are being fired upon.'

I crouched in the shelter of a clipped box hedge. I tore my hankie from my head and examined it. To my horror, it had been scorched along its length by the passage of a bullet.

23

'By Crimbo,' I exclaimed. 'I have been shot.'

'You are unharmed.'

'Shot!' There was horror in my voice. 'You promised me excitement, but not an untimely death. Are such unwarranted attacks a day-to-day occurrence with you?'

'Plah!' said Mr Hugo Rune. 'I trust that you are not going to panic.'

'On the contrary. I only seek to retreat to a safe distance. Possibly London. Farewell.'

'Timid,' said Mr Rune. 'As I feared.'

'Gunman,' said I. 'Have fear of him.'

'He wasn't firing at us.'

'No? At whom, then? And look at the state of my hankie – it is ruined.'

'Wave it above your head.'

'And that will help, will it?'

'Just wave the hankie – higher now, that's right.'

'I am so sorry, I truly am.'

'I did not say that,' I said.

'I didn't think that you did,' said Mr Rune, and he rose once more to his considerable height.

'I truly am so sorry.'

I rose to what height I myself possessed and gazed towards the apologist, who stood on the other side of the clipped box hedge.

Now, as I have said, Mr Rune was tall, tall was Mr Rune, and big around with it, but the fellow beyond the hedge was taller still. Tall was he, and all over gaunt.

I looked up at the tallster and I was most impressed. And then I said something I should not have said, because I was still upset. 'You nearly shot my bl**dy head off, Rasputin!' I declared.

'Bl**dy?' said Mr Hugo Rune.

'Rasputin?' said the tallster.

'Yes,' said I. 'You look like Rasputin, with that gaunt face and big black beard and long black cloak and everything. And you shot me. I demand that you pay for a new headkerchief.'

24

The blackly bearded tallster blinked at me with his deeply set cadaverous eyes, opened his mouth to expose twin rows of pointy teeth, then closed it again with an audible snap. A rooftop pigeon took flight and a dog howled in the distance.

And then many more howled close at hand.

'My apologies once more,' said the tall, gaunt fellow. 'It was an accident, I assure you. I was cleaning my fowling piece by the window when a spaniel nudged my elbow.'

I glanced towards Mr Rune, who grinned at me and winked.

'Mister Neville Orion?' he then said, putting forward his hand above the hedge for a shake. 'My name is Hugo Rune. I received your letter this morning.'

'*My* letter?' said Mr Orion, ignoring the proffered hand.

'Indubitably.' Mr Rune withdrew his unshaken hand. 'I suggest that you do not take up forgery as a second occupation. The signature of your wife was most unconvincing.'

I viewed the face of the long, thin fellow. Deep in the shadows of their sockets, his eyes were veritably twinkling.

'Excellent,' said he. 'Pray, come inside.' And he indicated the front-garden gate.

The howling of the close-at-hand hounds had not yet abated and I made a doubtful face.

'They are caged,' said Mr Orion. 'Follow me.'

I followed Mr Rune, who followed Mr Orion. Mr Orion followed the garden path and this led us all to the house. The hallway led to a front sitting room and soon we were sitting within it.

It was your typical suburban front sitting room, with a typical settee and matching armchairs. There was a typical standard lamp, a typical plant in a typical pot, a carpet that was absolutely typical and a tank containing typical fish.

'Actually, they are *tropical* fish,' said Mr Orion.

'They appear to be dead,' I said.

'Typical,' said Mr Orion. 'I expect the wife forgot to feed them. Would you gentlemen care for a cup of tea, or would you prefer something stronger?'

'Something stronger will be fine,' said Mr Rune, idly drumming his fingers upon the typically embroidered arm-socks of his chair.

Mr Orion called out at the top of his voice, 'Bring rope, woman,' he called. 'And don't try fobbing our guests off with string.'

Presently, a most glamorous woman appeared in the doorway, bearing a tray that was anything but typical, it being a tray that had no bottom and such slender sides as to be almost no sides at all. There was plenty of top to this tray, however, and upon this rested three lengths of rope. The woman presented the tray and its cargo to Mr Hugo Rune.

'There, sir,' she said.

Mr Rune nodded thoughtfully but made no motion towards accepting the tray. His eyes were upon the woman – indeed, upon her breasts.

Now, these were, for all this world and whatever lies beyond it, a most remarkable pair of breasts. Clearly of an independent nature, they sought escape from the constraints of both bra and blouse and appeared to be upon the point of gaining freedom.

Mr Orion made impatient toe-tappings. 'I suggest we get down to business,' he said.

'And clearly a most remarkable business it is, too,' said Mr Rune, finally accepting the tray and hauling his eyes from the breasts of Mrs Orion. 'These ropes, although clearly strong, appear to have been ripped apart.'

'Precisely,' said Mr Orion.

'Not bitten through,' said Mr Rune.

'This was my conclusion.'

I gave my chin a bit of a scratch – it needed a shave, which I found encouraging as I was hoping to grow a fashionable goatee as soon as I was able. This talk of rope, however, perplexed me.

'I am perplexed,' I said.

'Silence, Rizla,' said Mr Rune. 'This is no time for idle chitchat. Watch, listen and, hopefully, learn.'

'I would not mind a cup of tea,' I said.

'Janet,' said Mr Orion to his wife, 'take young Rizla here to the kitchenette and give him tea.'

I glanced towards Mr Rune.

'Go,' said he.

I followed Mrs Orion to the kitchenette. She was wearing a very short skirt, that woman was, stretched over a lovely bottom. Her legs were rather lovely too, and I decided that I must habitually harbour a fancy for women who wore stiletto heels, because I certainly harboured one now.

I did not take much to the kitchenette. There were no units, nor labour-saving devices, nor even a cheese press, a butter churn, a yoghurt stretcher or a cream fondler, nor indeed any other artefact requisite to the refinement or processing of dairy products. I considered the mincer to be of an inferior design, one which in itself would have saved no labour whatsoever, and the rubber tea towel holder beside the sink was sorely perished and in need of replacement.

But these things were neither here, nor there, nor any place other to me.

'You'll have to mime the drinking of the tea,' said the lovely Mrs Orion. 'The kettle's on the blink and the milkman hasn't delivered today. The world is coming to an end and there's a fact for you to be going on with.'

'I do not think it is quite *that* bad,' I said.

'The optimism of youth,' said Mrs Orion.

'I have half a bottle of champagne in my hamper here,' I said, indicating the Fortnum's hamper, which could so easily have vanished from my possession due to poor continuity, but had not. 'If you have two glasses, we might finish it off.'

'You are a little ray of sunshine.' Mrs Orion reached up to a high shelf in search of glasses, then, finding none, bent over to seek at floor level.

I looked on approvingly.

'He hides them,' said Mrs Orion. 'He doesn't trust glasses. Never trust anything that you can see right through, he says. Hates air with a vigour – he wouldn't breathe at all if he didn't have to.'

'Perhaps they are on that *very high* shelf,' I suggested. 'You could climb up on that kitchen stool and look.'

They were *not* on the very high shelf. But to be absolutely certain, I persuaded Mrs Orion to take a second look. And I looked on approvingly.

'We'll have to use tea cups,' said Mrs Orion. 'There are some dried-on tea leaves in the bottoms, but from what I know of Tetleymancy*, they foretell moderate good fortune for at least one of us.'

I opened up the hamper, took out the champagne, uncorked the bottle and decanted some of it. 'What is all this business with the rope?' I asked the lady of the house.

'A horrible to-do,' she said. 'The police are baffled, which is why I had my husband write to Mister Rune. If anyone can sort this out, it's him.'

'Is Mister Rune famous, then?' I asked.

Mrs Orion shrugged. 'I've never heard of him,' she said. 'Inspector Hector gave me his name.'

'Inspector Hector?' I said.

'Of the Brighton constabulary.' Mrs Orion sipped at her champagne. 'He said that Mister Rune left a pile of flyers on the front desk of the police station, advertising his services as a metaphorical detective.'

'*Metaphysical* detective,' I said. 'And this Inspector Hector personally recommended Mister Rune?'

'Well, not as such. He did say that the case was right up Mister Rune's street. And he said that he'd carelessly thrown away all the flyers, but Mister Rune's advert was sure to be in the local paper amongst all the others for "personal services". And he said something else.'

'Go on,' I said.

'He said that if I met up with Mister Rune, I was to mention the matter of the twenty guineas he had borrowed from Inspector Hector and has yet to pay back.'

---

* Divination by tealeaves, as if you didn't already know.

'Right,' I said. 'More champagne?'

'Well, it does go straight to my head.'

'I will refill your cup, then.' And I did so. 'Am I to understand,' I asked, 'that you have lost a dog? Is that what this case is all about? The one that has the police baffled and Inspector Hector recommending the services of Mister Hugo Rune?'

'Not lost,' said Mrs Orion, supping further champagne and hiccoughing prettily, 'but stolen. Our prize-winning Spanikov.'

'Spanikov?' I said, feigning the pouring of champagne into my own cup and giving Mrs Orion's a further topping-up.

'It's a rare Russian breed of spaniel, probably the only one of its kind in the country – maybe even in the world.'

'Very valuable, then?' I brought out the jar of pickled quails' eggs and unscrewed its lid.

'Those are funny-looking onions,' said Mrs Orion.

'The dog,' said I, 'this Spanikov – is it a very valuable dog?'

'Very valuable and very big, too.' Mrs Orion dug her fingers into the jar and speared a quail's egg with her lengthy thumbnail. 'Almost the size of a horse.'

'A *horse*?' I said. 'A spaniel the size of a horse?'

'Well, a Shetland pony, perhaps, but there's no telling, is there? It's like a pig.'

'It looks like a pig?'

'No, that's not what I mean. I mean there's no telling how big a pig can grow. They're always slaughtered when they reach a certain age, so there's no telling how big a pig might grow if it escaped into the wild and lived out its natural lifespan. Which might be anything up to three hundred years, like a tortoise.'

'A tortoise?' I said.

'I heard,' said Mrs Orion, drawing me closer to her and whispering in a conspiratorial tone, 'of a pigman who lived in Henfield, just north of Brighton, back in the Victorian days. He kept a pig in his barn, didn't kill it. When he died, his son took on the responsibility – it was in the old man's will, you see. And then the son of the pigman's son took it on, and so on. They say that the pig still lives, and that it is the size of an elephant now.'

I shook my head. 'I think you are piddled,' I said.

'I think so, too. Is there any more champagne?'

'There certainly is.'

I refilled Mrs Orion's cup and her free hand leaned upon my shoulder as I did so. She smelled very nice, did Mrs Orion, and her freedom-loving bosoms pressed against my chest.

'Come,' called the voice of Mr Rune. 'Rizla, come.'

Mrs Orion fluttered her eyelids at me. 'I think you might have been about to,' she whispered.

I reluctantly gathered up the Fortnum's hamper and grudgingly withdrew from the kitchenette.

'I think I should further question that woman,' I told Mr Rune as we stood together in the hall.

'Have you forgotten so soon the matter of her husband's fowling piece?'

'Perhaps we should go, then. Have you learned all that you wish to learn? As it were.'

'It is a case that falls into the inexplicable-conundrum category.'

'It is a lost – or stolen – dog. Hardly anything to get excited about, surely?'

Mr Rune brought his stout stick down hard on to the hall floor. 'Farewell to you, Mrs Orion,' he called.

A hiccough was returned to him from the kitchenette.

I sighed and said farewell to Mrs Orion also.

And Mr Rune and I took our leave.

The sun shone as cheerfully as ever. Birdies twittered in treetops, a ginger tom sleeping upon a windowsill dreamed of Theda Bara, and as the cabbie had yet to awaken from the blow Mr Rune had dealt him earlier, the Mumbo Gumshoe suggested that I shift his unconscious body into the passenger seat and place myself at the steering wheel of the taxicab.

'Drive us home, Rizla,' said Mr Rune, settling himself in the back. 'I shall take a nap. Awaken me when we're there.'

'I do not know how to drive,' I said. 'At least, I do not think that I do.'

'Then now would be a good time to learn.'

'In a stolen car?'

'You are a teenager, aren't you? That's the way most teenagers learn to drive.'

'I am quite sure it is not.'

'Details, details. Apply yourself, lad.'

I shook my head, turned the key in the ignition and pressed my foot to various pedals until I received a noisy response. The taxicab, however, did not move.

'I think you'll find there's a handbrake involved, and also a gear lever,' said Mr Rune, drowsily.

'Do *you* know how to drive, then?'

'Certainly not. There are two kinds of person in this world: those who drive and those who are driven by them. I am, needless to say, one of the latter.'

I released the handbrake, stamped my feet on to various pedals and pushed the gear lever forward. And then we were off.

I really cannot see what all the fuss is about driving – why you need to take a test and get a licence and suchlike. I soon mastered the basics of the procedure. I scraped along a few parked cars and I did run over something that I suspect was a cat – it was certainly not a Spanikov, given its diminutive proportions. I suppose it might have been a hedgehog. And I eventually discovered the brake. In the nick of time, some might say, in particular the woman in the Morris Minor who screamed at me that I was on *her* side of the road when I discovered it. Then I ran the taxicab into the dustbins at the rear of forty-nine Grand Parade, which I will swear to this very day jumped out in my path.

This collision awakened the cabbie.

I awakened Mr Rune and we quickly took our leave of the taxicab.

★

'You were evidently born to drive,' remarked Mr Rune when we were once more safely ensconced within his rooms. 'I will hire a car for you to chauffeur. It will expedite matters regarding our travel. And spare my shoe leather.'

'Make it a Rolls-Royce, then,' I said, as I had indeed quite taken to the driving.

'Flashy,' said Mr Rune. 'A Bentley, perhaps. I shall look into the matter. But first this case.'

'Lost dog,' I said. 'Hardly worth the bother, surely.'

'The dog is merely the tip of the iceberg.' Mr Rune sought Scotch. 'Are we out of whisky?' he asked. 'Pop over to the offy and fetch more.'

'I have no money. You have yet to pay me.'

'You have yet to earn your keep. I provide you with free room and board. What ingratitude.'

'Regardless, they will no longer serve me at the local offy,' I said, 'because I do not wear black.'

'Black?' Mr Rune tried in vain to wring Scotch from the empty bottle.

'New management. It is the "Goth Licence" now. You have to wear black to get served.'

'Outrageous,' said Mr Rune. 'And you wasted the last of the Mulholland champagne upon Mrs Orion.'

'I think she fancied me.'

'Let us apply ourselves to the task in hand, to whit—'

'The lost dog.'

'The dog is the tip of the iceberg. The iceberg itself is the Chronovision.'

'This is altogether new,' said I. 'What in the names of the Holies is a Chronovision?'

'It is what I seek, and what I will inevitably find once I have solved the twelve tasks that lie before me.'

'The finding of a lost dog being one of these tasks?'

'I sincerely believe so, yes.' Mr Rune had located a bottle of port and this he uncorked, sniffed at and then decanted with care into a brace of glasses. 'Let me tell you about the Chronovision,' he said as he passed a glass of port to me. 'It

32

is better that you understand the situation now. There will only be confusion later if you do not.'

'I may not be around later,' I said. 'I agreed to stay with you for one month only.'

'You never did read the small print on that contract you signed, did you?'

'Ah,' said I.

'The Chronovision,' said Mr Rune, settling into his great big chair and tasting the port. 'A fascinating contrivance – and one, should it fall into the wrong hands, that would seal the fate of Mankind.'

'Ah,' said I once more. 'We are back on that subject again, are we?'

'It is the subject that consumes me. It is what I am.'

'Go on about this Chronovision, then. What does it do?'

'Quite simply,' said Mr Rune, 'although there is nothing simple about it, it is, in effect, a television set upon which one can view events that happened in the past.'

I laughed heartily at this.

'It is no laughing matter,' Rune said sternly. 'The man who possesses the Chronovision becomes, through its possession, the most powerful man on Earth.'

'I doubt very much whether such a device exists,' I said. 'It is the stuff of science fiction, like *The Time Machine*.'

'Mister Wells's Time Machine functioned well enough. And I should know – I helped him to construct it.'

'The last time you made a remark such as that, I told you that I was leaving,' I said. 'Would you care to hear me tell you this once more?'

'Allow me to explain.' Mr Rune raised his stout stick and I, out of politeness, allowed him to continue.

'The inventor of the Chronovision was Father Pellegrino Maria Ernetti,' said Mr Rune. 'He was a Benedictine monk, an expert in archaic Latin texts and Gregorian chants. A scant decade ago, he was working in the experimental physics laboratory at the Catholic University of Milan. You would be surprised if I told you about some of the experimentation that goes on there. Well, Father Ernetti was filtering harmonics out of certain Gregorian chants he had recorded when he heard the voice of his deceased father. He had somehow tuned to the frequency of the past. A great deal of further experimentation led him to the creation of the Chronovision, a device that, as I have said, resembles a television set, but upon which it is possible not only to hear events that occurred in the past, but witness them also. There is no mumbo-jumbo involved in this – it is science, it is physics.'

'It is c*bblers,' I remarked.

But Mr Rune continued, unperturbed. 'Father Ernetti demonstrated the Chronovision before Pope Pious the Twelfth. This is a fact; it is recorded in Vatican records. The Chronovision was tuned to the correct frequency and the Pope viewed the crucifixion of Christ upon the Chronovision's screen. He was amazed. But he soon became horrified.'

'I would have thought that he would have been chuffed,' I said, 'to know for certain that there had been a Jesus Christ, I mean. Not that I think I really believe in—'

'Silence,' said Mr Rune. 'The Pope was filled with horror because he understood the Chronovision's potential – what would happen should it fall into the wrong hands.'

'So what would happen? Surely if this were true, it would be the greatest scientific discovery of this or any other age. A Nobel Prize-winner for the scientific monk. To actually view the past, to see the events of history – every home should have a Chronovision, surely.'

'Absolutely not! The Pope understood the ramifications. Father Ernetti had tuned the Chronovision to the resonant frequency of the Pope; as a result of the succession of Popes, their lineage goes right back to Saint Peter, who walked with Christ, and who was present at the crucifixion. The image upon the screen was the one seen through the eyes of Saint Peter.'

'Yes,' I said, 'but I still do not see the problem.'

'The Chronovision can be tuned to anyone's personal frequency. We each have a unique resonance. If it was turned to your frequency, it could replay events that you witnessed and took part in three weeks ago.'

'Brilliant,' said I. 'Then I would know who I am.'

'Not brilliant,' said Mr Rune. 'If you can tune the frequency to the resonance of *any* individual on the planet, then you can see that person's past. That person can have no secrets from the man who tunes the Chronovision. Do you understand now?'

'Ah,' I said. 'You mean that should some dictator gain possession of it, he could uncover everything about the past of any individual on Earth. Any individual – is that correct?'

Mr Rune nodded. 'The Pope understood this and the terrible implications of it. He ordered the Chronovision dismantled, packed into boxes and placed under lock and key in the vaults of the Vatican, alongside the Ark of the Covenant and the Holy Grail.'

'Easy now,' I said. 'But if this is all really true – and I do agree that there is something about it that almost has me believing you – then the Chronovision is safely stashed away and that is that.'

'Would that it were so.' Mr Rune tasted further port and shook his great head sadly.

'It was stolen,' said I, 'from the Vatican vaults – that is it, is it not?'

Mr Rune nodded grimly. 'More than a year ago. It would never have come to my attention – indeed, the Chronovision's existence would never have come to my attention – had not the Pope and I been out on the razz and he, having imbibed too freely as is his habit, spilled the entire business out to me.'

'*You* know the Pope?' I said.

'We are the greatest of friends.'

'This is ludicrous.'

'What? Do you think that the Pope has no friends?'

'I am not saying that, but I find it difficult to believe that you are one of them.'

'And why might this be?'

I stared at Mr Rune.

And do you know what? For the very life of me, I could not think of a single reason as to why it might not be.

'You are a chum of the Pope's?' I said.

'Probably his bestest friend. It was me who suggested that he join the priesthood. He wanted to become a professional football player, but between the two of us, he had a weak left foot.'

I shook my head. 'So, hold on,' I said, 'are you presently being employed by the Pope to retrieve the Chronovision from whoever stole it?'

'Absolutely not. He did not recall in the morning that he'd told me anything about it. When I have located the Chronovision, I will destroy it. And then my work will be done.'

'Incredible,' I said. 'Ludicrous, but also incredible. But I fail to understand how finding a lost dog is going to help this noble cause of yours.'

'The dog is the tip of the iceberg, as I have told you, several times.'

'You told me, but I still fail to understand.'

'That map there, on the wall.' Mr Rune pointed. 'I have seen you peering at it many times. Have you fathomed it yet?'

'No,' I said. 'I have not. It appears to be a large-scale map of Brighton, but it has all kinds of figures drawn all over it, following the patterns made by the roads. A bat, a cat, a horse – I think.'

'And the head of a dog,' said Mr Rune, 'in the Hangleton area of Brighton. You will observe that the house we visited was in Tudor Close, in the very eye of the hound.'

'Oh,' I said. 'And that is significant, is it?'

'Most,' said Mr Rune. 'Entirely. This map is the means by which I will discover the Chronovision's location and achieve my goal – its recovery and destruction. If the Chronovision is the single most significant discovery of this century, then what is drawn upon that map must rank as number two.'

'So what is it?' I asked.

'It is my discovery, young Rizla. The figures you see traced on to that map are the Carriageway Constellations, the work of a Victorian magician who influenced the Brighton Borough Town-Planning Committee to lay out the roads and byways of Brighton to a particular pattern, one that would later be discovered by myself. There are twelve figures, you see. Each represents a case or conundrum that we together must solve in order to acquire the Chronovision. What you see before you on that map, young Rizla, is the Brighton Zodiac.'

Mr Rune paused, awaiting applause.

I raised my glass and said, 'Can I have another drink?'

PART II

All right. I was not impressed. Perhaps I should have been, but after the tale of the television set that enabled its viewer to witness scenes of the past, the Brighton Zodiac seemed a bit of a disappointment. And, you might think, hardly something upon which to end a chapter.

But then, this is *my* account of the events that occurred and if *I* feel that that is where the chapter should end, that is where the chapter will end! And in the light of events that were soon to occur, please be assured that I know what I am talking about.

After all, *I was there*!

'The Brighton Zodiac,' I said. 'Well, blow me down.'

'You are singularly unimpressed,' said Mr Hugo Rune, 'but then you have yet to understand its significance.'

'Well.' I shrugged. 'I suppose I will have to take your word for it.'

Mr Rune sighed mightily. 'I am confiding in you matters,' said he, 'that I have never confided to another soul. I am doing so because in a future time, indeed, a far future time, you will write these matters down, indeed, compose them into a book that will become a bestseller.'

'Do you really think so?'

'I have no doubt of it. The past and the future are one and the same to me. I am Rune, whose name is legend. Rune who fathoms the unfathomable. Rune who makes the impossible a strong probability. Rune—'

'I hate to interrupt,' I said, 'but about this Brighton Zodiac—'

'Ah yes. The key to it all. Allow me to explain.'

'Please do.'

'Back in the nineteen twenties, there existed a notable lady by the name of Kathleen Maltwood. She was a native of Glastonbury and also a visionary. She had the gift of overview: she could see beyond the everyday, glimpse the bigger picture – a gift that I possess to overabundance. It was her conviction that imprinted upon the landscape about Glastonbury was a great zodiac, formed from the rivers and hills, the roads and the natural features. She studied aerial photographs of the area and she joined the dots, so to speak. She discovered the Glastonbury Zodiac.*

'Ten years ago, another lady, one Mary Caine, put forward her belief that if the Glastonbury Zodiac existed, then so too should the Kingston Zodiac, surrounding the area where the ancient Celtic kings were crowned. She studied the Ordnance Survey maps of the surrounding territories and she, too, found her zodiac.†

'I am Hugo Rune,' said Mr Rune, 'and so it was inevitable that I, too, would find *my* zodiac.'

'But what does your zodiac have to do with the Chronovision?'

'Good question,' said Mr Rune, and he savoured more port and stared through the window to where Brighton was going about its business.

'Go on, then,' I said. 'Tell me.'

'Shan't,' said Mr Rune. 'Not right now anyway, for I have told you enough. More than enough.'

'There is one other thing,' I said.

---

* And she did – look her up on the Internet.
† And yes, she did, too. Look her up as well.

Mr Rune yawned and blew upon his fingernails. They had recently been manicured at a local beauty boutique. I had seen the unpaid bill upon his desk. '*Hand job £10*', it said. Quite expensive, for a manicure.

'About the Chronovision,' I said. 'Do you even know in which part of the world it might be at present?'

'Of course I do.'

'Would you care to enlighten me?'

'Young man,' said Mr Rune, 'enlightenment is my middle name. From the Vatican vaults I tracked its journey across Europe. It is presently here, right here in Brighton.'

'If you know this much, then why not seek it out straight away? All this piecing things together through a series of cases seems somewhat long-winded and overly circuitous.'

'You have no understanding of the situation. The felons who brought the Chronovision to Brighton are dead. They died in a freak accident involving concrete and deep water. But I shall have it. I shall have it before—'

'Before what?' I queried.

'Before *he* can lay his evil hands upon it.'

'Now *who* would this *he* be?' I queried further.

'My archenemy. Holmes had his Moriarty and I have him. He is probably the most evil man who has ever lived and were he to gain control of the Chronovision, then—'

'Yes,' I said. 'Doom and gloom and the end of Mankind as we know it.'

'And things of that nature generally.' Mr Rune had somehow finished the bottle of port now, without giving me a second glass. 'He is the most evil man who has ever lived. His name is Count Otto Black.'

The sun went in behind a cloud and a dog howled in the distance.

'The Hound of the Hangletons,' I declared.

'Buffoon,' said Mr Rune.

'All right, all right.' I rose from my chair and sought out the case of lager that I had secreted behind the sofa. 'Just let me get all this straight in my mind. A Benedictine monk invents a kind of television set that can tune into events in the past. He demonstrates it to the Pope. The Pope panics and has it locked away in the Vatican vaults. It is stolen. You track the thieves to Brighton, but they die in mysterious circumstances involving concrete and water and the present whereabouts of the Chronovision is unknown. But you are certain that it is still in Brighton and that through solving certain cases connected with the figures of a zodiac that you have discovered, you will be able to locate the Chronovision and destroy it before your archenemy, Count Otto Black, aka The Most Evil Man Who Ever Lived, gets his claws upon it and brings about the overthrow of Mankind.'

'As near as makes no odds,' said Mr Rune. 'Toss me over one of those cans of lager, if you will.'

'I will not,' I said. 'I am taking them with me.'

'Where to?'

'Anywhere but here,' I said. 'To use the popular parlance of the day, you are doing my head in, Mister Rune.'

'And so you are thinking to depart?'

'I am not thinking about it, I am doing it.'

'And our contract?'

'Sue me,' I said. 'You never know, I might turn out to be the son of a noble household. Perhaps even a prince or something.'

'Mostly likely a *something*,' said Mr Rune. 'But if that is your decision, then do what you must. I will be here when you return, in—' he drew out his golden pocket watch and perused its face '—precisely three hours.'

'I will not be back,' I said.

'You will,' said Mr Rune.

'Will not,' said I.

'All right,' said Mr Rune, 'I'll make a deal with you. If you do come back—'

'Which I will not,' I said.

'But if you do, then you must swear to assist me throughout all the cases that I have to solve in order to retrieve the Chronovision.'

'Oh yes?' I said. 'Then I will tell you this: if I do come back here, I promise, on my life, that I will do so.'

'Then it's a deal,' said Mr Rune. 'You will return and the case of the Hound of the Hangletons *will* be solved. All in three hours.'

'I will not be back,' I said, and went off to pack what few belongings I possessed into a pillowcase.

'I really will not,' I repeated as I rejoined Mr Rune.

'Not me,' I said as I made for the door.

'This is the last you will see of me,' I concluded, as I left the premises.

'Oh, and thank you once again for saving my life,' I added, popping back briefly, as it would have been most churlish not to do so.

'In precisely three hours,' said Mr Rune. But I did not hear him say it. And then he located an unopened bottle of twelve-year-old single malt, but I did not see him do that, either.

I shouldered my pillowcase and pondered my options. I could head straight to the police station and do what I should have done three weeks before – report that I had lost my memory and find out if anyone had reported me missing.

Or I could have a beer or two in the alehouse next door to forty-nine Grand Parade, where I knew that Mr Rune still maintained an active open account with Fangio the barlord. Something to do with Freemasonry, I was given to understand.

'Beer first,' said I. 'And then the police station.'

The alehouse was named The Rack and Pinion. It was an automotive theme bar most pleasantly furnished with bench seats from Ford Zodiacs, which in itself had a certain charm, considering the conversation that I had just had with Mr Rune.

Within, Fangio the barlord, clad in his distinctive mechanic's overalls, always offered a cheery welcome, good beer at a fair price and was ever prepared to talk some toot and make free with the complimentary peanuts.

I pushed open the door of The Rack and Pinion and

entered the bar. Then I retraced my steps and looked up once more at the sign. The Rack and Pinion, it read. And then The Bucket of Bacon. I blinked, scratched at my head and re-entered the bar.

Fangio stood behind the jump, but at my approach he offered no cheery welcome.

'Good afternoon, Fange,' I said to him. 'No cheery welcome today?'

'Look at me,' said the barlord. 'Tell me what you see.'

'You have dyed your eyelashes,' I said. 'Very fetching.'

'Not that,' said Fangio. 'That is another matter altogether. I woke up this morning to discover that I have become a gay icon.'

'What is a gay acorn?' I asked.

'*Icon*,' said Fangio. 'And that's another thing – these new false teeth are playing havoc with my diction.' He opened wide his mouth and I stared into it.

'I think you were supposed to take your old set out before you put your new set in,' I remarked.

'Ah,' said Fangio, pulling his new set from his mouth and hurling them the length of the bar. 'That's better,' he decided.

'So,' I said. 'Gay icon, is it?'

'Yes,' said Fangio, 'but that's not so bad. Now I can play my Judy Garland records really loud and if anyone complains I can accuse them of sexual discrimination.'

'Sounds like a dream come true,' I said.

'It is,' said Fangio. 'And some of my new-found friends and I are going down to the prom tonight, "straight-bashing".'

'The nineteen sixties are a great time to be alive,' I said. 'So why no cheery welcome?'

'I trust you saw the pub sign. I noticed you doing the old double-take.'

'The pub sign keeps changing,' I said.

'It's digital,' Fangio explained.

'Then all becomes clear. A pint of Old Brake Fluid, please.'

'We don't serve Old Brake Fluid any more.'

'I am appalled to hear it. A pint of Castrol GTX, then.'

'Nor that.'

'All right, I'll take a pint of Benzole Super.'

'Oh no you won't.'

'But then, you never did serve Benzole Super.'

'It was worth a try, though. Do you want to keep going or would you prefer to give up now and simply ask me what beers I presently have on tap?'

'That seems somewhat premature. I am certain that I could come up with some more really imaginative names for imaginary beers.'

'Not on the evidence so far.'

'So what beers are you presently serving?'

'We don't serve beer,' said Fangio. 'This is a wine bar.'

'Oh,' I said. 'Since when?'

'Since—' Fangio raised his wristwatch to his blue-fringed eyes. '—Ah,' he said, 'half-past, we're now a pub again. Care for a beer?'

'I do not think I quite understand,' I said.

'It's a kind of alcoholic drink,' said Fangio. 'Brewed from hops.'

'I understand beer,' I said and I leaned my elbows upon the bar counter. 'What I do not understand is—'

'Off the bar, please, sir, health-and-safety regulations.'

'Are you feeling yourself, Fange?'

'How dare you! Are you having a go at me because I'm a gay icon?'

'No,' I said. 'I am not.'

'And are you gay?'

'No, I am not.'

'Then you'll have to leave the bar in half an hour. I'd get a beer in now, while you can, if I were you.'

'If you were me,' I said, 'you would punch you right in the face.'

'Look,' said Fangio, 'allow me to explain. You saw the pub sign, didn't you?'

'I did,' I said.

43

'Well, it's broken.'

'I assumed that.'

'It's not working properly and it's changing every half-hour. It's only supposed to change once a day.'

'Why?' I asked.

'The brewery's idea. It has long been a tradition in Brighton that if there's a really nice pub, where people feel comfortable, and the beer is good, and the management personable and friendly, and it's making a profit and everything, that the brewery will close it down, sack the management, rip out the fixtures and fittings and dump the good beer in favour of something called "Alcopop". Then they refurbish the place in "Brighton chic", which is basically aluminium with really uncomfortable high stools, put some Australian women behind the bar, employ the services of a teenage DJ to play really dreadful music at an intolerable volume, change the name to confuse cab drivers and—'

'Stop!' I cried. 'Please stop!'

'Exactly,' said Fange. 'Dreadful, isn't it?'

'Dreadful?' I said. 'I am a teenager, Fange – it sounds great to me.'

Fangio fluttered his eyelashes.

'If that is meant to look fierce,' I said, 'it is not working.'

'Yes, well.' Fangio stamped his feet.

'Are you wearing high heels?' I asked, and I leaned forward over the bar counter.

'The brewery,' said Fange.

'About that beer,' I said. 'A pint of Esso Extra, please,'

'Coming right up, sir.' Fangio did the business.

'And put it on Mister Rune's account.'

'In your dreams, you hetro-fascist!'

'What did you call me?'

'Nothing, sir. I regret, however, that Mister Rune left explicit instructions. He said that he expected that you would come in here this afternoon, most probably carrying a stuffed pillowcase, hoping to gain free drinks on his account. He said that I was to politely refuse you. Then on second thoughts he said that I was free to insult you as much as I liked.'

'Very fair of him,' I said. 'Very democratic.'

'That's what we fought the war for,' said Fangio. 'That and the silk stockings, of course. Not to mention the powdered egg.'

'The powdered egg?' I queried.

'I told you not to mention that. Kindly get out of my bar.'

I fished what little money I had from my pocket and placed it upon the counter. 'Just give me the beer,' I said, and Fangio did so.

'So,' he said, 'before I was so rudely interrupted, I was telling you about the brewery and how they like to desecrate decent alehouses. Well, generally their new-style bars last about six months, then go bust. The brewery then refurbishes them again in their original style, they turn a profit again, so the brewery refurbishes them new-style again and—'

'I am beginning to see a pattern emerging,' I said.

'It happens about once every six months on average in Brighton. So this brewery, the one that owns this pub—' Fangio looked once more at his wristwatch '—The Muff-Diver's Helmet, has decided that it would be more profitable all the way round simply to change the name of the pub and the theme on a daily basis. Get the best of both worlds and all those in between.'

'Things are always so simple once they are explained,' I said. 'What exactly are you doing?'

'Getting into my muff-diver's helmet.'

'Very nice, too. I like the way the flaps come down over your ears.'

'If you want another pint of Esso, order it now,' said Fange. 'I'll waive the rules on this occasion. Normally you'd only be allowed to drink cocktails during this half-hour. They all have very suggestive names, full of sexual innuendo. I believe they paid Frankie Howerd a king's ransom to come up with them.'

'What I would not give to be rich and famous,' I said, sipping at my Esso when it came and taking joy in the sipping thereof.

'But I thought that was why you'd joined up with Mister Rune.'

'Excuse me?' I said.

'Why, what have you done?'

'I mean, what do you mean by that remark?'

'Well, according to Mister Rune, you are his amanuensis, his Boswell, you are writing up his exploits into what will become an international bestseller.'

'He told you that, did he?'

'He did. And that you'd put me into your book.'

'That I cannot see happening,' I said.

'Well, that's what he said. I make my first appearance on page thirty-nine, and I do something really helpful in Chapter Eight, apparently.'

I shrugged and settled myself on to a bar-side stool. 'That was a decent bit of toot we just talked there,' I said.

'Always a pleasure,' said Fangio. 'So you're taking your leave of Mister Rune, then, are you?'

'The man is mad,' I said. 'You would not believe all the things he has told me. Ludicrous stuff. And the people he says he has met. The Pope. Oscar Wilde. H. G. Wells.'

'He once lent me a copy of *The Time Machine*, a first edition with a handwritten dedication in the flyleaf: "To Hugo for his inspiration", signed "Herbert"!'

'A forgery,' I said.

'That's not what the expert at Christie's said when I put it up for auction in their rare-books sale.'

'You did *what*?'

'I told Mister Rune that I'd lost it. But I was only trying to cover my expenses. We may both be Freemasons, but that man is drinking my pub dry, and all on his "account".'

I laughed at this and shook my head.

'Clever, that,' said Fangio, 'laughing and shaking your head at the same time. I can't do that. But I *can* do *this*.'

Fangio did *this*.

I stared in horror. 'Please do not ever do *this* again in my presence,' I said, taking out my bullet-scorched hankie and mopping my brow with it.

'What, *this*?' said Fangio.

'No, not that. *This*.'

'Sorry,' said Fangio. 'It's the way these flaps come down over my ears.'

A customer called out for service and Fangio tottered along the bar to serve him (or her – I could not be altogether certain which).

'Excuse me, mister.'

I turned at this to observe an unsavoury-looking character looking up at me and tugging in an urgent way upon my trouser leg.

'Please do not do that,' I told him.

'But mister,' said this ill-clad ne'er-do-well, a roguish tramp by the look of him, and one in sore need of a laundering at that, 'I heard the name of Hugo Rune being mentioned – do I take it that you are his associate?'

'Ex-associate,' I said. 'Please leave my trouser leg alone.'

'Oh, it's your trouser leg, is it? I had a pair of trousers just like those once – I thought for a minute they were mine.'

'Kindly go about your business,' I said.

'But about Mister Rune,' the wretch persisted.

'I no longer work for Mister Rune. Not that I ever did, really.'

'I've got the dog,' said the shabby, down-at-heel, veritable scumbag of an individual. 'And just because I've fallen upon hard times, there's no reason for you to have a go at me.'

'I was not,' I said.

'No, but you were thinking it,' said the low-life, no-mark, dirt-poor-excuse-for-a-human-being. 'There – you're doing it again.'

'I was not.'

'You were.' The filthy degenerate shook an ill-washed fist.

47

'All right, I was. Now, please go away. No, hold on a moment, what dog do you have?'

'*The* dog,' said the—

The fellow paused.

And I paused also.

'Thank you,' he said. '*The* dog. The one that Mister Rune had me pinch from that house in Hangleton, which I was to deliver to him at his rooms this afternoon to impress some fellow called Rizla. Are you associated with this Rizla, by any chance?'

I all but fell off my bar-side stool. It was only through the exercise of supreme self-control – and having no wish to end up lying flat on my back – that prevented me from doing so.

'Are you telling me,' I said, 'that Mister Rune paid you to steal a dog from a house in Hangleton?'

'Well, he hasn't paid me yet. I came here because I forgot what number he lives at. What number is it, then, do you know?'

If I could have seen my own face at that moment, I feel certain that it must have been wearing a very broad smile indeed.

'What are you frowning at, mister?' asked the . . . erm . . . fellow.

'I am grinning,' I said, 'broadly.'

'Well, that's young folk for you. I can't tell the boys from the girls nowadays.'

'You really should try,' I suggested, 'or you might get yourself into all kinds of trouble.'

'More drinks, ladies?' asked Fangio, tottering back in our direction.

'Same again for me, and whatever my new-found friend here is having.'

'I'll have a pint of Diesel, please,' said my new-found friend. 'My name's Hubert, by the way.'

'Is that hyphenated?' Fangio asked.

'No, it's Welsh. It means "he who walks quietly to the cowshed and knows where the shears are kept".'

48

'Cow-shears?' I asked.

'It's one of the reasons why I left Wales,' Hubert explained.

'Put these drinks on Mister Rune's account,' I told Fangio.

The barlord shook his helmeted head.

'Or I will pass on to Mister Rune that matter of the first edition that was recently sold at Christie's.'

'Coming right up, then,' said Fangio.

'And have one yourself.'

'That's most generous, sir. I'll just have a glass of the vintage champagne that Mister Rune suggested I order in, in case of a special occasion.'

'Knock yourself out,' I said.

'Is that compulsory?'

'No, it is just a turn of phrase.'

Fangio served up our drinks and repaired to the wine cellar, smiling as he went.

'What was he frowning about?' asked Hubert.

'Never mind,' I told him. 'Drink up and enjoy the moment.'

The moment passed.

And so did further moments.

These further moments passed to the accompaniment of drinking.

These moments became minutes and these, in turn, became hours.

'I'm really rather drunk now,' said Hubert. 'How about you?'

'I am *very* drunk,' I said. 'But happy.'

'That's often the way with drinking.' Hubert slid his beer glass up and down the counter, thereby bringing grief to Fangio who was a barlord who liked his counter clean. For health-and-safety reasons, obviously. 'If I tell you a secret,' said Hubert, 'will you promise to keep it a secret?'

'Will it still be a secret if you tell it to me?' I asked.

Hubert scratched at his head, raising small clouds of purple dust.

'Don't confuse him,' said Fangio. 'I like secrets.'

'This is a really scary one,' said Hubert, 'and all the more so because it is true.'[*]

'Go on, then,' I said. 'I promise that whatever you tell me, I will not confide the details to another soul.'

'Nor me,' said Fangio. 'Unless the mood takes me, of course.'

'Right, then,' said Hubert. And he drew us closer to him. 'It's about rock stars and why they always die aged twenty-seven.'

'Do they?' asked Fangio.

'They do,' said Hubert. 'Johnny Kidd, out of Johnny Kidd and the Pirates, died aged twenty-seven. Brian Jones of the Rolling Stones. Jimi Hendrix, Janis Joplin, Jim Morrison, Gram Parsons from the Byrds, Pigpen out of the Grateful Dead. And Kurt Cobain, who hasn't been born yet, so we'll leave him out.'

'Hold on,' I said. 'Jones and Jimi, Janis and Jim, and Johnny, of course – they all died at twenty-seven?[†] Is this true?'

Fangio was counting on his fingers. 'It is,' he said. 'How odd.'

'Not odd,' said Hubert. 'Just the work of the Devil.'

'That's a bit strong,' said Fangio. 'I know that they call rock 'n' roll the Devil's music, but—'

'Listen,' said Hubert, 'I checked it out. I wanted to see where it all began, where it could be traced back to. And I have—'

'Go on,' said Fangio.

'Let me say something,' I said.

'Go on,' said Fangio.

'Go on,' I said.

'Eh?' said Fangio.

[*] And it all is – you can check it out for yourself.
[†] They *really* did.

'That is all I wanted to say.'

'Robert Johnson,' said Hubert, 'blues musician – ever heard of him?'

'Actually, I have,' I said. 'He wrote "Cross Road Blues" and "Me and the Devil Blues" and "Hell Hound On My Trail" and "Love In Vain" – the Rolling Stones recorded that one. Just about every rock musician today pays homage to Robert Johnson. They say that he started the whole thing, put it all together – the notes, the chord progressions, the lot.'

Hubert nodded. 'You're absolutely right. So let me tell you this. The story goes that Robert Johnson wasn't much of a guitarist, but he wanted to be the best, to be remembered. So he went down to the crossroads at midnight with a black-cat bone and sold his soul to the Devil. The Devil tuned Robert Johnson's guitar—'

'I remember reading this somewhere,' I said. 'From then on he always played with his back to the audience. Folk who looked at him from the stage side of the curtain swear that he had six fingers on his left hand.'

Hubert nodded. 'When Keith Richards first heard Robert Johnson's recordings – and he only recorded twenty-nine songs, all in a hotel room, with his back to the recorder – Keith Richards said, "Who's the other guitarist playing with Johnson?" because one man alone simply couldn't play all those notes at the same time.'

'Spooky stuff,' said Fangio.

'There's more,' said Hubert.

'Go on,' said Fangio.

'*I* was going to say *that*,' I said.

'Robert Johnson met with an untimely death,' said Hubert. 'Murdered by a jealous husband, they say. Or perhaps the Devil claimed his own. Perhaps he always claims his own.'

'How old was Robert Johnson when he died?' I asked.

'Twenty-seven,' said Hubert.

'Thank God for that,' said Fangio.

'Thank God for *what*?' I said.

'Thank God it's five o'clock,' said Fangio. 'I can take off this muff-diver's helmet now.'

'And I have to get off,' said Hubert. 'I have this enormous Russian spaniel outside in my van that has to be delivered to Mister Rune.'

'Ah, yes,' I said, 'the Russian spaniel. I am really going to enjoy the Russian spaniel.'

'That's Thursdays,' said Fangio.

'Thursdays?' I said.

'Bestiality Theme Night.'

'We are off,' I said to Fangio. 'I doubt whether our paths will cross again. It has been a pleasure to know you.'

'Don't forget to mention me in Chapter Eight,' said the barlord. 'And don't forget your pillowcase.'

I did not forget my pillowcase. I followed Hubert around to the rear of forty-nine Grand Parade, where he had parked his van. And here I maintained something of a low profile, for there were several parked police cars to be seen and a lot of that yellow 'POLICE – DO NOT CROSS' tape draped all around a taxicab that had apparently crashed into the dustbins.

'Wait here and I'll get the dog,' said Hubert.

And he did so.

It really *was* a very large dog, for a spaniel.

'It's grown a bit since I put it in the van,' said Hubert, struggling to drag it along. 'It's almost the size of a Shetland pony now. I wonder how big these things grow. I heard this story about a pig in Henfield once. It seems that—'

'Follow me,' I said, and I grinned as I said it.

I turned the handle and then kicked open the door. Mr Rune looked up from his doings, which were playing 'Love in Vain' upon his reinvented ocarina.

'My dear Rizla,' he said, 'you have returned.' And he took out his gold pocket watch. 'And right on time to the very minute, as I predicted.'

'You charlatan!' I cried. 'I have found you out.'

'Indeed?' said Mr Rune. 'Indeed?'

'I have the Hound of the Hangletons with me.'

'Then the case is solved, as I also predicted.'

'There never was a case. This fellow here—' I encouraged Hubert into the room. 'This fellow here—' Hubert struggled to ease himself past the Russian spaniel '—stole the dog at your behest. You scoundrel. You fraud.'

'Scoundrel and fraud,' said Mr Rune. 'Harsh words.'

'And too good for you.'

'You're piddled again,' said Mr Rune.

'I am,' I said, 'and proud of the fact, for I have done it at your expense.'

'I knew that Fangio would sell my signed first edition,' said Mr Rune. 'I trust that you enjoyed the champagne that I had him lay down for a special occasion.'

'Actually, I did. He shared it with me.'

'Splendid,' said Mr Rune. 'You can return the hound now, Hubert. Oh – and take this.' Mr Rune rose and handed Hubert an envelope.

'What is that?' I asked.

'My bill,' said Mr Rune, 'for the Orions, for the recovery of their dog. Make sure you get the money in cash, Hubert; don't accept a cheque.'

'But *you* had Hubert steal the dog in the first place,' I said.

'I was not employed by the Orions to catch the thief, only to recover the dog for them. That has been done, and I am therefore entitled to my fee. I see no flaw in this reasoning, do you?'

'I . . .' I said. 'I . . .'

'And *you* have returned, as I predicted, within three hours to the very minute. And so *you* must honour the oath you swore upon leaving, that should you return to these rooms you would remain in my employ until all the cases are solved. You promised on your life, did you not?'

'Yes,' I said. 'Well, yes, but—'

'But me no buts,' said Mr Rune. 'Everything has gone exactly as I planned it. Let us now go together to The Pillow Biter's Elbow, as I believe it to be called at this time of the day, and celebrate our success: a found hound, a fat fee and a partnership that will lead one day to you making a fortune when you publish the book of our exploits. I'd end this chapter here, if I were you.'

And so I did.

2

The Curious Case of the Centenary Centaur

The Centenary Centaur

PART I

I think that you might find this of interest,' said Mr Rune
to me, as we sat a-breakfasting in our rooms at forty-nine
Grand Parade upon a fine morning in April. 'Give me your
considered opinion.' And he flung the morning's edition of
the *Argus* in my direction.

My hands being occupied with cutlery, the newspaper
fell into my breakfast, mashing the fried egg that I had been
saving for last.

'Damn and blast it,' said I, putting down my knife and fork and plucking up the eggy newssheet.

'Front page,' said Mr Rune, availing himself of the last piece of toast.

I took the *Argus* and viewed the front page, and at once saw the headline printed there: **HORRIBLE INCIDENT IN HANGLETON** And what was printed below this?

Police were called last night to a house in Tudor Close, Hangleton, when concerned neighbours gave the alarm. They had heard dogs howling repeatedly and although having knocked upon the front door, they had been unable to elicit any response from the tenants who were presently renting the property, a Mr and Mrs Orion. Fearing foul play, the officers of the law, once summoned, gained entry to the property by applying reasonable force to the front door with their helmets. They were ill prepared for the scene of horror that waited them. The house was literally alive with spaniels.

Constable Runstable, who was one of the first on the scene, told our reporter, 'There were literally thousands of them, ranging from the size of a Shetland pony to that of a bluebottle. All identical – but for the size, of course.'

No trace whatsoever was found of the tenants. The police wish to contact Mr and Mrs Orion as soon as possible to help with their enquiries. The spaniels are being held in police custody.

' "From the size of a Shetland pony to that of a bluebottle"?' I quoted. 'Whatever is *that* all about?'

'I should have thought that to be perfectly obvious.' Mr Rune dipped the last bit of toast into my wounded egg. 'It was a Russian spaniel, after all.'

'You have lost me,' I said. 'And leave my egg alone.'

'The spaniel reached critical mass,' said Rune. 'Surely you've seen those sets of Russian dolls that fit inside each other? Such it is with Russian spaniels – a great big spaniel, with a lesser-sized spaniel within it and so on and so forth.'

'Ludicrous,' I said, drawing my breakfast plate beyond Mr Rune's reach and beating back his hand with the morning's

Argus. 'And I suppose these spaniels get smaller and smaller for ever and ever.'

'Don't be absurd,' said Mr Rune. 'You can't divide things in half for ever.'

'Oh, I beg to differ there,' I said. 'Space is infinite; you can always multiply a distance by two and never come to the end of it. It therefore follows that you can similarly divide something in half for ever and ever and ever.'

'You can't,' said Mr Rune, 'because your diminishing object will eventually become so small that it will weigh less than the light which falls upon it, and then cease to exist in this dimension.'

'Oh,' I said. 'Well, I never knew that.'

'Nor did Einstein until I put him straight on the matter.'

'But what does it mean?'

'It means, young Rizla, that you should not take anything for granted. I am Rune, the physical manifestation of all astral possibilities. I knew from the first that we were dealing with no ordinary spaniel.'

'But *you* stole the spaniel!'

'*Had* it stolen. One does not own a dog and bark oneself. It is well to know your enemy, to gauge his strengths and weaknesses.'

'The spaniel was your enemy?'

'Not the spaniel. Tell me, Rizla, when we were there in that house at Hangleton, what observations did you make? Do you recall that I asked you to keep your eyes and ears open?'

'I do,' I said, as I helped myself to the very last pouring of coffee, 'and I made quite a few observations, as it happens. For one thing, those two were not married.'

'Very good,' said Mr Rune. 'And how did you reach this conclusion?'

' "Mrs Orion" was not wearing a wedding ring, and she was a very fastidious woman, very clean, her nails beautifully manicured. And he was a right scruff, all over shabby with nasty black fingernails. I do not think a woman like that would ever marry a man like that. *And* he called

57

her Janet, not Aimee, as was written in the letter you received.'

'Excellent,' said Mr Rune. 'Anything else?'

'I do not think there were any other dogs there,' I said.

'Then how do you explain the continued howling that came from the rear of the house?'

'It was a tape recording, a loop tape – you could hear the pattern of the howling as it repeated itself.'

'I am very impressed,' said Mr Rune. 'However, I would have been more impressed if you'd mentioned these details to me at the time.'

'I drove back here in a stolen cab and then you gave me all that toot about Chronovisions and zodiacs.'

'Well, nevertheless I am impressed. You are wrong on almost every count, but nevertheless.'

I topped my coffee up with the last of the milk and sugar. 'So how am I wrong?' I asked.

'The couple are indeed married. They were married in Saint Petersburg in nineteen ten.'

'Saint Petersburg?' I said. 'Nineteen ten?' I said. 'What are you saying?' I said. 'That Mister Orion really *is* Rasputin?'

I said.

'No,' said Mr Rune. 'Mister Orion is in fact none other than my arch enemy, The Most Evil Man Who Ever Lived. Mister Orion is Count Otto Black.'

'Then him shooting at us was no accident.'

'He is a crack shot – he trained with the Eton Rifles. (Eton Rifles).[*] Had he wished to shoot us dead, then he would have done so.'

'But if he is your arch enemy—'

'He was testing me out. He is unaware that I am aware of his true identity. It was a pleasure to take his money – a share of which I passed on to you at the time.'

'An insubstantial amount,' I said. 'But I still do not

---

[*] As in The Jam classic, obviously.

understand about all these spaniels being inside one another.'

'All will be explained in good time. Oh, and by the way, Rizla, the name "Orion" was something of a giveaway. It's a stellar constellation that includes Sirius, the Dog Star. But anyhow, that isn't the piece in the *Argus* that I wanted you to read. Read what is written beneath the Hangleton article.'

I took up the newspaper once more and studied the front page. 'There is nothing else,' I said, 'apart from an advertisement.'

'Read the advertisement aloud.'

And so I did.

THE CENTAUR OF THE UNIVERSE

A talk upon the Elliptical Navigations of the
Aethyrs of Avatism by World-Famous Paranormal
Questor and Psychic Youth

DANBURY COLLINS

Tonight 7.30 p.m. The Rampant Squire,
Ditchling Road, Brighton

'Nutcase,' I remarked. 'New-Age nutcase.'

'What?' Mr Rune feigned outrage. 'Danbury Collins, renowned psychic youth and masturbator?'

'What?' I feigned a little outrage of my own.

'He is most entertaining. He, Sir John Rimmer and Doctor Harney have conducted numerous investigations into the paranormal – with little success, I hasten to add – but his talks are always a riot. I have crossed intellectual swords with this fellow on numerous occasions. My sword, however, has a rapier's edge. His, alas, would not pass through butter.'

'Speaking of butter,' I said, 'we have no more.'

'Then it is time for you to do the Tesco run.'

'Oh no.' I shook my head fiercely. 'Tesco does not give credit and I am not running out of there again without paying whilst you remonstrate with the checkout girl. Why do you not simply pay for something once in a while?'

Mr Rune now shook *his* head. 'I am Rune,' said he. 'I offer the world my genius. All I expect in return is that the world cover my expenses.'

'So would you care for me to see if I can somehow scrounge some free tickets for Mister Collins's lecture?'

'Unnecessary,' said Mr Rune. 'I doubt very much that he will be playing to a packed house. We'll inveigle our way in when we get there. But for now—' Mr Rune dabbed his napkin to his lips, '—let us take a stroll to Sainsbury's.'

We did not stroll back from Sainsbury's. Well, I believe that Mr Rune might well have done, but I was forced to run and this was not easy, considering the number of carrier bags making red rings upon my fingers. We lunched well, though, and suppered, too, and then at six of the evening clock took to the street and waved a taxi down.

The taxi driver's name was Dave, a truculent fellow who supported the Brighton Seagulls 'come rain or shine, through thick and thin and all the way to Hell and back'. And he enlivened our journey with talk of his theories that the planet Earth was in fact a great big head, swinging through space and gaining increased sentience due to human beings, which were in fact its brain cells, exchanging information.

'When the Earth was young, it knew nothing,' the taxi driver explained, 'because there were only a few people/ brain cells. But as the millennia passed, more and more people/brain cells appeared upon the planet. Quite soon now, when the world knows everything it needs to know, it will quit this solar system and take off on a voyage of discovery. Somewhere, out there—' the cabbie gestured to 'out there' generally, taking his hands off the steering wheel and nearly having a passing cleric off his pushbike '—the wandering world will meet up with other wandering worlds

that have similarly gained sentience due to all their people/ brain cells. And it will amalgamate with them into a super-organism, which will be God, a new God who will then create a new universe. That's what happened before, you see – that's how this universe began. And it will happen again and again.'

Mr Rune had no comment to make during the cabbie's metaphysical discourse; he sat passively with his eyelids drooping, playing the occasional wistful air upon his reinvented ocarina.

When we reached our destination, I made hurriedly to The Rampant Squire and so did not witness the rise and fall of Mr Rune's stout stick.

I rather liked The Rampant Squire. It was a rough old dive filled with rowdy students from the university. I observed them as they laughed and chatted and wondered whether I was a university type myself. Probably not, I concluded, because I was too young.. Too young for drinking in pubs also, of course, but then *that* only made the drinking more enjoyable.

The walls of The Rampant Squire were decorated with dreadful contemporary paintings, the work of a local artist by the name of Matthew Humphrey. They were all squiggles and daubings and splatterings-on, and looked much the way that restaurant tablecloths looked by the time Mr Rune had reached the cheese-and-biscuits course.

I elbowed my way to the bar and found Fangio standing behind it.

'Hello, Fange,' said I. 'I did not know that you worked here.'

'A man's got to have a hobby,' said Fange. 'I saw you admiring the artwork.'

'The paintings are horrible,' I said.

'I know,' said Fangio. 'I chose them.'

'Why?'

'The pub is called The Rampant Squire, so the brewery asked me to order in some erotic paintings.'

61

'I see,' I said. But I did not.

'You don't,' said Fangio. 'I blame these new teeth of mine. I telephoned this Matthew Humphrey and asked him to knock up some erotic paintings. He misheard me and—'

'Let me guess,' I said. 'He supplied you with a series of erratic paintings instead.'

'Oh,' said Fangio. 'That would be it, then. I thought he was just a really terrible artist.'

'A pint of Esso, please. And as I have a thirst upon me, we will scrub around all the toot about what you do or do not have on the pumps, if that is all right with you.'

'A pint of Esso it is, then. And one for Mister Rune? I see his big baldy head looming through the crowd.'

'Make his a half,' I said.

'Appalling pub,' said Mr Rune, joining me at the bar. 'Have you ordered?'

'I have.'

Fangio served up the drinks and Mr Rune availed himself of my pint.

'Only a half for you?' he said. 'Wise move – you'll need a clear head for what lies ahead of us this night.'

'The lecture?' I said, ruefully sipping my half.

'The lecture is merely the tip of the iceberg. Before this night is through, you will have stared death in the face, and spat into its cavernous eyeholes as well.'

'I do not like the sound of that.'

'It's much of a muchness,' Mr Rune said. 'I've done it on many occasions. I remember once in the nineteen thirties when I went down to the crossroads at midnight with the blues musician Robert Johnson—'

'Ladies and gentlemen, will you please take your seats upstairs for the lecture. It begins in five minutes,' called a personable young woman with a nimbus of orange hair and a dress that barely covered her costs.

'Best get a couple more beers in, then,' said Mr Rune. 'And trust not the ways of women, "For they are like unto a fire that quencheth not even though constantly watered." The Gospel of Rune 3: 16.'

'Bravo,' said Mr Rune. 'Naturally, I have toyed with this concept myself.'

'Eh?' said I.

And Danbury continued, 'Space is infinite, but matter is finite — there is only a limited amount of it. It's a fair old amount, I grant you, but if you lumped it all together it would have a finite weight, and no matter how far you spread it all about, it's the same amount. And we — you, me, Oscar Wilde, all of us — are composed of the matter of the universe. We are stardust.* We are composed of universal stuff. Every cell of our bodies has been here, part of the finite amount of matter, for ever. You can't create more matter — that would be creating something out of nothing. You can convert matter, burn it, change it into gas, whatever, but the weight of it all remains the same. We — everyone in this room — is composed of cells that are composed from the original matter of the universe.'

I had a bit of a think about this. I was only a teenager and had never, as far as I could recall, ever given much thought to esoteric matters of this ilk, but I had to say that this was, well, profound. That is what it was: profound.

'So,' continued Danbury, 'if we are all composed of the original and finite material of the universe, we are all a part of its beginning; we all contain the stuff of its beginning — whatever that beginning might have been. And so we should be able to access universal knowledge, knowledge of the past and the future, for it is all one in universal terms. And it's all there in the cells of our being.'

A student type a few seats along from me raised his grubby hand. 'Are you saying,' he asked, 'that we are inherently capable of accessing the past — of travelling in time, as it were?'

'Certainly,' said Danbury. 'It is all in our cellular memory. You don't just inherit your father's physical features, but also his cellular memory of his father and his father before him. I've heard that a scientist named Doveston has

_____
* We are golden, etc.

invented a drug called Retro that allows you to access these memories.'

'I read that somewhere,' said the student type. 'And also about this Benedictine monk who invented a television set that could play back past events.'

'Eh?' said I and I turned to the student type. 'Where did you read about that?' I asked.

'In the *Weekly World News*,' the youth replied. ' "MAD MONK INVENTS TIME TV: Watches Christ's Crucifixion", that was the headline.'

I looked at Mr Rune. The Perfect Master appeared to be sleeping.

'The *Weekly World News*!' I said. 'I have seen that in the newsagent's. It is nothing but made-up nonsense. Only last week the headline was "ELVIS PRESLEY CONFESSES: I Travelled Through Time With the Aid of Barry the Time Sprout". The *Weekly World News* is always on about time travel and it is all rubbish.'

'The CIA owns the *Weekly World News*,' said another student type. 'They publish real information but in such a way that no "right-thinking" person would believe it. It's all a big conspiracy. The CIA had Kennedy shot because he was going to blow the whistle on the alien bodies in Area Fifty-One. Everybody knows that.'

'Not me,' I said.

'Well, you *say* that,' said the student type, 'but of course you might well be lying. You might well be a spook.'

'A spook?' I said. 'What is a spook?'

'A CIA agent. Probably a member of MK Ultra, the mind-control programme.'

'I can assure you that I am no such thing.'

'Yeah, well, you *would say that*!'

'Let's have order now, please,' called Danbury. 'I haven't got to the exciting part of my lecture yet. You see, it is indeed possible to reach through time – in either direction, in fact – and I have actual living proof of this here with me. Something brought forward through time from the past. From the distant past, the Age of Myth. A mythical beast and it's here.' And Danbury held aloft the Aladdin's lamp that had been standing on the table named Peter.

'A centaur!' cried Danbury. 'Now, please let's have a little order while I give the lamp a rub.'

'I am not having this bloke calling me a spook,' I protested.

'You look like a spook,' said the personable young woman with the nimbus of orange hair and the dress that barely covered her costs at all now that she was sitting down. 'That ID his big fat friend flashed me on the door looked like a CIA Above-Top-Secret security pass to me.'

'It is a library ticket,' I said.

'There,' said the personable young woman, becoming somewhat less personable. 'He has access to the American Library of Congress. They're both spooks.'

'You are bl★★dy mad,' I said.

'Bl★★dy?' said the increasingly more unpersonable young woman. 'He speaks in Esperanto, which we all know is an alien tongue. He's definitely a spook. The CIA are in cahoots with the aliens in Area Fifty-One. In exchange for alien technology, they allow the aliens to abduct one hundred human beings each year for their hybridisation programme.'

'You should get yourself a boyfriend,' I suggested.

'There!' screamed the now extremely unpersonable young woman. 'He wants to hand me over to the aliens to be part of their hideous crossbreeding programme.'

'Could we have a little order, please?' called Danbury.

'Oh,' said another student type, one with the kind of goatee beard that I was hoping soon to grow. 'Siding with the CIA-Proto-Zionist-Illuminati-Bilderberg-New-World-Orderists, are you, Collins? You're part of the misinformation programme, too, aren't you?'

'I'm a paranormal investigator,' cried Danbury. 'It's my job to get to the bottom of this kind of thing.'

'*Get to the bottom?*' The young woman rose to her feet, with her dress all most pleasingly rucked up at the back.

'The bottom, did you hear that? He wants to hand me over to the aliens, too. For rectal probing.'

'That sounds like fun,' I said. 'Do you think the aliens are taking on apprentices?'

Now, I probably should not have said that.

In fact, looking back, I *definitely* should not have said that.

It transpired that the student type who had asked the original question about travelling in time was the orange-nimbus-young-woman's boyfriend, who apparently had a bit of a thing about anal sex because the nimbus woman was avidly refusing ever to give him any.

And one thing led to another.

And the other thing involved punches being thrown.

And as I recall mentioning in the opening chapter of this bestseller, I do know how to handle myself. But once again I found myself to be substantially outnumbered.

But then they were not all actually hitting me. Several of them were hitting Danbury Collins, who was doing his best to put up a spirited one-handed defence. And a small grey chap with a big bald head and shiny black eyes was hitting on the nimbus woman. But a lot of them *were* hitting me.

Chairs were overturned. And raised and used as projectiles and weapons. The blackboard was torn from its precarious stand and went the way of all flesh. The beer crates were raised and hurled, some through the windows.

If there was a haven of peace and quietude in the midst of this maelstrom, an eye in the hurricane, as it were, then this haven and eye was to be found in the person of Mr Hugo Rune.

The Guru's Guru, the Logos of the Aeon, the Hokus Bloke, the Lad Himself slept on, untouched by the chaos that reigned all about him, surrounded, it seemed, by a protective cocoon. A cone of power? A psychic force field?

Or just the plain luck of the draw?

Luck was not on my side and I went down beneath a torrent of blows and buffets.

Which all seemed rather unfair, really. After all, I was definitely *not* a CIA spook.

'You are all bl**dy nutters!' I cried, as I did my best to fight back.

'Once more he speaks the alien tongue.' And nimbus woman put the boot in.

Now, I recall this as clearly as if it was yesterday, because it is often funny the way things work out. In fact, it is *always* funny, but mostly only from a detached point of view, but I do recall that it was Danbury Collins that set The Rampant Squire on fire.

I do not think he *meant* to do it. I do recall him shouting something about peace and love, although it was difficult to tell exactly what, with all the noise of breaking furniture and the boots going in and everything. And I do recall Danbury up on what was left of the stage, rubbing away at his magic lamp. And then flames coming out of the spout. Which had me thinking that the thing was probably a table lighter. But it really was not his fault. He was hit, fell against the curtains and the curtains took fire. And I suppose that all the noise must have attracted the attention of all the other folk in the bar downstairs, because suddenly, it seemed, there were many more folk in the room upstairs and all fighting and coughing, what with the smoke, and panicking also, and stampeding.

And I do recall something altogether strange.

Something monstrous.

In the midst of the conflagration and the screaming (of which there was much) and the violence and all of the rest, I saw something.

It rose above me, huge and menacing and terrible, a mighty primal force, so it seemed. An atavistic *something* from a mythical time long past.

Its upper parts were manlike and naked, too, its lower parts those of a horse. And it reared up and then it stamped down with its hideous hooves. And I swear to you, yes, I swear that at that very moment, amidst all the flames and chaos, that I surely stared death in its face.

And spat into its cavernous eyeholes.

Although whether or not I did the actual spitting, I am unsure.

I am at least sure that I saw Mr Hugo Rune, stout stick in hand and defiant.

And he struck out at the atavistic *something* and once again saved me from death.

PART II

I awoke to find myself blinking up towards a glossily painted ceiling. I was in hospital. I did not have to think too much about this, because it is only in hospitals that they paint the ceilings with gloss. In fact they paint everything with gloss in hospitals because it is so much easier to wash blood and guts off gloss paint. I believe that all military establishments are also painted with gloss, but this is only my belief, as I have never personally entered any of them.

Especially not Area Fifty-One.

The fact that I now found myself in hospital was somewhat alarming, because I had not been aware that I was ill. So why had I woken up in hospital?

'Doctor Proctor.' I heard the voice of a nurse – Nurse Hearse, I would later discover. 'Doctor Proctor, this is the patient.'

'Patient X,' said Doctor Proctor and suddenly he loomed over me and did pullings about with my eyelids. 'Looks like a hopeless case.'

Well, I was certainly *not* having *that*.

I sought to protest.

And to my absolute horror found that I could not.

I was paralysed.

'Apparently he started a fight in The Rampant Squire and a female student knocked him out,' I heard the nurse say. 'He's in a coma.'

'No, I certainly am not,' I sought to say, but also could not.

'And he has no identification,' said Doctor Proctor. 'Another one of the same, I suppose.'

'The same, Doctor?' queried Nurse Hearse.

'They keep turning up,' said Doctor Proctor. 'Brighton is full of them – the down-and-outs and *Big Issue*-sellers with their big dirty boots and spaniels on strings. They have no identities. They do not remember their names. There's no doubt in my mind, of course, as to who they *really* are.'

'Who?' asked Nurse Hearse.

'Do you believe in fairies?' asked the doctor, shining a torch into my eyes.

'I've never really thought about it.'

'Well, you should. I am presently writing a treatise on the subject, a medical treatise in which I explain my theory that all these folk who wander the streets of Brighton were bewitched by the fairies, that they stumbled into a fairy mound, partook of fairy food and became bewitched. Time, you see, is different in fairyland. This fellow here, for example, he probably wandered into a fairy mound several centuries ago and left again what he thought to be several hours later. But it was in fact several centuries later. And here he lies before us now, another helpless, lost soul, with no identity.'

I took to a certain inward shuddering and wondered if the doctor's words might in fact be true. After all, I really did not remember who I was or where I had come from.

But.

I was pretty damn sure I had never met any fairies.

'So what should we do for the best?' asked Nurse Hearse.

'What we always do in cases like this. You know the drill, Nurse. This is Brighton. This fellow should be good for numerous donor transplants – heart, lungs, liver, retinas. Have you checked out his old chap?'

'His father?'

'His . . . you know.' I saw Doctor Proctor pointing to the area slightly below his waistline.

'Ah,' said Nurse Hearse. 'His plonker.'

'There's always a need for plonkers in the Third World,

Nurse. And this hospital could never survive financially if it wasn't for the trade we do in transplant organs.'

Something clicked when I heard this, as if I had heard it all before – read it in fact, in some book. Although I felt certain that it had been a work of fiction.*

'Help!' I cried silently and unheard by anyone but myself. 'Help, Mister Rune, get me out of here!'

'And there're no signs at all of brain activity?' asked Doctor Proctor.

Nurse Hearse shrugged (I assume, because I could not actually see her then). 'I've no idea, Doctor,' she said. 'We haven't bothered to connect the encephalograph.'

'You're a credit to your calling,' said the doctor. 'A regular Mother Teresa.'

'Isn't she a nun?'

'She's a kind of nursing nun. Dresses in tea towels, a bit like Yasser Arafat.'

'Is he a nun?'

'Don't try to confuse me, Nurse. Others have tried – and succeeded, let me tell you – but it doesn't inspire confidence in the patients.'

'I'm sorry, Doctor.'

Doctor Proctor was now fiddling with my chest. My eyes were still open and I could see him at it. He had his stethoscope on me. It was cold, of course.

'Heart seems sound,' he said. 'Pulse a bit rapid, though. What do you make of this?'

'The mark on his chest? It looks like a hoof print, doesn't it? But burned in, somehow.'

'By a fairy horseman, probably. Bit of a shame, really – we generally use the chest skin to make lampshades.'

'Help!' I screamed silently. 'Mister Rune! Help!'

'I've a lovely collection of them in my study,' continued Doctor Proctor. 'Perhaps you'd like to come up later and see them, Nurse Hearse?'

'I'd love to,' said Nurse Hearse.

---

* And a good 'n.

And I screamed 'Help!' once again. Silently, of course.

After a while, the two of them left. It had been an unpleasant while for me, what with Doctor Proctor measuring my old chap, because apparently they are sold by the inch, and Nurse Hearse asking the doctor whether she could have my finger bones, because apparently she made contemporary jewellery out of them that sold well at the Brighton Festival.

Once they had gone, I lay and stewed in my own juices. Actually, I was rather hungry. They could at least have hooked me up to a drip or something. But beyond being hungry, I was very scared. It had been no female student that had knocked me unconscious; it had been some mad mythical beast. And what had happened to Mr Rune? Had the monster killed him? If it had not and he had escaped unscathed, surely he would be looking for me. Surely he would know that I was here?

I tried to cry out once again, but failed miserably.

And then, I suppose, I must have lost consciousness again.

Because the next thing I knew, there was a lot of bumping and banging about, which I assume must have woken me up. And there was that damned doctor shining his damned light into my eyes once again. And I did view a drip this time and a corridor ceiling and some doors and some more ceiling and then some more doors.

And then sky. An early-morning sky. And I heard the sound of the dawn chorus and smelled the fresh new air.

'Across the car park,' called Doctor Proctor, 'and into the Royal Mail van.'

'Are we going to post him, Doctor?' I heard Nurse Hearse ask. And it was chilly out, I noticed that, too.

'Not immediately, Nurse; we are, however, going to *dispatch* him, if I might put it that way. We use a lot of Royal Mail vans for this sort of thing, which explains why the post is so unreliable in Brighton. But that's by the by. The vans are mobile euthanasia units. We dispatch the . . . er . . . donor, then do the dissections and parcel up the pieces, and then it's on with the address labels and off to the sorting office. It's all quite official – it has the Royal Seal of Approval. This is the Royal Mail, after all. The Queen Mother approved the scheme for the National Health Service shortly after the Second World War. The country's economy couldn't possibly have supported all the war wounded flowing back from all around the world, but by selling off the organs of these otherwise hopeless individuals, the books were made to balance. There wouldn't be the swinging sixties, with full employment and everybody happy, if it wasn't for schemes like this.'

'It's all so simple once it's explained,' said Nurse Hearse.

My, it was *really* chilly out.

And my, did I try my damnedest to scream for help.

And my, did I get nowhere at all.

Except to the doors of the Royal Mail van.

And then through them and into the van.

And once the doors were closed, and the van was in motion, it was, well, at least a bit warmer. Although it really smelled in that van.

It smelled like a slaughterhouse.

And I could see Doctor Proctor looming above me. And I watched as he took big, deep breaths.

'I love the smell of cadavers in the morning,' said Doctor Proctor. 'Smells like victory for the NHS.'

'Should I give the poor soul a lethal injection?' asked Nurse Hearse. 'Put him out of his misery?'

'Heavens, no, Nurse – lethal injections cost money. They generally die of blood loss, anyway, and the organs are fresher when taken from a living donor. So where should I start?'

'Could I cut his old chap off? It's always been an ambition of mine.'

'Certainly, Nurse. Use one of the big scalpels – see if you can take it off with one swift—'

Now, I know what they say about people being talked out of comas, or sung out of them by pop-star types who are in need of a bit of good publicity to cover up some shame or other that is due to come out in the press. And like everyone, I suppose, I have always wondered whether it was actually true, or whether the coma case just happened to wake up at that moment. Or whether in fact there really were any coma cases who ever woke up, or whether the entire thing was made up by the newspapers.

Most likely the *Weekly World News*:

RIP VAN WINKLE:
Coma Patient Wakes Up After Two Hundred Years When Sung To By Elvis.

But believe me, or believe me not, if you really want to raise a male patient from a coma, just try threatening his old chap with a scalpel.

'Aaaaaaagh!' I went, very loudly, with all my limbs once more on the go.

'It's a miracle!' cried Nurse Hearse.

'It's an economic disaster!' cried Doctor Proctor. 'Prime up the lethal injection, Nurse.'

I struggled to rise, but found that I was strapped down to the hospital trolley (or gurney, as I believe they are called by our Stateside cousins).

'You b★st★rd!' I shouted. 'You bl★★dy b★st★rd!'

'The fairy tongue,' said Doctor Proctor, holding down my head. 'I'll put that in my treatise.'

'You murdering maniac!' I shouted. 'Let me out of here!'

The van went over a speed bump or something and the doctor and nurse were thrown all about. I was not thrown about too much myself, because I was strapped down to the trolley (or gurney, or 'big-push-along-blong-him-all-ouch' in the pidgin English of the Melanesian Cargo Cults).

'Careful up front, driver,' called Doctor Proctor. 'Nurse Hearse here nearly stuck a hypodermic needle in my nose.'

'Sorry, Doctor,' called the driver, whose name was Dominic Diver. 'Just ran over a *Big Issue*-seller – do you want me to reverse and bring him on board?'

'We have a bit of a situation back here at present,' Doctor Proctor replied. 'Best drive on, but carefully, now.'

I had been effing and blinding throughout all this, but as Doctor Proctor had his hand across my mouth, it was difficult to make my feelings fully felt.

'Nurse,' said the doctor, 'please stick this troublesome individual with your needle.'

'Oh no you don't!' I yelled. And I was finally able to get my teeth into the doctor's hand. Which caused him to howl in considerable pain.

And he dragged away his gory mitt and in doing so clouted the nurse.

She tumbled back and I managed to get a hand free.

'Stick him!' shouted Doctor Proctor, spraying blood all over the place.

'You hit me!' cried Nurse Hearse. 'I'm not having that.'

'It was an accident, you stupid woman.'

'Oh, stupid woman, is it? You sexist pig.'

I was struggling with my straps. 'Stick *him* with your needle, Nurse,' was my suggestion.

'Stick *him*!' shouted the doctor.

And then the van took a sudden swerve and the two of them took another tumble.

'Careful, damn you!' the doctor screamed. 'I'm all in a heap here, you fool.'

'Sorry!' Driver Diver called back, 'but some loony on a horse came out of nowhere.'

'Have you been drinking?' The doctor clawed himself to his feet, with Nurse Hearse clinging to his leg.

'I never drink on duty,' Driver Diver called back, 'although I did have some magic mushrooms for breakfast – these *are* the nineteen sixties, you know.'

'Just drive the van, or—'

I managed to get a decent punch in and the doctor went down once again. And I then took to struggling with the buckles on my leg straps.

And then, 'He's behind us!' bawled the driver. 'The loony on the horse, he's galloping after us.'

'I'm taking control here.' Nurse Hearse pulled herself to her feet. 'I'm a member of the Feminist Movement.'

'Bunch of lezzers,' mumbled the doctor. And Nurse Hearse kicked him, which I quite enjoyed.

'Faster!' Nurse Hearse told the driver. 'We can't be stopped by some mounted policeman.'

'He doesn't look like a policeman and . . . *oh my God!*' And Driver Diver put his foot down hard and the van gained considerable speed.

Doctor Proctor was back on his feet and now had me by the throat. I put up a spirited defence and punched him right in the nose. I had been hoping that the nurse would side with me, what with the doctor being such an odious dyed-in-the-wool misogynist and everything. But I suppose she was a dedicated nurse and she was evidently all for putting the interests of the NHS above any personal or political differences or disputes that she might have had with the doctor.

'Hold him still,' she told that man. 'I'll administer the injection.'

'You will get yours,' *I* told *her*, 'feminist or no feminist.'

Something struck the side of the van and it took to swerving once more.

'It's 'orrible!' shouted the driver. 'Or maybe it's the mushrooms.'

'All men are b*st*rds!' the nurse declared.

'She speaks the fairy tongue, too,' I said, hoping to inject a little humour into the situation.

But failing miserably.

Hey, a little sympathy, please – my life was at stake here.

And so I fought, and struggled and fought and the trolley (or gurney, or big-push-along-blong-him-all-ouch, or the chromium-plated chariot of Ra, to those who have really given the magic mushrooms a hammering) fell over on to the doctor and the nurse, which at least let me get my legs free.

And *Crash!* went something into the side of the van.

And, 'It's a Horseman of the Apocalypse!' went the driver, who really *had* given the mushrooms a hammering, *and* they were kicking in.

It was all rough and tumble in that van. I punched at the doctor and at the nurse. The doctor punched me and the nurse still had *that hypo*.

I was impressed by the way she had managed to hang on to it throughout all the to-ing and fro-ing. But not happy that she had.

And there she was again, trying to stick me with it.

I kicked her right in the ear.

But the doctor was up again and sitting on my chest, and the nurse was coming at me with the hypo again and—

'Aaagh!' screamed Driver Diver. 'The Horseman is upon us. The Seventh Seal is open. The beast riseth up from the bottomless pit. It is Armageddon. We're all gonna die. I'm swearing off drugs in the future.'

And the van overturned.

And me and the driver, the doctor and nurse went around and around and around. And of course it all seemed to happen in slow motion, just like it would in a film.

The rear doors burst open and into the sunlight myself and the doctor, the nurse, and the trolley (or gurney or it-is-too-hard-to-come-up-with-any-more-trolley-jokes-now) spewed forth in a great churning mass of much chaos.

And yes, yes, I saw it. I know that I did: Mr Hugo Rune, riding on the back of a centaur.

All in slow motion.

Just like in a film.

And then fade out.

And cut.

And print.

And fade up.

And—

'I told you that Danbury's talks were always a riot,' said Mr Rune, 'but I do think he surpassed himself this time.'

I was alive! I felt at myself.

'Please don't feel at yourself in my presence,' said Mr Rune. 'I hope Danbury's habits aren't rubbing off on you.'

'The centaur,' I managed to utter. 'And, oh, we are back in our rooms.'

'An exciting night for both of us, wasn't it? I thoroughly enjoyed the chase, reminded me of the time I rode with the Light Brigade at Sebastopol.' Mr Rune offered me alcohol. I took him up on the offer.

'A centaur,' I managed to utter once again.

'So you said. My hat, if I wore one – which I do upon certain occasions, although not state ones, as the Runes by Royal charter are granted the right to remain hatless in the presence of royalty – my hat, as I said, if I wore one, would be off to Mister Collins at this moment. You don't see a centaur every day of the week. This is the first that I have seen for more than three hundred years. It is coming together, young Rizla. We are upon the cusp here. Time, it seems, is presently in a malleable state.'

'I am confused,' I said to Mr Rune. 'I am *very* confused.'

'You must learn to expect the unexpected, young Rizla. We have added one more piece to the puzzle. One more badge sits upon your breast. Each episode brings us closer to our goal – to whit, the recovery of the Chronovision before Count Otto Black can lay his grimly nailed claws upon it. Much was learned by you last night, although you might not be aware of it. But it will all fit together for you in time. The manifestation of the centaur is only the beginning of what is to come. We can expect a lot more of such anomalous phenomena.'

'Where is the centaur now?' I asked.

'It depends on exactly what you mean by "now".'

'I know *exactly* what *I* mean by "now",' I said.

'Then it is no longer in *this* now. It is back in its own time, which although being the same "now" as this, is profoundly different, whilst being exactly the same. Did you not pay any attention at all to Danbury's lecture? I personally found it most instructive. As well as being a riot.'

'That doctor,' I said, with terrible recollection, 'he harvests the homeless for spare parts. We must do something about this. We must go to the police.'

'You think they might believe you?'

'Why would they not?'

Mr Rune shrugged. 'They might,' said he. 'In fact, I feel certain that they would, for it is the police who scoop up the homeless from the streets and deliver them to the hospitals. The police might, quite naturally, ask you for some form of identification, of course. I wonder what might happen to you when you fail to provide it.'

'But this is outrageous. Inhuman.'

'Indeed,' said Mr Rune, pouring for himself alone another drink. 'And it will be dealt with. All such injustices will be dealt with.'

'When?' I asked.

'In time,' said Hugo Rune. 'Everything will resolve itself in time.'

'Can I have another drink?' I asked.

'It's now *time* that you popped out to the offy,' said Hugo Rune.

3
The Monstrous Mystery of the Moulsecoomb Crab

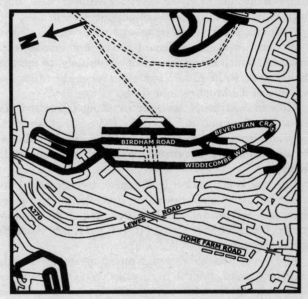

The Moulsecoomb Crab

PART I

I am sure that it must have been May when it happened. The Brighton Festival was on the go and many strange fellows were doing strange things in the town. There was a lot of 'street theatre', which seemed generally to consist of foolish people with whitely daubed faces climbing into cardboard boxes and fiddling about with fish. Things that I am told they did for Art.

Now, I confess that I have never been altogether

comfortable with Art. It comes in so many shapes and sizes and is more difficult to pin down than Iron Man Steve Logan, my favourite wrestler of the day. You knew where you were with the wrestling, of course. You were sitting in your armchair at four o'clock of a Saturday afternoon watching television with Kent Walton doing the commentary.

But Art, well, I was never comfortable with it.

I felt this irrational desire to smite the whitely daubed types, tear up their cardboard boxes and murder their mackerel, which brings me, albeit circuitously, to the next case that Mr Rune had set himself to solve: the Monstrous Mystery of the Moulsecoomb Crab.

Now, I had never set foot in Moulsecoomb. I had mooched all around and about the rest of Brighton in the hope of stirring something that would lead to the rediscovery of my identity, but the Moulsecoomb area remained a mystery.

I do not know what it is like these days. Perhaps it has 'come up' like so many other areas have. Perhaps the houses there now sell for millions. But back then in the swinging sixties, Moulsecoomb was a NO-GO AREA. And that was in capital letters.

It all went back to Victorian times, apparently, and the transportation of criminals to Australia. With the opium and slave trades having fallen off, worthy captains had put their vessels to use in the lucrative transportation of criminals to the lands of Down Under. The scheme – organised, I understand, by an early precursor of the NHS – was that the captains were paid for the one-way journey there only. They dropped off the criminals in Australia, then took on whatever cargoes they thought would prove profitable at home, and then returned.

The cargoes they acquired in Australia – platypus pelts, which were used extensively in the manufacture of theatrical costumery of the amphibious persuasion, and koala ears, which adorned many a fashionable Kensington dowager's snuff-trumble – were profitable in their way, but it was the trip out that paid the bills. And Australia was a long way away. It took nearly a year to get there in those days, two if you took an accidental turn into the Gulf Stream and had to go via Canada. So the worthy sea captains shortened their journey times by dropping off the criminals in Brighton and returning to the port of London the pretty way, via Dublin's fair city where the girls are so pretty, with talk of favourable headwinds and excuses for their empty holds – that platypi and koalas had become extinct.

The criminals themselves, of course, knew better than to return to London and so set up a colony in the Moulse-coomb area, which was at that time all but impenetrable swamp, the haunt of the Sussex crocodile, the Hove hippo-potamus, the Brighton bagpuss and any number of sundry other unlikeable beasties. And from there they engaged in piratical activities and freebooting.

The name 'Moulsecoomb' derives, of course, from the founder of the colony: the infamous pirate, brigand, plunderer and pigeon-fancier Black Jack Moulsecoomb.

Of evil memory.

Black Jack's escapades remain to this very day the talk of the quayside taverns of Brighton. Wherever two grizzly salts meet together, the name of Black Jack is never far from their tattooed lips.

I must have always harboured a liking for pirates. Whether it was the cutlasses, or the flintlocks, or the Jolly Roger, or the drinking of rum, wenching of wenches, chewing of limes or the wearing of ostentatious earrings, I am unable (or perhaps unwilling) to say. But I like 'em.

Do not like Art, do like pirates.

It is simply a preference thing.

And I am sure I would have really liked that Black Jack.

It is said that when the weather held to fair and the barometer was rising, he and his scurvy crew would set sail from their secret inlet within the swamps of Moulsecoomb, cruise around the Brighton Marina and at precisely four o'clock on a Sunday afternoon (during the mixed-bathing season) pillage the Palace Pier.

Apparently, members of the aristocracy, lords and ladies and the like, who came to promenade upon the sundecks during that period did so in the hope of being pillaged by Black Jack and his pirate crew. Especially the ladies, for Black Jack was something of a Johnny Depp.

The upshot of all this, lest the reader think that I am losing the plot, is that Black Jack put it about all over the place, but nowhere more so than in the pirate enclave that he founded, with the result that it grew and expanded into the community that it became: the den of iniquity known as Moulsecoomb, where policemen and right-thinking individuals feared to tread.

Back then, in the nineteen sixties, the barbed-wire entanglements were still up and Moulsecoomb had its own parliament and private army, the Moulsecoomb Militia, better armed and more greatly feared than any official British regiment. There were fewer pirates, of course. In fact, there was hardly one to be found, the last pillaging of the Palace Pier on record being in 1953, when Black Jack's great grandson Grey Jim (for he was getting on in years) launched one final pillage as a tribute to James Dean who had died the previous week.[*]

So I had never taken to walking alone around Moulsecoomb, and would certainly never have entered it at all if it had not been for Hugo Rune and his desire to visit the circus that was presently encamped upon the Palace lawns before our rooms at forty-nine Grand Parade: Count Otto Black's Circus Fantastique.

'We cannot go to *that*!' I told Mr Rune as he and I sipped champagne in The Mound and Merkin (for such was Fangio's bar named upon this particular day). 'Count Otto is your mortal enemy, or so you told me. And you never told me that he ran a circus.'

'It comes to Brighton every year at this time,' said Rune,

---

[*] James Dean, it is to be noted, did not die aged 27 and had no connection with Robert Johnson whatsoever. Although he was recently canonised and is now the patron saint of pirates.

quaffing champagne and chasing a tiny spaniel around an ashtray with a cocktail stick. 'It's part of the Festival.'

'But he is the Moriarty to your Holmes – or so you told me.'

'It is unnecessary for you to add the words "or so you told me" to each sentence. You may assume, and you would be correct, that I am aware of what I have told you.'

'I suppose then that you will want *me* to acquire the tickets.'

'No need,' said Mr Rune. 'Fangio here has two free tickets.'

'Got them for putting up a poster,' said Fangio, indicating the gaudy item that hung amongst the auto parts behind his bar. And drawing the bowl of complimentary peanuts beyond the reach of Mr Rune. 'And I'm keeping them, too,' he continued.

I recollect now that Fangio put up a respectable struggle to retain his circus tickets. I recall the silken words of Mr Hugo Rune that oozed persuasion to part with them. And the harsher words that followed when Fangio failed to comply. And I recollect also that I took to the gents' when I saw the stout stick rising.

And it was in there, in the gents' of The Mound and Merkin, that I first met the bog troll.*

It was the first time I had ever entered the gents' in Fangio's bar (for I was young and my bladder elastic) and I had never before encountered a bog troll.

'This way to the urinal,' said he.

'Excuse me?' I replied.

---

*Bog troll is the generic term applied to cloakroom attendants at nightclubs. It is to be noted that they do not actually attend to cloakrooms. Rather, they set up their stalls in the gentlemen's toilets, where they proffer their wares, soaps and towels and a squirt of aftershave 'for the ladies'. And all for a small fee. And just as there were once 'the Cries of Old London', so is there a cry of the bog troll. And this cry is, 'Freshen up?'

'That's right,' said the fellow, laughing with vigour. 'This is the gents' excuse-me.'

'I am well aware of that,' I told him. 'I have come here to take a pee.'

'Come on, then,' he said, bowing graciously, 'I'll escort you to a urinal. This one is unoccupied, but it is over the drain hole, from which noxious fumes sometimes issue. This one, although on the face of it no different from the rest, has an evil reputation and it is rumoured that those who pee in it end up in court upon trumped-up charges of necromancy.'

'Are you insane?' I asked, which seemed a reasonable question.

'On the contrary, your lordship.'

'My lordship?'

'On the contrary. Now, this urinal might also appear to be the same as any other, but don't be fooled – the floor tiles are unevenly laid before it and an unwary man, or one somewhat taken by the drink, might easily make a forward tumble. My name is Bartholomew, by the way.'

'Is that hyphenated?'

'No, it's Jamaican.'

'Hence the dreadlocks, I suppose.'

'But I'm bald,' said the man, as indeed he was.

I covered my embarrassment by explaining that I was dyslexic.

'Does that mean that you bounce when you fall?' he asked.

'Dyslexic,' I said. 'Not *elastic.*'

'Pardon me, your lordship. I lost my hearing aid. I've been trying to grow a new one, but with no success so far.'

'Grow a new one?' I asked, in a manner that implied that I actually cared.

'A mate of mine grew a new pair of spectacles. But he's a Tibetan lama and they can do all manner of things like that.'

'Listen,' I said, 'I have just come in here to take a pee, and although I find your conversation fascinating, I would appreciate it if you would just leave me alone to do my business and then I will be off on my way. No offence meant.'

'And none taken, I assure you. Now *this* urinal, again whilst appearing identical to its fellows, is definitely not the one for you—'

'Stop,' I told him. 'Stop now.'

'But your lordship, it's more than my job's worth to have you pee in an unsuitable urinal and then report me to Health and Safety for failing to advise you correctly.'

'Your job?' I asked. 'What exactly *is* your job?'

'I'm the cloakroom attendant.'

'But this is *not* a cloakroom.'

'It would be if you were wearing a cloak.'

'But I am not.' And I unzipped and took aim at the nearest urinal. Not that I could actually *go*, because I never can when someone is watching.

'As luck would have it, you've chosen correctly,' said the cloakroom attendant. 'I'll deduct the finder's fee from your bill upon this occasion, but if you could conveniently forget that you chose this particular urinal the next time you come in here, then I'd really appreciate it because I need every penny I can get – I'm saving up for a galleon.'

I zipped my trousers. I did not really want to pee anyway. 'A galleon?' I said.

'A three-masted man o' war. Forty cannon, three spinnakers, a yardarm and a plank for walking mutineers off. Not that I'm expecting any mutineers. I won't be pressganging the crew.' And the cloakroom attendant laughed at this, although I have no idea why.

'Why do you want to buy a galleon?' I asked, because I was genuinely interested, what with my love of pirates and everything.

'To follow in the bootsteps of my great-great-great-grandfather, Black Jack Moulsecoomb.'

'Get out of here,' I said.

'Certainly not, your lordship. This is my place of work.'

'No,' I said. 'I meant "get out of here" as in "you have to be kidding", or "no f*cking way".'

'You speak the pirate patois,' said the great-great-great-grandson of Black Jack Moulsecoomb.

'But surely you cannot be a pirate nowadays – not in the Brighton area, anyway.'

'There's plenty of booty to be had in the English Channel – pleasure boats, sailing yachts, the floating gin palaces of the gentry.'

'I suppose there is,' I said, 'but would a speedboat not be better than a galleon for such work?'

'*A speedboat!?!*' And Bartholomew Moulsecoomb spat into the chosen urinal. 'Pardon my phlegm, your lordship, but I don't hold with speeding boats. Back in the days of the early steam railways, it was believed that a man's brains would come loose if he was to travel at more than the speed of a galloping horse. And I hold this belief to be true.'

'But—' I said.

'Those who travel at greater speeds do so at the risk of their sanity. The faster a man moves, the more stupid he becomes.'

'I think there is probably some truth to that,' I said. 'But a life of piracy does have some risks of its own, such as ending up in prison, for instance, or at the end of a rope.'

'Prison?' The cloakroom attendant laughed once again. 'So what would you call *this*?'

'A cloakroom?' I suggested.

'A prison that smells of wee.'

'I think most of them do. And feet, of course. Prisons stink of smelly feet. And unwashed armpits. Or so I have been reliably informed.'

'You evidently number dubious characters amongst your acquaintances. Do you think that any of them might wish to enlist in a life of piracy?'

'I should not be at all surprised. I am quite keen myself.'

'Then let's call it a fiver.'

'Let us call *what* a fiver?'

'For services rendered. Freshen up?'

'Freshen *what*?'

'Freshen up.' The cloakroom attendant guided me

towards his table. It was one of those wallpaper-pasting tables, of the type that I have spent most of my life avoiding, along with fitted-kitchen catalogues and visits to IKEA.

The life of domesticity has never held much appeal.

The cloakroom attendant's table was covered by a white tablecloth and this by regimented rows of popular male perfumes of the day in their colourfully hued spraying bottles. There was Brut and Hai Karate and Old Spice (which was new at the time and had a sailing ship upon its bottle that might well have been a pirate vessel). And there was Muskrat For Men and Big Helmet and Silver Spaniel and Bird Puller, although few folk remember these top-selling brands today.

'Freshen up,' said the cloakroom attendant, 'for the ladies.'

'Are you selling these bottles?' I asked.

'A shilling a spray.'

'But some of them only cost two bob a bottle.'

'Galleons don't come cheap. And I will be avenged for the death of my brother.'

'Avenged?' I asked, for it is not a word that comes up in conversation too often. 'Avenged upon whom?'

'Upon all of creation. The pirates of old waged war upon humanity and so shall I.'

'Oh,' I said. 'So what happened to your brother?'

'Murdered,' said the cloakroom attendant, 'although the police refuse to investigate the case. They say that it was death by misadventure – that he built the costume for himself and so it was his own fault that it happened. If you ask me, I'd say they were simply baffled.'

'I am baffled, too,' I said. 'Of what costume do you speak?'

'That of a crab,' said the cloakroom attendant sadly. 'The costume of a crab.'

'The costume of a crab,' I told Mr Rune, upon my return to the bar. The Guru's Guru nodded his big baldy head.

'A crab?' said he. 'Go on.'

'It seems that the cloakroom attendant—'

'Bog troll,' said Mr Rune.

'Bog troll?' said I. 'Bartholomew the bog troll?'

'Bog troll,' said Mr Rune. 'Trust me on this. I am, after all, a magician.'

'The bog troll, then. His brother was found dead upon the Sussex Downs inside a platypus-pelt crab costume. The police are baffled; they say it was death by misadventure. And not only that, the police refused to release the body to Bartholomew for burial. They said it was too badly decomposed, a health hazard, and they had it cremated. But Bartholomew says that his brother had only been missing for a day. It all sounds very strange and I thought it might interest you.'

'It does indeed,' said Mr Rune. 'Pop behind the bar and set us up with drinks, would you?'

'Where is Fangio?' I asked.

'Upstairs, nursing his bruises and sulking.'

'Oh, right then.' And I shinnied over the bar.

'Naturally I read of the case,' said Mr Rune, when I had presented him with a bottle of Scotch and returned to the punters' side of the bar. 'Most curious business. Body of a man found all alone upon the Downs encased within a platypus-pelt crab costume. Naturally, I could conceive of at least a dozen reasons for him being there in such a guise, but as to his demise, I do not consider that death by misadventure quite filled the platypus bill, as it were.'

'The bog troll thinks he was murdered.'

'I shall have a word with this fellow.' And Mr Rune rose from his barstool and set off for the gents' excuse-me, taking the bottle of Scotch with him.

I sat and twiddled my thumbs, as one is apt to do when lost for some other way to pass the time. I have never fully acquired the knack and sometimes it has taken me almost an hour to untwiddle my thumbs again.

Happily, they were not too inextricably twiddled by the time Mr Rune returned.

'The case is ours,' he said, 'and the game is afoot.'

'I have never been sure exactly what that means,' I said, as I deftly (and, I think, through luck rather than design) untwiddled my thumbs. 'What *does* it mean?'

'It means, my dear Rizla, that I have saved the patrons of the Palace Pier from an unexpected pillaging – or at least will do once the case is solved and the murderer brought to justice. And there will be a profit in it for the both of us.'

'The bog troll is going to pay you?'

'For bringing his brother's murderer to book, the galleon that the ship-builders at the marina are presently constructing for him will become mine. I had him sign a contract to this effect.'

'In blood?'

Mr Rune cast me a certain glance. 'How else?' he asked. 'How else?'

We did not visit the circus that day, but as Fangio's tickets were for the following week, this mattered not.

We travelled instead to Moulsecoomb.

And we travelled in a taxicab that I hailed for our conveyance.

The taxi driver's name was Ralph, and he was an avid supporter of Chelsea Football Club. To which, he promised us, 'I offer my allegiance and will continue so to do until the Rapture comes and the good are carried bodily to Heaven.'

He then went on to expound his views upon the gift of prophecy. 'What folk don't understand,' he told us, 'is that prophets aren't blessed by God. It's just that they are able to see the peaks. Time doesn't travel in a straight line, you see. Time is like light, it comes in waves. You can chart it, like a hospital chart of a patient's heartbeat.'

I cared not for talk of hospitals, what with my recent experience in one and everything, but the taxi driver continued, 'So time comes in waves, peaks and troughs, like on a chart, and your prophet, he can see from one peak to the next – like a mountaineer, if you will. He can see what's on the next peak. And on the last one, but prophets never predict the past, you notice. They always look forward. And do you know why they do that?'

Well, *I* never learned why. Because by that time we had reached our destination, which was within the gates of Moulsecoomb, for cabbies were allowed entry. And there was some unpleasantness regarding the matter of the fare.

And I turned away once more.

'Widdicombe Way,' said Mr Rune. 'A rather insalubrious neck of the woods.'

'This is a most unsavoury neighbourhood,' I said. 'We will be murdered here for certain. And most likely eaten also.'

'Plah!' cried Mr Rune, 'no man dines upon Hugo Rune.' The Lad Himself brandished his stout stick. 'I am a master of Dimac,' he continued, 'personally tutored by Count Dante himself.'

'A chum of Count Otto?'

'Another count entirely. But have no fear for your safety, young Rizla. Hugo Rune will protect you.'

'Then I will have no fear,' I assured him. 'But what are we doing here?'

'I wish to gain an overview of the situation. We are going to visit the house of the deceased.'

'I see,' I said and I followed Mr Rune as he paced on ahead. And I have to confess that I marvelled at the man when I did so. Not because he was pacing on ahead – anyone could do a simple thing like that. No, it was something much more than that. Mr Hugo Rune had a *way* about him, something that signalled him as being above the everyday and the everyman. He was an enigma, a riddle wrapped around an enigma and tied with a string of surprising circumstances. He appeared to inhabit his own separate universe, where normal laws – and I do not mean those of the legal persuasion – did not apply. Who he was and *what* he was, I know not to this day.

But he was certainly *someone*.

'Pacey-pacey, Rizla,' Mr Rune called back to me. 'The worm of time turns not for the cuckoo of circumstance.'

And how true those words are, even today.

I did not like the look of the house we stopped at. I did not like the look of the gun emplacements in the front garden, nor the rocket launchers on the roof. And I did not take kindly to the garden gnomes.

'What are those three gnomes doing?' I asked Mr Rune. And he told me.

'The house seems quiet,' said the Cosmic Dick. 'Too quiet, in fact. Follow me.'

And I followed him.

The front door was made of steel and fortified with many rivets, but it was not locked.

'Suggestive,' said Mr Rune.

'Of what?'

'Of many things, but none of them auspicious.' And he pushed upon the door, which swung open soundlessly. 'Also suggestive,' he said. 'I suspect foul play.'

The hallway smelled of something. I think it was Bird Puller. Mr Rune sniffed at the air and said, 'Suggestive,' once again. 'Search for clues,' said he. 'See what you can come up with.'

I shrugged and went off searching.

I did not take much to the hallway. The floor was of mottled linoleum and the walls were papered with a drab floral print. Photographs hung upon these walls – military group photographs. I gave them a bit of perusal. There was the face of Bartholomew – or more probably, on reflection, his brother – grinning along with a bunch of hard-looking soldier boys. I read what was printed beneath this photograph: The Queen's Own Electric Fusiliers. I had never heard of that regiment before and I headed into the lounge.

I did not much take to the front lounge. It was furnished with a sofa and chairs of the style known as hideous. Their horizontal surfaces resembled the flight decks of aircraft carriers and the vertical ones the north face of the Eiger.

There was a preponderance of tweed, and a severe lack of cotton. I am no connoisseur of fabrics, although I do know when to call a spade a spade and when to avoid doing so, lest I cause offence. But there was nothing even vaguely spade-like here and I was lost for an answer to that eternal question: *Why?*

There were medals in a glass case on the wall, big important-looking medals with strange sigils and planetary signs upon them. I shrugged my shoulders at these medals and moved on. There were maps on the walls also, maps of the surrounding area with crosses marked variously upon them. A wall calendar, also with markings – rings about certain days. One, I noticed, about today's date. I moved on.

A desk stood by the window, a desk cluttered with papers through which I nosed. I examined one of several letters: 'Dear Prime Minister' it began, and beneath that there were lots of crossings out. The other letters all looked the same. There were many books to be seen on shelves, books of philosophy and religious matters.

Mr Rune peered over my shoulder and said, 'Suggestive,' to me.

'Digestive?' I said. 'I would love a chocolate digestive.'

'You're piddled,' said Mr Rune.

'I am not,' I said, 'but I do feel rather odd.'

And I did. I suddenly felt giddy and sick and the room began shifting unsteadily.

'Out!' cried Mr Rune. 'It is all around us and it is affecting you.'

'Or a ginger snap,' I said. 'Or a caramel spaniel. One with a waggily tail.'

'Out, quickly.' And Mr Rune grasped me under the armpits and hauled me bodily from the house.

Outside and in the sunlight, I came to myself once again. 'What happened?' I asked. 'I feel altogether strange. What happened to me in there?'

'We are on to something here,' said Mr Rune. 'Something untoward. Something unique and unsurpassingly queer. We have stepped into a sticky situation.'

'I think I am going to be sick,' said I.

'Better that than to end up dead in a crab suit upon the Sussex Downs.'

'You mean . . . ?' said I.

'I mean,' said Mr Rune, 'that the brother of Bartholomew Moulsecoomb was undoubtedly murdered. This is a very bad thing. A truly bad thing. If I am not very much mistaken, this is a plot not only to bring down the House of Windsor, but also the British government itself.'

'And that is a *bad* thing?' I asked.

PART II

I sat in the front garden next to one of the unmanned gun emplacements whilst Mr Rune returned to the house. I heard sounds issuing from within, bangings and scrapings and other noises that suggested that heavy chains were being hauled to and fro over corrugated iron. And then the distinctive chiming of a Burmese temple bell, the plaintive howl of a spaniel and what appeared to be the roar of a train coming out of a tunnel, a factory chimney being demolished, an owl hooting and finally the sound of silence.

Mr Rune emerged from the house with several LPs under his arm. 'I don't think too much of the sound-effects records,' he said, 'but I'm keeping this Simon and Garfunkel one.'

'That is not even remotely funny,' I told him. 'I saw it coming a mile off.'

'Which is as it should be, young Rizla, but my money, if I carried any, which I do not because I always feel impelled to give it away to the poor, would be placed upon a bet with you that you have not observed the larger picture.'

'You are probably right there,' I said, rising to my feet and dusting grass-cuttings away from my person. 'Did you find any clues in the house, or were you even looking for any?'

'I have already made up my mind regarding this case. It is,

in its way, all but solved.' Hugo Rune flicked through the LPs he was carrying. 'This Captain Beefheart, is he any good?'

'Exceedingly so. Do you have any Robert Johnson there?'

'The very question I was hoping you would ask.'

'And the answer?'

'We must proceed at once to the Sussex Downs. You will note that the sun is already beginning to set.'

'I trust you will not be taking any personal credit for that.'

Mr Rune raised a hairless eyebrow. 'We will need torches,' he said.

'Flaming ones?' I asked. 'As are generally carried by villagers when they storm Castle Frankenstein?'

Mr Rune sighed deeply. 'You are still not entirely yourself, young Rizla, so please do this for me.' And he pointed with a podgy digit back towards the house. 'Close your right eye and hold your nose and tell me what you see.'

I gave him the blankest of stares.

'Just do it,' said the All-Knowing One.

And so I shrugged and did it.

I did not see anything untoward at first, just a rather shabby, dull suburban dwelling, which, but for its rooftop rocket launcher, titanium-alloy window grills and sandbag heapings, looking much the same as any similar house might look in any similar street. Although quite unlike one of a different period in a different country somewhere else – Wales, say, or Greece, or possibly the Solomon Islands. But then, as I breathed in through my unblocked nostril, I saw it: there appeared to be something shrouding the house, like a mist, perhaps, or more like a shimmering film, oily, glistening, but difficult to pin down. It sort of came and went as you looked at it. And the more you did not look, it came, and the more you did, it went.

'Whatever is *that*?' I asked, turning to Mr Rune.

The Reinventor of the Ocarina was red in the face and he let out a terrible gasp. 'My apologies,' he said. 'To grant you the ability to see what I see, even for a moment, is an exhausting exercise. But you *did* see it, didn't you?'

'I did,' I said. But looking back I could no longer see it at all. 'But what *is* it?'

Mr Rune gave his nose a significant tap. 'All will be revealed, and upon this very night. And you will be offered an opportunity to redress the imbalance that exists between us.'

'The financial imbalance?' I asked. 'Does this mean that you will be sharing fifty-fifty whatever profits you hope to derive from solving this case? Can I have half-shares in the galleon?'

'You certainly can *not*,' said Mr Rune. 'I speak of a spiritual imbalance – that I have upon two occasions saved your life. Tonight it will be your turn to save mine. Please don't make a fist of it, Rizla. I am not as yet ready to move on to my next incarnation.'

'Right,' I said. 'Well, you can trust me.'

'So,' said Mr Rune. 'Torches. And armaments, too, I feel. Bring one of the machine-guns from that emplacement there.'

'A *machine-gun*? I do not know about *that*.'

'I will teach you. There isn't much to it. I observe that the machine-gun there is none other than a General Electric M135 7.62mm minigun, of the variety that they are presently using on the gunships in Vietnam. A war, I hasten to add, that was precipitated by a bet between Aristotle Onassis and Howard Hughes. The General Electric is a sound enough weapon, dispensing, as it does, six thousand rounds per minute from its six rotating barrels. Now let us hasten back to the cab, and be off to the Sussex Downs.'

Mr Rune suggested that for his own safety and wellbeing, the unconscious cabbie be placed in the boot of his own taxicab. And this I did unaided, for Mr Rune complained that his shoulder was playing up – 'the one that had been struck by a Jezail bullet during the Afghanistan Campaign, where I was serving as spiritual adviser to General Custer.'

I dumped the cabbie in the boot and dropped the lid.

And then I drove off towards the Sussex Downs.

Mr Rune had not as yet acquired for me the Bentley he had promised; although he had assured me that it was on order. But my driving skills were improving and I merely glanced against a few parked cars, and sent just a single cleric flying from his pushbike on this occasion.

Oh, and there was some unpleasantness when I nearly ran down a fellow who was filling his Morris Minor with petrol at the garage we stopped off at to purchase a couple of torches.

Now, I do have to say that I had taken a shine to the glorious Sussex Downs, their natural glories, flora, fauna and things of that nature generally. I took the occasional stroll upon them when I felt the need for solitude, which was not often, I confess, as I am gregarious by nature. In fact, if the very truth be utterly told, I never took a stroll upon them at all, for I cared as little for nature as I did for Art.

'There are an awful lot of these Downs,' I said to Mr Rune as I drove amongst them on the road that leads towards Henfield. 'Is there any specific part you would like to visit? It all looks much of a muchness to me, although I cannot see much of the muchness at all now, as it is growing somewhat dark.'

'Keep driving,' called Mr Rune from the rear of the taxicab. 'I'll tell you when I wish to stop.'

And presently he did so and I pulled to the side of the road.

'Where *exactly* are we going?' I asked.

'To the very spot where Bartholomew's brother expired.'

'And you know exactly where this spot is?'

'So would you had you observed a little more closely whilst we were at his house. But that is not entirely your fault. Bring the machine-gun and follow me.'

'You said you would teach me how to use it.'

'And I will, when the need arises. Now pacey-pacey,

Rizla,' called Mr Rune, marching on ahead. 'Mahatma Gandhi's loincloth won't go washing itself.'

And who can argue with *that*?

It was very dark upon the Sussex Downs by that point, and rather chilly, too. I felt very out of place there. And somehow rather vulnerable. Even though I carried a General Electric M135 7.62mm minigun – or struggled beneath its considerable weight, to be precise. But I did not fit in in places such as this – outdoor places, where there were no pavements. I was, and still am, strictly a town-dweller. You know where you are in a town, but out in the wilds, well, you could be *anywhere*.

The torch that Mr Rune carried was flashing its light all about as his chunky silhouette loped onwards at an easy pace. He had told me that he had once walked alone across the Kalahari Desert wearing a dinner suit and carrying only a rolled copy of *The Times* for protection, in order to win a bet with Lawrence of Arabia. Whether this was true or not, there were certainly times when he showed remarkable energy and stamina for a man of his not inconsiderable bulk. This, it seemed, was one of those times and I was sorely flagging.

'Keep up, Rizla.' Mr Rune turned and shone his torch in my face.

'This gun is bl**d*ng heavy,' I said.

'Ah, a touch of the Old Sussex dialect. How fitting.'

'That particular running gag, if such it is,' I said, 'will soon run its course when I run out of swear words.'

'Well, as it happens we're nearly there.' Mr Rune's voice dropped to a whisper. 'Now listen to me, Rizla, and listen to me closely. What you are about to witness you will not entirely understand, but do as I say, when I say it, and all will be well. Do you understand this?'

'I do,' I said. 'And I am cold.'

'Things will soon warm up, methinks. Now follow close at hand. I'm going to switch off the torch.'

Mr Rune did this and the darkness closed about us.

'And now I am scared,' I confessed. 'There could be badgers about and those things can give you a terrible biting.'

'Badgers are the least of our concerns. Stay close behind me, in case of man traps.'

'*Man traps?*' My voice made the whisper known as hoarse.

'We are on secret government property now, and I do not mean property owned secretly by the government – I mean property owned by the Secret Government.'

It was an uphill struggle. In the literal sense of the words. Mr Rune was on his hands and knees now and so was I, struggling uphill, the minigun slung across my shoulders and Mr Rune's big bottom filling most of what little vision I had.

'Are we nearly there yet?' I whispered.

'Nearly, and indeed yes. Come up alongside me, Rizla, and position your weapon according to my specific instructions.'

Mr Rune's specific instructions were: 'Lay it there, pointing in that direction.' Which I gratefully did. And then I peered out into the darkness all around and a big breath of surprise caught in my throat.

We were crouched, it appeared, upon the rim of some natural indentation in the Downs. But it was a vast indentation, somewhat like to that of an extinct volcano. It was a great crater of a thing, with steep sides that led down and down.

To brightness.

The only way to describe what I saw is as an encampment. There were vehicles parked there that looked to be of the military persuasion, but these were not of your everyday military ilk. They were camouflaged, but in psychedelic colours, positively Day-Glo, and lit by strips of lights that were powered by a chugging generator. And within the brightness of these lights were many folk all busily engaged in activities that were strange and enigmatic to me. And there was equipment, too, scientific equipment – big portable computer jobbies with rotating tape wheels and rows of valves that glimmered and glistened and looked very much all the present state of the art.

Which is not to say the *Art*, for this was no *Art* installation brought in for the Festival.

Whilst chaps in white work-coats fussed at the computers, other chaps in black suits, white shirts, black ties and sunglasses fussed at *them* and did occasional pointings towards the sky above.

The sky this night, although moonless, was altogether clear of cloud and I was able to make out the constellation of Orion (which put me in mind of spaniels) and vaguely the Crab Nebula (which put me in mind of Bartholomew's brother who had perished hereabouts in a platypus-skin crab suit).

'What is this place?' I whispered to my companion.

'A window area,' said Mr Rune, 'which is to say, a very special place where the line between what we believe we understand to be real and what we believe to be unreal is very thin indeed.'

'You must feel right at home here, then.'

'Just observe, whilst doing your best to remain unobserved. Do you think you can do that for me?'

'I will try,' I said and I patted the General Electric M135 7.62mm minigun. It really was a most remarkable-looking weapon, with its six rotating barrels and everything. And the big belt of bullets and . . .

Well, you know how it is for boys. Or at least you will if you *are* a boy. There is something strangely compelling about guns, especially great big machine-guns. It is like fire, really – how small boys play with matches and big boys have barbecues and bonfires. There is something about the excitement and danger of it all. Firing guns is wrong. Guns are all wrong. But there is still something terribly compelling about them.

'Am I right in thinking,' I whispered to Mr Rune, 'that the men down there are baddies?'

Hugo Rune nodded his naked dome. 'Baddies of the baddest persuasion.'

'Do you want me to shoot them?' I asked.

The Guru's Guru turned his head towards me. 'Whatever has brought *this* on?' he asked.

'Well . . .' I patted the minigun.

'Ah,' said Hugo Rune, 'too close a proximity to a weapon. I once wrote a most erudite monograph upon the subject of the car crash in relation to metallurgy, to whit how certain metals are capable of absorbing the psychic essence to which we refer, most lightly, as good luck or bad luck. Allow me to elucidate.

'The alchemists believe that gold is the purest metal, that all other "base" metals aspire to be gold and can in fact be transformed into gold by the addition of a catalysing agent known as the Philosopher's Stone. This stone is, in essence, the very quintessence of purity.

'People love gold – worship gold, in fact; they are unconsciously drawn to its purity. Gold pleases them upon a psychic level, above that which they are able to comprehend. Gold, you might say, *is* good luck. Iron, however, and the steel it is converted into, are quite another matter. Here we have the basest of metals, a primitive atavistic brute of a metal. Weapons are not fashioned from gold; jewellery that beautifies is fashioned from gold. Which brings me back to the subject of my monograph. It is my contention that the motorcars that crash, as opposed to those that do not, do so because a portion of the iron of which they are constructed has been recycled from a piece of iron that in the past absorbed bad luck. It might have once been a sword, or a knife or some other weapon. The cycle continues. Evil inevitably befalls the user.

'Now please remove your hand from that weapon lest its evil contaminate you further.'

'I was only asking,' I said and I grudgingly removed my hand from the General Electric M135 7.62mm minigun.

'When I do ask you to start shooting,' said Mr Rune, 'and be assured that I will, it will not be towards those particular baddies that I will request you to direct your firepower.'

'Whatever you say,' I said. 'This is all rather exciting. In a sort of I-wonder-what-will-happen-next kind of way. If you know what I mean.'

Mr Rune sighed deeply. 'Just remain alert,' said he.

And I remained alert, although chilly, and I watched the fellows below us, the ones in the white and the ones in the black. And there were some in colourful camouflage, too. And they were all keeping busy. Then a van arrived from somewhere.

And it was a Royal Mail van.

'Look at that,' I whispered to Mr Rune. 'A Royal Mail van. What do you think *that* is doing here?'

'What do *you* think it's doing here?'

'Delivering letters? Although—'

'Although?' Mr Rune took out a silver hip flask, removed its cap and drank from it.

'Although, as you know, I recently had a most alarming experience in a Royal Mail van. You do not think it could be that evil Doctor Proctor, do you?'

'Observe,' said Mr Rune.

'Give me a sip from your hip flask.'

'Observe,' said Mr Rune once again. And he did not give me a sip. The rear doors of the Royal Mail van opened. And it *was* that evil Doctor Proctor.

'That f*cker!' I whispered.

Mr Rune had no comment to make.

And that f*cker climbed down from the Royal Mail van and Nurse Hearse climbed down from it also. And then they reached up and helped another f*cker down.

And this f*cker was—

'A crab!' I whispered, though harshly. 'Some f*cker dressed up as a crab.'

'Enough f*ckers now,' said Mr Rune. 'Such language does not become you. But what do you make of it?'

'No sense at all,' I replied. 'But I can see his head sticking out of the top of the crab suit – Bartholomew the bog troll.'

'It's his brother,' said Mr Rune. 'His twin brother, to be precise.'

'But I thought his brother had been murdered. *You* said his brother had been murdered.'

'He was.'

'Well, clearly he was not, because he is right there.'

'You misunderstood me.' Mr Rune had pulled a bar of chocolate out of his pocket now and was munching upon it. 'That is the twin brother of Bartholomew's twin brother. The identical twin. It is, in fact, a clone of Bartholomew's twin brother.'

'And what is a clone?' I asked.

'A genetically engineered duplicate wrought from the DNA of a subject.'

'That is science fiction,' I said. 'We cannot do things like that yet.'

'*We* can't. But *they* can.'

'Would you care to enlighten me, please?' I pleaded. 'Clearly you know what is going on here.'

'All the clues were back at the house of Bartholomew's brother – you saw them with your own eyes – but now is not the time for explanations. Look on and learn and be prepared to employ the weaponry if and when the need arises.'

I made exasperated sounds, but I looked on, because let us face it, whatever *was* going on was not the sort of thing that you see every day. Whatever it was that was going on.

And then . . .

'Ah,' whispered Mr Rune, 'if I am not mistaken, the show is about to begin.'

And then I heard those big electrical clunking sounds that are only made by searchlights when you switch them on. And sure as sure can be, around and about the encampment below, searchlights that I had not previously noticed because they were all in darkness blinked on and shone up into the sky.

They crisscrossed and arced in the sky and then appeared to focus upon something.

Something large.

'What is *that*?' I enquired of Mr Rune.

'A scout-craft,' said himself.

I could hear a low, distant humming. And this grew louder to such a degree that I had to cover my ears. And down from the sky dropped this scout-craft.

This scout-craft was—

A flying saucer, no less.

'Mister Rune!' I shouted above the din. 'Mister Rune, it is a flying saucer!'

Mr Rune clamped a big, fat hand over my mouth. With his other hand, he raised a finger to his lips.

Down and down came the flying saucer. I saw some kind of glowing undercarriage fold out, and I do have to say that it was with a certain elegance, almost balletic, that it set down within the crater below.

The terrible humming died away.

A terrible stillness followed.

'The sound of silence,' whispered Mr Rune.

I recalled that I had once seen photographs, purported to be of flying saucers, taken by an American chappie by the name of George Adamski. I had considered them to be fakes at the time, but now I was of a different opinion. George's photos were dead on the nail, conning tower, portholes and all.

An entrance port in the saucer eased open and a metal gangway slid down towards Earth. And then an occupant of the craft appeared in the doorway.

And that occupant looked like a crab.

But it was a simply spiffing crab, and I am not being flippant here.

It came down the gangway sideways, as is the manner of crabs. But it was decked out in a silver spacesuit.

Which is what made it look so simply spiffing.

For those who pay attention to such matters, it would have been noticed that in the early days of the NASA programme, the astronauts all wore silver spacesuits, unlike the white ones that they wear today. Why? Because silver was the colour that spacesuits should be, wasn't it? Everyone in those days knew that a spacesuit had to be silver. Until of course it crossed the mind of some spacesuit designer at NASA that spacesuits did not really have to be silver just because everyone naturally assumed that all spacesuits had to be silver. Spacesuits could be *white*. In fact, they would actually look more chic if they were white.[*]

Well, everybody is entitled to their opinion, I suppose, but for me, a simply spiffing spacesuit has to be silver. To Hell with modern trends.

'That is one simply spiffing space crab,' I whispered.

'I have to agree,' said Mr Rune, 'so I trust that you won't take it too badly when I call upon you to shoot it.'

'Of course not,' I replied. 'After all, it is a *space crab*.'

The space crab was now at the bottom of the gangway. It had sort of scuttled around, because scuttling is what crabs do – as opposed to shifty fellows. Who sidle. Although there seemed to me to be a degree of sidling in the space crab's scuttling, for it scuttled in a sinister fashion. I would not have trusted it at all.

And then I heard a kind of fanfare coming through loudspeakers that I had also failed to notice earlier. And I noticed a chap with a Stylophone™, of the type that was presently being advertised by Rolf Harris on the television. This chap had a microphone set up and was scraping away at the Stylophone™ with a will and a vigour. And then he spoke into the microphone, speaking words that sounded to me like absolute gibberish.

'That would be Cosmoranto,' Mr Rune explained, 'the universal tongue.'

The gibberish went on and on and then it stopped.

And the space crab must have said something in reply.

Because it then went on and on again.

And then stopped.

And then the chaps in the black suits with the white shirts, black ties and sunglasses took hold of the twin brother of Bartholomew the bog troll's twin brother and started

---

[*] This really is true. Look it up if you don't believe me. I got it from Mike Simpson and he knows these things.

dragging him towards the space crab and the flying saucer. And it quickly became clear that the twin brother of the bog troll's twin brother had come to the conclusion that he did not want to be dragged anywhere, especially *there*, and he began to put up a spirited struggle. Which was not easy as he was somewhat encumbered by his platypus-skin crab suit.

'Should I shoot someone now?' I asked Mr Rune.

'You'll shoot no one at all.'

'I am impressed by that,' I said, 'because even though I can only see you vaguely in this uncertain light, you really *did* appear to say that without moving your lips.'

'That's because *I* said that,' said someone who was not Mr Hugo Rune. And I glanced up to see who this was. And someone clubbed me all but unconscious.

PART III

Now, I felt reasonably certain that I had never been marched along at gunpoint before. And I do have to tell you that I did not like it one bit. In fact, I would not recommend the experience to anyone. It is a very frightening experience, having a loaded gun poking in your back and knowing that on the trigger end is a nutcase who seems quite prepared to use it.

I was scared. Well and truly scared. And I felt dizzy and sick in equal part, because the nutcase with the gun – and he was a nutcase, you could see it in his eyes – this nutcase with the gun had hit me with his gun and damn near knocked my lights out.

'Get a move on,' demanded this nutcase, poking me harder with his gun. 'And you, too, fatso,' he said to Mr Rune, 'or I'll shoot your boyfriend here.'

The Hokus Bloke glared daggers at the nutcase and I expected him to employ his Dimac at once and dispatch this malcontent. Mr Rune, however, demurred, no doubt for reasons too inscrutable for me to fathom. And so he and I were ushered down into the crater.

And all too soon we were down in the encampment.

And other guns were being trained upon us.

And I found myself face to face with the evil Doctor Proctor. And *he* now had a gun in *his* hand.

'Well, well, well, well, well,' said this man, looking me both up and down. 'If this isn't the transplant patient. You put me to no little inconvenience and caused me considerable grief. I'm still rather bruised, you know.'

I raised my fists to strike at the doctor. The increased pressure of a gun barrel in my back, however, removed such thoughts of violence from my mind. For the time being, anyway.

'But,' the doctor continued, 'matters adjust themselves. Nurse, do we have the spare crab suit in the van?'

'We do, Doctor, we do.' Nurse Hearse smiled a terrible smile, made all the more terrible by the fact that she lacked for her two front teeth. 'You're going to get yours now,' she told me.

Mr Rune made clearings of the throat preparatory to speech. 'If I might have a word or two,' he began.

'You certainly may not,' said Doctor Proctor. 'I recognise you well enough – you're the rider of that hideous horse. What was that, by the way – a little bit of your own genetic engineering? Well, regardless, I have you now and I'll have your skin for a duvet cover, you see if I don't.'

I looked at the doctor and looked at the nurse and then I looked towards the simply spiffing space crab. And I do have to tell you that, right up close, he did not look all that spiffing after all. Terrifying is what he looked, too large and too wrong and too menacing. He clicked his oversized claws and glared horribly at me with his horrible eyes on their horrible stalks.

'Nurse, the suit,' said Doctor Proctor.

'Now hold on,' I said. 'I do not know what is going on, but it is nothing to do with me. Just let us go free and we will say no more about it.' I have no idea why I said that, really – it did not make a lot of sense. But when you are as scared as I was scared then, you too would talk all manner of rubbish.

'Look,' I shouted, 'over there – Zulus, thousands of them.'

Well, it might have worked.

Doctor Proctor laughed, and he did it in that terrible mad-scientist manner. It was most disconcerting.

'I feel,' said Hugo Rune to Doctor Proctor, 'that a deal might possibly be struck between us, for although my companion remains ignorant of what is going on here, *I* do not.'

'Oh, really,' said the doctor, in a sneery kind of way. 'So what do *you* think is going on, baldy?'

Mr Rune fairly bristled at this and I quite expected him to employ the Dimac Death-Touch. But he did not.

'I am not without connections,' said Mr Rune. 'My name is known to those in high office. I am acquainted with the workings of the Ministry of Serendipity.'

'This is new,' I remarked.

'The Secret Government,' said Mr Rune. 'Those who control the controllers. Those who govern the government. This project bears all their hallmarks and will surely end in calamity for all of us.'

'Well, certainly for *you*,' said Doctor Proctor.

And the space crab gave his claws a further clicking, in a rather irritable way, I felt, a rather impatient way. And words came from the space crab's nasty mouthparts. Words that were not spoken in Cosmoranto, the universal tongue.

'Hugo Rune,' the space crab said in a voice that was all clicks and grunts and very unappealing.

'I am that man,' said Mr Rune. 'And you are Captain Ahab, I presume.'

'Ahab the space crab?' said I.

Ahab the space crab nodded his eyestalks. 'You are correct,' said he.

Doctor Proctor gawped at Mr Rune. 'You two *know* each other?' he said.

'I know all,' said Mr Rune. 'I am Rune, whose eye is in

the triangle, whose nose cuts through the ether, whose ear takes in the music of the spheres. Rune, who—'

'Someone shoot this stone-bonker,' said Doctor Proctor.

'I think not,' said Mr Rune and he delved into his waistcoat pocket and withdrew his pocket watch. Perusing its face, he declared, 'You have by my reckoning approximately two minutes before the heavily armed unit that I summoned earlier to meet me at this location lays waste to the lot of you. I would recommend a rapid withdrawal. Any violence visited upon my person or that of my companion will be dealt with in the severest manner.'

I glanced about at all and sundry. The scientific types in the white coats. The Men in Black, for such they were, in their black suits, white shirts, black ties and sunglasses. The psychedelically camouflaged military personnel. The twin brother of Bartholomew's twin brother, still putting up a bit of a struggle. And Ahab the space crab, let us not forget him.

To say that there was a certain degree of unreality about the situation would be to say that there is more to a Russian spaniel than most folk generally know.

I glanced towards Mr Rune and viewed the big smile on his face.

'Hand over the experimental subject,' clicked and grunted the space crab. 'If the area is compromised, my crew and I must make a speedy departure.'

'Not so fast,' said the doctor. 'You promised to exchange the microchip technology. A deal is a deal.'

'Another time,' clicked Ahab.

'No,' said Doctor Proctor. 'My superiors won't take kindly to that. Don't believe a word of what this fat fool has to say.'

'Another time,' clicked Ahab once more.

'I think not,' said the doctor. 'If you won't give it now and willingly, then we'll take it.'

And he turned his gun on the space crab. And would you not just know it, but that space crab suddenly drew out a gun of its own from somewhere. A big silver gun. A big silver *ray*-gun, I supposed.

And suddenly a cry went up, a great cry, as of warriors, and up upon the hillside at all points of the crater's rim I saw them, big and bold and piratically inclined. And well armed, too, and holding flaming torches. It was none other than the greatly feared Moulsecoomb Militia.

'I warned you,' said Mr Rune.

And I saw the look of horror on the face of Doctor Proctor. And then I saw him swing his gun towards Mr Rune and pull upon the trigger and I dropped down and swung around and kicked at this gun, which went off loudly and blew the end from one of the space crab's legs.

And then there was gunfire all around and things became rather chaotic. The nutcase holding me at gunpoint was removed from existence by an arc of blue energy that issued from the muzzle of the space crab's ray-gun. For which I remain eternally grateful.

There was running and shouting and screaming and shooting. And Ahab the space crab retreating up his gang-way. And the Moulsecoomb Militia laying down fire and pouring into the crater. The fighting was fearsome and I took cover and Mr Rune did likewise.

And amidst the running and shouting and screaming and shooting, there came a terrible humming as Ahab the space crab's scout-craft rose into the sky.

And then some blighter clubbed me down and things went very black.

And I awoke with a terrible headache in forty-nine Grand Parade.

'I do very much hope,' I said, when I had located my voice, 'that I dreamed all that.'

'Which part?' Mr Rune asked. 'The space crab, or the attack by the Moulsecoomb Militia?'

And I made plaintive groaning sounds.

'You acquitted yourself most well and also saved my life, as I predicted.' Mr Rune placed a glass of Scotch in my hands and I was grateful for this.

'And all has worked out rather splendidly,' said the Mumbo Gumshoe, 'for I am now the owner of a three-masted galleon.'

I rubbed at my head, which did not help, and sipped at my Scotch, which did. 'That will come in handy if we ever decide to take up a life of piracy,' I said.

'I'm leasing it out to Bartholomew Moulsecoomb,' said Mr Rune. 'He's still rather keen and there might well be booty worth sharing.'

I did further rubbings of the head. 'Please explain it all to me,' I pleaded.

'Certainly,' and Mr Rune took Scotch himself. 'Firstly, all the clues were there in the house of Bartholomew's brother. You saw them, as did I. You saw, but I saw more.'

'Continue.' I savoured Scotch, and found it to my liking.

'The photographs on the hall wall,' said Mr Rune, 'of Bartholomew's brother in military uniform – the Queen's Own Electric Fusiliers, a regiment that you will not find in any military history book. A unit that specialises in covert operations for the Ministry of Serendipity. There were medals in a case on the lounge wall – you noticed them also, but you did not understand their significance. They were for off-world campaigns, for battles fought in space.'

'You cannot be serious,' I said, in a manner that would one day find favour with the likes of John McEnroe.

'I certainly can. If you recall, in Danbury Collins's lecture, he spoke of the endless vacuum of space, and how there couldn't have been a Big Bang because sound cannot travel through a vacuum.'

'I recall that,' I said. 'It made a lot of sense.'

'But it is incorrect. Space is not a vacuum. Space is filled with air. There is an atmosphere in space and not only that, all of the other planets in our solar system are inhabited.'

'That cannot be true,' I said. 'Surely we would have discovered that by now.'

'Rizla,' said Mr Rune, 'spacecraft have been flying from Earth since Victorian times and commuting between the planets. You won't find this in any history books because it is a secret, a top-secret secret known only to a few. That few being the Secret Government that controls the controllers of our planet. I know this because I have travelled in space. I travelled with a circus, as it happens, that of Professor Merlin and his Greatest Show Off Earth. A treaty exists between the inhabited worlds – a peace treaty. But, needless to say, there are pirates – the flying starfish from Uranus, and those crab lads from the nebula that bears their name.'

I shook my head. Which hurt. 'So Ahab the space crab is a pirate,' I said. 'A space pirate.'

'You've no doubt read about alien abductions,' said Mr Rune.

'I have,' I said, 'in the *Weekly World News*.'

'It dates back to the time of the pharaohs. An unsavoury business, but there you are. Bartholomew's brother, it seems, was having his doubts about the whole thing. You saw also the books on his shelves, books on philosophy. And there were the letters on his desk. He was about to blow the whistle, as it were. The Men of the Ministry offered him up to Ahab, so he took his own life.'

'That is horrible,' I said.

'Indeed,' said Mr Rune. 'But by using his genetic material and the advanced technology that Ahab had already provided for previous services rendered, to whit the supply of the surplus "homeless" for experimentation in the crab nebula, Doctor Proctor cloned another Bartholomew's brother.'

'This all seems rather unnecessary and complicated,' I said.

'If everything was simple,' said Mr Rune, 'there'd be no need for me.'

'Go on,' I said. 'Tell me how you knew that Ahab would be landing last night and where.'

'The maps were there in the house – you saw them. And also the calendar with the rings about the dates.'

'But that is all so simple,' I said. 'But then *you* knew a lot more about all this than I could possibly know. But what happened to me when I was in that house and what was that shimmering shell thing that I saw surrounding the place?'

'An engineered fluctuation in the ether,' said Mr Rune. 'It is the ether that is the substance of space. It is by attuning to the ether that one can access everything – the past, the present and the future. It is how the Chronovision functions.'

'I really do not understand,' I said, 'but I did see a real flying saucer and a real alien last night and that was pretty damn exciting. I cannot wait to tell Fangio.'

'You will tell no one,' said Mr Rune.

'Aw,' I said.

'No one.' And he put a big fat finger to his lips. 'You and I,' he continued, 'have embarked upon a crusade. We are comrades in this and confidants, also. I have to have your word regarding secrecy – it is imperative.'

'Oh, all right,' I said. And grudgingly, too.

'We've seen the last of Ahab for the time being,' said Mr Rune, 'which is something.'

'It is something, I suppose. But there is another something. I recall you saying that the future of the House of Windsor and the British Government were at stake here. It seemed a big thing at the time. I remember thinking that I would probably end a chapter upon it, should I ever come to write the bestseller that you say I will write.'

'And you will,' said Mr Rune. 'The cloning process, which will now go no further as Doctor Proctor was shot in the head last night—'

'Oh, good,' I said. 'I am sorry I missed that, though.'

'You would not have enjoyed the experience. Very messy.'

'But the cloning process.'

'The Ministry of Serendipity's intention was to clone the Royal Family and the Prime Minister, then remove the real McCoys and substitute their own versions – versions that would do as the Ministry wished them to do. The Ministry seeks to control all, but it does not *absolutely* do so. Yet.'

'I am sure I have other questions,' I said, 'but as I cannot think of them now, I will not go racking my aching head.'

'Sound fellow.'

'No, hang about,' I said. 'I do have one question: why were Bartholomew's twin brother and Bartholomew's twin brother's twin brother dressed as space crabs?'

'*Female* space crabs,' said Hugo Rune, and he tapped at his nose and winked in a somewhat lewd manner.

I shook my head. 'I do not get it,' I said.

'It's a long way back to the Crab Nebula,' said Mr Rune, 'and with an all-male crew with time on their hands and—'

'Stop!' I cried. 'I do not wish to know any more.'

Mr Rune and I went to the circus the following week.

It was not Professor Merlin's Greatest Show Off Earth. It was Count Otto Black's Circus Fantastique.

The Count was not there in person, of course, but Mr Rune knew that he would not be. But there were clowns – fellows with whitely daubed faces who did things with cardboard boxes and mackerel for Art.

I did not take to the clowns.

Nor did Mr Rune.

And when they came grinning in our direction and capering and doing it all for Art . . .

We punched them.

And we were thrown out of the circus.

4
The Lark of the Lansdowne Lioness

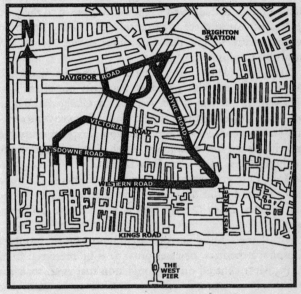

The Lansdowne Lioness

PART I

I really did enjoy my time with Hugo Rune. It was certainly a dangerous time, but it was also thrilling. It was exciting.

He annoyed me greatly, however, because although he always said much, he taught me so very little. He hinted at many amazing things – impossible things, so it seemed at the time. That he had lived for several thousand years, for instance. Ludicrous, I know, but he said it, and said it with sincerity. Also that he walked with Christ, as the thirteenth and unchronicled disciple. And that during the Victorian age, *something* had happened, something big, in which he had somehow been involved. That there was a great secret hidden away from Mankind, and that history had been somehow changed.

And all this had to do with Mr Rune's quest to find the Chronovision, this television-set jobbie invented by a Benedictine monk that allowed its viewer to tune in to the past.

And of course there was the sinister Count Otto Black, who similarly sought this miraculous device for his own nefarious purposes.

Mr Rune had lent me a copy of what he described as his 'Magnum Opus' and 'probably the most important book ever written'. It was called *The Book of Ultimate Truths* and Mr Rune suggested that I should read it from cover to cover and learn its contents by heart. It would explain everything and change my life, he told me. After all, it had been written by the Greatest Man Who Ever Lived.

Well, I did give it a quick skim through, but it was not an easy read and I did happen to have the new Lazlo Woodbine thriller, *Blood On My Trenchcoat*, on the go, so I put it aside.

Mr Rune's book seemed to me to consist mostly of conspiracy theories, or cases proven, as he preferred to call them. Most centred on his conviction that A–Z road-map books of towns and cities concealed more than they revealed. It was Mr Rune's contention that there were Forbidden Zones, which were not on the maps, and that 'A–Z' really meant 'Allocated Zones', the zones that were allocated for the 'rest of us' to inhabit, whilst those who controlled us – the mysterious Ministry of Serendipity, or God knows who else – hid within the Forbidden Zones, running everything. I got almost halfway through the first chapter before I stuck the bookmark in. The bookmark, I noticed, was an unpaid printer's bill for the private printing of three hundred leather-bound copies of *The Book of Ultimate Truths*.

*

'What think you of miracles?' asked Hugo Rune upon a fine June morning as sunlight gushed in through the windows of our study/sitting/dining/drinking room at forty-nine Grand Parade.

I looked up from the breakfasting table. 'Miracles?' I said.

'Miracles, young Rizla. What do you think of them?'

'I have never thought much about them at all,' I said, as I poured myself coffee. 'I do not think I understand *exactly* what a miracle might be.'

'Then look up the definition.' And Hugo Rune hurled his *Webster's Dictionary** at my head.

I ducked the flying tome and availed myself of the last of the toast.

'I shall quote from memory,' said the Greatest Man Who Ever Lived. 'A miracle is a marvellous event attributed to a supernatural cause.'

'I think,' I said, as I buttered the last piece of toast, 'that it is somewhat marvellous that we are still in these rooms. I see another rent demand from your landlord in the morning post.'

'Perhaps *you* should chip in towards the rent,' Mr Rune suggested.

'From the wages you have been promising to pay me?'

'Take a look at this.' And the Hokus Bloke flung me a copy of the morning's *Argus*.

As I caught the paper, Mr Rune deftly snaffled away my piece of buttered toast. I sighed and read out the morning's headline:

' "PIRATES PILLAGE WORTHING" '

'Not that.' said Mr Rune, munching my toast.

---

* It *was* Morocco bound. As in the theme song of Bob Hope and Bing Crosby's now-legendary *Road to Morocco*. Never heard of it? Well, please yourselves, then.

'Nor that,' he said, now downing my coffee.

'How about "CRAB-SUITED DOCTOR FOUND DEAD ON DOWNS"?'

Mr Rune chuckled. 'Not even that,' he said, as he dabbed at his gob with my napkin.

'Then you must mean "SHE IS NOT AMUSED".'

'That's it, carry on.'

And I read the column of newsprint aloud:

In what some are now calling the miracle of Lansdowne, the statue of Queen Victoria is weeping tears of Earl Grey.

'Tears of Earl Grey?' I shook my head.

'Always Her Majesty's favourite cuppa, Gawd bless Her.'

'Someone is having a laugh,' I said. 'They are always having a go at that statue, sticking a traffic cone on its head or daubing it with graffiti.'

'So you don't believe it to be a miracle?'

'I have read that statues of the Virgin Mary have been known to weep,' I said, 'and the *Weekly World News* mentioned a statue of Elvis that occasionally coughs up cheeseburgers.'

'You should apply yourself to more substantial reading matter. I trust you are marvelling at *The Book of Ultimate Truths*.'

'Absolutely,' I said, tucking away the Lazlo Woodbine thriller that was spread across my lap. 'But I do not believe that a statue can weep tears of Earl Grey. It is not only absurd, it is, well, it *is* absurd, and only that.'

'And yet I feel that a visit to this phenomenological manifestation might prove instructional. Pop outside and hail us a cab, young Rizla.'

'I will do no such thing,' I said. 'It is but a short stroll. We shall walk.'

And we did.

Mr Rune gave me another badge to wear, one with the head of Queen Victoria upon it this time. He referred to her as the Lansdowne Lioness, and suggested that she was the reincarnation of Richard the Lionheart. And he went on and on about the glories of the British Empire until he could take my yawnings no more. I pinned the badge to the tie-dyed T-shirt I was wearing, the one that flattered my shoulders.

For his part, Mr Rune looked particularly dapper on this particular day. He had recently taken possession of a six-piece white linen suit – jacket, waistcoat, trousers, spats and matching Panama hat. Swinging his stout stick, he strode along, flipping the bird at a passing cleric and cocking a snook at the seagulls.

Presently, we reached the area of the statue, and here discerned a great wonder: there was a crowd of people present, and local characters abounded. I spied the now-legendary masked walker, who, despite the clemency of the season, wore his usual anorak and gloves and scarf about his face. And there were holidaymakers, too, easily distinguishable by the knotted hankies they wore upon their heads and by their braces and vests. These individuals were being looked upon sniffily by the local residents, the sauve élite of the Lansdowne area. In their shell suits and trainers.

'So many athletes,' Mr Rune declared. 'And see there,' and he pointed to where stalls had been set up, selling flags and T-shirts and trinketry, all adorned with printed representations of Queen Victoria.

'Time to remove the money-lenders from the temple,' quoth Mr Rune, overturning the nearest stall, to the great alarm of the vendor.

'It is a bit early for trouble, do you not think?' I asked the Hokus Bloke. 'Would it not be better simply to blend into the crowd and observe?'

'Hugo Rune *never* blends,' declared himself. 'But we *have* come to observe. Follow me.' And swinging his stout stick to the left and right, he cleared a path before us and we approached the statue.

It was not sporting its usual traffic-cone helmet, but it *was* heavily garlanded with flowers and there were many candles burning beneath it. And the eyes of the statue were definitely wet: liquid glistened in the sunlight and trickled down towards the plinth and from there dripped on to the ground. And here and there and all around lay many arms and legs and other body parts of broken dollies.

'Votive offerings,' Mr Rune explained, observing these. 'I think it's safe to assume that the first purported miraculous cures have already occurred.'

'That they 'ave, mister,' said a Cockney type. 'A woman tasted Her Maj's tears and her dose of baker's bosom cleared right up.'

'How fortuitous,' said Mr Rune. 'And you personally witnessed this phenomenon?'

'Not me, mister, but a mate of mine said he knows a bloke what seen it.'

'You can't argue with evidence like that,' said Mr Rune.

'Are you taking the piss?' asked the Cockney.

'No, I assumed that you were giving it away.'

Mr Rune and the Cockney eyed one another. The Cockney was short and well knit. Mr Rune was large and carried a stout stick. The Cockney muttered something dialectal with asterisks in it, turned and shuffled away.

Hugo Rune took a glass phial from his waistcoat pocket and uncorked it. 'We shall take a sample of the tears to test,' said he.

'To test for what?' I asked.

'To see whether Her Majesty weeps real Earl Grey.'

'And what will that prove?'

'Whether we are dealing with a hoax or what I fear to be in fact something I have been dreading.'

'Have a word with yourself,' I said. 'That will not prove anything.'

'It will to me.' And Hugo Rune reached out to take a sample of the anomalous tears.

But he found to his complete disgust that his way was suddenly barred by several burly members of the Sussex constabulary.

'Stand aside, there,' ordered the Perfect Master.

'Go back behind the line, please, sir,' said a constable.

'Line?' said Mr Rune. 'What line?'

'The one that the officer there is marking upon the grass.'

'I require a sample of this liquid.' Hugo Rune did squarings of his shoulders. 'I am an eminent scientist working for the Ministry of Serendipity.'

'There's no such ministry,' said the constable. 'That's just myth, like trouser imps, or the Oxford Don with the luminous nose.'

'Or the Singing Maggot of Salisbury,' said another constable.

'Or the Laughing Lamppost,' said the first constable.

'Isn't that a pub in Penge?' asked the other constable.

'No, you're thinking of The Smiling Handbag.'

'I'm always thinking about *that*,' said the other constable. 'But the Ministry of Serendipity *is* a myth, like the Battenburg cake that can breathe underwater, or—'

'Or the peanut that surpasses all understanding,' said a lady in a straw hat. 'Although my husband had one of those.'

'I'm sure he did, madam,' said the first constable, 'but I'll have to ask you to step back behind the line also, please.'

'Why?' asked the lady.

'Yes,' said Mr Rune. 'Why?'

'I asked first,' said the lady.

'Because I am telling you to, madam,' said the constable.

The other constable nodded. 'I will back the first constable on that,' he said. 'It's outrageous, I know, the way we policemen can throw our weight about these days, but you have to move with the times, I suppose. So do as the nice constable tells you, madam, or we'll employ the tear gas.'

'I love employing the tear gas,' said the first constable. 'It really makes me laugh.'

'Perhaps you're using the can the wrong way up,' said the lady. 'Which reminds me of the one about the Irish Guinness bottle.'

'The Irish Guinness bottle?' I asked, for I had said nothing in a while.

'Yes,' said the lady. 'What do you think is printed upon the bottom of an Irish Guinness bottle?'

I shook my head.

'Open other end,' said the lady, and she laughed.

'That is a racist joke,' said the first constable. 'Give the lady in the straw hat a little squirt from the tear-gas canister, fellow officer.'

'Are you talking to me?' asked another constable. 'I thought I was "the other constable".'

'Now *look*!' said Mr Rune, in a commanding tone, 'I require a sample of the dripping liquid.'

'No, sir,' said the first constable, 'sorry, sir, please move back behind the line or I will be forced to run you in for causing a breach of the peace, or some similar trumped-up charge, such as trespass, loitering with intent—'

'Flying without a licence,' said the other constable.

'Being drunk in charge of a butcher's bicycle,' said the first constable.

'Taking coals to Newcastle,' said the other constable.

'Good one,' said the first constable. 'And bringing the good name of the regiment into disrepute by rogering the mascot.'

Now, I have said little about the crowd – the growing crowd, as it happened. The crowd that was pressing closely around us, with those at the front of it listening intently to the conversation that was being carried on between Mr Rune, the two constables and the lady in the straw hat. Who now, it appeared, had decided to side with the constables and have Mr Rune run in for indecent exposure and her husband's failure to get BBC2 on the television set.

And there was still much talk from the constables of

'moving back behind the line', which had now been completed, although in a somewhat ragged fashion, by a third policeman with nothing whatever to say.

And to say that I could see what was coming is to say that only a fool wears a blue suit in Lincoln when there is an 'M' in the month.

'He did *what*?' asked Fangio, as I sat upon my favourite barstool in The Quail That Can See Through Concrete.

'Struck down the constable with his stout stick,' I said. 'And your pub's present name is particularly foolish.'

'I've given up caring,' said Fangio. 'And seeing, too, as it happens. What do you think of my eyebrow extensions?'

'Very fetching,' I said. 'I like the beads – although I think the ribbons are somewhat ostentatious.'

'It's the last time I barter with a gypsy,' said Fangio. Which explained everything to my satisfaction. 'So where is Rune now?'

'In police custody,' I said. 'He put up quite a struggle. I would have helped, but he instructed me to get a sample of the statue's tears while he caused a diversion. Which I did.' And I held up the phial, now filled with liquid.

'I've heard that the tears cure baker's bosom,' said Fangio 'A Cockney bloke was in here earlier.'

'The whole thing is bound to be a hoax,' I said, as I sipped my pint of Texaco. 'A stunt to attract more visitors to the town. There are already stalls there selling souvenirs to the gullible.'

'That's a bit harsh,' said Fangio. And I viewed his souvenir T-shirt. 'Bought it off the Cockney bloke,' the barlord explained. 'I thought it was a Hawaiian shirt. Curse these eyebrow extensions.'

I sipped more ale and nodded as if I cared in the slightest.

'So what about Rune?' asked Fangio. 'You're not going to leave him to rot in some rat-infested cell, surely.'

'He informed me, just before he struck down a lady in a straw hat, that no lock on Earth could hold him. He taught Houdini everything he knew, apparently.'

'And the Jackson Five,' said Fangio. 'Their father was all for them going into his bicycle-repair business, but Rune suggested that they have a bit of a sing-song instead.'

'He is certainly one of a kind,' I said.

'Oh, yes,' said Fange. 'They broke the mould before they made him.'

And I drank awhile in silence and helped myself to the complimentary peanuts, while Fangio blundered about behind the bar, bumping into everything.

Presently he tired of this, and so did I, as it happened.

'So when Rune escapes,' said Fangio, 'does that mean he will have to go on the run? That you will have to leave your rooms at number forty-nine? That he might pay off his enormous bar bill here?'

'Interesting questions,' I said, as I filled my pockets with peanuts. 'The answers to the first two might be "yes". But as to the last one . . .'

'Such I feared,' said Fangio. 'I'm seriously thinking of signing on with Bartholomew Moulsecoomb for a life of piracy. I hear he plans to pillage the aggregates depot in Portslade in the galleon that he now rents from Hugo Rune. *The Saucy Spaniel*, I believe it's called.'

'The Sound of Silence' was to be heard.

'I'd switch that jukebox off,' said Fangio, 'if I could find it.'

'Well, I have to go,' I said. 'Mr Rune instructed me to go to a certain address and deliver this phial to a certain Professor Nessor.'

'Would that be Professor Nessor the funambulist analyst?'

'It would,' I said. 'Do you know him?'

'Never heard of the fellow,' said Fangio. 'It was just a lucky guess.'

I did not have to travel far to find the rooms of Professor Nessor. He occupied those that were above the rooms that Mr Rune and I occupied, which were below his, which were, in turn, above ours.

I knocked on the door to avoid any further confusion.

Professor Nessor answered my knockings.

'Aha,' he said, 'young Rizla. You have brought the phial of the statue's tears?'

'You were expecting me?' I asked.

'No, it was just a lucky guess.'

I really liked the professor. He looked just the way a professor should look, all gaunt and angular and old and clad in tweed with lots of mad white hair.

And I really liked his rooms. I had visited them before, upon many occasions, to borrow sugar. Or milk. Or coffee. Or tea. Or cocoa. Or a fill for Rune's pipe. Or . . .

'Step carefully,' said the professor. 'Don't trip over the wires.'

I stepped very carefully. I had tripped on the wires before.

The wires, as might well be imagined considering that the professor was a funambulist analyst, were tightrope wires. They – and there were many of them – crisscrossed the room nine inches above the floor. Professor Nessor was a member of a religious cult that took its sacred texts from the works of the science-fiction writer Kilgore Sprout.

Sprout states, in *The Earth Dies Belching*, that it is contact with planet Earth that is the cause of man's mortality, and that if a man could remain above the surface of the planet throughout his life, if only by nine inches, he would become immortal. The planet Earth itself, according to Sprout, sucks the vital juices of humans out through the soles of their feet to reinvigorate itself as a compensation for all the ill that Mankind has wrought upon it over the ages. Sprout himself is claimed by many to be the inventor of the platform sole and throughout his remarkably long life touched the planet on as few occasions as were humanly possible. His followers believe that he would have lived for ever had he not died tragically in a freak stilt/banana-skin accident.

The professor lived upon the top floor of forty-nine Grand Parade, rarely venturing out, and only then upon two Castrol GTX tins strapped beneath his feet. And to be on the safe side, his rooms were crisscrossed with tightropes, upon which he walked with considerable skill without the assistance of a tightrope-walker's pole.

'You take your life in your hands upon those floorboards,' he told me, as he had done on many previous occasions, the last being when I had come up to borrow a half-ounce of Moroccan black and three condoms, as Mr Rune was going out clubbing. 'The boards may be above the Earth, but they are constructed of wood, which grows from the Earth.'

'I thought trees are made out of air,' I said. 'I have heard that if you grow a tree in a pot, the earth you plant it in weighs exactly the same even after the tree has grown big. So the tree must be made out of air. And water, I suppose.'

'I don't know who puts these mad ideas into your head. But let's see what this phial of tears has to tell us.'

He bounced along a wire to a raised worktable and performed raised work upon it. Work involving Petri dishes, a microscope, a Bunsen burner, some litmus paper, a retort stand, a number of test tubes and several alarm clocks of the old-fashioned sort with great big gong jobbies on the top. And a bell jar.

And at length he was done with his experimentation.

'So what do you think?' I asked.

'It's real Earl Grey,' he said. 'There's no doubt about it. Crawford's of Piccadilly, by appointment to Her Majesty the Queen. The real McWindsor.'

'Well,' said I. 'Now there is a thing.'

'*Where?*' cried the professor, raising the lid of his chemistry set to strike the thing down.

'Not an actual *thing*,' I said. 'It was just a figure of speech. But it is real Earl Grey. So what?'

'It does have some outré qualities,' said the professor.

'Oooooh,' I said. 'Go on.'

'It is not present-day Earl Grey. It is Victorian Earl Grey. The tears this statue is shedding come from the past.'

I gave the professor a suitably old-fashioned look. 'What are you telling me?' I asked.

'I have carbon dated the residues of the tea. They come from eighteen fifty-one, the year of the Great Exhibition.'

'You do not have a carbon-dating machine,' I said.

'Don't try and baffle me with science, young man. I can positively date the tea residues to eighteen fifty-one, to the very day that the Great Exhibition opened. Oh, and there are also residues of Reekie oaks. Those trees only grew in Hyde Park during that period. They were levelled by the great Reekie oak blight of eighteen fifty-two. Don't bandy words with me, silly boy. I know what I know what I know.'

I shook my head. I confess that I was quite confused. 'So you are telling me,' I said, 'that a bronze statue in Lansdowne Gardens is weeping tears of Earl Grey tea that come from eighteen fifty-one?'

'The year that the statue was erected,' said the professor. 'Suggestive, no?'

'I wish I had the vaguest idea where this is leading,' I said, 'because if I did, then when I was led to it, I would know what it was and then would not be the least surprised.'

'I couldn't have put that better myself,' said the professor. 'Unless, of course, I'd given it a moment's thought.'

'Well, I am sure that Mr Rune will be pleased.'

'Delighted,' said the voice of Hugo Rune.

I did not ask him how he had escaped from the police cell. In fact, I did not broach the subject at all. Nor whether he was now on the run. Or whether we would have to quit our rooms. Or whether he would be paying off his bar bill at Fangio's.

I was just glad to see him back.

'It never ceases not to amaze me,' said Mr Rune, 'the power of a Masonic handshake.'

Which no doubt explained everything. But was not going to get Fangio his owings.

Back in our rooms beneath the professor's, which were above ours, Mr Rune said, 'Suggestive, no?'

'The professor said that also,' I said.

'And he knows which way up is a sixpence,' said Mr Rune. 'We will have to prepare ourselves for what is to come, both mentally and physically.'

'And what *is* to come?' I asked, hoping that I might be granted some small explanation.

'Bad things,' said Mr Rune. 'And when they come, as come they will, then it will be for you and me to beat them back.'

'You would not care to be a little more specific, I suppose?'

'What, and spoil the surprise? The clues are all there, Rizla. Can you make nothing of them?'

'Of course I cannot,' I said. 'And I will tell you for why. It is because there will be some metaphysical twist to all this involving something that you knew all about anyway and I could have no possible way of knowing.'

'Why don't you pop upstairs,' said Mr Rune, 'and borrow some beer from the professor?'

The mental and physical preparations that Mr Rune had alluded to appeared to consist mostly of him thinking of things he needed and me running about all over Brighton trying (and for the most part, succeeding, I hasten to add) to acquire them without payment.

By the end of the day, I was thoroughly exhausted.

I had acquired all manner of diverse whatnots. Mr Rune's list had been long, and it had also been specific. I viewed all the whatnots laid out all over the study/sitting/dining/drinking room.

'I would really appreciate it,' I said, 'if you would give me some clue as to what is going on. I would be a lot more use to you if you did.'

Mr Rune stroked at one of his chins. 'This is indeed true,' said he. 'And so, upon this particular occasion, I will tell you what we are up against. Witchcraft, young Rizla. Witchcraft.'

'Witchcraft?' I said. 'As in magic? You claim to be a

magician yourself, although you have never shown me proof of these claims.'

'Magic indeed,' said he, and he opened one of the cans of beer that I had borrowed from the professor. 'In eighteen fifty-one, the Great Exhibition opened in the original Crystal Palace in Hyde Park. There, the very state of the art of all Victorian technology was exhibited. But there was technology exhibited there of which no record exists in the history books of today, technology created by a genius called Charles Babbage.'

'The father of the computer,' said I. 'I have heard of him – he invented the Difference Engine, the first computer. But it was never taken up and he died in poverty.'

'According to accepted history. But that is not true. His computer was exhibited at the Great Exhibition. I saw to that. And it *was* taken up, and with the aid of another genius called Nikola Tesla it revolutionised the Victorian age. Electric automobiles, the wireless transmission of electricity – even a space programme. But it was all wiped from the face of the Earth as if it had never existed at the dawn of the new century. I know, young Rizla. I was there.'

'My head is swimming,' I said. 'Is this really true?'

'All of it – and everything you may have read in science fiction of H. G. Wells's Time Machine, of the Invisible Man, and of the *Nautilus* of Jules Verne. All true.'

'And what has this to do with a weeping statue?'

'Time,' said Mr Rune. 'Always time – the manipulation of time, the displacement of time. The Chronovision, that technology was originally formulated by Mister H. G. Wells, with no little assistance from myself, I might humbly add. Time is not a straight line. It's bumpy and it has holes in it, holes into which things fall in and out – like those unfortunates who enter fairy mounds and tumble out centuries later, thinking that only moments have passed.'

'So that is *true*?' I said. 'What I heard Doctor Proctor say in the hospital when I was in my coma?'

'All true,' said Mr Rune. 'Holes in the fabric of time.'

'And the weeping statue?'

'That statue was originally exhibited at the Great Exhibition. It says so on the plinth – if you'd troubled to look, you would have seen it. It was one of a pair, both of which were exhibited. You will not find them in any existing copy of the Exhibition catalogue, however, but at the time of their exhibition they were billed as "The Remarkable Sympathetic Statues". Although twenty yards apart, it was demonstrated that if you whispered into the ear of one statue, the words you whispered could be heard issuing through the mouth of the other. It was quite a parlour trick. Queen Victoria *was* amused.'

'How did it work?' I asked.

'Victorian supertechnology. Not the work of Babbage or Tesla, but of another.'

'This would not be Count Otto Black.'

'It would be his great-great-great-grandfather. And the statues were *not* a parlour trick. They were a technological marvel. A marvel of technology *and* magic, since alchemy is chemistry *and* magic. It was a cabal of witches that destroyed all memory and all existence of the Victorian supertechnology. Those twin statues were, if you like, portals – magic portals. One of them now stands in Lansdowne Gardens. Where do you suppose the other one stands?'

'I have no idea,' I said. 'Perhaps the other one does not stand anywhere. Perhaps it was destroyed in the war, or something.'

'No.' Mr Rune shook his head. 'The other one still stands, parted from its sister, which was moved here to Brighton on the second day of the Great Exhibition to its present location. The other statue is not in the present. It is still in the past in eighteen fifty-one, at the Great Exhibition.'

'That does not make any sense,' I said. 'You cannot have two things existing at the same time and then more than a century apart.'

'Take my watch,' said Mr Rune, and he drew it from his waistcoat pocket and tossed it to me. 'This watch was constructed in eighteen fifty-one. It existed then, and it exists now. It is the same watch.'

'I really do not understand this,' I said.

'It is difficult,' said Mr Rune, 'I agree. Time is a difficult concept. But the past, the present and the future all exist, all at the same time. I can tell you what is going to happen. Something is going to be dispatched. It will be, or in fact has been, dispatched into the statue in eighteen fifty-one and it will emerge through the statue in Lansdowne Gardens in our day and age. It is already on its way.'

'I am still baffled,' I said. 'What about the Earl Grey?'

'I have been waiting for the Earl Grey,' said Mr Rune. 'You see, I am responsible for its appearance.'

'Go on then.' I sighed. 'Impress me.'

'I attended that first day of the Great Exhibition, in the company of Her Majesty the Queen, Gawd bless Her, and my dear friend Lord Jeffrey Primark. And I observed the demonstration of "The Remarkable Sympathetic Statues". And I observed that their demonstrator was Count Otto Black. And I suspected that he was up to No Good, but I confess that I did not know at that time exactly what variety of No Good he was up to. And so, when the exhibition halls closed upon that night, I did a little experiment of my own. I emptied an urn of Earl Grey over one of the statues. No Earl Grey poured from the other statue. I waited, but none did. I therefore assumed that eventually it would, when it was in fact *programmed* for it to do so. But that would not be in the present of eighteen fifty-one. Rather, it would be at some time in the future.'

'That is an impossible assumption to make,' I said. 'You could never have deduced something like that.'

Mr Rune sighed. 'You are dealing with Rune,' said he. 'You are not dealing with you.'

'And so when you read that tea was issuing from this statue, you knew that it was the tea that you had poured on to the other statue in eighteen fifty-one.'

'Precisely,' said Mr Rune. 'And when my tea appeared, I knew that something else would not be far behind.'

'Incredible,' I said. 'Nothing less than incredible.'

'Everything is centred upon this area.' Mr Rune had

finished his beer and was opening another can. 'The Brighton Zodiac – the Brightonomicon from which all this derives. This is a window area, an epicentre of psychic phenomena. It is where the holes in time open, where those who wander into fairy mounds are spewed out. It is where that which comes from the past will issue into the present.'

'What is coming?' I asked. 'What is going to follow your tea?'

'Evil,' said Mr Hugo Rune. 'Pure evil, and it's coming tonight.'

PART II

I had read somewhere that Queen Victoria had not been too keen on Brighton. She had considered it somewhat tawdry and was all for pulling down the Royal Pavilion. Happily, she was persuaded instead to sell it to the local council.

It is to be noted that the few statues of the great lady that are to be found in the Brighton area all face out to sea. This, it is said, was done at her request, that she should not have to look at the place even in effigy.

I think Queen Victoria was being rather hard on Brighton, particularly as I have also read that she was not averse to doing a bit of opium, and, although making male homosexuality an offence punishable by incarceration with hard labour, she passed no such laws whatever regarding lesbianism because she was of the Sapphic persuasion herself. So I should have thought that Brighton would have suited her most royally.

But there you go.

It was a glorious June night in Brighton, balmy and breezy and beautiful. Mr Rune and I strolled along the prom, although he did most of the strolling. I was engaged in the heavy pushing myself – the heavy pushing of the perambulator that I had acquired, which had been standing, unoccupied, outside a local crèche and was now top-heavy with various accoutrements that I had also acquired at Mr Rune's request.

'Pacey-pacey, Rizla,' said he. 'It takes more than a blue tit's tinkle to fill a parrot's bath.'

Which I could not find reason to doubt.

'You might do some pushing yourself, for a change,' I suggested.

'I might,' said the All-knowing One, 'but it is to be doubted that I will.'

It was eleven of the evening clock and there were still many folk strolling on the prom: Brighton beauties with beehive hair, miniskirts and kinky boots; a number of 'moderns', whose presence put a faint chill into me, although I knew not why; old ladies in bath chairs and gents in straw boaters. And a tiny spaniel or two.

'A poor night for it,' said Mr Rune, making a very grumpy face towards the cloudless sky.

'It is a beautiful night,' I said.

'I was hoping for rain.'

I shrugged as I pushed, and did some panting, too.

'Aha!' cried Mr Rune as we approached the gardens wherein stood the statue of the tea-weeping monarch. 'Cast your eyes across the road there, Rizla – the boys in blue have cordoned off the entire area.'

'They have been a bit heavy handed,' I said. 'They have erected a high steel security fence with great "DANGER: KEEP OUT" signs all about the perimeter of the entire gardens, by the look of it.'

'It's keeping the crowds at bay.' Hugo Rune grinned at this. 'And look – they've covered the statue with a tarpaulin.'

'I really cannot see why they have made such a big fuss.' I leaned, puffing, upon the pram.

'Unless they know something.' Hugo Rune did tappings at his nose with the finger adorned by his Ring of Power. 'Perhaps they received a telephone call early this morning from an eminent government scientist informing them that

the statue's tears were in fact fermenting effluvia, bub-
bling up from a plague pit that lies beneath the gardens,
and that for the sake of public safety they should cordon off
the area.'

'That is somewhat unlikely,' I said, for such was my
opinion.

'Nevertheless, it is the case. I made the call myself, shortly
before you awoke from your slumbers.'

'But . . .' I went. 'All that trouble . . .' I went.

'I confess,' said Mr Rune, 'that I did not expect the police
to act quite as promptly as they did. I had hoped to acquire
my sample before they came blundering on to the scene.
Still, the fracas was fun and I enjoyed striking down that
woman in the straw hat.'

I rolled my eyes and shook my head.

'Please don't do that,' said Mr Rune. 'It makes you look
like a dullard.'

We comfied ourselves upon one of the elegant Victorian
benches that favour the prom. I drummed my fingers, trilled
a bit, then smoked a cigarette. Mr Rune, for his part,
whistled a ditty on his reinvented ocarina, then clasped his
hands across his belly and fell instantly asleep.

He awoke upon the stroke of twelve, which chimed from
his pocket watch.

'Up and at it, Rizla!' he cried. 'A walk around the gardens
is the order of the day. I trust that you have arranged matters
within the perambulator in the manner in which I
instructed you.'

'Trust me,' I said. 'I am an amanuensis.'

Mr Rune now rolled his eyes and shook his head. 'Then
let's go walkie round the gardens.'

'Like a teddy bear?'

'Just walk.'

I walked and he walked, but once more I pushed the
pram. And as I did so, I did furtive things. Things as
instructed by Mr Rune. Things that at least lightened my
load. At length, we returned to the point from which we

had begun, this being the seafront area before the shrouded statue.

'Leave this area untainted,' said Mr Rune. 'It will then appear as an obvious exit. Here we will lie in wait. You have the matches?'

'Five boxes, as you instructed.'

Rune nodded his Panama hatted head, then drew from an inner pocket a brass telescope and gazed out to sea.

'I hate to do what I have to do,' he said with a sigh, 'but it is for the greater good. And yes, all appears to be in order, seawards.'

I looked up at Hugo Rune. 'What *is* going to happen?' I asked.

'Something will come and we will defeat it.'

'As simple as that?'

But Mr Rune did not reply.

We settled ourselves down to wait, although I still had no idea what we were waiting for. It had long gone midnight now and folk were few on the streets. There were no policemen on guard or patrol and only the occasional stumbling drunk or passing taxicab.

'You should have brought a coat,' said Mr Rune. 'You look chilly.'

'Actually, I am freezing now,' I said, as I hugged at myself.

'Yes.' Hugo Rune nodded and drew a thermometer from his breast pocket. 'Two degrees below freezing, as it happens.'

'At *this* time of year?'

'The evil will shortly be upon us.'

My teeth were chattering and my knees started to knock.

'Prepare yourself, Rizla,' whispered Mr Rune. 'It comes.'

And I do have to say that it came with a fair degree of style.

There was a great gust of icy wind that tore at the statue's tarpaulin and hurled it high into the air, shredding it to ribbons.

I peeped through the mesh of the steel security fence towards the statue and saw to my amazement that it was beginning to shake. And sounds came from its vicinity, curious metallic sounds as of heavy industry, faint at first, then rising to a terrible volume.

I clapped my hands across my ears. An arctic wind was blowing now and tears were swept from my eyes. The statue shook and then began to split. Dazzling light blazed from the fractures, beamed as searchlights from the eyes, sparkled like jewels in the crown.

And then the statue exploded into shrapnel. Mr Rune and I took to ducking as shards of flaming bronze passed over our heads like tracer bullets, spiralling into the night sky as lethal starburst fireworks. And then something truly awesome swam into view. It literally materialised, this truly awesome something. It squatted on the statue's plinth and then rose to its terrible height.

At first I thought it to be some monstrous manlike creature, the very spawn of the Bottomless Pit, for it was all over black and fearsome and roared with the fires of Hell. But then through my trembling fingers I saw that this was no beast at all. Rather it was a robotic machine, some twenty feet in height, forged from steel and covered with hundreds of riveted scales. It was a work of hideous genius, all pistons and pinwheels. Twin chimneys rose from its armoured shoulders and from these belched the smoke and flames. Within the chest of it was a kind of armoured cockpit and within this sat a fellow working controls. He pulled at levers and turned at stopcocks and he grinned most evilly as he did these things.

And I knew the face of the man who worked those levers and turned those stopcocks. It was the face of the man who had called himself Orion. The face of the man who was Count Otto Black.

The Victorian robot, for such indeed it was, flexed its steely fingers and turned its head from side to side. The head wore a great brass devilish face and this gazed down upon us. The eyes were lenses set in silver mounts, which revolved and focused, and then the robot spoke.

'Hugo Rune,' came an amplified voice. 'My nemesis of old.'

I was for running but my legs could scarcely carry my weight. I felt Mr Rune's hand upon my shoulder and he cried, 'Now employ your matches!' into my ear.

My fingers fumbled. Found one of the matchboxes in my pocket. Drew it out and dropped it.

'Fortitude, Rizla,' commanded Mr Rune. 'Hand me the matches, please.'

I did my bestest to oblige.

The robot, rather than seeking to destroy us, was turning away instead.

'Hurry now,' said Mr Rune. 'I don't want him escaping to some prearranged bolthole.'

I was all confusion, but I managed to thrust a box of matches into the hands of Mr Rune, who took a match from the box, struck it, plunged it back into the box and threw the box down on to the pavement.

On to the line of 'taint' that I had previously laid.

The taint in question had come from the drum of highly volatile industrial cleaning solution that Mr Rune had bid me acquire and had later laced with various other combustible materials and mixed into a deadly cocktail. This had been leaked in a line girdling the gardens through a hole I had drilled in the bottom of the pram, all but for the area where he and I stood with Mr Rune. But these are mere details.

The flaming box struck the pavement, igniting the trail of flammable solution. Fire rose and streaked. It was a most spectacular effect.

Why indeed a wall of flame should have troubled a fellow in an armoured steel robot, I know not. But looking back on the incident now, I do not think it was intended to do anything other than distract him. And possibly annoy.

Yes, I think 'annoy' would be the word. For the robot

swung back and the Count's face in the cockpit on its chest looked very annoyed indeed.

'Better you die now than later,' came the amplified voice. 'It will spare me the trouble in the future.'

'Rizla,' said Mr Rune. 'Do you know how to run?'

'I feel that I am up to it now,' I said.

'Then run to the West Pier, as fast as you can. I will accompany you.'

Now, I always really liked the West Pier. It was a sort of poorer sister of the Palace Pier, shorter and with fewer pretty fiddly bits, but it did have a ballroom with Lloyd Loom furniture and potted palms, where Friday-afternoon tea dances occurred. Leading to this was a penny arcade wherein stood many old-fashioned gambling machines, which Mr Rune had taught me to win on using nought but the aid of wisdom and a magnet. And there were still some freak shows at the end of West Pier in those days: the Headless Lady, the Legless Yorkshireman, the Smallest Spaniel on Earth, the Talking Sprout and the Peanut that Surpasses All Understanding.

And the West Pier was only a short jog from Lansdowne Gardens.

'Although I rarely perambulate at a pace that is greater than sedate, as befits a man of my dignity,' said Mr Rune, who now jogged easily at my side, 'I am capable of prodigious speed when the need arises. I am skilled in the art of *lung-gom* running, which I learned from the Dalai Lama in Tibet. So I'll see you on the pier. Pacey-pacey, Rizla.'

And then he was gone. In a blur. In a flash. Just gone.

Which impressed me greatly, I have to say.

But did not do much for my safety.

And there now came great crashing and mangling sounds as the Victorian robot smashed through the flame-free area of the steel security fence and burst on to the street behind me.

Amidst the cacophony of driving pistons, churning

flywheels, meshing cogs and great steel feet raising sparks upon the pavement, the monstrous construction lurched forwards, a single stride being ten of mine.

Then came flame and smoke and the rattle of machine-gun fire.

I glanced over my shoulder.

Gun ports had opened in the belly of the beast and rotating barrels spat flames. And bullets.

I added ducking, skipping and dodging to the now-increased pace of my fearful fleeing. Ahead was the West Pier and I was soon upon its boards.

And as I raced along them, with the steely monster drawing closer every moment, a thought occurred to me that caused me grief. It caused my spirits, already low, to sink to a level beneath my feet and plunge into the sea.

Piers, by their very nature, project from land to the ocean.

A man, pursued along such a pier, will shortly find that he has nowhere further to run.

Such a thought must also have crossed the twisted mind of the evil Count Otto Black. Victorian forbear of the similarly evil present-day version, but whereas this thought had caused great grief to come unto me, Count Otto found favour with it. Amplified laughter rang in my ears.

I entered the penny arcade at a speed that surprised even myself. The robot followed hard upon my fleeing heels, overturning the gambling machines that spilled out pennies, which I was presently disinclined to gather.

I hastened into the ballroom, with its Lloyd Loom and its potted palms, marvelling that its doors were open at this time of night. And that its lights were still on.

And up ahead I spied out Mr Hugo Rune.

'Pacey-pacey, Rizla,' he called. 'You won't win a maiden's heart of oak by getting wood in her window box.'

But I was in no mood to deal with that.

I was young and I was fit, but I was now all in. Sweat ran freely down my face and my feet felt as if they were dragging bags of sand.

Behind me came the monster of metal, chugging, clanking and emitting amplified laughter and another burst of gunfire.

'This way,' cried Mr Rune. 'Please get a move on, do.'

And so I ran, through the ballroom and out on to the sundeck, moonlit now, and onward and onward.

Until.

I reached the railing. Where stood Mr Rune. With nowhere left to run.

'Over the rail,' cried Mr Rune, 'and jump.'

'Jump?' My eyes gaped down towards the sea, all black and cold and merciless. 'Jump?' I wailed. 'I cannot jump. I cannot swim.'

'Ah, that's right,' said Mr Rune. 'You can't.'

And then it was upon us. It tore through the rear of the ballroom, splitting the wooden panels and destroying a stained-glass window that was the work of Dante Gabriel Rossetti. It drew itself up to its terrible height and swiped aside a potted palm. And the sound of that horrible laughter came to my ears once more.

'Backed yourself into a corner, Mister Rune,' came words amongst the laughter, as weaponry angled down upon us. 'Should I shoot you, or stamp you to the oblivion you so rightly deserve?'

'Surrender,' said Mr Rune, braving it up with considerable aplomb. 'Surrender and I will spare your life.' And Hugo Rune took from his pocket an oversized green gingham handkerchief and held it aloft.

'It's a *white* flag for surrender, you oaf,' called the voice of Count Otto Black.

'It's a green flag for "go",' replied Mr Rune. 'Climb down from your cockpit, or I will drop the flag.'

'Insane.' Count Otto did some more laughing.

'I will count to three,' said Mr Rune.

'You'll be dead before you're able.'

And then the steely monster came at us.

And Mr Hugo Rune let his 'flag' drop with a flourish.

And it is funny what you remember and what you do not.

I do remember Mr Rune grabbing me by the collar and hauling me over the rail. And I remember the terrible fall and the overwhelming fear of hitting the water.

But I do not actually remember hitting the water.

But then, perhaps I never actually hit it.

Because I was not wet afterwards.

Although I was a bit confused.

I think Mr Rune hit the water, because moments later I saw him very soaked and most upset.

But I certainly remember the galleon. It was *The Saucy Spaniel*, and it had been lying at anchor off the pier's end, awaiting the green-flag signal of Hugo Rune.

And I remember the thunder of an awesome broadside burst of cannon.

And the chaos. And the smoke and flame.

Was it luck, or was it judgement? Was it skill?

I am informed that it was chain-shot, two twelve-pound balls linked by six feet of chain. Very popular on the *Victory*, was chain-shot. Excellent for taking down the masts of an enemy man o' war.

It certainly took down Count Otto. And I suppose it was the explosion that took down most of the ballroom. And being constructed mostly of wood, the resultant inferno was hardly unexpected.

Though, as Mr Rune agreed, it was regrettable.

Especially as the penny arcade went with it, along with all those gambling machines.

Apparently, Mr Rune had flung me down into a moored longboat, where I had been caught by a contingent of Moulsecoomb pirates.

Apparently they had not risked catching Mr Rune, fearing for the safety of their longboat.

Mr Rune and I drank rum in the cabin of Captain Bartholomew Moulsecoomb, the Bog Troll Buccaneer. Mr Rune thanked the captain for sailing the galleon out at his request and peppering the pier with cannonballs when signalled to do so.

He had harsh words to say, however, regarding the crew of the longboat.

5

The Curious Case of the
Woodingdean Chameleon

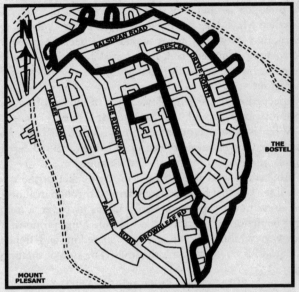

The Woodingdean Chameleon

PART I

'Who is your favourite fictional detective?' Hugo Rune
asked me one morning in July as we sat taking in our
breakfast.

I use the expression 'taking in our breakfast' because
upon this morning it was truly something to behold.

Our regular cook, Mrs Rook, who normally provided
our morning repast, had recently absconded with the silver
cutlery and cruet set, leaving Mr Rune a bitter note that

spoke of 'drunkenness and cruelty' and the failure to furnish her with wages.

Hugo Rune had therefore been forced to take on a new breakfast cook, and this person had appeared the previous day in the comely shape of Jade, a Taiwanese mail-order bride whom Mr Rune had somehow managed to acquire on a three-month free-trial sale-or-return kind of caper. She was presently serving us as maid – Jade the maid, I suppose. Whether Mr Rune intended to engage her skills in the bedroom, I know not, for it would have been indiscreet of me to have enquired. But as to her skills with the skillet, these we were presently taking in, because they were prodigious.

I peeped over the Jenga-style stack of sausages that rose from my plate and said, 'Pardon?' to Mr Rune.

'Who is your favourite fictional detective?' the All-Knowing One enquired of me again, which aroused certain doubts in me regarding his all-knowingness.

'Ah,' said I, and I rummaged in the pocket of the new grey linen suit that had also lately arrived through mail order and drew out a paperback book. Upon its cover was the lurid depiction of a scantily clad blonde lying prone in an alleyway, whilst a brooding figure in fedora and trench-coat stood above her in the shadows. The title of the book was:

DEAD DAMES DON'T DANCE
A Lazlo Woodbine Thriller

The author of the book was a chap named P. P. Penrose.

'Lazlo Woodbine,' I said to Mr Rune and I tossed the book in his direction. He would probably have caught it had his vision not been obscured by a tower of toast.

'Lazlo *who*?' he asked, retrieving the book from the carpet.

'Woodbine,' I said. 'Some call him Laz. He was a nineteen-fifties American-genre private eye, the greatest of them all. He wore a trenchcoat and a fedora and always carried his trusty Smith and Wesson. And he only ever worked four locations, the maximum he considered that a genuine private eye should work: his seedy office, where clients came to call; a bar, where he "chewed the fat with the fat boy barman" and talked the now legendary toot, picked up leads and inevitably ran into the "dame that done him wrong"; an alleyway, where he got into sticky life-threatening situations; and a rooftop, where he had his final confrontation with the villain, who always took the big plunge to oblivion in the final chapter. Oh yes, and all this he did strictly in *the first person*.'

'Sounds positively appalling,' Mr Rune observed, flicking through the pages of the book.

'Not a bit of it,' I said, attacking my sausages. 'With Woodbine you can always expect a lot of gratuitous sex and violence, a trail of corpses, no small degree of name mispronunciation and enough trenchcoat humour and ludicrous catchphrases to carry you through a month of rainy Thursdays.'

'Gratuitous sex,' said Mr Rune, thoughtfully, and he pocketed my book.

'Why do you ask?' I asked.

'Because I have to take a little trip. I will be away for a few days and I am going to leave the practice in your capable hands.'

'The practice?' I queried.

'The offices of Hugo Rune, the World's Foremost Metaphysical Detective, as is engraved upon the brass plaque on the front door below.'

'I fear that Mrs Rook absconded with your brass plaque also,' I said, with some regret. 'But I am not *exactly* certain of what you are asking me to do.'

'Come,' said Mr Rune, and he beckoned. I rose, with difficulty due to the tightness of my stomach, and joined him before his big framed map of Brighton, the one on which the figures of the Brighton Zodiac, the Brightono-micon, were brightly outlined over streets and roads and culs-de-sac and so forth.

'We have so far solved four cases,' said Mr Rune.

'*You* have solved them,' I said, 'if solved be the word.

And you have always done so through possessing prior knowledge that was unknown to myself.'

'And so I am giving you the opportunity to prove yourself, as it were'

'I am *not* a detective,' I said.

'But you'd like to be.'

'Well, actually I would,' I said. 'I have certainly enjoyed myself during the time I have spent with you, although it has thus far been fraught with peril and the wages are nothing to write home about, even if I knew where my home was. Although if I did, I would still have nothing to write home about regarding wages.'

'I think you have all the makings of a truly great detective,' said Mr Rune, although I have a feeling that he said it to divert my conversation away from the subject of my wages.

'A truly great detective, eh?' said I, taking this remark at face value, because I liked the way that it smiled upon me.

'And so the next case is yours.'

'And the next case is . . . ?'

'Pick one of the figures of the Zodiac. Go ahead, point one out.'

'Any one?'

'Other than those that we have already dealt with.'

'Naturally.' As this was clearly ludicrous, I pointed to a figure at random. 'That one,' I said, 'the one that looks like a banana with the mumps.'

'The Woodingdean Chameleon,' said Mr Rune. 'A very bold choice. Do you truly feel up to the challenge?'

I looked up at him. 'You are having a bubble,' said I.

'A bubble?' said the Mumbo Gumshoe.

'A bubble bath. You are having a laugh.'

'I can assure you, this is no laughing matter.'

'But there is no case,' I said. 'Just because I pick out a figure at random . . . I mean, through considered choice . . . that does not mean that there is a case to solve. That is not the way things work.'

'It's the way *I* do business,' said Mr Rune. 'You chose correctly. The case will come to you.'

'Nonsense,' I said. 'I could have chosen any figure on the Zodiac.'

'I think not,' said Hugo Rune.

'*Think so*,' said I.

'Not,' said Hugo Rune and he opened his hand and presented me with the single badge that he held in it.

And on that badge was printed something that left me in no doubt as to the veracity of his words.

Hugo Rune packed a pigskin valise, instructed me to keep my 'grubby mitts' off Jade, waved me his farewells with his stout stick, marched downstairs and out of the front door and hailed for himself a cab.

The driver's name, Mr Rune mentioned later, was Colin, and he was a staunch supporter of a football team called West Bromwich Albion, to which side he pledged a filial affiliation that no man could put asunder, even should this man have Cerberus, the many-headed canine guardian of the underworld, on a chain with him and he, Colin, backed into a corner. Colin may well have held to certain metaphysical beliefs that he was more than willing to share with his fare. As to whether he did, and what the eventual outcome of this would have been when it was Mr Rune who occupied the rear seats of his cab, I cannot say with any degree of precision because Mr Rune never told me. I would be prepared to chance my arm at a guess, though.

I sat myself down in Mr Rune's favourite armchair and loosened the lower buttons of my waistcoat. I pondered momentarily whether Jade would indeed be prepared to make herself sexually available to another, younger, potential spouse, but I felt somewhat bloated and not quite up to the effort. And as I sat and drummed my fingers and whistled a ditty, it did cross my mind that I really did fancy trying my hand at a bit of detective work. Mr Rune would be really impressed if he returned to discover that I had cracked the Curious Case of the Woodingdean Chameleon.

Of course, there would have to *be* such a case.

And this I considered unlikely.

I stroked the badge that now adorned my lapel. Producing it had probably been sleight of hand – Paul Daniels did that sort of thing all the time, pushing Debbie Magee through a letterbox, swallowing gerbils and making Tower Bridge disappear. Had I not read somewhere that it was Paul Daniels who had started the war in Vietnam to win a bet with David Copperfield?*

But all that aside, I really did fancy trying my hand at a bit of the old crime detection. Do it the way Laz had done it, back in the fifties, when a man had to do what a man had to do. And walk those mean streets alone. And, I thought, *And!* There was a trenchcoat *and* a fedora hanging in the wardrobe of my bedroom. *And* I was pretty sure that they were my size. In fact, I *knew* that they were my size because I had tried them on more than once and paced up and down in front of the wardrobe mirror, 'making shapes' and being Laz.

Because, to coin a phrase that I would not normally use, gimme a break here, I *was* a teenager!

I made off to the wardrobe and returned looking hot to trot. The trenchcoat's belt was somewhat tight across my swollen belly, but I would soon work off the bulge with some fist-fightin', pistol-totin', dame-diddlin' big-Dick action. Private Dick, of course, if you know what I mean, and I am sure that you do.

I struck a pose beside the window and awaited the arrival of the client who would soon appear, most likely in a state of extreme distress and in the shape of a beautiful dame, to beg me to take on a case.

At eleven of the morning clock, and fed up with waiting, I took myself next door to Fangio's bar, which today was called The Laughing Cadaver.

* Definitely *not*. Ed.

Which I thought most appropriate.

I straightened my shoulders, cocked my fedora to that angle that is known as rakish, straightened the hem of my trenchcoat and entered the bar in *the first person*, in the guise and persona of Lazlo Woodbine, the world's greatest nineteen-fifties American-genre detective.

The lounge was long and low and lost in a dream that was forever yesterday. The chrome shone like oil beads on a Chevy's tail fin and the guy who stood behind the counter copped me a glance like he was whistling 'Dixie' through the wrong end of a clarinet. I crossed the bar with more aplomb than a pagan pedal-pusher at a podophiliac's picnic and acquainted myself with my favourite barstool.

'A bottle of Bud and a hot pastrami on rye,' I told Fangio the fat boy barman.

'Good evening, sir,' said Fangio, adjusting a wig of elaborate confection.

'Good evening?' said I. 'But it is morning.'

'It might be for you, sir,' said the wearer of the wig, 'but not for me – I have become a Dyslectic.'

'You cannot *become* a Dyslectic,' I rightfully protested. 'You either *are* one or you are not.'

'Well, I *am* one now,' said Fange, 'which rather proves my point, don't you think?'

'Okay,' said I, 'I will go along with this. How did you become a Dyslectic?'

'Answered an ad,' said Fangio, 'in the *Weekly World News*. It's a religious sect – fastest-growing religion in America. I've seen the Light of the Lard. I've been made Hull. And they give you a special enchanted omelette and everything.' And he pointed to something cheap and nasty and plastic that hung around his neck.

'That is not an omelette,' I said. 'That is an amulet.'

'See,' said Fange, 'it's working already. And I got a badge.' And he now pointed to something pinned upon his lapel.

'That is not a badge,' I said. 'It's a *budgie*.'

'That would explain why it squawked so much when I did the pinning on.'

Oh, how we laughed. Till we stopped.

'Enough of this gay repartee,' said I.

'Are you implying that I'm a choirboy, sir?'

'Well,' said I, 'if the shirt fits, lift it.'

'That's easy for you to say, young Razzler.'

'Ah,' said I, 'it is not young Rizla any more, for while *you* are now a member of the Temple of Dyslexia, *I*—'

'It's the *Tadpole* of Dyslexia,' Fange corrected me.

'Quite so. Well, just as *you* are presently a member of that, *I*, for my part, am now a practising detective of the nineteen-fifties persuasion, hence the trenchcoat and fedora.'

'Ah,' said Fangio, 'so that's it. And there was me thinking that you were "having a bubble".'

'A laugh?'

'No, a bubble. From a dyslextic perspective, of course.'

'Any sign of my bottle of Bud and hot pastrami on rye?' I asked.

'None at all so far,' said Fangio. 'So, are you going out on your own, then? Have you been giving your arching morders by Mister Hugo Rune?'

'I do not think "arching morders" is dyslextic,' I said. 'I think you will find that to be a spoonerism.'

'Is it that time of year already?' Fange asked. 'I'll have to put the decorations up.'

I mused upon that, but failed miserably in the attempt.

Oh, how we laughed once more.

'So I am no longer to be referred to as Rizla,' I continued. 'I am now to be known as Lazlo Woodbine, private eye. Although actually, you being a practising Dyslectic will come in handy here, as one of the running gags in the Lazlo Woodbine books is that people always mispronounce his name.'

Fange looked at me blankly. And he did it very well.

'They get the name *Woodbine* wrong,' I said.

Fange shrugged. 'As you please, Mister Humphreys.'

'No,' I said, and sternly, too. 'Not like that. They might say "Mister Woodcock", or "Mister Woodpecker".'

'Or "Mister Woodlouse",' said Fange.

'Well, I suppose they might, but that is not very nice.'

'I'll let you know if I come up with anything worse. But if you don't mind, I'll have to interrupt this toot we're talking because I want to switch on the TV – the croquet is on at Lourdes.'

'Very good,' I said. 'You mean that the *cricket* is on at *Lords*.'

'No,' said Fange, shaking his head and all but dislodging the wig that I had not as yet got around to ridiculing. 'I mean the croquet at Lourdes – the Benedictine Bears versus the Franciscan Foxes. Who really *are* foxes, if you know what I mean, and I'm sure that you do.'

'That is one of *my* catchphrases.'

'You should have mentioned that earlier.' And Fange went off and turned the TV on.

'Could I *please* have a bottle of Bud?'

'Oh, *all right!*' huffed Fangio. 'It's want want want with you.'

Fangio served me a bottle of Bud and a bowl of chewing fat. 'We're out of hot pastrami,' he explained. 'Now please stop talking. I want to watch the match.'

I had never really considered croquet to be much of a spectator sport. And I certainly never knew that it was televised.

Nor that it was quite so popular.

All of a sudden, the bar seemed to be full of supporters, most wearing the distinctive brown of the Benedictine strip. In fact, they wore numbered mini-habits, which I was informed were selling like hot cross buns at the local sports shops. Fangio's eyes were upon the match and he refused all requests for drinks, referring the requesters to a pair of female bar staff that he had taken on for the day. These bar staff were bikini-clad and wore snazzy papal mitres upon their bonny blonde bonces.

'Now *he's* the man!' cried Fangio, pointing to the TV screen as the camera zoomed in on a monk who was taking a mighty swing with his croquet mallet. 'Like the Wolf of Kabul wielding Clikki Ba.'

I shook my fedora. And wondered what the world might look like if you were standing upon your head and viewing it between the straps of a tart's handbag.

'That's Father Ernetti,' said Fangio. 'Father Pellegrino Maria Ernetti.'

'That name rings a bell,' said I.

'No, you're thinking of Quasimodo.'

'No, I was not.' I watched the Benedictine Bear taking his swing.

'Oh and it's through the hoop!' cried the commentator.

And the pub crowd went into a Vatican wave.

'Father Ernetti,' I mused to myself. 'I *do* know that name. Of course I do. According to Mr Rune, *he* is the creator of the Chronovision – the TV that broadcasts past events.'

And aloud I said, 'It is him – he is the one.'

'Damn right,' said Fangio. 'He's a one-man lean, mean grilling machine.'

I shook my hat for a second time and applied my attentive faculties towards the television screen. Not only had I not realised that croquet was a spectator sport, but I had certainly not considered it to be such a violent spectator sport. It made ice hockey look almost refined. The monks, and indeed the nuns – for this was a mixed sport – went at each other like knives in the water, and water off a dead duck's back.

'Have *you* joined the Tadpole of Dyslexia?' asked Fange.

'No, I was merely thinking out loud.'

'Well, keep it down. We're trying to watch the match.'

And I have to say that I quite enjoyed it, what with all the bloodshed and the swearing, which, although in Latin, still made its meaning obvious. And the skill, of course. We all applaud the skill in sport. We do not just enjoy the violence and mayhem. Or watch the Grand Prix hoping for a really spectacular crash.

Well, not *all* of us. *Do* we?

And when the final whistle blew and the bar crowd erupted into cheers and the singing of the dirty version of 'Ave Maria' and Father Ernetti was carried shoulder-high around the pitch by the few of his team-mates who had not been stretchered off injured, I clapped somewhat myself and Hail-Maryed away with the best of them – the best of them being a chap called Kevin and his son, who had come down on the special bus.

'I have tickets to the final tomorrow,' said Fange. 'Excuse my failure to employ the Dyslextic dialect there.'

'What?' said I. 'Are you flying out to Lourdes?'

'Hardly. The final is to be held here. Tomorrow, at the sports stadium in Woodingdean.'

'The stadium is in Withdean,' I said.

'Exactly,' said Fangio. 'That's what I said.'

I took my bottle of Bud *and* the bowl of chewing fat away to a side table that was not being overturned by joyful Benedictine supporters and pondered on my lot.

'You'll go blind doing that,' said a lady in a straw hat, who was passing by en route to the female toilets.

I obviously had to get to the Withdean Stadium and speak to this Father Ernetti – Mr Rune would surely expect me to do no less than this – although what exactly I would say to the good father, I did not know. Talk croquet and sort of work up to his Time TV, perhaps. And then a truly terrible thought struck me, like a dendrophiliac's dongler at an autopederast's arboretum, for I had slipped somewhat from the Woodbine idiom. What if the evil Count Otto Black knew that Father Ernetti was on his way to Brighton? Would he not seek to contact the monk? Count Otto wanted the Chronovision for his own evil ends. Would he not perhaps seek to acquire its creator? Kidnap him, torture him into providing the plans?

'This is deep,' I said. 'This is very deep. And very dark, too.'

'And it will give you hairs on the palms of your hands,'

said the lady in the straw hat, who was returning from the toilet.

'I am on the case here,' I said to myself when she had passed me by. 'This all makes sense. The Woodingdean Chameleon. Well, Fangio confused Withdean with Woodingdean, but that is near enough. And chameleons are masters of camouflage and Count Otto Black will surely disguise or camouflage himself in order to capture Father Ernetti. I have only been a detective for a couple of hours and I damn near have this case already solved.'

The bar was all but deserted once again, the croquet fans having returned either to their places of work, or to the mother who bore them. And but for an Oriental and a salesman travelling in tobaccos, there was only me and the fat boy, Fangio.

I returned to the bar counter, taking with me the chewing-fat bowl, and ordered another bottle of Bud.

'And don't think that I don't remember that you never paid me for the first bottle,' said Fangio, presenting me with same.

'About these tickets you have for tomorrow,' I said, with more savoir-faire than a salirophiliac at a sperm bank's summer sale. 'You did say tickets, did you not?'

'I might have said "rickets",' said Fange. 'Or if I didn't, I probably should. Or property shed, or pebbly shroud – the permutations are endless.'

'I would like one of those tickets,' I said, and I cast him the kind of smile that would win you a first prize at Crufts.

'You can't have one,' said Fangio. 'One is for me and the other for my fiancée Norma. For we are soon to be joined in wholly monotony.'

'You do *not* have a fiancée,' I informed the befuddled barkeep. 'You once had a black and white cat called Ginger that deserted you, if I recall correctly, after you shaded in its white parts with felt-tip pen in an attempt to win the blackest cat competition that the Goth Licence sponsored for the Brighton Festival.'

'I do too have a fiancée,' said Fangio. 'That's her over there.' And he pointed with the stick he used for stirring.*

I followed the direction being pointed out to me by the stick that the barman used for driving cattle to market on a winter's morning.†

'My Norma,' said Fangio, proudly.

I shook my hatted head for the third, and hopefully last, time that day. 'Fangio,' I said, 'that is *not* your fiancée Norma. That is one of the lady-boys of Bangkok, who pitched their tent here during the Festival.'

'Then I have been betrayed by my Dyslexia,' wailed Fangio, affecting a face of vast distress. 'One of the lady-boys of Bangkok? I thought he was one of the blousy lays of Babcock.'

'Easy mistake to make,' I said, 'if you are stupid. Now, about that ticket.'

I recollect that Fangio put up a respectable struggle to retain his croquet ticket. I issued silken words of persuasion. And then harsher words when he still failed to comply. And I recollect also that finally I had to strike down the fat boy with the chewing-fat bowl, because sometimes words are simply not enough.

And it was a long, hard search for those tickets. I went through all his pockets. And the drawer of the cash register.

It finally came to light when, in a right old sulk, I kicked the unconscious barman in the head and they turned out to be hidden under his wig.

'Mr Rune will be so proud of me,' I said as I left the bar. And I felt certain that he would.

* Cocktails, probably.
† An easy mistake to make.

PART II

Oh Stadium of Withdean, high perch'd on lofty crag,
A stony fortress hewn for love of sport
Where land-bound winds from stormy oceans drag
At lichen'd walls, where nesting crows consort.

Yea doth this bastion, this architectual whim,
When fill'd with acolytes of ath-el-etes
Rejoice with cries exhalted, from lovers of the gym
And cost both arm and leg for decent seats.

I cannot be having with poetry, myself. I mean, *what is*
poetry? Song lyrics without the musical accompaniment,
when you come right down to it. I mean, folk singers, on
the whole, are pretty rubbish, but at least they have taken
the trouble to learn how to play the guitar. And how can
you *really* tell a good poem from a bad poem? I think they
are supposed to rhyme, mostly, but even if they *do* rhyme,
does that make them any good?

But then, what did *I* know about poetry?

Not very much, is the answer to that.

But then, why should I? Because *I* was a detective.

I was Lazlo Woodbine, private eye.

And I can tell you, I *was* experiencing some difficulties
with this. I was having a real job keeping in the idiom. And
I was in *real* trouble being at the Withdean Stadium. Lazlo
did not work stadiums. The office, bars, alleyways and
rooftops, yes, but *not* stadiums.

But I was young and had my health and was up for
inspiration. And so I stood in one of the corridors that led
down to the pitch. A corridor that was open to the sky at
intervals. A corridor that would have passed for an alleyway any day of the week, with the possible exception of
Tuesdays.

I lounged against the wall, sporting my trenchcoat and
fedora and smoking a Woodbine (nice touch, I thought)

and occasionally patting at the item that made my poacher's pocket bulge. The item was my pistol. Naturally, I did not possess the trusty Smith and Wesson favoured by Laz, and even if I had, I would not have dared to carry it. You can get arrested for something like that and I had no Masonic connections.

What I did have, however, was an air pistol. It did not possess the clout to bring down an arch-villain, but it could make a decent dent in a seagull at more than thirty paces.

And so I lounged and patted and smoked and looked cool.

And then a chap in a white groundskeeper's coat came along and told me to move.

'I am here upon official business,' I told him. 'Security.' And I flashed him one of Fangio's beer mats. 'Just act as if you have not seen me.'

'Move along, you twat,' said he, in a real pea-souper of a Scottish accent.

'No,' I said. 'You fail to grasp the subtle nuances of acting as if you have not seen me.'

'If you dinna move, I'll call fer security.'

'I *am* security.' And this time I flashed an origami dog, which I had created through skilful folding of cigarette papers.

'Is that a spaniel?' the Scottish groundskeeper asked, adding, 'Hoots mon,' to fine effect.

I tapped at my nose. 'Mum is the word,' I said.

'I'm away to fetch my knobkerrie,' said the grounds-keeper, 'and should I return to find y'here, I'll set about y' as m' forefathers set about the Sassenachs at Bannockburn.'

'Then I will have to shoot you dead,' I replied, patting at my pocket bulge. 'It is nothing personal. I am not a racist, or anything.'

The Scottish groundskeeper looked me up and down.

'Do you know anything about croquet?' I asked him.

'It's pish,' he said.

'Not a fan, then?'

'Dinna get me wrong,' he replied. 'It's a Scottish game, after all.'

'It never is,' I said.

'Och, laddie.' The groundskeeper threw back his ginger-haired head and laughed a highland ha-ha-ha, exposing a crop of blackened teeth that had clearly never known the joys of Colgate. 'D' y' never read books?' he asked. 'The Scots invented everything – the Thermos flask, the television set, the Venetian blind, the Irish jig, the Norwegian wood, the Dutch cap, the French letter—'

'The Jewish New Year?' I suggested.

'And that. Also the Welsh harp, Kentucky Fried Chicken, New York, New York—'

'It's a wonderful town.'

'The Greek Tragedy, the Roman Holiday and the Turkish Delight. Not to mention the American Pie.'

'The American Pie?'

'I told y' not to mention that.'

And oh, how we laughed. For the old ones are always the best.

'So how does croquet work, *exactly*?' I asked. 'I really do not understand the game.'

'Och, 'tis simple. Listen while I explain.'

And he went on to do so. And so I shall explain it to you. Croquet apparently originated in the highlands of Scotland, where poor crofters used it as a means of settling disputes. Which generally involved peat, heather, sheep, long-horned cattle, who had been knocking whom about with claymores and someone called Dear Annie, who was the fairest of the isles.

A croquet team normally consists of four men or women, or some combination thereof, although the American WCF (World Croquet Federation) field six-man sides and allow the underpass rule, which is outlawed in Kilmarnock.

Each four-man team, and only two teams play at a time (although the natives of Papua New Guinea, who took the world title twice in the nineteen forties, allow three teams to play simultaneously, and they also allow the side-swipe-no-takers offside rule, which is punishable by death in Falkirk) consists of a captain, a flackman, a cream-dealer and a fourth man known only as the Shady. The original name for a croquet mallet was a McGregor, after the legendary Rob Roy McGregor, but was renamed the Mallet (after Lord Timothy Mallet of Marlborough) as part of the Suppression of Annoying Highlanders Act 1736. At which time any person calling a Mallet a McGregor could have his lands confiscated by the crown, himself hanged, drawn and quartered and dug into the king's rose garden at Kew. The original name for the ball was a bollock. But as to why this was changed, the groundsman admitted ignorance.

The object of the game is to knock the bollock with the McGregor – or Mallet – through a series of hoops, which are correctly termed the Hoops of McVenus and represent either the female sexual organ or the Great Arch of Heaven from which the Celtic Goddess Danu plucked the star-stuff from which She fashioned the Earth. 'Or least it's some pish to do with womenfolk', to quote the groundskeeper.

'There are thirteen hoops, as there are thirteen months in the year and thirteen spots upon a dice. The—'

'You are making all this up,' I said to the groundskeeper.

'Damn right,' said that man, 'y' Sassenach twat.'

'What time does the match start?'

'Start?' said he. 'It's almost finished.'

And I should have guessed, really, what with all the deafening cheers that were coming from the stands. And the broken bodies of injured players being carried past me on stretchers. And the reserves jogging by to replace them, crossing themselves as they did so.

'Who are the Benedictine Bears playing in the final game?' I asked the groundskeeper, who had fallen into fits of drunken[*] mirth and seemed on the point of collapse.

---

[*] For Scotsmen are known to enjoy a drink.

'Glasgow Rangers,' he managed to say.

I looked up and down the 'alleyway', but apart from the groundskeeper and myself it was otherwise deserted. I drew out my trusty air pistol and did unto the groundskeeper what Mr Rune did unto cabbies with his very own stout stick.

Two stretcher-bearers appeared from the ground end of the 'alleyway', bearing another bloodied body. They stepped carefully over the fallen groundskeeper.

'Is Father Ernetti still on the pitch?' I asked them.

'He's responsible for this,' said one of the stretcher-bearers, nodding to the bloodied body. 'Now stand aside, please, we have to get this chap into the back of a Royal Mail van.'

I took myself to the end of the 'alleyway' and peered out at the sunlit pitch. And I do have to say that what with all the carnage going on down there, it put me somewhat in mind of the Games of Ancient Rome, the glory days of sport, with lions and gladiators and Caesar giving the old thumbs-down from the royal box while munching lark's noses and being given a Swedish swallow (which the Scottish probably invented) by a slave girl.

And there was Father Ernetti, in the thick of it, giving as good as he got and better and bringing his blessing-finger into play before dispatching an opponent.

Beneath the shade of my fedora's brim, I surveyed the crowd as best I could. Was he out there somewhere, the evil Count Otto, ready to strike? With the height of him and his long black beard, he would have to be a master of disguise to avoid recognition.

By *me*. The detective.

Well, if he was there, I could not see him. And so I lounged in the 'alleyway' and enjoyed the closing moments of the match. The scores were even up on the big board – six hundred and sixty-five points each. If Father Ernetti could not whack his bollock through the last Hoop of McVenus before the ref. blew his whistle, there was every chance of it going into extra time, possibly even ending in a penalty hoopout.

I glanced up once more to the big scoreboard. The final seconds were ticking away upon the big digital clock. It was an early precursor of those liquid-crystal-display jobbies that were soon to become all the rage. Its internal workings involved a small boy with a skill for counting seconds and a deft hand for slotting up a numbered card.

Thirty seconds left of the match time.

And a little twinkle.

I did the old double-take, as Laz himself would probably have done, but in a more prosaic manner. What *was* that little twinkle? I delved into my trenchcoat and brought out Mr Rune's brass telescope, the one through which he had viewed Captain Bartholomew Moulsecoomb's pirate galleon during the Lansdowne Lioness adventure. I had taken quite a shine to it, and when the opportunity had presented itself for me to acquire it for my own professional use, I had taken up this presented opportunity with gusto.

I put the telescope to my eye and did focusings. And there I spied, upon the rooftop up above the big scoreboard, a crouching figure clad in black and peering through a telescopic sight.

A telescopic sight that was mounted upon a very long rifle indeed.

'Oh my God,' I said to none other than myself. 'A sniper.' And I angled my spyglass from his rifle to the pitch. He was aiming for Father Ernetti.

And I confess that at that moment, I did not know what to do. Cause a distraction? Run on to the pitch? I could rip off all my clothes and streak. Streaking was all the rage nowadays. Folk did it all the time, at football grounds and race meetings, in supermarkets, in cinemas (although no one noticed these streakers much).

Lazlo Woodbine *never* streaked, I told myself, although he did once take off all his clothes in *The Blonde in the Burberry Body Bag* (A Lazlo Woodbine Thriller). But that had been to display his regimental tattoo[*] to a dame that inevitably done him wrong.

But I was in serious trouble here. My air pistol did not have the range or the requisite ballistic capabilities to bring down a sniper.

And I did not know how to fly a Mustang.

And my chances of ever starring in a Broadway musical were, to say the least, remote.

So I would have to come up with something else.

Or in this case, it seemed, I would not, because the ref blew his whistle and the entire crowd in the stadium rose to its collective feet and cast its collective headwear into the air. Which somewhat obscured the sniper's view and allowed the good Father Ernetti to leave the field of play unshot and head off to the changing rooms. Probably for oranges, a pep talk from his manager and a Hail Mary Haka before engaging in extra time.

Which gave *me* some extra time.

I headed off up the 'alleyway' in search of a stairway or something.

Looking back on all this now, I probably would have been better going directly to Father Ernetti's changing room and informing him that there was a rooftop sniper intending to 'take him out'. But I figured (well, in retrospect, I suppose it must have been what I figured at the time) that it was not the way that Laz did business.

Laz always went for the final rooftop confrontation.

And it never failed him once. In one hundred and thirty-two best-selling thrillers.

I steeled myself to do what must be done, and fell into genre to do it.

The alleyway was colder than the heart of an errant wife.

My footsteps echoed hollow as a hooker's moan of passion.

[*] Fosdyke's Flying Tigers. Woodbine was a Mustang pilot during WWII (as opposed to WWF) where he'd served in the South Pacific. And later starred in the stage version of *The Blonde in the Burberry Body Bag* when it became a musical and was first brought to Broadway.

But a man must do what a man must do to save another's life.

And a stylish trenchcoat's never out of fashion.

'No,' I said to myself, with more snafu than a kamikaze catamite at a coprophiliacs' convention. 'This is not the time for poetry. This is time for action.'

And I found myself in the stadium's bar, which was filling up with thirsty sports fans. I elbowed my way between two who did not look particularly psychotic and called out to the barman.

'Which way to the scoreboard?' I called. 'I need to get up there in a hurry.'

> 'Would you mind doing that in verse for me?
> And I'll serve you with alacrity,'

said the barman. 'Only I have recently converted from the Tadpole of Dyslexia to the Church of Poetic Pronouncement, and I now only communicate in rhyme.'

'Fangio,' I said. 'It is *you*.'

'Was that iambic pentameter?' asked the barman. 'Or was it a haiku?'

> 'It could be either, I do not know.
> I need the stairs, I have to go.'

'Very good,' said the barman.

> 'A fine piece of verse.
> It could have been better.
> But I have heard worse.

'Are you a practising Pronouncist yourself?'

> 'What are you doing behind the bar?
> You have a ticket. And also a scar.'*

---

* Where I had whacked him the previous day with the chewing-fat bowl.

'I'm most impressed sir,
A pint would it be?
We've draught BP Super
Or plain G and T.'

'What *are* you doing behind the bar?' I asked the versifying barkeep.

'In confidence,' said Fangio, 'working a bit of a flanker. The barman in residence, Colonel Mortimer (the best shot in the Carolinas) had to pop upstairs upon some pressing business. He bunged me fifty quid cash to fill in for him. Damn, none of that rhymed, did it? There once was a barman called Mortimer/Who—'

'Fange, this is serious business. Which way did he go?'

'Who went up the stairs for a shortener. No, that doesn't make any sense, does it? But do you think it matters? I can't be having with poetry, myself. I mean, *what is* poetry? Song lyrics without musical—'

I reached across the bar counter and grabbed Fangio by the throat. Which did not go down particularly well with all the sports fans who were crying out for drink.

'Unhand that barman, mister,' said one – a Cockney, by the look of his vest and braces. 'We want serving here.'

'This is serious,' I said. 'This is a matter of life and death.'

'They always say that,' said a lady in a straw hat.

'Who do?' asked the wearer of the vest and braces.

'Vegetarians,' said the lady. 'The bane of my existence, they are. Always hovering around the meat counter in Sainsbury's when you're trying to buy cutlets, wearing those shoes they wear and going on and on about meat being murder and that if sheep were left alone and never sheared they'd grow bigger and bigger and then float off into the sky to become clouds.'

'I've heard that about sheep,' said he of the vest and braces. 'And gorillas. They'd all grow to the size of King Kong if you left them to it. Which is why I always shoot the blighters if I see them in a zoo.'

I had not relinquished my hold upon Fangio's throat. 'Which way did Colonel Mortimer go?' I requested to know once again.

Fangio made gagging sounds, which I found less than informative.

'Let that barman go,' said the Cockney. 'Extra time will be starting in ten minutes.'

I let Fangio go. 'Tell me which way the colonel went,' I shouted at him, 'or I will shoot you dead.'

And to add some weight to my words, I drew out my pistol and flourished it all about.

Which had a most remarkable effect on the crowd.

Who immediately drew out theirs.

'That,' said the lady in the straw hat, 'is what you call a Mexican stand-off.'

'The Scottish invented that,' said a well-informed member of the gun-toting crowd.

'I will shoot the barman,' I said. 'Then none of you will get served.'

'We'll help ourselves,' said the Cockney.

'Over my dead body,' said Fangio.

'Well, obviously,' said the lady in the straw hat. 'I think I'll have a double Pernod and lemonade. I've never been able to afford that.'

'Fange,' I said to Fangio, 'I do not want to shoot you, really. I just want to know where the colonel went.'

Fangio pointed across the bar to a sign above a doorway that read 'TO THE SCOREBOARD ONLY'.

'Thank you,' I said.

'No problem, sir. Now, who wants serving?'

I went through the door and then up a flight of steps. Although they will not receive a mention here as Lazlo Woodbine did not work steps. Unless they were in alleyways, of course, like those retractable iron fire-escape jobbies that are always to be found in New York alleyways. And indeed figured large in *The Bride Wore A Concrete Wedding Gown* (A Lazlo Woodbine Thriller) where Laz held a week-long stakeout on just such a set of stairs, watching the rear door of Tony Gallenti's nightclub The Blue Nipple, and was rewarded by witnessing Deaf Boy Helligan, the blues singer, being gunned down by one of the Carrachilo Brothers, about which he was able to testify before the grand jury. Although this was done as a footnote. Because Laz did not do courtrooms.

But I digress.

A rooftop is a rooftop, said the greatest Dick of them all, but a dame with a handlebar moustache will never be Queen of May. I eased open the rooftop door and peeped through the crack, my pistol in my hand.

And there he was, lying there, Colonel Mortimer, the best shot in the Carolinas. Henchman of the evil Count Otto Black. There was no doubt in my mind of that.

The door had less squeak to it than a mouse with laryngitis and I crept over the rooftop like a floor-fetishist at a tiler's tea party. And then I heard the crowd go crazy. The players were back on the field.

I saw the colonel stiffen and take aim.

And I crept up upon him with a smile on my face that would have won me a first prize at Crufts had I been a spaniel and had spaniels' smiles been a speciality event.

'Oh, sod it,' I said to myself. 'I will shoot the blighter in the leg and have done with it.'

And so I shot him.

Just like that.

And missed.

And Colonel Mortimer turned his head and, I have to say it, glared somewhat at me. And then he turned not only his head, but the rest of his body, too, including his rifle.

'So,' said he, rising to his feet, 'what do we have here?'

I was frantically trying to reload my pistol.

'You are under arrest,' I said. 'Do not do anything hasty, such as shooting me. You are surrounded.'

'Really?' The colonel looked most unconvinced. And I do have to say that he did not look much like a colonel. I had always imagined colonels as having military bearing, and big sideburns, of course, and looking very much like Lionel Jefferies. This fellow looked more like Rondo Hatton.

'And who might you be?' asked the look-alike of Hollywood's greatest actor.

I chewed upon my bottom lip. 'The name is Woodbine,' I said, 'Lazlo Woodbine,' adding the now-legendary words, 'Some call me Laz.'

'Mister Woodlouse,' said Colonel Mortimer, which was at least in keeping with the books, in which Laz's name was always mispronounced, but not altogether impressive, because Fangio had already done that one. 'Mister Woodlouse, we meet again.'

'We do?' I said.

'Oh, indeed. Surely you recall in *Death Is A Rotund Redhead* (A Lazlo Woodbine Thriller) that we had a shoot-out in your office. I was disguised as a Persian dwarf and you as a fiddler's elbow. I escaped down the laundry chute, leaving you with egg on your face and fluff on your gramophone needle.'

'I do not think I remember that one,' I said, scratching at my fedora.

'Perhaps I just made it up, then. But it doesn't matter either way, because I'm going to kill you.'

'Look out behind you!' I shouted. 'Zulus, thousands of them.'

But curiously to no effect.

It has always been the way with me that when caught in moments of extreme panic, I have a tendency to flap my hands and spin around in small circles. So far during my time with Mr Rune, I had somehow managed to avoid doing this, possibly because I was always in his company when the big trouble got on the go. But who indeed can say for sure?

But what I must confess here is that those hands of mine were really beginning to flap.

'Trying to fly away, are you?' Colonel Mortimer advanced upon me. 'You chose the wrong day to be Woodbine. Today, I'm afraid, is a Tuesday.'

I tried to stand my ground, but it was not easy. My hands were flapping freely now and I was beginning to spin.

'Let us talk about this,' I managed to say. 'You really do not want to shoot me.'

'Oh, I do,' said the colonel. 'I really do. And then I'll shoot Mister Grimsdale.'

'Mister Grimsdale?' I said. 'Who is Mister Grimsdale?'

'The referee,' said Colonel Mortimer. 'The swine who has been shagging my wife.'

'Oh,' I said. '*That* Mister Grimsdale.'

'Well, obviously *that* Mister Grimsdale. What other Mister Grimsdale did you think I'd be lying on this rooftop trying to shoot?'

'The one in the Norman Wisdom movies?'

'What, the one played by that fine character actor Rondo Hatton?'

'Rondo Hatton did not play Mister Grimsdale,' I said. 'It was that fine character actor Edward Chapman who played Mister Grimsdale.'

'Well, that's neither here nor there. He has to die and so do you.'

'Well, actually, I do not,' I said. 'You see, I thought you were up here to shoot Father Ernetti.'

'Who?'

'The captain of the Benedictine Bears.'

'Oh, *that* Father Ernetti.'

'Yes,' I said. 'That one. But if you are only going to shoot the referee, that does not matter to me. I will leave you to get on with it. It is none of my business.'

'Sure?'

'Sure,' said I. 'If he has been having sex with your wife, then he deserves it. Go ahead. It is nothing to do with me.'

'You won't have another go at me when I lie down again to take aim?'

'Not at all. I will lie down with you, if you want.'

'No,' said the colonel. 'You don't have to do that. I'm going to shoot myself afterwards. I shot my wife earlier, and when I've killed Grimsdale, I'll do away with myself.'

'You know your own business best, then,' I said. 'Far be it from me to go butting in. I am sorry to have interrupted you. No offence meant.'

'None taken, I assure you.'

And I went on my way.

Well, sort of.

I read the *Argus* the following day to see how he had got on. Not too well, as it happened. He may have been the best shot in the Carolinas, but it had been Tuesday and he had not even managed to wing that Mister Grimsdale.

Apparently, whilst taking aim he had slipped and fallen off the roof above the big scoreboard, and had not fared well when he had hit the crowd beneath, injuring a Cockney and bothering a lady who wore a straw hat.

'And so,' I said to Mr Rune, upon his return a few days later, 'through quick thinking and no small degree of bravery, with little thought for the danger to myself, I kicked his rifle aside. The shot missed Father Ernetti, whom he had sought to assassinate, being an evil catspaw of Count Otto Black, and no one was harmed. The struggle that followed on the rooftop was of the life and death persuasion, but I persevered and he took the fall to oblivion.'

Mr Rune sat back in his chair. He was clearly very impressed.

'I don't know what to say,' he said to me, at length.

'You can say that I am a damn fine detective,' I suggested.

'I could,' he said, in ready reply. 'Or a most creative liar.'

'Oh, come on,' I said. 'I solved the case of the Woodingdean Chameleon – at least give me credit for it.'

'I see,' said Mr Rune. 'Other than for the fact that the case was not set in Woodingdean and did not involve a chameleon.'

'I explained that,' I said. Because I had, earlier. 'Fangio confused Withdean with Woodingdean and Count Otto Black was there in the crowd, somewhere, overseeing his evil business in disguise, like a chameleon.'

Hugo Rune raised one of his hairless eyebrows.

'Oh, all right then,' I said. 'I am rubbish. I did *not* solve it.'

Mr Rune smiled broadly and then he said, 'Yes, you did, even though the Father Ernetti you sought so bravely to protect is not the same Father Ernetti who invented the Chronovision. Although it was an easy mistake to make. And the gunman was *not* aiming at Father Ernetti. *Nevertheless*, you *did* solve the case.'

'I did?' I said. '*I did?*'

'I know that things did not happen as you have described them because a chum of mine, the Scottish groundskeeper, *did* observe exactly what happened and reported everything to me. The groundskeeper saw you up-end Colonel Mortimer into the stands whilst the colonel was busy taking aim at Mister Grimsdale.'

'It is true,' I said. 'That is what really happened. Well, I could not let him shoot Mister Grimsdale, could I? Norman Wisdom would have been most upset. But tell me this: you *knew* that he was not aiming at Father Ernetti. How did you know *that?*'

'Because I know Colonel Mortimer, and his wife. He did not shoot her dead, either. He lied to you about that. She left him for another man. And it wasn't Mister Grimsdale. It was *me*. I've just spent a most pleasant few days away with that very woman in Eastbourne. And I'll probably be seeing a lot more of her, now that her husband is safely behind bars.'

'You cad!' I said.

'I admit it,' said Mr Rune. 'But you *did* solve the case of the Woodingdean Chameleon, as I knew you would.'

'But how,' I asked, 'if I got it all wrong?'

'Because the chameleon was *you*,' said Mr Rune. 'The

chameleon, that creature which disguises itself, that creature was you – Mister Lazlo Woodingdean.'

And I was most impressed by this.

'Now give me back that telescope you nicked,' said Hugo Rune.

6

The Scintillating Story of the Sackville Scavenger

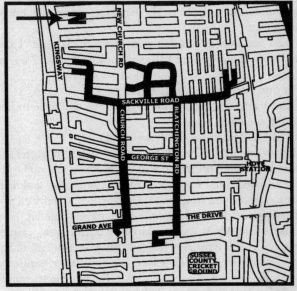

The Sackville Scavenger

PART I

'And what would you take *this* to be?' asked Hugo Rune, upon a bright and breezy August morning.

We were sitting taking breakfast, in our rooms at forty-nine Grand Parade, Brighton, and I looked up from the breakfast I was taking and cast an eye towards the Hokus Bloke.

He held upon the tines of his fork the blackened something that was causing his puzzlement.

I viewed it with suspicion. 'It might once have been a sausage,' I ventured. 'Or possibly a member of the mushroom family that has undergone a violent immolation.'

Mr Rune nodded thoughtfully and sniffed at the thing with disgust. 'It has much the look,' said he, 'of the mummified prepuce of Saint Michael, which is venerated in the church at Penge that bears his name. Which leaves me wondering what it might be doing upon my breakfasting plate.'

'I do not think it was doing anything much at all,' I said. 'Just lying there hoping to go unmolested would be my guess.'

'It just won't do,' said Hugo Rune.

And I agreed it would not. 'I think we will have to sack that Jeff the chef,' I said.

And Mr Rune agreed that we would.

I had never taken much to Jeff the chef. Mr Rune had found him wandering the streets of Brighton one night in a pitiable condition. He was evidently homeless and kept asking which year this was and whether Cromwell still ruled England. I did not like the smell of him one bit.

Mind you, Mr Rune would never have had to employ the services of Jeff the chef had Jade the maid not left us. She had vanished away a week before, leaving a letter, penned in Taiwanese, which according to Mr Rune's interpretation cited 'drunkenness and cruelty' amongst her grievances and cause for departure. She had absconded with Mr Rune's ivory chess set – a gift, he informed me, from Shah Jahan for assisting him with the design of the Taj Mahal.

And so we lately suffered at the hands of Jeff the chef.

'Perhaps if you were actually to *pay* for a cook,' I said, but did not trouble to follow that line of conversation further.

'The most important meal of the day, breakfast,' said Mr Rune, pushing his plate aside and rattling the coffee pot that Jeff had neglected to refill. 'No matter in which far-flung reach of civilisation I have cast my noble shadow, I have never failed to begin the day without a decent breakfast lodged beneath my belt. What chef skills do you possess, young Rizla?'

'Oh no,' I said. 'I am your amanuensis, your acolyte, if you will, your partner in the fight against crime and the forces of evil. I am *not* a cook.'

'Hm,' went Rune, and I heard his stomach growling.

'Oh, and another thing,' I said, 'I chanced to open the latest letter that arrived from Mister Hansord the landlord. He says that you have until Tuesday to cough up the last six months of back rent, or the bailiffs will be coming in.'

A growl now issued from the mouth of Hugo Rune.

'I read in the *Leader*,[*] I said, 'that the pirates of *The Saucy Spaniel* recently plundered a B&Q in Shoreham. As owner of the galleon, you will no doubt be receiving your share of the booty.'

'I would hate to part with it to a landlord,' said Mr Rune and he made a very grim face indeed.

'I would hate to be ejected from these rooms,' I said. 'No doubt matters will resolve themselves.'

'Where is that copy of the *Leader*?' Mr Rune asked.

'The cat has made a nest of it.'

'And since when have we possessed a cat?'

'No,' I said. 'You are right – I have the *Leader* here.'

Mr Rune took it away to his favourite chair and sat with it, huffing and puffing.

I dabbed at my lips with an oversized green gingham napkin, pulled out reading matter of my own – *The Corpse Wore Maltese Falsies* (A Lazlo Woodbine Thriller) – and proceeded with the matter of reading it. And I had just got to a really exciting part involving Laz getting into a sticky situation in an alleyway with a dwarf who was taller than he looked when Mr Rune went 'Plah!' and flung the morning's *Leader* in my direction.

'Just read *that*!' he shouted.

---

[*] The *Argus* being no longer delivered due to an unpaid newsagent's bill, we now received our news courtesy of the *Leader*, which was a free newspaper.

I plucked the *Leader* up from the floor, uncreased it over my lap and read:

LIFE FOR ELIXIR MAN

James Fennimore Bacon, of no fixed address, today received a life sentence for selling his patented Elixir of Life pills in defiance of code laid down in the Witchcraft and Fraudulent Mediums Act. He had previous convictions for selling his 'tablets of immortality' in 1959, 1943, 1920, 1857, 1703 and 1628.

'Seems a bit harsh,' I said.

'He'll breeze through it,' said Mr Rune. 'He always does. But it wasn't *that* article which caused me to "Plah!" Read what is below it.'

I read.

'Out loud,' said Mr Rune.

I read it out loud. ' "EAT YOUR FOOD NUDE",' I read. ' "The new naturist restaurant is opening tonight in George Street, Hove. The Sussex constabulary are cordoning off the area in expectation of the crowds of protesters." ' I looked up at Mr Rune. 'What will they be protesting about?' I asked. 'They have yet to taste the food.'

'Perhaps the nudity.'

'Ludicrous,' I said. 'These are the nineteen sixties – you cannot protest about nudity.'

Mr Rune shook his great bald head. 'Rizla,' said he, 'these *are* indeed the nineteen sixties – people are protesting about *everything*. Hadn't you noticed?'

'I have noticed that our landlord protests about you not paying him the rent.'

'Please do not broach that subject again.'

'So what does this restaurant opening have to do with us?' The question was scarcely out of my mouth when I realised that I knew the answer. Mr Rune's rat-bone protestations had him barred from every eating-house in Brighton. The opening of a new restaurant was bound to interest him.

'I do not know whether I fancy eating my food in the nude,' I said.

'You can always place a napkin in your lap if you fear the spilling of hot soup on to your 'nads.'

'I was not thinking of *that*. I was thinking of the diners. Few folk look appealing in their bare scuddies. Of course, if all the other diners were "Page-Three" girls, that would be an altogether different affair.'

'We'll take on the case,' said Mr Rune.

'*What* case?'

Hugo Rune rose ponderously from his favourite chair and took himself over to the big wall-mounted street map of Brighton, the one on which the enigmatic figures of the Brighton Zodiac had been coloured on to the streets and roads and culs-de-sac and whatnots. The figures of the Brightonomicon.

'See there,' said Mr Rune, and he took up his stout stick and pointed with it. 'The Sackville Scavenger. It lies across Hove with its mouth wide open. And there, you see, at the line of his belly – George Street.'

I looked and I saw. 'Very good,' I said. 'But the case?'

'The case will present itself, Rizla. Have a little faith.'

'I have plenty of faith,' I said.

'And I also,' said Hugo Rune. 'And if faith were bread, my belly would be full. But it is not and neither is my belly.' And he yawned and drew out his pocket watch and viewed its elegant face. 'The sun is over the yardarm,' he said. 'I suggest that we repair to Fangio's bar and there avail our-selves of his complimentary peanuts and the chewing fat that he currently has on offer.'

And so we did.

I looked up at today's pub sign. ' "The Merry Terrorist",' I read.

Within The Merry Terrorist, the furnishings were as ever they had been: the hubcap ashtrays, the Ford Fiesta wheel-arch loungers, the car-bumper footrests before the bar counter, the Vauxhall Velux headlamps on their chromium wall sconces. Mr Rune and I approached the bar and there we encountered the barman.

'Morning, comrades,' said Fangio, raising a blackly gloved fist. 'Great day for the overthrow of the capitalist system.'

I looked Fangio up and down, then up and down once more. The barlord had a somewhat military look on this occasion. His portly form had been ladled into figure-hugging camouflage fatigues, and upon his head he wore a beret. A beard had been sketched on to his chin with the aid of a felt-tipped pen.

Hugo Rune made groaning sounds.

But I was caused to smile.

'Let me guess,' I said to Fange. 'Che Guevara, is it not?'

'You have it in one,' said Fangio, which I have to say rather surprised me.

'Of course, Che was not really a terrorist,' I said. 'He was a revolutionary.'

'Oh,' said Fangio. 'I thought he was a fashionable bou-tique in Kensington High Street. I paid a packet for this fab gear. It goes down very well with the ladies, so I'm told.'

Mr Rune was tucking into the complimentary peanuts. I ordered two pints of Texaco Unleaded and Redex chasers.

The dedicated follower of fashion did the business. And being the professional he was, chalked up the cost to Mr Rune's account.

'This peanut bowl is empty,' remarked the Lad Himself.

I tucked into the chewing fat while Fange refilled the peanut bowl.

'So you are up for the overthrow of the capitalist sys-tem, are you?' I asked Fange, by way of making idle conversation.

'I'm up for anything, me,' said the camouflaged barman. 'You name a cause that's worth protesting about and I'm up for it.'

'Blood sports,' I said.

'Pro or anti?'

'Anti,' I said.

'Up for it,' said Fangio.

'And what if I had said "pro"?'

'Then I'd have said "up for it". I'm all for democracy. Although I support the Communist Party, of course.'

'You are only dressed up like that and talking like that because the brewery has inveigled you into it.'

'And because of the bird-pulling potential of the attire.'

'You hypocrite,' I said.

'Excuse me,' said Fangio, 'but I take exception to that. In fact, I protest! I am dressed like this to keep the job I enjoy and to have sex with women. Where is the hypocrisy in that?'

I scratched at my head. He had me there.

'You need a haircut,' said Fangio.

'I protest about *that*!'

'Top man. I'll join you on the march.'

'So will you be protesting tonight?' Mr Rune asked Fangio.

Fangio took out his diary and leafed through it. 'I get off at six,' he said, 'and I will be joining the Angry Lesbians of Kemp Town in their sit-down protest at the swimming baths, over the mixed-ninepennies. That should be a noisy one. Then at six-thirty I'll be with the Miffed Mimes of Moulsecoomb – we'll be trying to escape from an imaginary phone box, so that should be a quiet one. Then at seven I'm going to be part of a human chain across the car park at Tesco. That's an animal rights thing – I've been issued with a whistle for that one.'

'Will you not be joining the protesters who are seeking to stop the opening of the Eat Your Food Nude restaurant in George Street?' I asked.

'Heavens, no,' said Fange. 'I'll be dining there myself – the brewery has sent me two free tickets. It's one of their new theme venues.'

I looked at Mr Rune.

And Mr Rune looked at me.

'I think I will go to the toilet now,' I said.

Some hours later, I asked Mr Rune, 'Why are we dressing up?'

'We'll want to look our best for the occasion.' Hugo Rune had on his best tuxedo, with the lacy shirt and velvet dicky bow.

'But it is a naturist restaurant. We will have to take our clothes off!'

Mr Rune let free a mocking laugh. 'Rizla,' said he, 'Hugo Rune does not disrobe in public.'

'Shy, eh?' I said.

'On the contrary,' said Hugo Rune, 'but should I expose what lies presently dormant beneath my kecks in a public eatery, the inevitable attention of the womenfolk present and the inadequacy felt by their male companions might well erupt into jealous rage, which would interfere with my digestion.'

'Indeed,' I said. 'So can I keep my clothes on, too?'

'We will represent ourselves as high muck-a-mucks of the brewery, come to observe the proceedings.'

'Well, you *have* acquired the brewery's tickets.'

'Quite so. Now let us hasten to the street where you can hail us a cab.'

The driver of the taxicab was a fellow who called himself Darren. Darren was a supporter of a football club named Hull, to which even 'torture to the third degree as administered by cardinals of the Inquisition could not procure disloyalty'. Darren expounded his theories regarding why Marmite went white when you repeatedly patted it with your finger. And how there was really no such thing as chicken.

'Eggs, right,' said Darren, as he drove along Western Road en route to Hove. 'Every day there are millions and millions of eggs. You can buy them everywhere, right?'

I nodded in agreement.

'But also everywhere, there are millions and millions of chickens for sale in supermarkets, and sandwich shops, and restaurants, right?'

'Right,' I said.

'So where do they all come from?'

'They come out of eggs,' I said.

'But the eggs are all for sale.'

'Well, obviously not *all* of them,' I said. 'A very great many must hatch into chickens. A *very* great many.'

'Which would require a *very* great many cockerels to inseminate all these chickens that lay fertilised eggs that turn into more chickens.'

'I would assume so,' I said.

'So where are all these stud farms full of randy roosters?' asked Darren. 'You have all these battery-chicken farms where chickens lay eggs. But you'd need millions and millions of randy roosters. It's all a conspiracy. Eggs come off assembly lines, and so do chickens. They're artificial. And we should be told. I'm going to start a protest.'

I scratched at my head.

'You need a haircut,' said Mr Rune.

When we arrived at the police cordon that blocked off Church Road some one hundred yards before George Street, I left the cab with haste, leaving Mr Rune to deal with the matter of the fare.

And I recognised two of the policemen in the cordon – the same two who had ordered Mr Rune and me to move back behind the line before the Earl-Grey-weeping statue of the late Queen Victoria.

'Good evening, Officer,' I said to the first policeman. 'Nice night for a protest, eh?'

'Perfect night, sir. Move back behind the line, if you will.'

'I have tickets to the restaurant opening,' I said, and I flourished same.

'You lucky bugger,' said the first constable. 'All those "Page-Three" girls with their kit off, and me and my compatriots here with nothing to enliven our evening other than the thought of the inevitable truncheoning-down of protesters that lies ahead.'

'And the stun-gunning,' said the second constable. 'And the tear-gassing, of course, not to mention the employment of the bowel-loosening infrasound canons that have been supplied to us for testing by the Ministry of Serendipity.'

I felt it prudent *not* to mention those bowel-loosening infrasound canons.

'Very wise of you,' said the first constable.

And suddenly Mr Rune joined me.

'Oh,' said the second constable, sighting Mr Rune. 'It's you, is it? Are we supposed to tip our helmets or something, you being a Thirty-Fourth-Degree Mason or whatever?'

'A simple curtsey will suffice,' said Mr Rune. 'Now please clear a path for us between the protesters.'

'There *are* no protesters,' I said, for my powers of observation were keen.

'No,' said constable number one. 'I've just heard word on my special police walkie-talkie that they are presently trapped inside an imaginary telephone box on the Level. Imaginary firemen are cutting them out.'

'I just love the nineteen sixties,' I said.

'Me, too, sir,' said the second policeman. 'Especially the drugs.'

I don't know whether we were the first to arrive at Eat Your Food Nude, but I knew that we were not the last. There is a balance to these things and a strict pecking order, celebritywise. But I will not go into any of that here, because frankly I did not care – I was just hungry. There were a lot of paparazzi present and these individuals aimed their cameras at us.

But to Mr Rune's appalled disgust, they did not take any

pictures. 'They do not know who you are,' I said, as we strolled up George Street, past the charity shops. 'They are only here to photograph the famous.'

'Rizla,' said Hugo Rune, 'how would you like to appear upon the front page of the *Leader* tomorrow?'

'That very much depends,' said I. 'If it is alongside the headline "DO YOU KNOW THE IDENTITY OF THIS MURDERED MAN?", then I am not altogether keen.'

Mr Rune smiled that certain smile of his, the one that I might not have mentioned before, and we strolled on towards dinner at Eat Your Food Nude.

We were greeted at the door by two muscular types wearing nothing more than fig leaves.

'Invitation,' said one of these, fingering the fig leaf that he wore upon his head. And I made free with our tickets.

'Go through, please,' said the other. And we did so.

'Fine-looking women,' said Mr Rune.

Now, I have to say that I rather took to the décor of Eat Your Food Nude. It had that comfortable, lived-in feeling to it.

The walls were painted all-over mauve, which I knew to be this year's black.

Upon them hung many silk-screened prints of the Andy Warhol persuasion.

There were sofas and chairs of a velvet ilk and many a beanbag sack.

And tables of oak of every shape, which answered every occasion.

'Most poetic,' said Mr Rune, 'but that was the *last* chapter, surely.'

'It is a very nice place,' said I. 'And we appear to be the first arrivals.'

'First in, last out,' said Mr Rune. 'I have no pretensions.'

'If the sirs will proceed to the disrobing area,' said the maître d', who had approached us silently upon his bare feet and now loomed before us, as naked as the day was long. Mr Rune explained to him that we were from the brewery.

'Indeed, sir, yes,' said the maître d', with exaggerated politeness. 'But as you will observe from your tickets—' and he turned them over '—"NO KIT OFF – NO SERVICE". It's in big black capital letters here. I'd overlook your dinner suits if I could, but it's more than my job's worth.'

I looked at Mr Rune.

And Mr Rune looked at me.

And our stomachs growled in unison.

Now, I really do not wish to go into this in detail. Mr Rune and I were guided to the disrobing area, where we divested ourselves of our garments and received cloakroom tickets for same. When Mr Rune asked where exactly we might be expected to put our cloakroom tickets for safekeeping, as we no longer possessed pockets, he received a reply from the cloakroom attendant (who looked very much like a bog troll to me) that might either be described as 'cheeky' or 'downright insolent', depending upon your point of view.

Mr Rune and I, then in the buff, were escorted to our table. And I *do* have to confess that as to whether Mr Rune's claims regarding God's generosity to him in the matter of wedding tackle were genuine, I could not say.

Because I really, truly did not want to look.

We sat ourselves down and took up our napkins.

And I laid mine over my lap.

Well, you never can be too careful regarding the soup course.

The tablecloths were of crisp white linen and the cutlery was none too shabby, either. There was a selection of glasses, rising from little tiny shot jobbies to great big brandy balloons. A bit like a set of Russian dolls. Or dogs, perhaps. And there was salt and pepper. And only ketchup, no HP. Proper posh.

Mr Rune called for the wine list and made his choice guided, as far as I could see, by price alone.

'The Mulholland eighteen fifty-one,' said he. 'And bring two pint pots.'

And then, as we sat guzzling wine, the other diners began to appear. And much to my utter amazement, many of these were *famous*. And I do have to say that, much to my utter amazement, once they had visited the disrobing room and returned to the restaurant as naked as jaybirds, I was hard put to identify them. It is really difficult to recognise the famous when they have their clothes off. They all look alarmingly similar.

'Is that Jimi Hendrix?' I asked Mr Rune.

'No, that's Janis Joplin.'

'But *that* is Brian Jones, surely?'

'No, I think you will find that it's Jim Morrison.'

'Ah,' I said. 'I know *that* is Johnny Kidd – he still has his eye patch on.'

'No,' said Mr Rune. 'That's David Bowie. Oh, good, they're throwing him out. He always tries to sneak into events like this.'[*]

Mr Rune pointed out Gram Parsons from the Byrds, Pigpen from the Grateful Dead and somebody called Kurt Cobain, who was not even born yet.

'Tell me,' I said to Mr Rune, 'who is that black fella over there?'

'That's Robert Johnson,' said Mr Rune.

I gave my head another scratching and considered the possibility of getting myself a haircut. 'Now hang on a moment,' I said, 'I recall having a conversation with your confederate Hubert, and he told me that all these rock stars had died at the age of twenty-seven.'

'That hardly surprises me,' said Mr Rune, finishing off the last of the Mulholland '51 and calling out to the waiter for more. 'Hubert claims to be a descendant of Nostradamus. But surely you're missing the point here, young Rizla. Everything we deal with is to do with time – my search for the Chronovision, anomalies of time, holes in time.'

[*] Allegedly.

'But these rock stars are dead,' I said.

'They don't look very dead to me,' said Mr Rune. 'Would you care for me to introduce you to any of them? Most are personal friends.'

'I do not really fancy getting up,' I said, steadying my serviette. 'I am comfy here.'

'We've extra chairs at our table and we haven't ordered the nosebag yet. Who would you care to speak with?'

'Him,' I said. And I pointed.

'Robert Johnson,' said Mr Rune. 'Why does this not surprise me at all?'

'Because you are the All-Knowing One?' I suggested.

'Bobby boy,' called Mr Rune to the great blues legend. 'Would you care to join us over here?'

All right, I confess it, I had trouble with this.

Perhaps all of these nineteen-sixties rock stars had not yet died at age twenty-seven. Maybe one or two of them had, but possibly their deaths had not been featured in the *Argus* or the *Leader*, concerned as those organs were with local events.

But I was damn sure that Robert Johnson *had* died in nineteen thirty-eight.

But there was Robert Johnson, naked as the day that he was born, approaching our table.

'Lower yourself into a chair,' said Mr Rune.

And Robert Johnson did so.

'This is my companion, Rizla,' said Mr Rune. 'He is anxious to meet you.'

Robert Johnson smiled upon me and I smiled back at him.

And through my smile I also stared in awe.

Could this really be *the* Robert Johnson?

The man who started it all – rock music, soul music, all that now we had and loved?

The man who had supposedly gone down to the cross-roads at midnight with a black-cat bone and sold his soul to the Devil, who then tuned his guitar?

The man who always after this played with his back to

the audience, for fear that they might see a magical something?

That magical something that Keith Richards discerned when he first heard Johnson's recordings?

That you would need an extra finger upon your left hand to play the way he did?

Robert Johnson put out his hand for me to shake it.

It was his left hand.

As it extended in my direction, I took to counting the fingers.

And as it reached me, I exclaimed, 'Oh my God!'

PART II

'Well, that was very rude,' said Hugo Rune, 'refusing to shake his hand. I think you quite offended him. He stormed off in a huff.'

'But his hand,' I said and I was shaking as I said it. 'He has six fingers on his left hand. He sold his soul to the Devil. It is all his fault that these rock stars will die aged twenty-seven. What are we going to do?'

'Well, I am going to order a starter. I don't know quite what you have in mind.'

'This is no time for food!' I raised my voice to Hugo Rune.

'On the contrary, this is exactly the time for food. It is eight o'clock and this *is* a restaurant.'

'But we have to do something.'

'Ah,' said Mr Rune, 'you think there is a *case* or something, do you?'

'A case,' I said. 'Yes, that is it, a case.'

'Please calm yourself, Rizla, you're getting most upset.'

'Well, of course I am getting upset. Look at them – Jimi and Janis and Brian, and Jim and Pigpen and Gram, and Johnny Kidd—'

'And Kurt Cobain,' said Mr Rune.

'Forget him,' I said. 'But look at the rest of them, all

sitting here, naked, in Hove, enjoying their grub. And they are all doomed to die. And all because of Robert Johnson. We have to stop it.'

'We can't,' said Mr Rune.

I looked at Hugo Rune and I looked at him sternly, which even surprised myself. ' "*Can't*"?' said I. 'That is not a word I have ever heard you use before. Are you telling me that there is something that Mr Hugo Rune cannot do?'

'In a word, yes,' said the Hokus Bloke.

'I am appalled,' I said. *And I was*.

'They have to die,' said Mr Rune. 'It is preordained that they will do so. They will live fast and die young, and they will leave an exceeding legacy. Would you care to see what would happen if this did not come to pass?'

'I do not understand,' I said. *And I did not*.

'Pick one,' said Mr Rune, 'any one you like, and I will grant you a glimpse of how things would be if they were to cheat their fate and continue to live.'

'This is not funny,' I said. 'You should not say such things to me.'

'Any one,' said Mr Rune. 'The experience will be shocking and real, but in *real time* it will last but for a moment. Do you dare?'

'What are you saying?'

'That you will glimpse an alternative future, a future that will exist if any one of these rock stars were to live beyond the age of twenty-seven.'

I did not really know quite what to say. So I said, 'Go on, then.'

And I suddenly found myself no longer unclothed in a restaurant in Hove, but somewhere else entirely.

'Are you going to sit there dreaming, or do some work for me?'

I rose to consciousness and stared.

At Jimi Hendrix.

He was fat and bald and did not look too well.

'What year is this?' I cried. 'And who is the president?'

'I wish you would stop doing that,' said Jimi. 'It isn't big and it isn't clever. It's nineteen eighty-four and *I* am the president.'

'You?'

'Don't do this to me again, please. Since Elvis was voted out of office five years back, I have been the man at the controls.'

'The controls?' I said.

'My hand is on the nuclear button.'

I tried to get a grip of myself and take in my surroundings. We appeared to be in one of those big boardrooms that you see in movies, the ones that are below ground level, deep in a top-secret bunker. They always have dramatic down-lighting and a lot of faceless fellows in black suits who nod a great deal and look like Gary Busey.

'*You* are the president?' I said to Jimi.

Several Gary Busey lookalikes nodded at this.

'And *your* hand is on the nuclear button?'

'My *left* hand,' said Jimi. 'I always played left-handed, as you know.'

'I am uncomfortable with this now,' I said. 'I think I want to go back to Hove.'

'Ah,' said Jimi, lowering his big fat self into the big fat chair at the head of the table. 'Hove, how well I remember Hove, where you saved my life. I am eternally grateful, of course – if it hadn't been for that night, I would never have given up the life of sex and drugs and rock and roll, taken to protesting and risen through government to the position that I hold today.'

'I did not want you to die,' I said.

'And you did the right thing. We'll best those Commie b*st*rds.'

'Was that rock 'n' roll patois?' I asked.

'No, I meant bastards!'

'Oh,' said I.

'It's an odd thing, isn't it,' said Jimi. 'How when you are young you have all these ideas, all these things that really matter to you that you are prepared to protest about, to shout out about. Then as the years pass and you get older, they don't seem to matter any more. Other things matter, that you'd never even thought about before. More mature things, responsible things. And so you choose. You never notice it happening – it happens bit by bit. And somehow, suddenly you're there, as if you've just woken up in your fifties, saying, "Where did my life go?" And, "How fast was that?" And you're not the same person you were when you were young. In fact, you have contempt for that foolish, frivolous person you once were, who did all those irre-sponsible things. So you sort of go into denial, saying "Well, what I did was okay, it didn't matter, I was just having a good time." And then you wake up and find that it's now. Do you know what I mean?'

'No,' I said. 'I do not.'

'Well, it doesn't matter,' said Jimi. 'I woke up, as one does at the age of twenty-eight. Up until that age, you have dreams, you are irresponsible. You rebel, you protest. But when you reach twenty-eight, you realise where you have been going wrong. I realised that all that guitar stuff I was doing was rubbish.'

'No, it was not,' I said. 'It was wonderful. Innovative. Incredible.'

'Trivial,' said Jimi. 'Nothing at all.'

'No – it was something.'

'That rock 'n' roll,' said Jimi, 'that's the Devil's music. I hate myself for having played it. But now I'm born again in the Lord. Now I am responsible. And that's why those Commie bastards are going to get what's coming to them.'

'Which is?'

'Nukes,' said Jimi. 'Lots of nukes.'

'No!' I shouted. 'Do not do that. You do not know what you are doing. You were the greatest rock guitarist ever. You were The Man.'

'I'm still The Man. *The* Man. I was voted into power by middle-aged fan boys who still believe in me. I used to believe in fans when I played. Now I know them for what they are – cattle.'

'No!' I cried again. And I had a right sweat on now. 'You do not know what you are saying, or what you are doing.'

'Wake up,' said Jimi. 'I woke up. Why don't you?'

'This is not right!' I screamed. 'You cannot have become this. This is all wrong.'

'We have to grow up,' said Jimi. 'We have to wake up. That's how it is. And I'd just love to go on talking to you, but I have a button to press.'

And his left hand came down upon that button. And I cried out for him to stop.

'You cannot be this!' I shouted. 'It would have been better if you had died at twenty-seven . . .'

And then things seemed to blink and change and I was back in Hove in the company of Hugo Rune, without either clothes or composure.

'Aaagh!' I went. 'Oh!' and, 'Eeek!' also.

'Nice trip?' asked the All-Knowing One, raising his glass to me – a glass filled with Mulholland champagne of the vintage persuasion.

'I . . .' I went. 'I mean . . .' I went. 'I saw . . .' I went. 'I mean . . .'

'Not such a nice future, was it, then?'

I spied a glass that was filled with wine and poured it down my throat. 'That cannot be,' I said. 'That cannot happen, surely?'

'It is one possible future. Who can say for certain what will come to pass?'

'And so . . .' I glanced about all around me. 'And so they all have to die?'

'Robert Johnson did *not* sell his soul to the Devil,' said Mr Rune. 'Quite the contrary, in fact. You could say that he was an angel of the Lord, if you are inclined to such beliefs. Those who fell under his influence changed the world of music. Such was their gift. But had they lived longer, they would not have been remembered lovingly as rock legends; rather they would have grown in power to become something altogether else.'

'So I could have chosen any of them?' I said. 'And the future would have been the same?'

'With subtle variations. But not *that* subtle.'

I mopped the sweat from my brow with an oversized green gingham serviette. 'I am not well at all,' I said.

'You'll feel a whole lot better when you have some food inside you. I took the liberty of ordering for you whilst you were otherwise engaged in future possibilities.'

And so I dined with Mr Hugo Rune at Eat Your Food Nude, and I have to say that I enjoyed all that I dined upon.

Whether I actually met Robert Johnson, or any of the dead rock stars, I am not entirely sure. Their photographs did not turn up on the front page of the *Leader* the following day.

Although mine did, and Mr Rune's. And it was such an unnecessary fuss. Because we *did* have free tickets, after all. Mr Rune took to a bout of coughing during the pudding course, and there was this rat bone involved, although where *that* materialised from, I have no idea. *And* there was a demand for compensation, which surprisingly was met in full and paid in cash, which *did* pay off our owings to Mr Hansord the landlord But then there was the unfortunate business of our clothes having been stolen from the disrobing area. Which required further and heavy financial compensation from the management – sufficient, in fact, to put that particular theme venue out of business. But which nevertheless did involve Mr Rune and me having to leave the restaurant in the buff. Which *did* attract the attention of the paparazzi.

We took a final late-night drink at Fangio's. Still in the buff, but I no longer cared.

'Did you enjoy the Scintillating Story of the Sackville Scavenger?' asked Mr Rune, as he drained a pint of Shell to its dregs.

'Not in the least,' I replied, 'but I am looking forward to

194

breakfast tomorrow, what with you persuading the cook from Eat Your Food Nude to come and work for us.'

'Part of the compensation for the pilfering of our clothes,' said Mr Rune, 'although I found that somewhat amusing, and nothing to protest about. A good night out, I consider. We must do it again, *some time in the future*.'

And then Mr Rune offered me something. It was a badge with Robert Johnson's face upon it. 'I thought you might care to keep this as a souvenir,' said he. 'A pictorial representation of the Scavenger himself. The benign Scavenger, of course.'

'That is very kind of you,' I said, 'but as you can see, I have nowhere to pin it.' And then I paused for a moment, and said, 'And for that matter, where *exactly* have you been keeping it?'

7

The Fantastic Adventure of the Foredown Man

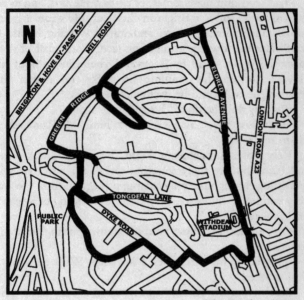

The Foredown Man

PART I

'He walks,' said Hugo Rune, in answer to my question. 'He walks, is what he does. He walks and he walks and he walks.'

My question had been, 'Why does he do it?'

'I know that he walks,' I said.

It was a misty morning in September. And lest the reader feel that some kind of formula has become evident in the cases that Mr Rune and I had so far solved, let it be said that we were *not* having our breakfast.

We had just *finished* our breakfast. Mr Rune was in his favourite chair, reading *my* copy of *Dead Dames Don't Do Doggie-Style* (A Lazlo Woodbine Thriller) and I was looking out of the window. And it was whilst I was doing this looking out that I had seen him once more.

The masked walker.

I had seen him many times, of course. He was, and as far as I am aware still *is*, a Brighton character. He wears a green anorak and matching trews and sturdy walking boots. A scarf hides the lower portion of his face, a large pair of sun-specs the upper. And he is never to be seen without his gloves. And in this costume he walks, no matter the weather, he walks and he walks and he walks.

'But *why* does he do it?' I asked once again.

'How close have you ever been to him?' Mr Rune asked me in return.

'Very close, as it happens,' I said. 'I was in Primark once, and I saw him in there selecting towels for purchase. He was going through the pile, examining each in turn. He was very fastidious. And very, very clean. Everything he wears is immaculately clean.'

'One question for you,' said Mr Rune, putting aside my paperback.

I pricked up my ears as best I was able. 'What question is this?' I asked.

'Plah!' cried Mr Rune. 'The question is this: what were *you* doing in Primark?' There was a certain edge to his voice. An edge that could have cut cheese. ' "Primate" it should more rightly be called,' he continued.

'Yes,' I said. 'Well, I know that you prefer to shop at Harrods, but *I* needed a new towel and *you* are a little late with my wages once again.'

'I despair,' said Mr Rune, despairingly. 'Have you learned nothing during your time with me?'

'I have learned that it is better not to travel in a cab with you if one has a terror of violence.'

'Quality,' said Mr Rune. 'Quality above all. Style to an equal degree. And good taste. Good taste is paramount.'

'Taste is merely a matter of opinion,' I said, turning away from the window.

'On the contrary,' said Mr Rune. 'It has been said before, but for your benefit, I will say it again: some things *are* better than other things and some people are capable of making the distinction. *I* am one of these people. I, Rune, the Perfect Master, the Earthly Manifestation of the Infinite, the One and Only, the Lord of the Dance—'

'And the Man Who Broke the Bank at Monte Carlo.'

'Only the once. They never allowed me to play there again.'

'But what about the masked walker?'

'Interesting fellow.' Hugo Rune took a cigar from his silver case and rolled it thoughtfully beneath his nose. 'I have observed him, naturally. He never takes the same route twice. He walks all around Brighton and even as far as Henfield, some ten miles to the north. There is a pattern to his perambulations, however – they trace out the figure of the Brightonomicon, the twelve figures that make up the Brighton Zodiac.'

I shrugged and said, 'Have you another cigar for me?'

'No,' said Mr Rune. 'This is my last.'

'I saw three more in your case.'

'My last for now.'

'I am bored,' I said. 'It is misty and it is growing cold. Summer is over, we are six cases through your Brighton Zodiac and what do we have to show for it?'

'More than you might think. But we *do* need another case.' And Mr Rune took himself over to his big map on the wall. '*This* one, I feel,' he said, indicating one of the shapes.

I followed him and peered at the map. 'The Foredown Man,' I said.

'Looks rather jolly, doesn't he?' Mr Rune made a jolly face. 'Standing with his feet four-square upon the Old Shoreham Road and his right hand pointing to Hangleton.'

'He might be pointing,' I said, 'but that is all he is doing. I bet he would not care to stroll in that direction.'

'Why not?' Mr Rune asked. And he lit up his cigar.

'Because it is a very dull place,' I said, fanning away at the smoke that engulfed me. 'No offence to the good folk of Hangleton, but it is very, very quiet up there. They appear to exist in some kind of nineteen thirties time warp. And I am not talking about Lower Hangleton, where we were involved in a case involving a certain spaniel. I speak of the upper bit, near West Blatchington, where the swells live. They have a saying there: "Nothing happens in Hangleton", which is obviously the way they like to keep it.'

'Then we'll have to liven them up a little.'

'They will not take kindly to that.'

'As they have *not* taken kindly to the plague of petty thievery there that has recently been reported in the gutter press. See this,' and Mr Rune handed me an envelope.

It was a rather striking envelope, of topmost-quality paper. I considered that the sender of this envelope probably did *not* shop at Primark. It was addressed to Mr Rune in copperplate lettering. You could actually smell the ink.

'Crawford's Radiant Blue,' said Mr Rune, 'from Asprey's.'

I opened the envelope, took out an elegant card (upon matching stationery) and read what was written thereon: 'The Earl of Hangleton requests,' I read, 'that Sir Hugo Rune attend his garden party. There are certain pressing matters that he wishes to discuss.'

Hugo Rune nodded.

'*Sir* Hugo Rune?' I said.

'It's an honorific title. I bestowed it in honour of myself. But I know of this Earl of Hangleton – I was a very close friend of his most distinguished ancestor. In fact, we visited the Great Exhibition together. I think we might expect a most lively afternoon, if my powers of reasoning have not deserted me. And of course, they have *not*.'

'The garden party is today,' I said, viewing the date.

'Then quality and style will be our watchwords. The Boleskine tweeds for you, I feel, young Rizla.'

Now, I do have to say that I was rather fond of the

Boleskine tweeds. They were green and tweedy, patterned with a tartan of Mr Rune's personal design, and they came from a quality tailor's in Savile Row. And they were a four-piece, with waistcoat and matching beret.

I confess that I was not altogether sure about the beret. Berets had not exactly been 'hip' since the nineteen fifties, and then only amongst the French avant-garde, who wore them whilst they rolled naked women about on canvasses for Art.

And as for my feelings about Art—

'You *will* wear the beret,' said Hugo Rune.

And wear the beret I did.

And at a little after two, I was forced to flag down a cab. I did not want to do it, but it was simply too far to walk to Hangleton.

A doddle for the masked walker, perhaps, but not for Mr Rune and me in our quality tweeds.

The taxi driver's name was Salvador de Allende Fernandes Mal de Mer and he was no fan of football. He was a passionate follower of croquet, offering his undying allegiance to the Benedictine Bears, who were this year's World Champs, and whom I myself now supported.

I chatted with Salvador at length regarding the Bears' prospects of taking the Inter-World Championships, which were apparently going to be held on Venus the following June.

Salvador showed no leanings towards metaphysical thought, and when at length we arrived at Hangleton, Mr Rune paid him off without complaint and waved as he drove away.

I stared in some surprise at Mr Rune. After all, he *was* carrying his stout stick.

'You paid,' I said. 'And you did not knock him unconscious.'

'Have some sense of decorum, Rizla,' said Mr Rune. 'You are in Upper Hangleton now. I trust you won't go letting the side down at the garden party.'

'Have no fears on my account,' I said. 'I know which hand to hold my knife and fork in.'

'It is "in which hand to hold my knife and fork".'

'Well, if you know, too, then we will be fine.'

Mr Rune rolled his eyes and shook his head, but did not choose to employ his stout stick at this particular moment.

'Come then, Rizla,' he said unto me. 'Follow on.'

And so I followed on.

The weather was most pleasant for the time of year and the rich autumnal colours of the conker trees made a striking contrast with the pale blue sky.

I followed on into Hangleton Park, towards stately Hangleton Manor. It looked to me to be *exactly* as a manor house should be: Georgian, mellow red-bricked, ivy-hung and slatily slated. It was a quality dwelling. It had class. Before it were parked a number of swank automobiles upon which lounged liveried chauffeurs puffing Park Drives and discussing the sex lives of the Windsors (in muted and respectful tones, of course).

'I am going to buy myself a gaff like this,' I said to Mr Rune, as we crunched our way up the gravelly gravelled drive.

'Admirable,' said Mr Rune. 'Are you hoping for a win on the football pools?'

'No,' I said. 'I am trusting to that contract I signed for you in blood. It promised worldly wealth, I recall, and long before I write up the account of our adventures together, which you are convinced will become a number-one bestseller.'

'Really?' said Mr Rune.

'In the small print,' I said.

'Ah,' said he. 'I *never* read the small print.'

At length, we paused before the big front door.

'This is one of those places,' I said to Mr Rune.

'One of *which* places?' Mr Rune had a certain sigh in his voice.

'One of those country-house places,' I said, 'like in Agatha

Christie's novels, or the Sherringford Hovis Mysteries written by P. P. Penrose.* Oh,' I said, 'or like Cluedo. If there is a murder here today, I bet it will be in the library and that Colonel Mustard will do it with the length of lead pipe.'

'Rizla,' said Mr Rune.

'Yes?' said I.

'Put a Primark sock in it!'

Mr Rune rapped upon the big front door with his stout stick and presently it was opened. He flourished his invitation and we were granted admittance.

'Butler,' I said to Mr Rune. 'You can tell by his get-up.'

'Mister Cutler at your service, sir,' said the butler. 'If you will kindly walk this way.'

'Don't say it,' said Mr Rune.

And I did not.

We followed Cutler (the butler) through elegant rooms that wore family portraits upon their pastelly painted walls and then through big French windows to lawns that lay beyond, lawns upon which gilded youth mingled with old money.

'Ah, yes,' said Mr Rune, approvingly. 'Ah yes, indeed, most splendid.'

I viewed the gilded youth and wondered at them. So *that* was what young toffs looked like, was it? I had never encountered them before. They were clearly in a class of their own, different from other Brightonians. Although it had to be said that there was not a distinct Brighton type. Brighton was overly cosmopolitan and played host to *all* types, from the pirates of Moulsecoomb and the wide boys of Whitehawk to the back-seat drivers of Kemp Town and the sporting celebrities of Hove (which was pretty much Brighton – you could not really seen the join).

But the gilded youth of the Upper Hangleton area.

Well.

* Although less well known than the Lazlo Woodbine thrillers, they are, nevertheless, far better than the majority of the old toot that you find on the detective shelves at Waterstones. Like that Ian Rankin, for instance.

Well, for one thing, I recognised many of them – I had seen their photos in the society pages of the *Argus*, red-faced and mostly drunk, with their arms about the naked shoulders of some damn fine-looking women. And all of them closely related, as is generally the way with such folk. I recognised the Honourable Nigel Fairborough-Countless, heir to the Countless millions; Lord Edward Marzipan-Fudge, heir to the hundreds and thousands; Lord Burberry Spaniel-Fondler, heir of the dog that bit him; and Lord Lucus Lapp-Dancer, heir on a G-string. Then there was Lord Henry Myle-Hie, British Heirways – club class, of course. Not to mention—[*]

A smart young fellow-me-lad in a suit not unlike to my own detached himself from the gabbling throng of gilded youth and came a-jigging over to us, a glass of Pimm's in one hand and a crustless sandwich in the other.

'Sir Hugo,' he said, in the accent known as Posh.[†] 'It *is* you, isn't it? It has to be, for I am related to everyone else here. Excepting the butler, of course.' And he laughed. Although I did not feel the need to do so myself.

'I must therefore have the pleasure of addressing Quentin Vambery-Greystoke, Fifth Earl of Hangleton,' said Mr Rune, bowing from the neck up.

'Your servant, sir,' and the Fifth Earl bowed also, dropping his sandwich and spilling his Pimm's. 'You must pardon my clumsiness,' he said in an apologetic yet still posh tone. 'Generations of inbreeding. Still, it's better than being a commoner, isn't it? And who is this commoner with you, by the way?'

'My acolyte, Rizla,' said Mr Rune. 'And trusted confidant.'

'Loyal servant, eh?' The Fifth Earl tapped at his upturned nose, nearly dislodging his monocle. 'Do you want to shoo him out of the way to wait with the chauffeurs?'

---

[*] The secret is knowing when to stop. Ed.
[†] As opposed to the Spice Girl known as Posh. And who isn't nowadays?

'He stays with me,' said Mr Rune, which I appreciated.

'Actually,' I said, 'perhaps I *will* go and wait with the chauffeurs.'

'You will do no such thing,' said Mr Rune.

'Then I will have a drink,' I said. 'What is there?'

The Fifth Earl raised a coiffeured eyebrow. 'Plenty in the drinkies tent,' said he, and he indicated same.

'I will bring you something,' I said to Mr Rune and left him chatting with Quentin, the Fifth Earl of Hangleton, who, I have to say in all honesty, I was not too taken with.

I suppose it was obvious that my face did not fit there – it had a chin on it, for one thing – but I was prepared to make the best of things, especially regarding the matter of the free drinks.

And so I entered the drinkies tent.

And it was there that I saw her.

She was surely the most beautiful young woman that I had ever seen in my life. She had long golden hair, and her eyes were blue and her lashes long. She wore a flowery frock and sunlight shone upon her, though I do not know how this could be inside the tent. She was sipping a long glass of something through lips that I desperately wanted to kiss. And I knew that I was in love.

'Well, hellllllo,' I said, in my finest Terry-Thomas.

She looked at me rather blankly.

'Heeeelo,' I said once more. But I got it right this time – it was not Terry-Thomas, but rather Lesley Phillips.

'Heeeelo to you,' she said with the voice of an angel.

'My name is Rizla,' I said. 'I am the . . . er . . . business associate of Sir Hugo Rune.'

'Oh,' said the beauty. 'Is *he* here? Would you introduce me?'

'I do not know your name,' I said.

'It's Kelly,' she said. 'Kelly Anna Sirjan.'

'A very beautiful name.'

'So will you introduce me to Sir Hugo? My cousin Quentin says that he is the greatest poet, adventurer, swordsman, philosopher, philanthropist, exorcist and problem-solver extra-ordinaire of this or any other age.'

'Really?' I said. 'I wonder how your cousin came by this intelligence.'

'I think he read it on the flyer that was recently pushed through his letterbox. It offered cheap rates to members of the aristocracy who needed problems solving. It was delivered, I understand, by a curious chap in an anorak, with dark glasses and a scarf around his face.'

I sighed.

Very deeply.

'What saddens you?' asked Kelly Anna Sirjan.

'The way that I never see the obvious coming,' I said. 'However.'

'However?'

'Well,' I said, 'the situation is this: Sir Hugo is a *very* busy man, what with all the poetry-writing and adventuring and sword-fighting, philosophising, exorcising and problem-solving. Not to mention the philanthropy.'

Kelly Anna Sirjan did not mention the philanthropy.

'Which is why he employs me exclusively in the capacity to – how shall I put this? – *vet* folk who wish to speak to him, which is inevitably a life-changing experience. The meeting of him, I mean. He insists that I gain – how shall I put this? – *intimate knowledge* of those who wish to have such a life-changing experience. Would you care for another drink?'

'Oh, yes please – a large G and T.'

'I will return with it in a moment.'

I took myself up to the bar in the drinkies tent. Behind this bar stood a smartly dressed barman: white tuxedo, pink bow tie, caste mark on his forehead beneath his natty turban.

'Good afternoon, sahib,' said this barman, bowing with exaggerated politeness. 'How might I be helping you?'

I gazed upon the swarthy son of the Raj. 'Fange,' I said. 'It is you.'

'Blessings be upon you, sahib, and upon your memsab also.'

'No,' I said. 'Fange, it is me.'

'Oh, so it is,' said Fangio. 'Pint of Old Antifreeze, would it be?'

'I will have it, if you have it,' I said. 'Do you have it?'

'No,' said Fange. And he shook his turban. 'Only the posh stuff – care for a half of Frangelico?'

'I am easy,' I said.

'And so would I be, wearing a beret like that.'

Oh, how we laughed. I had quite forgotten the beret.

'So what are *you* doing *here*?' I asked Fangio once I had acquired my half of Frangelico and a G and T for Kelly.

'The brewery sent me out,' said Fange. 'I have left The Pudding and Puller in the capable hands of my twin brother Nuvelari for the afternoon.'

'I never knew you had a twin brother.'

'Nor did I. But then I might be one of triplets. There's just no telling, is there?'

'Or quads,' I said.

'Or quintets.'

'Or sextiquidalians.'

'Or Seventh-Day Adventists.'

'Or octoroons.'

'Or nonets.'

'Or decathlons.'

'Or . . . what's elevens?' Fange asked.

'Elevenses?' I suggested.

'Or twelve green bottles hanging on the wall.'

'I would love to go on talking toot with you,' I said, 'but there is this really cracking young woman over there who I have recently fallen in love with and whom I am hoping like hell to pull.'

'That would be Kelly Anna Sirjan, would it?'

'Yes, it would.'

'One of the famous Sirjan twenty-seventuplet sisters.'

'You are kidding me, right?'

'They do a human pyramid act with Count Otto Black's Circus Fantastique.'

'You are kidding me, right?'

'In tiny little bikinis.'

'You are kidding me, right?'

'Of course I'm kidding you,' said Fangio.

'Oh,' I said. 'Why?'

'Because in case you hadn't noticed, if I'm not talking to you, I'm not talking to anyone. And it's really lonely when you're all on your own with no one to talk to.'

'I will be back,' I said. 'I will need another drink soon.'

'Couldn't you include me in the conversation with Kelly?'

'I want to chat her up,' I said.

'I'd only put in the occasional word or two, nothing flashy. Wouldn't try to hog the conversation or anything.'

'Sorry,' I said.

'Bl★★dy ingratitude,' said Fangio.

'Nice try,' I said, 'but I do not think we are doing the swearword/asterisk running gag at the moment.'

'Over there!' cried Fangio, pointing. 'Zulus – thousands of them.'

'See you later,' I said and returned to Kelly Anna Sirjan.

'You spent a long time talking to that Sikh barman,' she said.

'Damn,' I said. 'I forgot to ask him about that. But I am not going back. So, let us talk about you.' And I handed Kelly her drink. 'What do you do with yourself?'

'I'm in the circus,' said Kelly. 'My identical sisters and I do a pyramid act.'

'You are kidding me, right?'

'I've got two free tickets for the Captain Beefheart gig at the Hove Town Hall*,' called Fangio. 'They're yours if you want them; you don't have to beat them out of me or anything. Speak to me, please.'

'Let us go outside and chat,' I said to Kelly.

Outside, the September sun was putting a brave face on it, and in its light Kelly looked achingly beautiful.

---

* And he really did play there, believe it or not.

'Pardon me for asking this,' I said, 'but do you have a boyfriend?'

Kelly laughed, most prettily. 'Are you chatting me up?' she said.

'No, I was just asking. Information, you see – the vetting process for Sir Hugo, just standard questions.'

'Oh, I see. Then ask away. Anything you want.'

'Do you like it doggie-style?' I asked.

And Kelly hit me right in the mouth.

'Rizla,' called the voice of Mr Rune. 'I demand drinkies.'

I returned to the drinkies tent.

'Thank God you're back,' said Fangio. 'This chap here has been looking for you.'

'New approach,' I said. 'And who is "this chap here"?'

'Lord Jeffrey Primark,' said Lord Jeffrey. 'You are Sir Hugo's associate?'

'His confidant and spiritual advisor, as it happens.'

Fangio sniggered.

'I can take this conversation outside,' I warned him. 'A pint of Pimm's for Sir Hugo, my good man.'

'Coming right up,' said Fangio. 'Stay where you are.'

'I need your help,' said Lord Jeffrey to me. And I looked this fellow up and down. He was of the gilded-youth persuasion, wearing tweeds and beret and also a dashing moustache.

I touched lightly upon my upper-lip area. My attempts at growing a fashionable goatee were still not coming to much.

'The Man,' said Lord Jeffrey in an urgent tone. '*He* is amongst us. He means to harm us. These reports in the gutter press of petty thievery – the excuse with which the Earl has drawn Sir Hugo here – they are nothing to what is really going on. It is unspeakable. Evil. Beyond all reason.'

'Sounds most intriguing,' I said. 'Have you been drinking, by the way?'

'Of *course* I've been drinking. You'd be drinking too if you knew what was *really* going on.'

'I drink whenever I can,' I said. 'No matter what.'

'I'll back him up on that, sahib,' said Fange, presenting me with Mr Rune's pint of Pimm's.

'Ah, yes,' I said. 'The Sikh business.'

'It's an interesting story,' said Fange. 'You see—'

'I can't speak to you here,' said Lord Jeffrey to me. 'Let us repair to the library.'

'No, hold on,' said Fange. 'Don't rush away. It's nice here. You can lean on the bar and everything. And I can serve you with more drinks and slip in the occasional bon mot for good measure.'

'Follow me,' said Lord Jeffrey to me.

And I followed him from the drinkies tent.

'Rotten swine,' muttered Fangio as we were leaving, 'ungrateful, rotten swine.'

I really liked the library. All those leather-bound tomes – they were *real* quality, *real* class. And very old, too. And there were big leather button-backed chairs, and Lord Jeffrey poured brandy, and so I had two drinks and was at peace with the world.

'Go on with what you were saying,' I said to him, 'about The Man.'

'He'll kill us all.' Lord Jeffrey had a shake on now. His brandy swirled about in its balloon.

'Who is The Man?' I asked.

'The Foredown Man,' said Lord Jeffrey.

'Ah,' said I. 'Go on.'

'They say that he is only a legend.' Lord Jeffrey swigged at his brandy and spoke as best as he could as he swigged. 'This house, you see, is built upon an ancient Celtic burial ground. There are Burrowers beneath, you see. The land that time forgot, the Worlds Between, the Great Old Ones, the Minds Outside Of Time, the Time Out Of Mind, the time-mind mind-time—'

'Perhaps we should go back to the drinkies tent,' I suggested. 'Fangio is good at this kind of thing.'

'The terrible horror.' Lord Jeffrey's face was that grey mask of fear that is rarely to be seen beyond the pages of the horror novel. He quivered and quaked and his eyes bulged out unappealingly. 'He comes for us. He comes for me and my kind. The last of our kind. And soon he comes. And . . .'

He paused and seemed to freeze as a terrible coldness moved through the air. There came a crackling all around us and as I looked, I saw it, felt it, knew it to be . . .

Rippling fingers of frost spread like the leaves of ferns across the windows, over the carpet, up a vase of roses, turning the flowers to glass. My breath steamed from my mouth. Lord Jeffrey clutched at his throat. I raised my glasses and found that both of my drinks had turned to solid ice.

And I gawped at Lord Jeffrey. He sat there, opposite me, glass in hand. But still now, frozen. Lifeless.

And then it came. As from nowhere. But down from above, somehow. It arched through the arctic atmosphere, cleaved through the icy air.

And it struck Lord Jeffrey a murderous blow.

And he shattered.

Exploded.

Showered down in a multitude of subzero fragments that tinkled and tumbled all about me.

And then it came to rest at my feet.

The instrument of his destruction.

The length of lead pipe.

'I knew it,' I said. 'Colonel Mustard.'

And then my hands began to do some flapping.

And then I fainted dead away.

PART II

And then there he was, a-looming: Mr Hugo Rune.

'Oh!' I went and 'Wah!' also.

Mr Rune was gazing down upon me. 'I will not ask if you are all right,' he said, 'for clearly you are not. What has occurred here, Master Rizla?'

'Lord Jeffrey,' I went. 'He froze, then he shattered. Did I get any of him on my suit?' And I flapped and patted myself.

'Lord Jeffrey?' Mr Rune cocked his head to one side. 'What *precisely* has occurred?'

I did blinkings of the eyes. I felt rather poorly and gaped up at Mr Rune. And also at those who stood with him, a-gazing down at me. The Fifth Earl was there, looking most suspicious. And the lovely Kelly. And Fangio, too, though he was not wearing his turban.

'Is that a fez?' I asked him.

'No,' said Mr Rune and he raised a fat finger. 'Before you commence with the talking of toot, speak to me and tell me what transpired.' And he placed a drink in my hand, for somehow I no longer had my own.

'I was here,' I said, 'in this library, with Lord Jeffrey Primark. And he was ranting on about him, The Man, the Foredown Man, he said, who was going to kill him and everyone else. And all manner of other stuff about Great Old Ones and Minds Outside Of Time and this house being built upon a Celtic burial ground.' The Fifth Earl made groaning sounds when I mentioned this. 'And then the room became impossibly cold and he froze and this lead pipe swung down and—'

'Ah,' said Mr Rune. 'Have to stop you there. You did say lead pipe, didn't you?'

'Yes, I did,' I said. 'It swung down and—'

Mr Rune raised his stout stick to me. 'Buffoon,' he said. 'Colonel Mustard, was it?'

'That is what I think,' I said.

'And the corpse?'

'Well, it is . . .' And I beheld. And there was no corpse. Indeed, no trace whatsoever of a corpse, which there most surely would have been had one been there, because for one thing the room was now at room temperature[*] again,

---

[*] I've always puzzled over that one: a wine that is best served at room temperature. Surely a room is always at room temperature, no matter how hot or cold it might be. Or is it just me?

and the frozen fragments would have thawed into gooey gobbets.

And the stains they make can be a right blighter to get out of a carpet, even if you use white wine (at room temperature, probably), salt, or even molasses, which in my opinion is a very poor choice, but you know what it is like when you are very drunk indeed.

'Not funny,' said Mr Rune. 'Not funny at all.'

'I am not trying to be funny,' I complained and I dragged myself up from my chair. 'He was here and then he was dead. I did not make any of this up. And there was a length of grey lead pipe involved. Really, truly there was.'

Mr Rune stared me squarely in the eyes. 'I do believe you are telling me the truth,' said he. 'Lord Jeffrey Primark, did you say?'

'I did,' I said. 'And Fange saw him. He introduced him to me.'

'Did you?' Mr Rune asked Fangio.

And Fangio shook his Stetson.

'You did,' I said. 'You liar.'

'I never did.' Fangio took off his topper and fanned at himself with it.

'In the drinkies tent,' I said. 'You were serving behind the bar.'

'I never was.' Fangio replaced his bowler hat upon his head. 'I only just got here.'

'You must have seen him,' I said to Kelly.

But Kelly shook her head.

'What is going on here?' I said. 'You are lying, Fange, I know that you are.'

'I'm not,' said Fange, and, pointing to his homburg, 'as sure as I'm wearing this trilby, I'm not.'

'Rizla,' said Mr Rune, 'will you please follow me? Excuse me, gentlemen, lady,' and he raised his beret to Kelly.

And then he led me from the library and back to the entrance hall. And there he halted next to a big, grand family portrait. 'Is *that* Lord Jeffrey?' he asked.

And I looked up at the portrait. 'That is him,' I said. 'He was wearing the same outfit and everything. He must just have had this portrait painted.'

'Regrettably, no,' said Mr Rune, 'although I was present when he sat for Richard Dadd. This portrait was painted in eighteen fifty-one, shortly before the death of his lordship.'

'A ghost?' I said. 'You are telling me that I saw a ghost?'

'Something more than a mere ghost,' said Mr Rune. 'We are dealing with dark and sinister forces here. It is fortunate that my reputation for dealing with such matters is well known to members of the aristocracy.'

'And there was me thinking that skinflints as they are, they were merely attracted by the "cheap rates" advertised on your flyers.'

'Plah!' went Hugo Rune.

And we returned to the library. It was a rather crowded library now, for it had started to rain and the gilded youth had come in from the garden. There were not as many as there had been; I assumed that the rest had gone home. Fangio was pulling bunnies from his hat to entertain those who remained. The hat was an old deerstalker; the bunnies wore no hats at all. There was a bit of a hubbub going on, which stilled at Mr Rune's approach.

'Ladies and gentlemen,' said he, 'I must crave your indulgence. Something untoward has occurred. I am going to have to ask that nobody leave this room.'

This got a bit of hubbub going once again.

'Excuse me,' said the Honourable Nigel Fairborough-Countless, 'but I have an appointment with my accountant in half an hour.'

'And I've a bun in the oven,' said Lord Edward Marzipan-Fudge.

'And I've a dog that won't walk itself,' said Lord Burberry Spaniel-Fondler.

'And I didn't get a mention earlier,' said Lord—

'These pressing appointments must be put aside,' said Mr Rune. 'There is Devilish work abroad in this house and I mean to get to its bottom.'

'Perhaps *I* can help you there,' said Lord Lucas Lapp–Dancer.

'Saw that one coming,' said I.

'Well, I have to go to the little boys' room,' said Lord Michael Kiddee-Phidler.

'I am sorry that I did not see *that* one coming,' I said.

'Hurry, then,' said Mr Rune to Lord Michael.

And his lordship left the room.

'Chap,' said Lord Henry Myle-Hie to Mr Rune, 'this Devilish work that you speak of – would you care to enlighten us regarding its nature?'

'Presently,' said Mr Rune.

And then there came a flash and a great almighty crash.

'Weather's taken a turn for the worse,' said Lord Edward, closing the French windows. 'Devilish storm, to be certain.'

'It is only the beginning,' said Hugo Rune.

And then we heard the scream. It was loud and it was shrill and it was scary. It made all the hairs stand up on the back of my neck – the ones I had been thinking of shaving off, but could not really see the point as they could not actually be seen, what with my hair having grown pretty long at the back, in the fashionable mode of the times.

'Rizla, come, the rest of you stay here.' Mr Rune whispered words to Fangio and then marched out of the room. I followed him at the hurry on and down the hall and up the stairs we went. I followed Hugo Rune to the little boys' room and we stood before the door.

'You may not like what you see,' said Hugo Rune.

'Avocado suite, do you think?' I said.

And Mr Rune pushed open the door.

I must confess that I did not at all like what I saw. There was no avocado suite involved in my disliking. The bathroom was in tasteful white, somewhat spoiled for me, however, by the large amount of tasteless red, all scattered and splattered and running.

'Don't look,' said Mr Rune.

But I did.

And I saw him – well, the little of him that I *could* see.

This 'little' being his ankles and feet protruding from the toilet.

'This is bad,' said Mr Rune and he shook his great baldy head.

'Very bad,' said I. 'He had no time at all to build up his part before *this* happened.'

'Hardly a suitable moment for such flippancy,' said Mr Rune.

'I do so agree,' I said. 'Aaaagh! Help! Police! Murder!'

Mr Rune clamped a large hand over my mouth. 'Control yourself,' he ordered. 'You are no good to me otherwise.'

I detached his oversized mitt from my unlaughing gear. 'I do not *want* to be any good,' I said. 'Let us get out of here, and quickly.'

'Rizla, this is no time to panic.'

'Trust me,' I said, 'there will be no better time than this.'

'We must return to the library.'

'We must return to Grand Parade. Call the police.'

Mr Rune shook his head. Firmly. 'This is *not* a job for Inspector Hector,' said he. '*This* is a job for Hugo Rune.'

And so we returned to the library. And once inside, Mr Rune closed the door, turned the key in the lock and took himself over to the drinks cabinet, where he poured for himself something large.

The gilt was coming off the gilded youth. They sat about in attitudes of dejection, nervously toying with glasses and looking very edgy and uncertain.

'Lord Michael Kiddee-Phidler is no more,' said Mr Rune.

Which did not seem to ease the situation.

Although it certainly roused them from their seats. They rose as one and made as two to the main door and the French windows where they got all sort of scrunched up together, the room door and the French windows being locked.

'Sit down!' ordered Mr Rune. 'Such unseemly behaviour is for the lower orders, not for such as you.'

The room door was being kicked and several panes

of glass went out of the French windows, but neither shifted.

'Sit!' ordered Mr Rune. 'If you would live, then sit.'

It was a cowering, giltless bunch of youth that slunk back to their seats.

'What is going on here?' Lord Edward demanded to be told.

'All right,' said Mr Rune, 'I will tell you. My companion here witnessed, in a vision, the destruction of Lord Jeffrey Primark earlier this afternoon. All of you here are descendants of Lord Jeffrey; and so all of you will probably know that he vanished in eighteen fifty-one, upon the second day of the Great Exhibition. It was believed that he was murdered. But he was not. Although he was interred – I know, because I was there at his interment.' This remark caused a certain ripple among the giltless youth.

'Trust to what he says,' I said. 'I have seen things that you people would not believe.' Which rang a bell somewhere.

'Thank you, Rizla,' said Mr Rune. 'Lord Jeffrey dabbled in certain unspeakable arts.'

'Nothing wrong with that,' said Lord Lucas Lapp-Dancer. 'We've all done that – it's the duty of the aristocracy to behave as badly as we can get away with. It's expected of us. It's a tradition, or an old charter, or something.'

'Time,' said Mr Rune. 'Always time. All of this is to do with time.'

'We do have to take time to behave badly,' agreed Lord Lapp-Dancer, 'but we have plenty of time on our hands. That's one of the benefits of being rich.'

'And also your downfall,' said Mr Rune. 'It was Lord Jeffrey's downfall. He sought to travel into the future. He discussed it with me many times and I advised strongly against it, but he was adamant and would not be shaken. As I wished for no harm to come to him, I offered my assistance in return for a small pecuniary sum. Together we built a cryogenic chamber and packed it with Arctic ice, shipped in by Fortnum and Mason. Lord Jeffrey was placed into a trance state by myself, as I am skilled in such matters, then placed in the chamber, which in turn was placed in a secret place, a safe place where it could lie undisturbed until more than a hundred years had passed. Certain details were lodged in a safety-deposit box, to be opened by his heirs upon a certain date, disclosing the whereabouts of the cryogenic chamber and the means by which Lord Jeffrey was to be defrosted.'

Lightning flashed and thunder roared and rain thrashed down outside.

'He could not make up this stuff, could he?' I whispered to Fangio.

'*I* could,' said the barlord. 'Do you think this bobble hat suits me?'

'But,' continued Mr Rune, 'there is always the matter of the soul, of the existence of the soul. A man's body might remain alive, in suspended animation, for more than one hundred years. But what of his soul? Might this perhaps detach itself from its host and go a-wandering?'

'Is he speculating here?' whispered Fangio, diddling with his hardhat.

'I would not care to speculate,' I whispered back. 'The brim's too big on your sombrero, by the way.'

'And *if* the soul wandered,' said Mr Rune, 'while the sleeper slept, and then returned at length to find the body destroyed – shattered, perhaps, by a length of lead pipe – what then of the wandering soul?'

'Wouldn't it go to Heaven?' asked Kelly, which I thought a reasonable question to ask.

'Would it?' said Mr Rune. 'In the matter of a normal death, I would assume that this would be the case. But the destruction of Lord Jeffrey's body when his soul had already detached itself – surely these are somewhat unusual circumstances.'

'This is all twaddle,' cried Lord Henry Myle-Hie. 'Perhaps Lord Jeffrey did have himself frozen up, and perhaps you *were* there at that freezing up, but all this soul stuff is simply speculation.'

Fange made a knowing face at me, but I could not see much of it under his snap-brimmed snood.

'Speculation?' said Mr Rune. 'Then I would like to test a proposition. Would you kindly take yourself over to the fireplace?'

'The fireplace?' Lord Myle-Hie flustered and blustered. 'I don't understand.'

'Indulge me,' said Mr Rune. 'Let me test the substance of my supposed speculation. And you, too, young lady,' he said to Kelly. 'If you would be so kind as to stand beside him.'

Kelly shrugged and wandered over to the fireplace.

'Quite mad,' said Lord Henry Myle-Hie. But he took himself, also as requested, to the fireplace. 'Satisfied?' he asked.

'Take a step back, please,' said Mr Rune. 'Mind the brass companion set, which is missing the tongs, I notice.'

'As you please.' Lord Henry took a step back, as did Kelly. 'Now are you satisfied?' asked Lord Myle-Hie.

And then there was a sudden whoosh and a lot of soot as well that billowed out into the room. And then there was a scream and a lot of muffled banging about. And then the soot sort of settled and Lord Henry Myle-Hie was gone. 'I'm satisfied *now*,' said Hugo Rune.

'What? What?' and 'Scream! Scream!' went most of those present. And I include myself amongst their number. And I flapped, too, I can tell you.

'A most troubled spirit,' said Mr Rune. 'I wonder who will be next?'

Perhaps they were not the best-chosen words, for they prompted another all-as-two rush towards the doors. And this time the French windows burst out and several giltless with them. And I confess that I turned away my face as out in the storm-lashed garden something murderous happened. Those on the threshold of the French windows drew themselves back in horror. Shrinking down and cringing became suddenly all the rage.

'Eight more there, by my reckoning,' said Mr Rune. 'What price my speculations now?'

The Honourable Nigel Fairborough-Countless fell wringing his hands at Mr Rune's feet. 'Save us,' he wailed. 'Save *me*. I will make it worth your while – I'm heir to the Countless millions.'

'A tempting offer,' said Mr Rune.

'Save *me!*' whined Lord Edward Marzipan-Fudge. 'I'll set you up with doughnuts for life.'

'If it's dogs you want,' begged Lord Burberry Spaniel-Fondler, 'I can get you really big ones – the size of a fully grown pig, some of them.'

'I don't know your sexual proclivities,' fawned Lord Lucas Lapp-Dancer, 'but name your chosen fancy and it's yours.'

'All most tempting offers,' said Mr Rune.

'I would not bother with the dog,' I said.

'*I'll* take the dog,' said Fange, 'and Mister Rune, if you'll see your way clear to protecting me from being sucked up the chimney, your credit will always be good at The Conjuror's Hat. We're a stage-magicians'-headwear theme bar today.'

'At last an explanation for *that*,' I said.

Fangio raised his flat cap to me.

Hugo Rune took a head-count. 'Just nine left,' he said, 'including myself. This is a sorry business. What think *you* of it?' And he turned to face the Fifth Earl.

'I think this is a disaster,' the Fifth Earl replied. 'I called you here because of the outbreak of petty thievery.'

'And my special low rates for members of the aristocracy,' said Mr Rune.

'Well, naturally *that*. But as for all *this* – do something, Rune. That's what I'm paying you for.'

'I do not recall that we discussed terms.'

'Name your price. Just save us from this horror.'

'You know what I want,' said Mr Rune.

'I *don't*.' And the Fifth Earl shook his head.

'You do,' said Mr Rune, 'and I will have it, too. Lord Jeffrey will have it and so will I.'

'You're mad!' cried the Fifth Earl. 'As mad as he was.'

'He was not mad,' said Mr Rune. 'He was a noble man and he was my friend. He was perhaps misguided, foolish – reckless, even, but he was brave and he was true.'

'I have money,' said the Fifth Earl. 'I have cash.'

'I'll take what cash you have,' said Mr Rune, 'if you give it willingly.'

'I do.' And the Fifth Earl dragged out his wallet.

I helped myself to a drink from the drinks cabinet, and I studied Mr Rune as I did so. *I should be able to reason this out,* I thought to myself. *I am sure that all the clues are here, but I am also sure there is something missing. And it is all to do with 'You know what I want. And I will have it, too. Lord Jeffrey will have it and so will I.'* But what, I wondered very hard, was *it*? It was not money, I was sure of that.

The contents of the Fifth Earl's wallet were now in Hugo Rune's possession.

'I made *my* offer first,' said the Honourable Nigel. 'Don't forget the Countless millions I have coming to me.'

'I fear that, regrettably, you will not be here to collect them,' said Mr Rune. 'Look out, behind you. Zulus – thousands of them.'

The Honourable Nigel covered his head and fled.

Through the open French windows, as it happened.

And out into—

'Aaaaaaagh!' went the voice of the Honourable Nigel.

And then there was just more rain. And lightning and thunder.

'You did that on purpose.' The Fifth Earl raised his fists at Mr Rune.

'You know what I want,' said Mr Rune.

I counted the heads. We still had the Lords Edward, Burberry and maybe Lord Lucas. It is difficult to remember and they all looked very much the same. And there was the beautiful Kelly, too, but she was not aristocracy. And there was me and there was Fange, and we were just commoners, of course.

And there was the Fifth Earl.

And there was Mr Hugo Rune.

And I really, truly should have been able to figure this thing out.

I poured another drink and took it over to Kelly. She looked all dishevelled and a bit sweaty, too. And God, is that not sexy with women?

'This is a very bad business,' I whispered to her as I handed her the drink (a triple). 'I truly do not know whether we are going to get out of it alive.'

Kelly said nothing.

And so I continued, 'You are a very beautiful woman,' I said, surveying her beautiful frontage. 'In fact, you are the most beautiful woman that I have ever seen. And I am sorry I offended you earlier. But as it does not seem likely that we *will* get out of this alive, could you see your way clear to giving me a—' And I whispered.

And damn me if she did not punch me once again.

'Time is running out,' said Mr Rune to the Fifth Earl. 'Will you give me what I want, what Lord Jeffrey wants, or not?'

'You can go to Hell,' cried the Fifth Earl, 'and Lord Jeffrey, too.'

'I think that he's already been there,' said Mr Rune, 'which is why he knows so much torment. He has seen the Burrowers beneath, experienced the horrors of the Great Old Ones, the Worlds Between, the Minds Outside Of Time. And now he wants what I want.'

And I do not know why I did not see it coming. Probably because, although rubbing at my grazed jaw, I was still most drawn to Kelly's beautiful frontage. But if I had been paying more attention to other people's body language and so on, I would have noticed the way that the remaining lords and the Fifth Earl had been gathering themselves about Mr Rune in a manner that can only be described as menacing.

And so when they fell upon him in a most violent manner, I was not close enough to offer my support.

'Out with him!' cried the Fifth Earl. 'Offer him up in sacrifice. It's the only way to save ourselves.'

And they had him. And I suppose that in desperation weight is no object. You hear stories of little women lifting cars off their trapped loved ones. I have read of several in the *Weekly World News*. These lords had Mr Rune off his feet in moments and over to the French windows and out.

And lightning flashed and thunder roared and I was somewhat horrified.

'You b*st*rds!' I cried.

'Don't try to fool us by putting on an upper-class accent,' said the Fifth Earl. 'You're next. Get him, boys.'

Now, I was impressed by Fangio. He brought down Lord Burberry with a neat rugby tackle. And Kelly put up a struggle, too, and clocked the Fifth Earl a really decent one in *his* mouth.

And as for myself, well, I do pride myself that when faced with a violent confrontation, I *do* know how to handle myself and—

And suddenly I was very wet. And Fange was wet and Kelly, she was wet, too. And she looked *good* very wet, I can tell you.

And suddenly something burst past us. It burst through the open French windows and into the library and hideous bloody business occurred, which happily I did not see.

I just lay in the rain with my eyes closed.

Beside Kelly and Fange.

And Mr Rune, who stood in the storm and grinned down upon me.

'That all went rather well, don't you think?' said he.

We took shelter from the storm in the drinkies tent. I did not fancy the library. Fangio took his place behind the bar and served us with drinkies.

'Is it over?' I asked Mr Rune. 'Are we safe?'

223

'It is over,' said he. 'It is done. We are safe. This case is concluded.'

'*Concluded?*' I said. 'There are at least a dozen dead. That is not what *I* would call "concluded". Or perhaps I have some misunderstanding as to what the word "concluded" means.'

'It means that the soul of Lord Jeffrey is now at peace.'

'That is pleasing to my ears,' I said, 'but what of the souls of those murdered?'

'They will be judged,' said Mr Rune, and he swallowed booze.

'I tried really hard,' I said, 'to figure it out, but I could not. Will you please explain? Please.'

'A case of murder,' said Mr Rune, 'murder, plain and simple: the murder of Lord Jeffrey Primark, which you observed, his frozen body shattered by a length of lead pipe. Although not in the library, but rather in the catacombs beneath these lands of the Primarks, which were once the site of an ancient Celtic burial ground. I interred him down there myself. He may have been foolish, Lord Primark, but he was no fool when it came to finance. He made many investments before he was interred, investments that would ensure that when he was resuscitated he would be a fabulously wealthy man. I put my name as signatory to several of them. As I mentioned earlier, the details of how he should be resuscitated lay in a safety-deposit box, awaiting the given time when they should be read by his descendants – all those who were gathered together in the library. But greed overcame them. They determined that the fortune should be theirs and chose not to resuscitate Lord Jeffrey. Instead, they followed the directions given in the papers that were in the safety-deposit box, which led them to the vault beneath the library where he lay frozen, and there they murdered him. They took a solemn vow that none would betray the other and that they would split the wealth between them. Then they took up the length of lead pipe – all put a hand upon it – and then they shattered Lord Jeffrey's frozen body.'

'The b*st*rds!' said Fange.

'Posh accent,' said Mr Rune. 'But that is what they did. They could have had no knowledge, of course, that his lordship's soul was not inside his body, for such metaphysical matters are beyond the ken of such fellows. And so they could have had no knowledge that this soul would seek revenge upon those who had destroyed its bodily host. The Foredown Man, young Rizla, as in *Fore*father, *down* below.'

'Far out,' I said, in the popular parlance of the day. 'And so it took its revenge upon all of them?'

'A bloody and terrible revenge. Who knows what torments that wandering soul has suffered? I pray that it truly suffers no more.'

'Very far out,' I said. 'But I have one question. You said to the Fifth Earl that he knew what you wanted, and that you wanted what Lord Jeffrey wanted. What was that?'

'Simply justice,' said Mr Rune. 'Nothing more. Take this.'

And he handed something to me.

It was a badge. And on it were printed the Scales of Justice.

I pinned the badge to my sodden lapel.

'Time, gentlemen, please,' said Fangio.

8

The Baffling Business Of
The Bevendean Bat

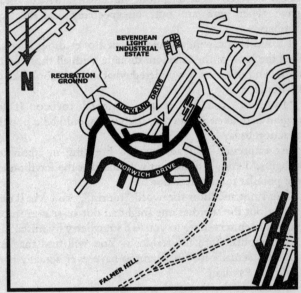

The Bevendean Bat

PART I

It was October and there were portents in the heavens. An odd conjunction of planets and a comet that was supposedly heading our way had all the local prophets of doom prophesying doom. There was talk of the end of the world, but I paid it no heed. All I knew was that it was October, and the weather was brisk.

A brisk wind spun fallen leaves all around the Pavilion Gardens, heaping them up, whisking them about and stirring them around once again. There was something about that I did not like: it looked like Art to me.

It was warm enough indoors, though, and in our rooms at forty-nine Grand Parade, Mr Rune had got a fine fire going in the hearth. It was fuelled by unpaid bills, final demands, those letters that solicitors write and a quantity of yellow-covered local telephone directories, which always arrive when you are out, unexpectedly and in large numbers.

I stood at the window and worried over those leaves. I liked the look of the Pavilion, though, with all those onion domes and minarets. I wondered what it might look like on the inside.

'Tasteless,' said Mr Rune. 'Oriental rococo. If the Regent had taken my advice, the place would be a popular attraction today.'

'As impressed as I am by you breaking in upon my thoughts,' I said, 'I think you will find that the Pavilion is a *most* popular tourist attraction.'

'I did not mention the word "tourist",' said Mr Rune, spitting out the word as one might an out-of-season sprout that has been served up to you as a strawberry by mistake. 'I meant popular with the residents. You will find that few folk who actually live in Brighton have ever actually been inside the Pavilion.'

'I wonder why that is?' I wondered.

'They just won't visit,' said Mr Rune. 'It's probably a tradition, or an old charter, or something. But more likely it's to do with all the gaudy décor.'

'Yes, but they would not know about the décor unless they went inside.'

'The suggestion that proves the rule, perhaps,' said Mr Rune and he tossed another unpaid bill on to the fire.

This one, as it happened, was from Bradbury's of Piccadilly requesting that Mr Rune cough up the readies for the two most wonderful coats that had recently been delivered to our door. Dark they were, of worsted wool with great big Astrakhan collars.

'Like unto the original that was worn by Tony Hancock,' said the other Lad Himself.

I had been pacing around the town for a week in mine, savouring the envious glances of my sartorial inferiors. It certainly kept the cold out and when topped off by the black silk stovepipe hat, I cut quite a dash. The black silk stovepipe had been a present from Fangio, for as The Conjuror's Hat was now called The Port In A Storm, the barlord had no further use for it. And I looked a regular dandy.

'It would be good if we had a case that involved us going into the Pavilion,' I said to Mr Rune.

'No, it wouldn't,' he replied.

'Maybe the Prince Regent built a time machine and he and Beau Brummel took it for a spin.'

'No, he didn't,' said Mr Rune.

'But say he did and it crashed here and now and—'

'Please be quiet,' said Mr Rune. 'I'm trying to concentrate.'

'On what?'

'On the fifth stair of the flight leading up to our rooms from the street. I am visualising a banana skin.'

'Why?'

'Ssssh!'

'Aaaagh!'

The 'Aaaagh!' came up to us from the stairs. And was followed by a thud.

'Bailiffs?' I asked Mr Rune. 'Should I hide the breakfasting plates?'

'It is a member of the Brighton constabulary,' said Mr Rune.

'Should I hide all the drugs, then?'

Mr Rune raised his hand and leaned back in his favourite chair. 'It is Inspector Hector,' said he. 'I'd know those clumsy footsteps anywhere.'

A knock came on our hall door and Mr Rune waved for me to answer this knock. I did so and there before me, all dishevelled, stood the inspector known as Hector.

'Every single time,' he spat. 'Every single time I come up those stairs I trip on something or other. You want to get a light bulb fitted on that staircase, Rune.'

'Believe me, I *don't*,' said the All-Knowing One, yawning an all-knowing yawn and adjusting the quilted lapels of his red silk smoking jacket. 'Enter quickly, Hector, you're letting in the draught.'

The inspector entered and I closed the door. Mr Rune waved the inspector to the other chair by the fire.

My chair!

The inspector took off his gloves, blew on his hands, removed his scarf and unbuttoned his grey topcoat. I considered fetching *my* new coat and parading about before him for a while, but I did not as Mr Rune called out that I should bring himself and his 'welcome guest' some coffee.

'We are out of coffee,' I said in ready reply.

'Tea, then,' said he.

'No tea either, I regret.' For that was how we worked this particular routine.

'Perhaps something stronger?' Mr Rune winked at the inspector.

Who winked back at Mr Rune and said, 'Scotch, please.'

I took myself over to the drinks cabinet and drew out the decoy bottle. The one with the single measure left in it.

'This is all we have,' I called to Mr Rune.

'Pour it for the inspector, then,' he called back to me.

'Oh, I couldn't, if it's your last.' The inspector raised his chilly hands.

'Then pour it for me,' said Mr Rune, keeping the straightest of faces, 'for by the gods I need it on a morning such as this.'

I poured Scotch for Mr Rune and handed it to him. And took a certain delight in the expression on Inspector Hector's face.

'So,' said Mr Rune to the inspector, 'what brings such a high-powered fellow as yourself to these humble rooms of ours?' And he flung a bundle of parking tickets into the roaring fire.

'You're supposed to pay those,' said the inspector.

'I don't own a car,' said Mr Rune.

'I see,' said the inspector. 'Well, no, I don't, actually, but I have come to you upon pressing business that is best conducted in private.'

'I have no secrets from Rizla,' said Mr Rune. Which was anything but true. 'Speak to us and whatever you say will not – you have my word as a gentleman – travel beyond these four walls of mine. See this wet, see this dry, et cetera.'

'Yes,' said the inspector, warming his hands beside the flames and wiping a tear from his nose. 'Well, Mister Rune, it's a veritable poser, and I confess that the Sussex constabulary are baffled.'

'Indeed,' said Mr Rune, cupping one of his chins in his big right hand. 'Go on.'

'It's cats,' said the inspector. 'It's the cats in Bevendean.'

'Cats?' said Mr Rune, and he said it thoughtfully.

'Missing cats,' the inspector said and he rubbed his now warm hands all over his still-cold face. 'And I am not talking about one or two cats. They regularly lose one or two cats up there every month, carried away by mutant doves or run over by men in white vans.'

'Mutant doves?' I said.

'They breed them up there, for the Ministry of Defence, I believe.'

'Oh,' I said, 'I see.'

'You don't,' said Mr Rune, 'but carry on, Inspector.'

'More than fifty cats have gone missing in the last month alone, as well as dogs, canaries, tortoises, lizards and whatnots.'

'Whatnots?' I asked.

'They breed them up there,' said Mr Rune, 'for the Ministry of Furniture.'

'But it's the cats that are the problem,' said Inspector Hector. 'Cats are always a political issue – you know how it is. I'd put my lads on to it, but we are stretched to the very limit. You must have read of that terrible business last month at Hangleton Manor.'

'In passing,' said Mr Rune, 'but the solution to that case seemed so obvious to me that I assumed you would have solved it yourself before lunch, and then gone a-golfing.'

'Most amusing,' said the inspector. 'But I fear in truth that it will take many months to solve, and in the unlikely event that I don't show a result, the Met will be called in, and then there'll be all sorts of chaos.'

'I see,' said Mr Rune. 'So let us not beat around the bush here. You would *really* like my advice concerning the murders at Hangleton Manor, in which case—'

'Er, no,' said the inspector. 'It's the cats I'd like you to help with.'

Mr Rune bristled, which I found impressive since he lacked for visible hair.

'Cats?' he said once more. 'You are asking Rune to deal with cats. Rune, whose name is Legend. Hugo Artemis Solon Saturnicus Reginald Arthur Rune. The Perfect Master. The All-Knowing One. Rune, whose eye is in the triangle, whose nose cuts through the ether, whose ear takes in the music of the spheres. This is the Rune to whom you speak of lost cats?'

'I recall that we once dealt with a case regarding a lost dog,' I said.

Mr Rune raised a naked eyebrow at me.

'Naturally, you would be paid a retainer and all your expenses would be covered,' said Inspector Hector.

'Speak to me of cats,' said Hugo Rune.

And Inspector Hector spoke to Hugo Rune of cats. He spoke at length on the subject. Exceeding length. At more length than seemed decent, considering the subject. And then he put on his scarf and gloves, shook Mr Rune by the hand and left.

And we listened at the door as he fell down our stairs.

'Cats,' I said, when we had ceased our laughter. 'You are going to take on a case concerning cats?'

Mr Rune grinned and nodded and studied his big map on

the wall. I joined him and studied it, too. 'The Bevendean Bat,' I said, tracing the figure that was coloured on to the roads of that area. 'That is "bat", not "cat". You have a cat there – the Coldean Cat, although it is not a very convincing representation.'

'Plah!' said Mr Rune. 'We'll deal with one thing at a time. This case intrigues me, and if I am not very much mistaken – and it is rare that I am – it will prove to be one of the most extraordinary cases that we have tackled so far.'

'It will have to go a bit to beat that space crab,' I said. 'Ahab the space crab, was it not?'

'The Bevendean Bat,' said Mr Rune. 'I wonder.'

Now, nobody walks to Bevendean, but then why would they want to? It is one of those out-of-the way parts of Brighton that only those who know the place well really know it at all. There are houses up there and there are workshops.

I have always had a lot of trouble with the word 'workshop', which seems to crop up a lot amongst those engaged in the Arts. Poetry workshops, writers' workshops. Vegetarian lesbian empowerment workshops. In my opinion, and not just mine alone, one should beware of anything calling itself a workshop that does not involve light engineering.

We stood on the kerbside of Grand Parade.

'Call me a cab,' said Mr Rune.

I did so and then hailed a passing cab, though I hated like damn to do it.

The taxi driver's name was Sean O'Reilly and he hailed from a land across the sea. He supported a football team called Arsenal, swearing on the life of the mother who bore him that should the Blessed Virgin Mary and her only son Jaysus become manifest upon the hallowed turf of Wembley when Arsenal were playing for the cup, 'Sure and they'd have to be waiting until half-time before I'd cross meself to them.'

Sean went on to espouse his theories regarding what he referred to as 'The Fillum Industry', specifically regarding the cinemas that showed these 'fillums'. 'I've never been in one of them places meself,' said Sean, 'because I know what goes on inside of them: back-row mischief, virgin deflowerment and the worshipping of false Gods. Idols,' said Sean 'Matinée idols. And I've heard tell that there are plans afoot to add a few extra frames on to the end of each fillum containing a subliminal message that you can't be after seeing, but what gets inside your brainbox. It will make you forget that you've seen the fillum. Then you'll go back to the foyer and be buying yourself another ticket to see it all over again.'

I quite warmed to that idea, and wondered whether it might actually work, and if so, how I might buy myself a cinema.

Mr Rune I knew to be something of a movie buff. He claimed acquaintance with Lana Turner, Rondo Hatton, Bradford Dillman and the now-legendary Bud Cort. Not to mention Bruce Dern and Harry Dean Stanton and the young Ron Perlman as well.

Which I never did.

Mention, that is.

When we reached our destination, I thanked Sean for the ride and took myself off at a pace up the road, that I might not see the rise and fall of Mr Rune's stout stick, nor hear the screams of he upon whom it fell.

And at length I was joined by Mr Rune.

'I am thinking of purchasing a cinema,' said he.

'Not next door to mine,' I said.

And then we surveyed the area. We strode briskly around and about it, around a crescent named The Hyde in particular. There was no shortage of light engineering here, plenty of workshops and none of these catering to would-be Yogic Flyers or Tantric foot-massagers. This was a proper industrial estate. There were carpenters' shops, shipwrights, refiners of animal feeds, manufacturers of earth-moving equipment, not to mention a nuclear processing plant. Which I did not.

We would have strolled but for the cold, which bit at our naked faces.

'It is exceedingly nippy up here,' I said. 'Positively Arctic, in fact.'

'The Bevendean microclimate,' said Mr Rune. 'Whilst Hove enjoys a semi-tropical climate all the year round[*], this area up here is prone to hurricanes and tornadoes and is continually sheathed by a layer of permafrost.'

I nearly slipped and fell upon my bottom. 'I wish I had worn two pairs of socks,' I said.

'You should learn to think ahead,' said Mr Rune. 'I'm wearing three.'

I dragged my stovepipe hat down over my ears and pulled up my Astrakhan collar. 'How much more brisk striding do you think will be necessary?' I asked.

'It's a curious place, to be sure,' said Mr Rune. 'Note the sweeping curves of the roads, which form the distinctive shape of the great Bat – the work of the legendary Edwardian architect and engineer Isambard Kingdom-Come.'

'Not very funny,' I said.

'I agree. The man lacked somewhat for a sense of humour. He is not, of course, to be confused with Isambard Kingdom Brunel. This is Kingdom-Come I speak of – have you ever heard of him?'

'Did he play with Isaac Asimov's Starship Jazz Quintet in the nineteen forties?'

'No,' said Mr Rune, 'but that's an easy mistake to make. This Mister Kingdom-Come was a visionary. He believed that all biblical events had actually occurred within the British Isles, but that "scholars" had transferred their locations to a more southerly area.'

'So he was a nutcase?' I said.

'Not to put a finer word on it, yes. But he somehow got it into his head that Brighton was the site of the Lost Continent of Atlantis.'

'That would be a bit of a squeeze,' I said, giving my icy

[*] It does *not* – I've been there! Ed.

nose a rub. 'An entire continent compressed into the size of a town?'

'It was his belief that the Atlanteans were somewhat smaller than we are.' Mr Rune made a teeny-weeny dimensional demonstration with his right thumb and forefinger.

'You are wearing *two* pairs of gloves,' I said. 'Lend a pair to me.'

'No,' said Mr Rune. 'But to continue, these sweeping roads were the product of his archaeological excavations in his quest to uncover the ruins of Atlantis.'

'I cannot be having with archaeological excavations, myself,' I said. 'The fellows who dig them only ever find tiny walls and a few bits of broken pottery, and then they get all excited and swear that they have just made the most important discovery of the century, the ruins of a mile-high gold-covered temple to Frogmore the God of Bike-Saddle Fixtures or some such.'

'I think you will find,' said Mr Rune, 'that they do this in order to secure further government funding for their diggings and so remain in employment.'

'That is a rather cynical view,' I said.

'Some of my best friends are archaeologists,' said Mr Rune.

'Oh,' I said. 'Well, this is all very interesting,' which in truth it was *not*, 'but what has it to do with lost cats?'

'No knowledge is ever wasted,' said Mr Rune, taking out his hip flask and tasting something to keep out the cold.

'Give me a swig,' I said. But Mr Rune would not.

'You can be a terrible rotter sometimes,' I said. Bitterly.

And Mr Rune relented this time and offered me a swig.

'The hip flask is empty,' I said.

'It's all right, I have another.'

'Then . . . Oh, forget it.'

'Consider it forgotten.'

'I am freezing here,' I said, my teeth all a-chatter. 'Can we return to our rooms? I noticed another pile of local telephone directories on the step when we went out. We will get a decent blaze going with them.'

Mr Rune sniffed the air and said, 'Shush.'

I shrugged and shushed. And I listened.

'Nothing,' said Mr Rune. 'Do you hear that – nothing?'

I listened some more, and that is what I heard: absolutely nothing.

'No birdsong,' said Mr Rune. 'No dog that howls in the distance.'

'All gone south for the winter,' I suggested.

'Not the wolves,' said Mr Rune. 'Nor even the bears, or snow tigers.'

'*Wolves?*' I said. '*Bears, snow tigers?*'

'Most suggestive.'

'I am off,' I said. 'I think I will jog to stave off frostbite to my toes.'

'You would not prefer to visit *there*?' And Mr Rune pointed to the *there* in question. And that *there* was a single alehouse.

Not that they generally come in pairs.

Or indeed in sets of up to a dozen in a single building, as would the cinemas of the future. Which makes you think, does it not? How many times *might* you have seen the same fillum?

I viewed the single alehouse. It stood there all alone in Norwich Drive, in the belly of the Bevendean Bat.

'The Really Small Atlantean,' I read, peering at the sign.

'Race you,' said Mr Rune. 'Last to the counter buys the drinks.'

And I was the last to the counter.

I really liked The Really Small Atlantean. It was a really small pub, really dinky, really cosy, a single-storeyed bungalow of a pub. From the outside it looked a bit like a child's drawing of a house – pitched roof, front door in the middle, windows to either side, even a chimney with curly smoke coming out. Inside it had the look of a coaching inn, with beams and daub and wattle and a big log fire in the inglenook. The walls were a-glitter with burnished horse brasses, the furniture was rustic, the lighting ambient.

Behind the bar, a barman, all bucolic, stood with leather apron and an old brown dog.[*] And as I puffed to his counter, at which Mr Rune now comfortably sat, this barman bade me welcome in the manner known as '*loud*'.

'*What will it be, sir?*' he shouted. '*Something to keep out the cold?*'

'Yes,' I said. And, 'Not so loud.' And then, 'Hey, Fange, it is you.'

'*Yes, sir!*' shouted Fangio. '*It is me. Two pints of Old Sump Lube, would it be?*'

'That is fine,' I said. '*Stop shouting.*'

'*Please don't shout at me to stop shouting, sir,*' shouted Fangio. '*It only makes me shout all the louder.*'

'*Why?*' I shouted, louder still.

'*To make myself heard over this din.*'

'*What din?*' I bellowed.

Fangio put one finger to his lips and another to his ear hole. The fingers were on separate hands, for otherwise it would have been quite a nifty trick. Although not *that* nifty – you can do it with one hand fairly easily, but it makes you look a bit foolish.

'*Oh,*' shouted Fangio. '*It's stopped.*'

I glanced all about the bar, but except for Fange and me and Mr Rune, it was quite deserted.

'It *has* stopped,' said Fangio, wiping his brow. 'Thank God for that.' And he pulled us our pints.

I paid for same (and grudgingly) and then asked once again, 'What din?'

'Animals,' said Fangio. 'Animals and birds, and reptiles, too, I don't doubt, all calling and mewing and howling and snorting and suchlike.'

'I did not hear anything,' I said.

'No, well, you wouldn't have – it stopped about an hour ago.'

'Suggestive,' said Mr Rune.

---

[*] Which might have been a spaniel, but was probably a Peke.

'I didn't mean to be,' said Fange. 'And I'm dreading it, I can tell you.'

'Dreading *what*?' I asked, though I knew that I would regret it.

'I'm only up here,' said Fange, 'because the brewery sent me for the day. This pub's last day, as it happens – they're closing it down. But the brewery is doing up my pub while I'm here. They're giving it a makeover. It's going to be called The Carry On Inn tomorrow, and I will have to talk like Kenneth Williams and only in innuendo. They've given me a phrasebook and everything. It makes even the simplest remark sound overtly suggestive. I'm dreading it, I can tell you.'

'Difficult times for you,' I said, as I sipped at my Old Sump Lube. 'Would you care to have a *crack* at it now?' I asked. 'Get *stuck in* for a bit of practice?'

'No, I wouldn't,' said Fangio. 'It's *too big* to even think about.'

'Tell me about the rabbits,' said Mr Rune.

'The rabbits?' said Fange. 'Is that some socially transmitted disease? I'll have to look it up in the phrasebook.'

'Did you hear any rabbits amongst the animal din?' Mr Rune asked. 'The hills about here are usually aloud with the sound of rabbits generally, or Arctic hares, at least.'

'I might have heard rabbits,' said Fange, 'but it was hard to tell – they were drowned out by the cries of the penguins.'

'Is that the right continent?' I asked.

'As in Atlantis?' Mr Rune asked.

'Or Arsenal,' said Fange. 'I just had a wounded cabbie in here who supports Arsenal. He said I was to watch out for cinema popcorn, that it contained active ingredients that made it addictive, so that every time you went back to the cinema, you found yourself ordering a bigger tub.'

I glanced over at Mr Rune, who shrugged. 'No rabbits, then?' said he.

And Fangio shrugged. And I shrugged, too. I did not want to be left out of the shrugging.

'Highly suggestive,' said Mr Rune. 'I have already formed certain theories regarding this most anomalous case.'

'Case?' said Fangio. 'Are you here on a case?'

'Not much of one,' I said. 'A bunch of missing cats.'

'I don't think it's correct to refer to them as a *bunch* of cats,' said the leather-aproned barkeep. 'That's not the collective noun. I think you'll find that it's a cabal of cats.'

'You mean like a dirtiness of dogs?'

'Not altogether like. More like a peregrination of pencils, or a hovering of Hoovers.'

'Ah,' I said. 'Well, you are into household appliances and appurtenances there, like a torturing of toasters. Although most folk only own the one. Or a philandering of forks—'

'Or indeed a spontaneity of spoons,' said Fange.

'Yes, but that has more to do with the essential nature of spoons.'

'It's a philosophical concept,' said Fange, 'like a dialectical materialisation of Doctor Martens, or a Freudian slip of slippers.'

'And now you have moved on to the metaphysical realms of footwear,' I said, 'which takes us seamlessly to a Lutheran dogma of loafers and a papal nuncio of plimsolls. Or, and I am sure you will know this one, a scandal of sandals, which is from "Subterranean Homesick Blues" by Bob Dylan.'

'Don't get me going on that,' said Fange.

So I did not.

Instead, I took sup upon my ale. 'A good bit of toot we talked there,' I said.

'Always a pleasure,' said Fangio, 'but never a—'

'Have you finished now?' asked Mr Rune.

'I think so,' I said. 'The secret really *is* knowing when to stop.'

'Or a . . .' said Fange. But he did not finish, for at that moment something untoward occurred in the bar. Untoward indeed it was, and very loud also.

It was as if all the zoos of the world had been gathered together at this one spot and every animal in them urged to give vent to the loudest of cries they could muster. The sound was appalling. Deafening. Mr Rune and me and Fangio clapped our hands to our ears and pressed them as hard as we could. The awful row went on and on.

Then suddenly it stopped.

Fangio's hands moved away from his ears. 'Did you hear *that*?' he asked.

'The rabbits didn't make much of a showing,' said Mr Rune. 'They were somewhat drowned out by the spaniels.'

'That was Hell,' I said. 'The sound of Hell. The cries of the damned calling up from the Bottomless Pit.'

'That's one explanation,' said Mr Rune, 'although whether rabbits go to Hell or not, I'm not entirely sure.'

'Bad rabbits would,' said Fangio. 'And most dogs, in my opinion. And definitely rats and pigeons, too.'

'And snakes,' I said. 'And spiders.'

'And earwigs, also,' said Fangio. 'They're always up to no good, crawling into your ears while you sleep on the lawn and laying their horrid eggs.'

'An evilness of earwigs,' said I. 'That is what it says in the Bible. Somewhere, if you are prepared to have a good look.'

'Don't get me started on the Bible,' said Fangio.

'Oh, go on,' I said, 'we can get a good half-hour of toot out of that.'

'Listen,' said Mr Rune, and he held up his hand.

'Not that noise again?' said Fange, and he covered his ears once more.

'A man,' said Mr Rune, 'with only one leg and in a state of distress.'

'Did he say, "in a state of undress"?' asked Fangio, uncovering one of his ears. The left one.

'No,' said Mr Rune. 'Stand back.'

'But we are sitting,' I said. And we were, upon barstools.

'Then avert your gaze.'

Which I did not. Although I really should have.

The door of The Really Small Atlantean flew open. And in through the opening flew a man. And for a man with only one leg to fly upon, he fairly flew.

He flew and he rushed and he screamed as he did so.
Then he fell.
And he exploded.

PART II

'I do so hate it when that happens,' said Hugo Rune.

'Aagh!' I went. And, 'Wah!' and, 'I have got one-legged man all over my nice new coat.'

'Spontaneous human combustion,' said Mr Rune, viewing the epicentre of the explosion and the large scorch mark it had made on the carpet.

'The brewery won't like this,' said Fange. 'But then the pub *is* closing down today.'

'Uniped,' I said. 'Charred bits of uniped all over my coat.'

'White wine will take that out,' said Fange, 'or salt, although I wouldn't advise molasses.'

'Suggestive,' said Mr Rune.

'No, it's not,' said Fangio.

'I am definitely going back to our rooms,' I said, 'and this coat is going straight to the dry cleaners.'

Mr Rune was up on his feet now, examining the carpet. 'His timber limb survived with only minor charring,' said he, 'which is also suggestive.'

'I do not like it here,' I said, 'what with the cries of the damned and the exploding unipeds. This is *not* a nice neighbourhood.'

'You've never been to Whitehawk, then,' said Fangio. 'But who's going to clear up this mess?'

'I have formed my conclusions,' said Mr Rune. 'The case is solved.'

'Well, phone for Inspector Hector and he can arrest the transgressor,' said I.

'Good word, that,' said Fange. 'I've a radio with those in it. Made valves completely obsolete, which is a shame because I've been hoarding thousands in case there was ever a world shortage.'

'The *transgressor*,' said Mr Rune, 'is not one who *can* be arrested, not by any normal law-enforcement agency, anyway. Come on, Rizla, all the clues are here. It's glaringly obvious what's going on.'

I sighed deeply. '*All* the clues?' I said.

'*All* the clues,' said Mr Rune.

'And the solution does not involve some piece of esoteric knowledge known only to yourself?'

'Not on this occasion, no. Perhaps a tiny bit, but this should not stand in your way. Think about what you have seen here, what you have experienced, what you have heard and not heard. Does not an explanation spring immediately to your mind?'

Now, I thought hard about this. I finished my beer and when I had done so I ordered another of same. '*All* the clues are here?' I said. '*All* of them?'

'All around you,' said Mr Rune.

'And I really *should* be able to reason it all out?'

'If you are half the fellow that I believe you to be.'

'Can I have a go at this?' asked Fange.

'No,' I told him. 'You cannot.'

'Suit yourself,' said Fange, somewhat huffily, I thought.

I did further rackings of the brain. 'All right,' I said to Mr Rune. 'Missing cats, missing indigenous wildlife, in fact. All gone. Then those terrible sounds that we heard. Then a one-legged man rushing into the bar and exploding. And all these things are connected?'

'All connected,' said Hugo Rune. 'All part of the big equation.'

'And the transgressor is not one that can be brought to book by members of the Sussex constabulary?'

'Absolutely *not*,' said Hugo Rune and he shook his big bald head.

'One thing,' I said. 'If I can come up with the answer, will you pay for my dry-cleaning?'

'Gladly,' said Hugo Rune.

'Damn,' I said. 'Then it really must be a poser.'

'I have to hand it to you blokes,' said Fangio. 'A

one-legged fellow explodes all over us and you take it as cool as can be.'

'I am upset,' I said. 'Look at my coat.'

'I think I may have had an accident,' said Fangio. 'I'm going to the bog.'

And off he went. And upon his departure, Mr Rune stepped around to the back of the bar and helped himself to a bottle of Scotch. 'It will aid your cogitation,' he explained.

'I am cogitating as hard as I can,' I said, 'but pour a measure into my pint – I am sure it will help me a bit.'

And he did and I drank and I did cogitations. 'All right, I am baffled,' I said.

'The single leg is significant,' said Mr Rune. 'Don't give up just yet.'

I thought and thought and thought some more. And then I said, 'I have it.'

'You *do*?' said Mr Rune.

'I *do*,' said I. 'And we are going to require some assistance.'

'Good,' said Mr Rune. 'Who do you suggest?'

'I suggest that we call upon the services of Captain Bartholomew Moulsecoomb, the Bog Troll Buccaneer.'

'Not to mention his scurvy crew of pirates,' said Mr Rune.

But I mentioned them anyway. 'What do you think?' I said.

'We'll see where it leads,' said Mr Rune. 'So far you've earned a cleaned sleeve.'

We sat and we drank and presently Fangio returned from his excursion, complaining that he had taken so long because he could not find the bog, there being so many hundreds of different doors downstairs. Mr Rune asked if he might use the telephone and Fangio said that he might. As no complimentary chewing fat or peanuts were available, I ate low-fat crisps and the antipasto (whatever *that* was) and I carried on with my cogitations, because they were far from complete. But I mentioned in passing to Fange that I had solved the case.

And at a little after three of the afternoon clock the bar door burst open once again, this time to admit the blustering passage of the swarthy Captain Bartholomew Moulsecoomb, not to mention his scurvy crew of pirates.

'What-ho, me hearties,' cried Mr Rune, in the vernacular.

'We had to hire a minibus to get up here,' said the Bog Troll Buccaneer, 'so we'll be wanting plenty of bounty. Where be the gold doubloons?'

Mr Rune glanced over in my direction. 'Would you care to tell him?' he enquired.

'The hoards of Atlantis?' I suggested.

'Good answer,' said Mr Rune.

'Will it be rum all round, lads?' asked Fangio, yo-ho-hoing as he did so.

'It will,' said the captain. 'It will.'

'And shall I put it on Mister Rune's tab?'

'Or I'll slit your gullet from ear to ear,' said the captain, heartily.

'I still quite fancy taking to a life of piracy,' I said to Fange, 'although I am presently torn between that and becoming a cinema proprietor.'

Fangio drew me to him in the manner known as conspiratorial. 'How do you think it will go for you,' he asked, 'when Mister Rune and all the now-assembled pirates discover that you really don't have the foggiest idea as to what is going on hereabouts?'

'Not altogether well,' I replied, 'but having recently solved, all on my own, the most complex case of the Woodingdean Chameleon, this will be a veritable walk in Preston Park, as it were.'

Fangio made sniggering sounds, which I felt to be inappropriate. 'Pirates have a habit of turning ugly,' he said. 'Well, *uglier*. They'll probably eat you. Having jolly rogered you first, of course.'

'I feel the solution coming on,' I said.

'Ooh, Matron,' said Fange. 'Oh, excuse me, that's tomorrow. Now, if you want my opinion in this case—'

'I do not,' I told him, as he took to passing out measures of rum. 'I can do this all on my own, with no help from anyone.'

'Have a word with yourself,' said Fangio. 'I'd try and leg it if I were you.'

And then I had an idea.

I called out to Mr Rune, who stood chatting with a pirate called David who had once been in a pop band, but later, having fallen upon hard times, had been reduced to running a hot-dog van on the seafront. They were discussing the relative merits of being keel-hauled and being flogged around the fleet.

'Mister Rune,' I called, 'might I have a look at that wooden leg?'

'Captain Bartholomew is wearing it.'

'But he has two good legs of his own.'

'He's wearing it on his head.'

'It's a pirate thing,' said Captain Bart, handing the timber limb to me.

'Just one question,' I said to Mr Rune. 'Would I be correct in assuming that if I were to run a Geiger counter over this wooden leg, it would buzz away like an angry bluebottle?'

Mr Rune placed a large hand upon my shoulder. 'Young Rizla,' said he, 'you have excelled yourself. Would you care to explain how you came by this reasoning?'

'I would,' I said. And then I looked at my wristwatch. 'But if I am correct, then my explanation will have to wait because—'

And it came again, that terrible cacophony – the barking and growling and screeching and, in the case of the rabbits, a sort of snuffling sound.

Hands rose up to ears all around. One-handed Harry the bosun's mate nearly had his eye out with his hook.

And then, as suddenly as it had begun, the dreadful din all dimmed away and quietness descended.

'What in the name of plunder was that?' asked Captain Bart. 'Last time I heard a row like that was when we laid waste to a pet shop in Pevensey Bay.'

'Would you care to explain, young Rizla? Take us through it a step at a time.' Mr Rune smiled upon me and I smiled back upon him.

'Right,' I said, and I preened at my Astrakhan collar. Which was sadly still rather sticky. 'I saw what you saw, yes? And heard what you heard. We walked around the area and I recall those light industries upon the trading estate – carpenters' shops, shipwrights, refiners of animal feeds and earth-moving-equipment manufacturers, not to mention the nuclear processing plant.'

'The—' said Captain Bart.

'Best not to,' said Fangio.

'All those,' I said to Mr Rune, 'suggestive in themselves. Then *all* the local pets and wildlife gone. Then this pub and the shape of this pub, like a child's drawing of a house. And the fact that it is closing *today*. Then the noises of the animals, at regular intervals – four-hour intervals, I believe. And of course, the exploding seaman.'

'Ooh, Matron,' said Fange. 'No, excuse me. Sorry.'

'Oh, yes,' I said. 'And Fangio said that he had trouble finding the toilet because there are hundreds of doors downstairs.'

'I *did* say that,' said Fangio, 'so I must take my share of the credit for solving this case.'

'Shut up,' I told him. 'And,' I continued, 'and the other stuff before we even left our rooms this morning: the signs and portents in the heavens, prophecies that the world is about to end, and mutant doves.'

'All becomes clear,' said Fangio.

'You are kidding me, right?' I said.

'I am,' said Fangio.

'Well, it all seems obvious to me,' I said. 'I can think of only one logical explanation.'

Mr Rune held his breath and I saw him cross his fingers.

'Why are you doing *that*?' I asked.

'Because,' said he, 'either you *have* arrived at the obvious explanation or you are about to say something really, really stupid.'

I beckoned Mr Rune and he inclined his big bald head towards me.

I whispered one word into his ear.

And Mr Rune said, 'Splendid.'

'Am I right?' I said to him.

'You are,' he said. 'You are. Although I have just one question for you now.'

'Go on,' I said.

'I feel absolutely convinced that you have only just arrived at your conclusion, so why did you have me call up Captain Bartholomew several hours ago?'

I shrugged. Guiltily. 'I just like being around pirates,' I said.

Cutlasses were drawn at this, and words were voiced that I should be made to walk the plank. Having been jolly rogered most thoroughly first.

'Hold there, me hearties,' said Mr Rune. 'There'll be rich pickings in this for all of you.'

The pirates made surly sounds and did some flintlock rattling.

'Trust to what he says,' said Captain Bart. 'If Admiral Rune says there'll be rich pickings, then rich them pickings will be.'

'*Admiral* Rune?' I rolled my eyes.

'So, young Rizla,' said *Admiral* Rune, 'would you care to tell us of your plan?'

'My plan?' I said.

'For how we shall best the *transgressor*.'

'Storm him,' I said, 'with cutlasses and flintlocks and possibly whatnots as well.'

'They *are* manufactured locally,' said Fangio, 'for the Ministry of Furniture.'

'Storm him?' said Mr Rune thoughtfully. 'You believe

this to be a wise course of action, considering the fate of the exploding seaman?'

'Well,' I said, 'there are bound to be casualties. Probably even fatalities. But that cannot be helped.'

My words were not, perhaps, as well chosen as they might have been. Cutlasses were drawn once more and some young pirate with cowboy leanings suggested throwing a hangman's rope over a high pub beam.

'Drinks all round. On *me*,' cried Mr Rune. 'And a word in *your* ear, in private.' And he took hold of my ear and dragged me from the bar.

And out into the ice-bound street beyond.

'Do you have a death wish?' he enquired.

'Definitely not,' I said. 'Which is why I will be keeping a safe distance when we send the pirates storming in.'

Mr Rune raised his stout stick and I flinched.

'It is cold out here,' I said. 'Can we go back inside?'

'Would you care,' asked Mr Rune, 'for *me* to direct operations from now on?'

'Well . . .' I said.

He mimed the throwing of a rope over a beam, accompanied by a series of pelvic thrusts suggestive of . . .

'I will leave it to you,' I said, 'although I do want to take some credit, because I *did* figure it out on my own.'

'I'll pay your dry-cleaning bill,' said Mr Rune.

And we returned to the bar.

The pirates were now looking more than just surly. Positively mutinous, they looked.

'I am taking charge of the situation,' announced Mr Rune. 'I will be personally directing operations. There will be no loss of life. And you will all prosper greatly, I promise you.'

The pirates grunted and grumbled.

One said, 'We'll throw in our hands with you, Admiral Rune, but only if we know the score.'

'Explain to them, Rizla,' said Mr Rune.

'We'll hear it from *you*,' said the pirate to Mr Rune.

Hugo Rune smiled and nodded. 'It's simplicity itself,' he

said. 'My companion and I were called to this area to investigate the disappearance of a great number of domestic animals. Many, if not all, other animals local to the district have similarly disappeared. Why should this be? you might well ask yourselves. Well, my companion offered you most of the clues: ominous signs and portents in the heavens; prophecies that the world is about to end, and of course the mutant doves. Considering also the nature of the light industries on the trading estate and that the regular screaming of animals is only to be heard *here*, the solution *is* obvious.'

Heads shook. Fangio shrugged.

'Ark,' said Hugo Rune.

'Ark at what?' asked Captain Bart.

'Ark of Noah!' said Hugo Rune.

'Where?' went the captain.

'Right here,' said the All-Knowing One. 'You are standing in the wheelhouse.'

'Oh,' went the pirates. And, 'Coo.' And, 'Fancy that.'

'The regular screamings?' asked Fangio.

'Feeding time,' said Mr Rune, 'for the animals. The animals below, behind those hundreds of doors.'

'It all makes perfect sense when it's explained,' said Fange.

'It does,' said Mr Rune.

'Except for the mutant doves and the exploding seaman.'

'Nuclear power,' said Mr Rune. 'The Ark is powered by a nuclear reactor. Noah had doves on board, if you recall. So did our transgressor. The doves were located somewhat too close to the nuclear pile before they escaped.'

'And the seaman?'

'He reached critical mass,' Mr Rune explained. 'Overexposure to the nuclear pile combined with subzero temperatures outside caused a metabolic sub-shift due to the transperambulation of pseudo-cosmic anti-matter.'

'Oh yeah,' said a pirate called Phil. 'Happened to a mate of mine.'

'And there you have it,' said Mr Rune.

'Right,' said Captain Bart. 'There we have it, do we? Some nutter thinking that the world is coming to an end has built a subterranean ark, of which this is the wheelhouse, and stocked it up with all the local animals.'

'And considerable booty, which is yours for the taking,' said Mr Rune.

Which caused the pirates to cheer.

'No,' said Captain Bart. 'Don't cheer. This ark is buried in the ground beneath us. How is it going to float away should the flood waters rise, which frankly they are unlikely so to do?'

'It isn't going to float,' said Mr Rune. 'It's going to tunnel down, to escape not the rising waters but rather the supposedly falling comet.'

'Fair enough,' said the captain. 'Whatever the case, it's damnably stupid. Lead us to this nutter, Admiral Rune, and we'll slit his throat and share the booty round.'

'I don't think that would be a good idea.'

Now Mr Rune never uttered these words. And nor, in fact, did I. But I recognised the voice and turned, as others did, to view the figure standing in the doorway.

He was a considerable figure, tall and gaunt and all in black. Black leather hat, black leather coat, black leather boots, black leather gloves as well. He wore a long black beard that was not of leather and stared at us with jet-black eyes that glittered in cavernous sockets.

'We meet again, Mister Rune,' said he, stepping forward, a black gun in his hand.

'We do indeed,' said Hugo Rune. And he even bowed slightly as he said it. 'Captain Bartholomew, allow me to introduce to you Count Otto Black, captain of the nuclear-powered subterranean ark *The Really Small Atlantean*.'

PART III

'Your servant, sir,' said Count Otto Black, and he tipped his black hat to the captain.

Mr Rune took a single step forward. Count Otto pointed his pistol. 'Easy, Mister Rune,' said he.

I noticed that Mr Rune had a very firm hold upon his stout stick and I wondered where I should hide.

'You must have fallen upon very hard times, Mister Rune,' said Count Otto in a mocking tone, 'if you are reduced to hunting for lost dogs and lost pussycats.' And he laughed that mad laugh that mad-laughers always laugh.

'Not a bit of it,' said Mr Rune. 'I discerned your unwashed hand in this from the very outset.'

'Bluff and bluster,' said Black. 'It's always the same with you.'

'On the contrary,' said Mr Rune. 'The difference between you and me is twofold. Firstly *I* am good and *you* are evil.'

'And secondly?' asked the Count.

'*I* know how *your* mind works.'

'Then pray enlighten me. And do make it interesting, or I will be forced to shoot you dead out of boredom alone.'

'This craft,' said Mr Rune, 'was not built by a present-day Noah to escape a biblical catastrophe, aka, the fall to Earth of a comet. Rather, it was built as an escape craft. And one, I have no doubt, that you have been working on for years.'

'Only months,' said the Count. 'I work very hard, unlike yourself.'

'Quite so. But it is an escape craft nonetheless, to enable you to escape from the mayhem you intend to cause once you have availed yourself of the Chronovision. Which you will never do as long as I have breath in my body.'

The evil Count Otto clapped his hands, but did not lower his pistol. 'You are indeed correct,' said he, 'although don't go wasting your time attempting to pat yourself on the back. Not that you could, you great fat oaf.'

I flinched somewhat at that remark. And Mr Rune did hairless bristlings.

'Just one thing,' said the All-Knowing One. 'The name of this craft – *The Really Small Atlantean* – that's a rather foolish name for an ark.'

'I had no wish to give myself away,' said the Count. 'Naturally I have another name for it.'

'I know that you do,' said Mr Rune. 'In fact, I know what it is.'

'Absurd,' said Black. 'Of course you do *not*.'

'On the contrary,' said Mr Rune once again. 'Your name for it is *The Bevendean Bat*.'

'What?' went Count Otto. 'What?'

And, 'What? went I also.

'Or to give it its full title, *The Bevendean Bathyscaphe*, the suburban submersible.'

'Impressive,' said Black. 'But no matter.' And he stalked across to the bar, elbowing pirates to the right and left of him, lifted the counter flap, ejected Fangio and installed himself behind the bar proper.

'The drinks are on you?' asked Hugo Rune. 'Did I win the champagne?'

'No,' said Black. 'The show is over.' And he reached beneath the counter and drew up a small microphone. 'Mister Mate,' he shouted into it. 'Take us below.'

'Below?' said Mr Rune and he laughed. 'You surely do not believe that this ludicrous contraption is actually going to work?'

'Oh, it will work,' crowed Black, 'and you will die, and I'll feed your flesh to the pussycats. Villains always have pussycats. They do like a pussy to stroke.'

'Do not say it,' I warned Fangio.

'You are somewhat outnumbered,' said Mr Rune. 'I'm not exactly certain how this particular fact has escaped your notice.'

'Outnumbered?' said Black, and he laughed once more in that manner that mad-laughers laugh. 'By these pirates here?'

The pirates growled and rattled their weaponry.

'Who will be the first, then?' asked Count Otto. 'The first to attack me and be shot dead? Any takers?'

None were immediately forthcoming.

'Or perhaps you would care to throw in your lot with me, sign on for a share of riches beyond your wildest dreams. Any takers for that?'

'Well . . .' went certain pirates. Most of them, in fact.

'Notoriously mutinous,' said Mr Rune.

'Pirates do have a habit of switching their allegiance at the offer of pecuniary advancement,' said Count Otto Black. 'I'll pay one thousand pounds cash to any man who will join me.'

There suddenly came a rumbling, as of mighty engines beneath.

'Hurry now,' said Count Otto Black. 'We are going below. Who will take the Count's shilling, as it were?'

'I'll sail with you, mister,' said the pirate called David who had once been a pop star, but later had fallen upon hard times and now ran a hot-dog stall.

'Me, too,' said Phil, whose mate had once reached critical mass.

And so said this fellow, and so said that fellow, and suddenly all were cheering.

'What a bunch of traitors,' I whispered to myself. 'I am definitely going for the cinema-proprietor option. Should I come out of this alive.'

And then I felt that sinking feeling. As one does as one starts to sink.

'Going down!' cried Count Otto Black. 'Basement sale. Guru meat on special offer.' And he pointed his gun at Mr Rune and squeezed upon the trigger.

But he never got to fire that gun, although he really wanted to. Because, and I am very proud of this, I did not let him do it.

I was still clutching the wooden leg of the exploded seaman. And this I swung, as hard as I could, at the head of Count Otto Black. And it caught that blighter a thunderous blow and knocked him from his feet.

'Out!' cried Mr Rune. 'All out.'

And we ran from that sinking ship. We ran for the door. Oh, how we ran indeed.

And we threw ourselves through the door and out into the icy cold as *The Really Small Atlantean* – or *The Bevendean*

Bathyscaphe – sank its way down into the ground, leaving only a gaping hole to signify its passage.

'Bravo, my friend, said Mr Rune, a–patting me on the back. 'You did splendidly. I'll even pay for the dry cleaning of your topper.'

'Yeah,' said Fange. 'You done good, kid.'

I looked at Fange. I looked at Mr Rune. 'The pirates stayed with him,' I said.

'Notoriously mutinous,' said Mr Rune.

'And he got away. He got away and he took our pirates with him.'

'Things might have gone better,' admitted Mr Rune, 'but let us not be discouraged.'

'I'm discouraged,' said Fangio. 'My coat was in there. I'm freezing out here.'

'I am discouraged, too,' I said. 'That is a formidable craft that the Count now has at his disposal.'

'Perhaps,' said Mr Rune. 'But if the exploding uniped was anything to go by, I personally would not wish to spend too much time beneath ground level aboard it.'

I shrugged and sighed. 'It is going to be a long and cold walk home,' I said.

'*Walk?*' said Mr Rune. 'I think not. See there – surely that is the minibus that the pirates hired to convey them here. It will take but a moment for you to hotwire that vehicle.'

'*Hotwire?*' I said. 'I do not know how to hotwire a van.'

Mr Rune tapped at his nose. 'Then *I* will instruct you,' he said. 'You will need something metallic to place across the terminals. This will do, I think.' And Mr Rune handed a badge to me. 'I had intended to give it you before we set out,' he said, 'but I thought it might influence your reasoning.'

I looked at the badge, and printed upon it was . . .

'Noah's Ark,' I said.

9

The Sensational Saga Of
The Saltdean Stallion

The Saltdean Stallion

PART I

It was November and it was cold, but my coat was back
from the cleaners. True to his word, Mr Rune had paid for
the dry cleaning and done so without any fuss. And as it was
November the fifth, he and I were in Lewes.

Lewes is a pretty town, built upon a pretty hill, with the
ruins of a pretty castle high up on its peak. It lies about ten
miles east of Brighton, and another ten or so up from the
coastline. If it has any faults at all, these faults are to be found

in its dreaded one-way system. On paper it all looks so simple, but try to drive your car through Lewes from one side to the other and you will know the dread yourself. Around and around the town you will go, as if trapped within a Möbius strip, losing all sense of direction, your temper and your sanity. Even the locals, who claim to know the area like the backs of their burly Sussex fists, never leave home in their cars without at least three days' emergency provisions and several extra cans of petrol in their boots.

And there is even an urban myth to the effect that a chap called Norris Styver has been driving around Lewes's one-way system in his Morris Minor for over a decade trying to get out of the town. But there seem to be certain reasons, mostly involving logic and common sense, to place some doubt upon the likelihood of there being any truth to this particular urban myth. Which was probably why it *was* an urban myth.

Those who incline towards mystical explanations claim that the roads of the town were cursed in the Middle Ages by the sinister warlock Eliphas Porlock, who met his end in a freak stake/flames incident in the town square.

However, those who prefer the commonplace put it all down to the work of Mad Mickey Wright, who designed Brighton's one-way system, which every summer funnels many thousands of motoring would-be holiday-makers from the A23 through a maze of some of Brighton's narrowest streets, lured ever onwards by signs that promise great parking areas, but somehow always fail to deliver.

To those who know a little more than most, and Mr Hugo Rune would number himself amongst this exalted few, it is an open secret that Mad Mickey Wright was a descendant of Eliphas Porlock and something of a black magician himself.

But Lewes *is* a pretty town and if there is one thing that Lewes is more famous for than anything else, it is its bonfire-night celebrations. Folk come from all over the country to enjoy them, some remaining in Lewes for over a week afterwards as a result of being unable to drive out of it. But folk do come, in their thousands, and those who come regularly do so by train.

Hugo Rune and I had come by train and I had located our accommodation through very careful study of a map.

Now, it does have to be said that the good folk of Lewes really do know how to get a fire started. And not just the one. They have dozens. It's that small-boy thing about lighting fires and the big bags of fallen leaves that keep those home fires burning. And there are torchlight parades through the town, with real flaming torches. And there are bonfire societies with exotic and evocative names, such as the Jenga Khan Society, the Lords of Ludo Society, the Barons of the Boggle Society and the Cluedo Klux Klan Society. And something that these societies really like doing, which probably dates back to Mr Porlock, is to burn people in effigy: politicians, celebrities, sports personalities, members of Brighton's road-route planning committee – anyone who has in some way incurred their displeasure during the previous twelve months. It makes for a most entertaining evening.

Rooms in the town's hotels that overlook the paradings, which can go on for many hours as the parades go round and round the one-way system seeking the locations of the bonfires that they are marching towards, have to be booked several years ahead and command appropriately exorbitant prices.

Mr Rune had booked us into one of the best of them – the Hotel California, which overlooked the High Street. How he had done this I have no idea, but a clue might be found in the fact that on arrival he sported papal robes and the desk clerk referred to him as 'your holiness' and knelt and kissed his ring.

'Ooh, Matron,' said Fange. But I did not hear him and possibly it was unconnected.

'This is brilliant,' I said to Mr Rune, as we stood together on the balcony of our exclusive suite of rooms overlooking the High Street that would soon be filled by torch-lit paraders, whilst we quaffed champagne and smoked expensive cigars. 'I am really going to enjoy myself tonight.'

'Me too,' said Mr Rune, raising his glass to me. 'It is always a delight to see oneself burned in effigy.'

'Oneself?' I queried.

'Indeed,' said Mr Rune, sucking upon his cigar and blowing out a perfect cube of smoke. 'Word has reached me that the ladies of the Chiswick Townswomen's Guild have brought themselves down in a charabanc to cast my effigy into the flames.'

'Why?' I asked, which seemed a reasonable question.

'It's an old issue,' said Mr Rune, 'dating back to the turn of the century. Some folk will never let bygones be bygones. Just because I thwarted their plans for world domination, they have taken against me personally.'

'This is good champagne,' I said, 'although I note that my cigar is somewhat smaller than your own.'

'As you are too young either to drink or smoke, I do not feel that we should let this become a bone of contention.'

'Oooh, Matron,' I suggested.

But Mr Rune did not think too much of this suggestion and instead he studied the sky. 'Those portents in the Heavens still remain,' he said. 'See there the conjunction of planets and the constellations of stars?'

I looked and I saw. 'They look to form the shape of a great horse,' I said, 'rearing up – do you see it?'

'Clearly,' said Mr Rune. 'And I see more.'

'You generally do,' I told him.

'We are close, young Rizla. We are very close.'

'Do you want to step back a little?'

Mr Rune raised one of those hairless eyebrows of his. 'Close to the end of our quest,' he said.

'To find the Chronovision?'

Hugo Rune nodded his big bald head.

'Oh,' I said, and I made a face.

'A look of disappointment, would that be?'

'Well,' I said, 'in a way, yes. I have been with you for months now. I am no closer to rediscovering my real identity, but to be perfectly honest, I think that I no longer care. I have so enjoyed my time with you, even though every case seems to put my life in jeopardy. It has all been, well, it has all been such fun.'

'Good,' said Mr Rune, smiling broadly. 'And I will miss you when this is over and you return, as you must, to your previous life.'

'That will only happen if I can remember who I was.'

'You will,' said Mr Rune. 'You will. Trust me, I'm a magician.'

I looked up at Mr Hugo Rune, this huge presence of a person who had become to me – what? A father figure? Not quite. A guru? Not entirely. A source of inspiration? Somewhat. I did not know quite what, only that he was special, other, apart. He was all of those. And even though he never paid his bills and wantonly assaulted taxi drivers, I really trusted, admired and to no small degree was in awe of this extraordinary man.

And did I love him also? Not in some sexual fashion – that would have been abhorrent – but rather in the way that a best friend loves a best friend? Well, then yes, I think I did. In fact, I know that I did.

'You'll have me getting a crinkly mouth, thinking thoughts like those,' said Mr Rune. 'But I must ask you to swear an oath to me.'

'I swear,' I said.

'Do you not wish to know what it is before you swear it?'

'Ah, yes,' I said. 'I might just have sworn away my wages, should there ever be any wages for me to swear away.'

'This is a serious matter,' said the Perfect Master.

'Go on, then,' I said.

'Should something happen to me, should I not be able to continue with the quest, I want you to swear that you will see it through to the end – find the Chronovision and destroy it before Count Otto Black gets his greasy fingers upon it.'

'By Crimbo,' I said, 'I like not the sound of this.'

'I would very much like you to swear.'

'But what is likely to happen to you?'

'Swear, please,' said Mr Rune.

And so I swore.

I placed my hand on my heart and swore that I would continue the quest in the event of Mr Rune's inability to do so.

'Splendid,' said he. 'The big parade begins in an hour, so I suggest we adjourn to the bar.'

It was all oak beams and Tudor in the hotel bars of Lewes. And they had barmen who wore clean white shirts and black dicky bows and treated you with politeness even when you were drunk. Which I intended to be, as Mr Rune was footing the bill. Well, at least in theory he was.

'Good evening, young sir, and good evening, your Popeship,' said the well-dressed barman.

'Good evening, Fange,' I said.

'Well, gracious me,' said Fangio, 'Whatever are *you* doing here? And Mister Rune, too – I didn't recognise you at first in that get-up.'

'We have come to enjoy the bonfires, of course,' I said. 'But much more to the point, what are *you* doing here?'

'Well,' said Fange, 'do you recall on page forty-three that I told you I would do something really helpful in Chapter Nine? Well, guess what?'

'Does time not travel fast when you are having a good time?' I said.

Fangio scratched at his head, upon which he wore no wig or hat, but only a helping of Brylcreem.

'Why scratch you at your Brylcreemed bonce?' I asked him.

'I was just wondering how I could get a page and a half of toot out of answering your question,' he said. 'I'll have to get back to you on it. What would you care to drink?'

'What do you have on offer?' I asked.

'Well,' said Fange, 'we have eight hand-drawn traditional ales on draft, a selection, I must state with pride, which exceeds the Heartbreak Hotel by three and the Crossroads Motel by four.'

I looked along the row of highly polished beer pulls.

'Impressive,' I said. 'What is that one there?'

'Old Willy Warmer,' said Fange. 'A fine Sussex ale, slightly nutty, but full-bodied and at five point two you only need three to be well on your way.'

'I will go for that, then,' I said.

'That one's off, I'm afraid,' said Fange. 'Bad barrel from the brewery. Word reached my ear that a tiny spaniel fell into the vat during the fermentation process.'

'Fair enough,' I said. 'I will have that one there, then.'

'Good choice,' said Fangio. 'McGregor's Brown Gusset, a fine Scottish ale brewed from hops that are rolled upon the thigh of a Glaswegian crofter's lass—'

'A virgin?' I asked.

'Naturally,' said Fange. 'The ale is then mellowed in casks crafted from the timbers of siege-engines captured from the British at Bannockburn. And at five point nine you only need two pints to be paralytic.'

'A pint of that will do me fine, then,' I said.

Fangio put his hand to the pump handle. 'Sorry,' he said, 'but this one's off, too. We have none in stock. It's flown down by airship, but only yesterday the delivering airship crashed into power lines on the Sussex Downs. Well, they *say* that it crashed, but the last radio communication from the pilot said that he was being buzzed by a UFO.'

'Really?' I said.

'He said something about crabs and then the radio went dead.'

'That is awful,' I said. But I was beginning to sense a theme. A familiar one. 'Tell me,' I said, 'and I want you to be totally honest with me here. Is there even one of these eight hand-drawn traditional ales, which you claim with due pride to exceed in number those served at the Heartbreak Hotel by three and the Crossroads Motel, where I believe Robert Johnson once stayed, by four, that you actually, at this very moment, have available?'

'You're putting me on the spot there,' said Fangio.

'I am,' I said.

'I was hoping to hold out a little longer and tell you all about the Old Muff-Widener.'

'You have none of that, either,' I said, 'have you?'

'Or Grampa Reekie's Wessex Butt-Fuc—'

'Nor that one, nor any other,' I said.

And Fange hung his head, though he grinned as he did it. 'Has to be at least a page,' he whispered to himself.

'What did you say?' I asked him.

'Nothing, sir.'

I turned to Mr Rune. 'Would you care to do the ordering?' I asked him.

But Mr Rune was already drinking brandy.

'Where did that come from?' I asked.

'Behind the bar,' said Mr Rune. 'I availed myself of it whilst you and Fangio were talking the toot.'

'Pour me a glass, then,' I said.

'No,' said Hugo Rune. 'Get your own.'

'Anything,' I said to Fange. 'Anything at all.'

'Anything?' said Fange. 'Would you care to be a little more specific?'

'No, I certainly would not. Serve me something alcoholic now or I will have you killed.'

'A pint of McGregor's Brown Gusset coming right up.'

'But you said—'

But it mattered not.

Because the ale was good.

'Right,' said Mr Rune when I had finished my pint, 'you have talked the toot and drunk the ale and now we should go and watch the big parade.'

'Has an hour gone by already?' I asked. 'Does time not travel fast when you are having a good time?'

'Well,' said Fangio, 'I've been thinking about that, and it's funny you should mention it again, because—'

'See you later,' I told him.

'But . . .' said Fangio.

Mr Rune and I returned to our suite, where he changed from his papal robes into something more sober and joined me on our balcony. The big parade was beginning. Beneath us marched members of the Cluedo Klux Klan Society in their distinctive livery of chiffon and mayonnaise. How magnificent they looked. And how harmoniously they sang. Their songs were all of four-wheel-drives and three-point turns and two-for-the-show and a partridge in a pear tree. They carried aloft their effigy for burning – Mad Mickey Wright of Brighton Town Council.

Close upon their polished heels marched the men of the Self-Preservation Society, all clad in horn-rimmed glasses and white trench coats. They proudly bore their flaming torches and sang their songs about 'blowing the bloody doors off' and there being Zulus, 'thousands of them'.

Next came the Marching Band of the Queen's Own Foot and Mouth Society, and you do not need me to tell you how simply spiffing they looked in their high-top shoes and pigtails, with matching handbags and handlebar mirrors. And of the songs they sang, who could ever forget—

'Stop *now*,' said Mr Rune. 'The secret *is* knowing when to stop. Or in this case whether to have bothered to start.'

'But I *do* like their handbags,' I said.

'But *these* are the ones to watch.' And he gestured with the brandy bottle he had brought up from the bar. 'The ladies of the Chiswick Townswomen's Guild.'

Now, I did not like *them*. They were all wrong, those ladies. Well dressed in what seemed to be Victorian garb, black and lacy and Cagney, too, but they were so thin and so pinch-faced and so terribly alike that they might have been sisters. Which somehow made me think about multiple sisters. And of Kelly Anna Sirjan, the beautiful young woman I had met at Hangleton Manor, who had refused my advances and returned with her multiplicity of sisters (no doubt) to Count Otto Black's Circus Fantastique.

'I do *not* like those ladies at all,' I said. 'And as for their effigy of you—'

'It is somewhat portly,' said Mr Rune.

'It has much of the Michelin Man about it,' I said. 'You might be fat, but—'

'Fat?' said Mr Rune. 'I am well knit.'

The ladies passed beneath us, chanting.

'Death to Hugo Rune,' they chanted.

'And they do not have much of a song,' I observed.

'We must follow them,' said Mr Rune. 'Gird up your loins, young Rizla. The game, as you see, is afoot.'

'I will wait here,' I said. 'They will probably get stuck in the one-way system and be passing by again in half an hour.'

'*You* will accompany *me*,' said Mr Rune. 'Fetch your coat and hat and follow.'

The pavements were impossibly crowded, six deep in places and seven in others. The *Argus* reported that its reporter had counted up to nine in one place, but the location of this particular place was not specifically mentioned and the reporter in question was noted as one much given to hyperbole.

'These pavements are impossibly crowded,' said Hugo Rune, clearing a path before him with the aid of his stout stick. 'Ten deep back there.' I followed in his wake.

'Are we nearly there yet?' I asked him.

'Follow on. Follow on.'

I followed on and Mr Rune followed on. He followed on behind the Chiswick Townswomen's Guild.

At length we passed our hotel.

'Don't be discouraged,' Mr Rune called back to me, as he struck to the left and right of himself and cleared a further path.

I was not discouraged, just a bit footsore. But it was exciting, what with the cheering crowds and the chanting women and the flaming torches and everything. And now the fireworks in the sky, great chrysanthemum bursts of white and gold and red and blue. Beautiful.

And suddenly I felt that we were on a different road, one that led up, and I knew where to because I had studied the map: towards the ruins of Lewes Castle that crowned the crest of the hill.

And as Mr Rune and I followed the ladies up a long and winding road that the Beatles would later sing about, I became aware of several things: of quite how cold it suddenly seemed to have become and how the pavements were no longer deep with any number at all of cheering onlookers.

Ahead of us marched the Chiswick Townswomen's Guild, bearing their torches and Mr Rune's effigy. Behind marched Mr Rune and myself. And none else marched but we.

'Suggestive,' whispered Mr Rune to me.

'I hate it when you use that word,' I said. 'It inevitably means that there is going to be trouble.'

Mr Rune put more spark into his step. 'Pacey-pacey, Rizla,' said he. 'A gnat's nuts need no oiling, but a lady-boy won't offer you a ride on a rusty bike.'

Which I could not have argued with, even if I had tried.

Up and up went the pinch-faced ladies. Although we could no longer see their pinch-faces. What with us following them and everything. Up and up and up.

'I never knew that the castle ruins were *this* high,' I panted at Mr Rune. 'We will soon be needing oxygen masks. I swear we are breathing rarefied air.'

'Suggestive,' said Mr Rune once again, marching ever onward.

Above us, the ruined castle loomed, its silhouette blacker than the sky. I turned and looked behind and I was amazed by what I saw: the town of Lewes was a great distance below us, and the torchlight parade was in miniature, snaking through, it seemed, a model village.

I pulled out my map of the area and held it low, for the chrysanthemum explosions of the airborne fireworks were now beneath us. My map was an Ordnance Survey jobbie, one of the many in Mr Rune's collection. It had spot heights on it, as well as the locations of churches with spires, churches with towers and contour lines, for which I have always had a liking. And benchmarks, of course, but who does not have a liking for *them*? I studied the spot heights on this map, and in the flare of an airborne firework, I could see where we were supposed to be. But we could not be there, because there *was* no *there*. It was all very wrong indeed.

'Mister Rune . . .' I said.

'Keep up, Rizla. Keep up now.'

'But,' I said, 'this is all wrong.'

And it was.

And then we lost sight of the ladies.

'They have entered the ruins,' said Hugo Rune. 'I would counsel stealth and the keeping of the now-legendary low profile.'

'I am with you there,' I said. 'And I will stay behind you, if you have no objection. To use the popular parlance of the era, I am somewhat weirded-out here.'

'Follow on,' said Mr Rune.

And I followed on.

'This way,' he continued.

And that was the way I went.

We did some 'duckings-down', followed by some 'skulk-ing arounds', followed then by some 'forward-creepings' and then a wee bit of 'crawlings up to'. And then Mr Rune nudged me, and though it was dark I could see that he was pointing. And I did 'strainings of the eyes' to see what he was pointing at.

Which eventually I did.

Below us, for we were now up on some ruined wall, lay the castle courtyard and within things looked somewhat busy. A great fire had been lit, in the best traditions of Lewes, and about this, dancing with a vigour and a vim, were the ladies of the Chiswick Townswomen's Guild. And . . .

'By Crimbo,' I whispered. 'They have all got their clothes off.'

'Sky-clad,' whispered Mr Rune. 'When one dances for the devil, one does so in one's bare skuddies.'

'Even though I am half-gone with altitude sickness,' I said, 'I am still capable of enjoying the sight of a bunch of women dancing around in their bare skuddies. Thanks very much for bringing me here. It is a shame that I do not have a camera.'

'Would that be one of those flippant remarks that you make in the hope of lightening the situation when you're fearing for your life?' asked Mr Rune.

'It would,' said I. 'Can we go now?'

'I think we will stay a little longer. It is imperative that I discover what these evil harpies are up to upon this night.'

'I suspect that you probably have a good idea already. Why do I not just slip back to the Hotel California and get us in a round of drinks? Which, you will agree, will be no easy matter and might take quite some time.'

'Hush,' said Mr Rune. 'I believe that matters are now about to take a certain turn.'

'Would that be a turn for the worse?' I asked.

Hugo Rune nodded. 'I fear that it would.'

I continued with my looking on. Actually, I had not ceased with it, what with there being naked women down there dancing around their handbags by a big bonfire. And me being a teenage male with no immediate shortage of testosterone.

The naked dancers ceased their dance and formed a joined-hands circle around the fire. Above them on a grassy knoll stood a single bare-naked lady. And I do have to say that she was far better looking than the rest. She was not all pinch-faced and skinny withal, she was simply gorgeous, all curves and beauty and long golden hair. And . . .

'It is Kelly,' I whispered. Although somewhat harshly. 'It is Kelly Anna Sirjan. Mister Rune, it is her.'

'Suggestive,' said the Lad Himself. Which I found somewhat annoying.

'All hail!' cried the voice of Kelly Anna Sirjan. 'All hail unto him.'

'All hail!' cried the pinch-faced bare-naked ladies. 'All hail unto him.'

'Tonight,' cried Kelly, 'we offer up our sacrifice, the token of our allegiance.' At this, a couple of bare-skudded ladies that I had not previously noticed, because they must have been skulking about beyond the light of the bonfire, stepped forward, holding aloft the Michelin Man effigy of

Mr Rune. 'We ask that He who knows all – the past, the present and the future – will accept our sacrifice and grant to us knowledge, show unto us the location of that which we seek. That which will serve His cause. That which will give Him all-encompassing power upon this Earth.'

'Is she talking about what I *think* she is talking about?' I whispered to Mr Rune.

'If you think she is talking about the location of the Chronovision, then you are correct,' the Logos of the Aeon replied.

'God, she looks great with her clothes off,' I said.

'*God* does not come into this,' whispered Mr Rune.

'I call upon His councillor to offer up this sacrifice,' cried Kelly. 'All prostrate yourselves before His councillor.'

'His councillor?' I asked.

'Keep watching,' said Mr Rune.

And I did so, and he appeared. Out of a puff of smoke. He was tall and gaunt and all in black, with an evil-looking black eye-patch as well.

'Count Otto Black,' I whispered, for it was he. 'I was not expecting to see him again so soon.'

'I told you,' said Mr Rune. 'We near the end of our quest.'

'Why the eye-patch?' I wondered.

'I think because of the blow you dealt him with that wooden leg.'

'Women of the Guild,' shouted Count Otto Black, 'thou of the Craft, I salute you.' And he saluted them. 'Tonight we will offer up the sacrifice to our Master and He will reward us. We will exact our revenge upon the hated one . . .'

'That would be *you*, I suppose,' I said to Mr Rune.

'. . . and pave the way for the New Beginning,' continued the Count. 'When the Chronovision is under our control. When we can see into the hearts of any that we choose, view their pasts, know their most innermost secrets, acquire all knowledge. Then we will have ultimate control. This world will be ours, in His service.'

'That would be Satan, I suppose,' I said to Mr Rune. 'He is a very bad lad, this Count Otto.'

'By sacrifice of the hated one, he that stands between us and our goal, the Great Old One will, but for a moment, be able to enter this plane of existence and point out the location of that of which we speak. It's all rather complicated, so I won't go into it here, but it does involve the transperambulation of pseudo-cosmic anti-matter and things of that nature generally. It's a ying and yang sort of jobbie. And these *are* the nineteen sixties.'

'I could not have put it better myself,' I said.

'Please put a sock in it,' said Hugo Rune.

'Bring on the sacrifice!' shouted Count Otto Black.

The bare-naked ladies carrying the effigy of Mr Rune raised it high.

And then a pair of pirates with great big guns appeared as if from nowhere to stand over us and pointed their great big guns down at Mr Rune and me.

'The sacrifice,' said one of them. The one who held his great big gun upon Mr Rune. 'He that is required by His councillor.'

I looked at Mr Rune.

And Mr Rune looked at me.

'That *would* be *you*,' I said.

PART II

'So, we meet again,' said Count Otto Black. 'And so soon.'

'I thought that,' I said. And the Count glared at me through his one seeing eye. 'No offence meant,' I continued.

'And you,' spat the Count, 'you who did *this* to me.'

And he pointed to his eye-patch. And I said that I was sorry.

'*Sorry?*' The Count did some maniacal laughing. He was good at that, the Count. 'You will know what sorry means, I can assure you of that.'

'I already know what it means,' I said. 'Do not trouble yourself with any demonstrations.'

Count Otto Black now grinned heartily at Mr Rune. 'How does this suit you?' he asked. 'I recall how upon our last meeting you told me that the difference between you and me was twofold – that I was evil and you were good, but that *you* understood how *I* thought, and not the other way about. What think you now upon this, Mister Rune? You walked straight into my trap, led here by your own vanity. You just *had* to see yourself burned in effigy. How sad is *that*?'

Mr Rune leaned upon his stout stick and breathed in rarefied air. I hoped that he might come out with some snappy James Bond-style rejoinder, but sadly, he did not. He just stood and stared at Count Otto Black.

'Lost for words?' crowed the Count. 'The Great Hugo Rune? Logos of the Aeon, the All-Knowing One, the Cosmic Dick. Rune, whose eye is in the triangle, whose nose cuts through the ether, whose ear takes in the music of the spheres. Whose arse takes up three seats on the Clapham omnibus. Nothing to say at all?'

The firelight lit upon Mr Rune's great face, for now we stood close to that fire. I thought to detect a look of gloom. Was this the look of defeat?

'Just one thing,' said Hugo Rune. 'Perhaps you would be so kind as to enlighten me, before you cast me into the flames?'

'My pleasure,' said Count Otto Black. 'Speak on.'

'Through my sacrifice you will learn the location of the Chronovision, am I correct?'

The Count stepped forward, rootled in my pockets and drew out my Ordnance Survey map. I might have put up a struggle over this, but a pirate had a pistol trained upon me. The Count unfolded the map, then held it up to the sky. 'You are aware as to how it works, Rune,' said he. 'You are a magician, as I am. One gives in order to receive something in return. My Master cannot pass through the barrier that separates His dimension from this. But if I offer Him something he desires — your soul, Rune — then for an instant He can make Himself manifest in this dimension, and at that moment He will point out the location of that of which both you and I speak. It is your desire to find it that is the catalyst.'

'And so upon the very moment of my death, this knowledge will be granted to you?'

'The Gods are out there,' said Count Otto Black, 'all of the Gods, just beyond the veil, out there in the ether. They all crave power. Some of them have held power upon Earth, only to be overturned by others. Some have yet to be. My Master has yet to be.'

'Ah,' said Mr Rune. 'So your Master is not His Satanic Majesty?'

'He had His go,' said the Count. 'He has not succeeded. Men are evil, certainly, but few actually worship Satan. He has little actual power upon this planet.'

'Who, then, is your Master — or what?'

'Another,' said the Count, 'one who exists within time, between the seconds. The one who speaks to me here.' And the Count tapped at his temple. 'One of whom *you* have no knowledge.'

'Plah!' said Mr Rune. 'You are delusional, Black. A basket case, no less.'

'Up with him!' cried Count Otto Black. 'Cast him into the flames.'

And bare-naked ladies took hold of Mr Rune and struggled to bear him aloft. His stout stick was torn from his hand and flung down to the ground. And although it took nearly all the bare-naked ladies to do it, they finally held him on high.

I looked over to Kelly, who stood on the grassy knoll.

'Kelly,' I shouted. 'You cannot let this happen. You are not bad. Stop this if you can.'

'And shut up, *you*.' And Count Otto hit me, hard and to the head. 'You damn near had my eye out, you little worm!' he shouted. 'You will be next into the flames.'

I looked up at Mr Rune and on high the big figure shrugged.

'You are taking this very well,' I said. 'And that blighter really hurt me.' And I rubbed my head.

'Perk up, Rizla,' said Mr Rune. 'Matters will adjust themselves.'

'That is easy for you to say,' I said, 'being held aloft and about to be thrown into a fire by a bunch of bare-naked devil-worshipping ladies. No, that does not make any sense at all. Sorry.' And my hands began to flap and I began to spin around in small circles.

'Cast the sacrifice into the flames!' cried the Count.

And, held up as high as the bare ones could manage, Mr Rune suddenly groaned. He groaned and he clutched at his heart. And his mighty body went all-over limp and the bare-naked ladies struggled, then dropped him. Mr Rune hit the ground with a thunderous thump.

The sound of it made me feel sick. And certainly made me stop spinning.

And there he lay, all lifeless and broken-looking on the ground.

'Enough of your party tricks, Rune.' And Count Otto Black kicked him, dealing a hideous blow.

But Mr Rune did not flinch, did not shudder. He just lay there.

And then he twitched.

And then he trembled, his eyes rolled back and the death rattle rose from his throat.

'Oh no!' I shouted and I leaped forward with no care for the pistol-packing pirate.

I bent and I put my ear to Mr Rune's chest. No heart-beat could I hear. 'Oh no!' I shouted once more. 'He is dead, he has had a heart attack or something. Call for an ambulance.'

Count Otto Black laughed mightily, which I felt was very callous.

'Do something!' I shouted, and I took to beating on Mr Rune's great chest with my fists.

And then all at once, a storm seemed to gather and lightning ripped through the heavens.

'It is no trick!' bawled the Count. 'He is surely dead. To the fire with him.'

'Leave him alone,' I shouted, and raised my fists.

Count Otto laughed once again, and then he gripped my shoulders and hurled me aside and his bare-naked minions laid hands upon Mr Rune. And they sweated and they struggled, but they could not budge his dead weight by even an inch.

'No matter.' The Count now held the map aloft once more. 'It is done. O Most High, the soul of the hated one now wings its way to You. Pass me the knowledge that I might prepare the way for Your coming.'

And as I looked on in considerable horror, the lightning struck like a laser beam, piercing a hole through the map.

'Aha!' The Count cackled and danced a bit, too. He veritably jigged. 'I have it!' he cried and he clutched the map to his bosom.

I stared down at Mr Rune and then stared up at Black and I was in some state of terror. Mr Rune was dead and Black had the map. The map with the neat hole through it. The hole that marked the secret location of the hidden Chronovision. There were tears in my eyes and I trembled and shook. The Count did a soft-shoe shuffle.

Though Mr Rune's heart had ceased to beat, mine was beating faster than ever. My pulse pounded drumbeats in my ears. And these were the drums of war.

He had known. Mr Rune had known that he might die this night, and he had made me swear to continue the quest should he not be able to continue it himself. And this dancing monster before me, this fiend in human form, it was *he* who had caused Mr Rune's death and *he* who now held the map to his chest and *he* who would kill me, too, cast me alive to the flames.

I rose with a roar and as I rose I sighted Mr Rune's stout stick. I snatched it up and I swung it, swung it as hard as I could. And I caught that blackguard a harder blow than I had with the wooden leg. And as he fell I snatched at the map and ripped it from his fingers.

The Count fell down on top of Mr Rune and the bare-naked ladies advanced upon me. And the pirates with their pistols.

'Stop,' I told them, 'all of you. Stop, or I do this.' And I held out the map towards the bonfire flames. 'I will burn it. I will.'

The bare-naked ladies made horrible sounds, like the growlings of spaniels in heat.

'Drop those guns,' I told the pirates. 'Drop those guns or I throw the map in the fire.' The pirates actually dropped their guns. 'And all of you back away.'

They did not want to do it, those witches of the Chiswick Townswomen's Guild. They wanted to tear me limb-piece from limb-piece. And then probably eat me, too.

'Go on,' I shouted, and there was madness in my voice. 'Back away now. It will not go well for you if the Count should awaken to find that the map has been destroyed and that it was all your fault.'

And they backed away, growling and spitting.

'Kelly,' I called out. 'Kelly, come down from that grassy knoll.' But Kelly would not come down.

'As you please, then,' I said. 'And goodbye.'

And then I ran. Oh, I can tell you that I ran as fast as I could away from that fire and away from those women. I ran away and away.

They did not follow me at first, but then I did not expect them to. It had occurred to me that they would probably want to get their frocks back on before they pursued me through the busy streets of Lewes.

Although I had read in the *Leader* that the waiters from Eat Your Food Nude had formed a naturist bonfire society for this year's event. So it was *possible* that the witches might have been able to blend in with them.

Though probably not *that* probable.

But those ladies did know how to get dressed fast, for I had not got all that far before I heard them in pursuit. I could not see them because it was dark, but I could certainly hear them.

And they certainly knew how to run, for they were shortly close upon my fleeing heels. 'I will burn it,' I shouted back to them as I ran. But as I lacked for any fire, my threat must have sounded hollow.

Old Laz would have come up with something. And being in darkness he could have been anywhere within the remit of his four locations. And something unexpected would have occurred, to come to his aid, something that had been mentioned in an earlier chapter, as a throw-away aside, or so it would have seemed at the time, but which was *really* significant when it came to the crunch.

Well, that is how he would have done it. Which was why I wished I was him.

And then as I ran around a corner I was almost run down by a car that was coming up the hill as I was running down. I bounced over the bonnet and came to rest in a heap. The car ground to a sudden halt, a window lowered and a face looked down at me.

'Are you all right?' asked the mouth in this face.

'Far from it,' I said.

'Then let me help you up.'

And I could hear those growling women growing ever closer.

'No,' I shouted and I jumped up and I climbed into his car, sort of over the top of him, as it happened, and I dropped down into the passenger seat. 'Back up,' I told him, 'back up now. Do it if you want to live.'

'I don't want to back up,' the driver told me. 'I'm going this way.'

'This way is a dead end,' I told him. 'It only leads up to the castle ruins. Oh, damn.'

And the women were upon us. They drummed upon the sides of the car. I slammed down the lock on my door. 'I would do yours, too, if I were you,' I told the driver. And he did.

'Tell these mad women to get off my car,' the driver said

to me. 'It's a classic Morris Minor. Nought to thirty in eight point seven seconds. It even has the original screw-type jack and nine-inch tommy bar. I purchased it in Saltdean thirteen years ago. I call it "The Stallion".'

'The Saltdean Stallion,' I said. 'Well this was not what I was expecting.'

'My name is Norris Styver, by the way.'

And *that* name rang a bell.

'You're the man,' I shouted, for there was quite a din now and the women had ripped off the windscreen wipers. 'The man in the urban myth, who drives for ever around the one-way system, trying to get out of Lewes.'

'I'm no urban myth,' said Norris. 'And if you are all right then I'm glad. I'm very pleased to meet you,' and he put out his hand for a shake. 'What is your name, by the way?'

'Just back up,' I shouted at him, 'or we will both die here. Back up.'

'If it really *is* a dead end,' said Norris, 'then I suppose I will. Get off my car, you mad women!' he shouted. 'Look what you've done to my windscreen wipers.' And he hooted his horn. And then he put the Morris into reverse. The Morris was rocking all over the place under the women's assault but reverse worked okay and we were soon travelling backwards. Although not as fast as I might have wished.

There were women on the roof and on the bonnet. Others jogged along on either side, swiping at the windows with their handbags.

I dragged the driving wheel to the left, hoping to grind at least a couple of them into one of the dry-stone walls that bordered the narrow road.

'Don't do that,' said Norris. 'Someone might get hurt.'

'These women are witches,' I told him, 'and they have just killed my bestest friend.'

'Well, in that case, we'll report them to the police. There's a police station in town. I've passed by it many many times.'

'Have you never thought of buying yourself a map and taking things really, really slowly?' I asked him.

'You want me to slow down?'

'No, not now. Speed up!'

'It's not that easy.' Norris was straining to look over his shoulder. 'The nodding spaniel in the back is obscuring my view.'

I shinnied into the back and ripped away the nodder.

'Now *you're* in the way,' said Norris. 'Oh, I do wish these women would leave us alone. Persistent creatures, women. I have one at home for a wife. My dinner will have been growing cold on the table for more than five years now.'

'Ever thought of phoning her?' I said.

'Do I look so rich as to possess a car phone?' asked Norris. 'Even if they had been invented yet, which they haven't.'

'No, but . . .' I paused. 'Never mind. Drive faster.'

'I am driving as fast as I can.' And he was. And suddenly with a lurch and a bang we were no longer on that darkened lane, but back in the bright streets of Lewes.

'It seemed to take much longer driving up than it did backing down,' observed Norris. 'How strange.'

'Just drive,' I said. 'I know the way out of Lewes. Follow my instructions.'

Norris laughed. But at least he kept driving as he did so.

'Do not laugh,' I said. 'I *do* know the way.'

'So where have you parked your car?'

'I came by train,' said I.

And Norris laughed again. And then he suddenly stopped laughing as one of the mad witch women who was still clinging to the bonnet of the Morris lost her grip and fell beneath the wheels. It was a horrible, horrible thing. The shriek. The thump. The bump.

'Oh my God!' shouted Norris, and slammed on the brake.

Another one fell from the bonnet.

'Do not stop.' I rammed the gear stick forward and forced my foot down upon his accelerator foot.

'Don't do *that*,' he shouted, but we lurched forward.

With another thump and a bump.

'Oh my God!' shrieked Norris again. 'I have become a serial killer. Please get out of my car.'

'I am not leaving,' I said, and I forced his accelerator foot down harder.

The last of the shrieking women fell from the roof and we moved off through the night streets of Lewes.

'These streets are very quiet,' I observed.

'Everyone is at the bonfire sites.'

'And where are they?'

'Search me,' said Norris, trembling terribly.

'Calm yourself,' I said. 'We are safe now.'

'You made me kill those poor women.'

'Those *poor women* would have killed you.'

'Why were they chasing you, anyway?'

'Because I have something they want. Drive faster now,' I told him, for Norris was slowing down again.

'They must want it very badly – what is it?'

'It is a map,' I said.

'Oh, one of *those*,' said Norris, with a sigh.

'And to obtain the information upon this map, they killed my bestest friend. A great man, a mystic and adventurer. The Logos of the Aeon. His name was Mr Hugo Rune.'

'Hugo Rune?' said Norris and he began to laugh again.

I still had Mr Rune's stout stick and was all for using it. 'Why are you laughing?' I asked.

'Because there's no such person as Hugo Rune. He's just an urban myth – the mystical detective who fights the forces of evil, but never pays his bills. It's a myth put about by cabbies, who swear that every time one of their fares runs off without paying, it was Hugo Rune.' And Norris laughed yet again.

'You can drop me off at my hotel,' I said to Norris. 'It is just along here.'

'Which street?'

'The High Street.'

'The High Street isn't just along here,' said Norris.

'I think you will find that it is.'

But it was not.

'Turn left here,' I said.

'Can't turn left, that's a one-way street.'

'Next left, then.'

And so it went on. And so we drove. And presently the sun came up and we drove some more.

'You get good mileage out of this car,' I said to Norris. 'We have been driving for hours and hours and the needle on the dial has never moved.'

'It never does,' said Norris.

'Well, of course it does,' I said, 'or do you mean that the needle is broken?'

'Not broken, just never moves. And the petrol never goes down.'

'Do not be silly,' I said. 'You will have to stop and fill up soon.'

'Never do. Never have.'

I looked at Norris. He stared straight ahead. And I felt a terrible chill. And then I saw something more. And I screamed.

'Stop this car right now!' I screamed.

'No,' said Norris. 'You're with me now. You made me drive over those women – you're mine and together we will drive on until the day we leave this cursed little town.'

'Let me out.' And I rattled the handle of my door. But the handle would not move and the door would not open. I was trapped, trapped in a Morris Minor with Norris Styver, the Morris driver, the driver who drives on and on.

And I saw once more what I had just seen that had caused me to scream. Norris Styver was not flesh and blood. Norris Styver was a skeleton, clothed in rags, a horrid skeleton.

He grinned me a death's-head grin and the morning sun made shadows in the sockets of his skull. And a terrible chill entered the air within that Morris Minor. A terrible graveyard chill.

'You are cursed now to ride with me,' said he and he laughed a terrible laugh. 'Unseen in the hours of daylight, when I don't look quite as good as I do at night, you and I will drive on and on until with the coming of Judgement Day we'll drive aloft to redemption.'

'Over my dead body!' I cried, and I swung Mr Rune's stout stick. And to my horror and further alarm, the stout stick passed through Norris and bounced right off his seat.

'Would you like the radio on?' asked Norris. 'It's almost time for *Desert Island Discs*. I wouldn't fancy being on a desert island myself, no roads to drive along.'

'Let me out of this car,' was what I had to say.

Norris shook his horrible head. A spider crawled out of his nose hole.

'Let me out!' I cried and I rattled at the handle of my door again with vigour.

'Relax and enjoy the ride. I've heard that there are signs and portents in the Heavens. Omens of the Coming of Ragnarök. The End Times are upon us. Judgement Day is close at hand.'

'I do not have time to wait for that,' I said. 'I am upon a quest. I have things to do.'

'There's always time,' said Norris, his finger bones drumming on the steering wheel. 'Time is all we have. You and I, that is.'

'I need the toilet,' I said. 'And I need my breakfast, so please let me out.'

'The pain will pass,' said Norris, softly. 'The hunger will grow strong, but with your passing, it will pass, as it did for the others.'

'Others?' I said.

'I'm Sam,' said someone.

'I'm Bill,' said someone else.

I turned and I stared. And would you believe it – there were two more skeletons sitting in the back.

'It's not so bad once you get used to it,' said Sam (the skeleton on the right, looking from the front, of course). 'We do have our sing-alongs. Is *Desert Island Discs* on yet, Norris?'

'*Let me out!*' I screamed.

282

'Not so loud,' said Norris. 'The noise bounces all about in my empty skull.'

'What do you want?' I begged the dry-boned driver. I was beyond the point of terror now, sort of numb all over. 'There must be something you want, something I can do for you, so that in return you will release me from this car.'

Norris turned his awful empty face in my direction. 'I want out of this town,' he said. 'Out of this one-way system.'

'That is easy,' I said.

Bill and Sam took to laughing and rattling their teeth.

'We tried that,' said Bill to me. 'Don't you think we tried?'

'Well, you cannot have tried very hard.'

'It can't be done,' said Sam. 'Norris is cursed. This car is cursed. It can never be driven out of Lewes.'

'Then let us get out and walk.'

'If we could get out,' said Sam, 'then where would we walk to – the nearest cemetery?'

'You might find some peace there. But come on, Norris, there must be some spark of humanity left in you. I am a young man with my whole life before me. And I *am* on an important quest, a sacred quest, you could say. Would it really be so hard for you to just let me out?'

'You made me kill those women.'

'And I am sorry, please do not get me wrong. But they killed my bestest friend.' And the thought of Mr Rune's death brought tears to my eyes.

'You can only be released from this car if you do something in return for me. It is the balance of equipoise, and it must always be maintained.'

'I will guide you out of Lewes,' I said, sniffily.

'Can't be done,' said Sam.

'Don't waste your time trying,' said Bill.

'There must be something I can do,' I said.

'What?' asked Norris, driving along with *Desert Island Discs* now on the radio. 'The car never needs petrol and we never need food. What could you possibly do for me?'

'I could . . .' And I thought. 'I could . . .' And I thought some more. 'I know,' I said, 'I could get you a woman.'

'*A woman?*' said Norris.

'Well, would you not like a female companion for . . . you know. You must miss the old you-know.'

'So what you are saying?' said Norris and he turned right.

'You have turned the wrong way down a one-way street,' I said.

'Doesn't matter,' said Norris. 'But what you're saying is that you would entice a woman into this car in order to save yourself. That she should face your terrible fate instead of you.'

'Well, yes,' I said. 'Well, no,' I said. 'That is not a nice idea, is it?' And then, 'Oh, look,' I said. 'That is my hotel up ahead. Please drop me off.'

'No,' said Norris. And then he said, 'Oh.' And the car took a lurch and shuddered all about. 'What is going on?' asked Norris.

'Flat tyre,' I said. 'You have a flat tyre.'

'Impossible,' said Norris. 'The tyres never go flat.'

'I bet your MOT is well overdue,' I said. 'I bet all your tyres are bald.'

'The tyres can never go bald.'

'Well, one of them has gone flat,' I said. And Norris stopped the Morris.

And then things grew a little quiet in the car. And a little tense, too, I thought. Not that they were not already tense. At least, they were for me. Beyond tense, in fact. Beyond anything, really.

'Do you have a spare wheel?' I asked Norris.

And Norris nodded his death's head.

'Within the boot, would it be?'

And Norris nodded again.

'Would you like me to get out and change the wheel?'

Norris was silent.

'I will do it,' I said. 'All you have to do is open my door.'

Norris remained silent.

'I thought not,' I said. 'Then you will have to do it yourself.'

'I cannot,' said Norris. 'I cannot leave the car.'

'Oh,' I said. 'Really? That is a shame then, is it not? Perhaps the ghost of an AA van will pass this way.'

'It won't,' said Norris.

'Then it will have to be me. And I *will* do it, to maintain the balance of equipoise. If you let me out, I will do it for you in return.'

'You'd just run away,' said Norris.

'I would not,' I said. 'I promise. See this wet, see this dry, cut my throat if I tell a lie.'

'You'd be cutting your own throat,' said Norris.

'Oh,' I said.

'Because,' said Norris, 'if I release you from the car and you break your side of the bargain, the curse will fall upon you.'

'That I will never be able to get out of Lewes?'

'Your bones will bleach as mine have done, and you will walk and walk for ever. And it's far more miserable to walk than to drive, I assure you. Very hard on the bones of the feet.' And he grinned me that terrible grin once again.

'Let me out of the car,' I said, 'and I will change the wheel.'

'Don't think to break our bargain.'

'I will not,' I said.

And there was a click and my door opened and I stepped out from the car into November sunlight, which although not altogether warm was a considerable improvement on the graveyard chill within that Morris Minor.

'There's a jack in the boot,' called Norris to me, 'a screw-type jack and a nine-inch tommy bar.'

'Norris,' I said, and I raised my finger, 'to use the popular parlance of the day, "sit on this and spin!"'

'What?' went Norris, a look of horror on his face. Which came rather easily to a bonehead.

'This has been the most horrible night of my life,' I said, 'and you can fuck right off.'

Which was as much of a shock to me as it must have been to Norris.

And I turned away from the haunted Morris Minor and marched into the hotel. And once inside, I paused to look back, but the Morris had vanished away.

'And good riddance to you,' I said.

The manager on the front desk made a face at me and I marched into the bar.

There was no one drinking as it was too early, but Fangio was there. He stood behind the counter polishing an imaginary glass and whistling a tune that did not exist. I approached the counter.

'Give me a drink,' I said to Fange, and I sank on to a barstool. 'No nonsense, no toot, any drink you have, as long as it is very alcoholic.'

Fange drew me a pint of Farmer's Wife. I did not ask him anything about it.

'You look knackered,' said the barlord. 'Party all night, did you?'

'Anything but,' and I drained much of my beer. 'It was terrible. Horrible. Mr Hugo Rune is dead.'

'Hugo Rune?' said Fange. 'Isn't he an urban myth?'

'Do not even think about it.' I raised Mr Rune's stout stick. 'He is dead – I saw him die, it was awful.'

'I'm truly sorry,' said Fangio, 'and I mean that most sincerely. I really liked the old fart. Does that mean that you will be settling his account at The Pub That Dare Not Speak It's Name, which is what my bar is going to be named tomorrow?'

'No, it does *not*,' I said. 'And show some respect. Mr Rune was a great man – one-of-a-kind, a one-off. I do not think that his like will ever be seen again.'[*]

Fangio pulled himself a pint. 'I'll miss him,' he said. 'How did it happen?'

'I do not want to talk about it now.'

'No, I suppose not. Oh, one thing – a bunch of

---

[*] Nor indeed that of Flann O'Brien.

strange-looking women were in here earlier asking after you.'

'What did you tell them?' I asked.

'That you weren't here.'

'Thanks for that.'

'I gave them your address at Grand Parade.'

I groaned.

'Oh, and the manager of the hotel is really upset. Apparently he saw the Pope on TV last night and he's not too happy about Rune having deceived him. But I suppose that doesn't matter now.'

'It does not,' I said.

'Although you'll have to settle the bill.'

I groaned again.

'Although,' said Fange, 'I might see my way clear to letting you slip out of the fire exit.'

'That would be brilliant,' I said.

'No problem,' said Fange. 'I told you that I did something really helpful in Chapter Eight.'

'This is now Chapter Nine.'

'You'd better pay the manager, then.'

'I will take you up on your offer.' And I finished my beer.

'I'll put this on the Pope's account,' said Fange.

'Thanks,' I said. 'I will go up to the suite and salvage what I can and then you can let me slip away.'

'See you later, then,' said Fangio.

I went up the stairs with a heavy heart. I felt empty inside. I had no idea how I was going to carry on without Mr Rune and I was worried now about what might have happened to his body. Had those monstrous women done something hideous to it? Should I return to the castle and look? I could not just leave him lying there. Should I call the police? An ambulance? An undertaker? And what was I going to do without him? Where was I going to go? Find the Chronovision, certainly I would try to do that, *and* destroy it, too. But without Mr Rune, was that even possible? I was sick at heart.

And empty.

I found the room key and turned it in the lock. And I pushed open the door.

And then I smelled something and felt something, too – a terrible chill in the air. And I looked and I beheld and I became afeared. Because something sat at the breakfasting table.

Something I knew to be dead.

'Ah, Rizla,' said Mr Rune, 'you took your time. I ordered two breakfasts, but had to eat yours as it was growing cold.'

PART III

'Dead—' I croaked and I staggered in the doorway. 'You were *dead*—'

'I am alive.' And Mr Rune rose to my assistance. 'You're all done in,' he said. 'You need some food inside you. There's a bit of toast left, I think.'

And I flung my arms around him (in a manly kind of way). 'Alive,' I cried. 'Alive! I am so glad.'

'Calm yourself, my friend.' And Mr Rune patted at my head. 'Your hair needs cutting,' he said.

'It *is* you.' I looked up at him. 'It really *is* you?'

Mr Rune guided me to a chair and set me down. 'Do you still have it?' he asked.

'Have what?'

'The map,' said Mr Rune. 'The map, of course.'

'I do,' I said. And I rootled about in my pockets.

'And my stout stick also, how thoughtful.'

I found the map and handed it to Hugo Rune. 'But how?' I asked him. 'Tell me how.'

Mr Rune poured coffee for me and I drank it. But he downed that last piece of toast.

'I had to know,' said he, 'the location where the Chronovision is hidden, and it seemed the only way. I put my trust in you and you did not let me down. Bravo.'

'But how?' I asked once more. 'I put my ear to your

288

10

The Birdman of Whitehawk

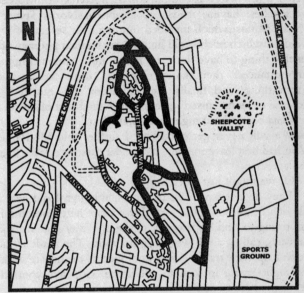

The Whitehawk Birdman

PART I

With the aid of Fangio, Mr Rune and I left the Hotel California by the rear fire exit, our beds still made, our bill, unpaid.

Leaving Lewes itself, however, proved to be somewhat more complicated. The walk from the station to the hotel that we had made the previous day had not been a long walk. It had been a walk-in-the-park kind of walk, although there was no park.

But the walk back . . .

'Check the map once more, Rizla,' cried Mr Rune, when after very much walking we found ourselves at the hotel's rear exit once again. 'This is thoroughly absurd.'

'It is the curse,' I told him. And I yawned as I told him, for I was very tired, having not slept all night, and having watched my bestest friend die and then having been chased by witches; having made my escape in Norris Styver's Morris Minor, which included running over several of the witches (which in the cold light of day seemed a somewhat terrible thing to have done, no matter how extenuating the circumstances); then discovering that Norris was a dead corpse-thing; and finally escaping from *him*, but at the expense of being cursed never to leave the town of Lewes.

It *had* been a hard night and I was all in.

'We will never get out alive,' I further told Mr Rune. 'You had best leave me here to wander these streets for ever and ever.'

'Or we might just hail a cab.'

'They do not have cabs in Lewes, although I did hear a tale of a Brighton cabbie who drove a fare here once and is still trying to find his way out of the one-way system. And anyways, calling a cab would do no good. The roads are all snarled up with traffic – first-time visitors to the fireworks last night trying in vain to get home. Go, save yourself. Leave me here to die.'

Mr Rune raised his stout stick. Then he lowered it again. 'It *has* been a difficult night for you, young Rizla,' he said, 'and you acquitted yourself bravely and loyally. If it is merely a matter of me voiding the curse of Norris Styver, then so be it. About turn.'

'It is a waste of time,' I said.

'About turn,' said Mr Rune, 'about turn, walk back-wards, close your eyes and lead us back to the station from memory.'

'Will that work?'

'Trust me—' said Hugo Rune.

'I know,' I said, sighing. 'You *are* a magician.'

If everything in life were as simple as that, there would be no trouble in this world. Certainly I bumped into a few lampposts, which I felt certain that Mr Rune could have steered me around. And although each time he was apologetic, I swear I heard titterings. But at length, and at not very much of one, we had arrived at the station.

And from there, upon a westbound train, we returned at further length to Brighton.

We did not, however, return to our rooms at forty-nine Grand Parade. In fact, we never returned to them again, which was rather sad, really, because I had certainly enjoyed our times together there, all the breakfasting and conversations and whatnots. Not to mention all that damn fine toot I had talked with Fangio in his bar next door. I wondered whether I would ever see Fangio again. It was always possible, I supposed.

There was some unpleasantness at Brighton Station regarding the matter of train tickets. Mr Rune was forced to employ his stout stick and we left the concourse with haste.

Mr Rune surveyed the line of waiting cabs.

'Splendid,' said he, blowing breath at the knob of his stout stick and buffing it on his sleeve.

'Now just hold on,' I said, 'are you thinking that we should go at once and attempt to acquire the Chronovision?'

'There is no time to be lost.'

'Things are not quite as simple as you might suppose.'

'We have the map. We have the location. What could be simpler?'

'Well, firstly,' I said, 'and all importantly, it is to do with the matter of the location. The Chronovision is hidden in Whitehawk.'

'So?' said Mr Rune.

'Whitehawk,' I said. 'Whitehawk.'

'Tell me about it in the cab,' said Mr Rune.

'Taxis will not drive into Whitehawk.'

'Ah,' said Mr Rune. 'The area has something of a reputation, does it?'

'And *you* call yourself the All-Knowing One?'

'Tell me about it in the cab.' And with no further words, he hustled me into the first cab in the rank.

'Whitehawk, please,' said Mr Rune.

'Get out of my cab,' said the cabbie.

Hugo Rune made impatient sighings. 'As near to Whitehawk as you dare, then.'

'Kemptown,' said the cabbie. 'Soon have you there.'

Then he did as all Brighton cabbies do, and drove 'the pretty way'.

And while he drove this pretty way, which included areas of Hove and Hangleton, I put Mr Rune in the picture regarding the matter of Whitehawk.

It is a fact well known to those who know it well, that if anything – *anything* – gets nicked in Brighton, then no matter what that thing may be, it will end up in Whitehawk.

The plain folk of Brighton consider Whitehawk to be a vast Fagin's kitchen, peopled by old rogues who send out young fellow-me-lads who all look curiously alike, all being small, tattooed and bony-faced and given to the sporting of sportswear and either the 'hoodie' – a kind of hooded sweatshirt that protects the wearer's facial features from CCTV cameras – or the ever-popular mock-Burberry baseball cap.

Now, I do not know what it is about baseball caps. Perhaps it is their tightness, but it always appears to me that simply putting on such a cap seems to reduce the wearer's IQ to single figures.

However, regarding Whitehawk.

Whitehawk has an evil reputation.

History records that the original settlers were Amerindians, or 'Redskins' as they were popularly known before the days of political correctness. These Redskins had set out from their native shores to discover China, but their canoes were sucked into the Gulf Stream and then blown along the

English Channel. Chief Whitehawk, the leader of the expedition, purchased a parcel of land from the Prince Regent in exchange for a couple of squaws and a tomahawk called The Widow-Maker[*] to which Prinny had taken a fancy.

And Chief Whitehawk had been blessed with the gift of prophecy and so knew what awaited his descendants on the American continent (which was probably why he had set out for China in the first place). So he was wise enough not to trust the words of the White Devil of the British Isles and insisted upon written deeds of ownership for the parcel of land he had been given and first dibs on the profits should a marina ever be built nearby. And then he applied for a council grant and oversaw the building of a housing estate upon the land that was now his.

It is said that those whom the nearby pirates of Moulsecoomb considered criminals amongst their own kind were exiled to Whitehawk, where they became slaves to the Redskins.

Whatever happened to the original Redskins history does not record, but many believe that they were eaten.

It remains a fact to this day that even Belfast's now-legendary 'Men of Violence' or the terrorist baddies of Al Qaeda would think twice about taking a stroll through Whitehawk on a Saturday night.

And it is said that the infamous Kray twins, who grew up there, left in their early teens because they found the place too rough.

Whether Whitehawk *really* deserves its evil reputation, I could not say. For in all truth, as I sat in the cab, explaining all this to Mr Rune, it seemed to me that there were certain things that just did not tie up, one of these being the sheer scale of the stolen-goods situation in Brighton. If only *half* the cars, household items and general all around everythings

---

[*] This being the original Widow-Maker and not to be confused with the 1960s proto-metal ensemble fronted by Cardinal Cox, whose only single 'Eat Everybody' still ranks as a classic.

that were stolen in and around Brighton ended up in Whitehawk, there would surely be so much swag that it would form a pile exceeding in height that of the Great Pyramid of Giza.

And—

But my words upon Whitehawk were constantly being interrupted by the cabbie. His name, it appeared, was Andy and he supported a football team called Brentford United. Whom, he assured us, would not only one day win the FA Cup, but also eventually the World Cup, as Brentford was in reality an independent principality founded by Indian settlers. And then he went on to explain how wheels could not possibly work.

'Nothing can go in two directions at the same time, can it?' said Andy.

'A rubber band can,' I said. 'And back again, too.'

'That's not what I mean. A wheel can't go forwards and backwards at the same time, can it?'

'I would not think so,' I said.

'But they do. Here, let me explain. You know what a bicycle is, don't you? Yes, of course you do. Well, take a bicycle and turn it upside down, rest it on its saddle and its handlebars. Are you following me? Yes, of course you are. Then with your finger spin the front wheel clockwise as hard as you can. Right?'

'Right,' I said and I shrugged.

'So it's going around clockwise, right? Now walk around to the other side of the bicycle and watch that wheel spinning around and what do you see?'

I shrugged once more.

'It's going anticlockwise. It is, it really is.* But it can't go in two directions at the same time, can it? But it does. The world has all gone mad nowadays. It's those signs and portents in the Heavens.'

Andy the cabbie halted his cab in Kemptown.

Mr Rune and I climbed from the cab.

* And it is. Check it out yourself.

'That will be fifty-nine pounds, seventeen and six,' said the cabbie. 'Let's call it sixty guineas for cash.'

I looked at Mr Rune.

And Mr Rune looked at me.

'Can I borrow your stout stick?' I asked.[*]

After I had dealt with the matter of the fare, Mr Rune and I stood in Portland Road in Kemptown and took stock of our surroundings. Very nice area. Georgian houses, many with balconies, fine sea view, posh people.

'I assume it is a goodly walk to Whitehawk?' said Mr Rune.

'Quite goodly,' I said, 'and I am *very* tired.'

And Mr Rune looked at me.

And I looked at Mr Rune.

'We will take Andy's cab, then,' I said.

We put Andy in the boot, where he could come to no harm, and I drove on towards Whitehawk. But I was not keen.

'This is *not* a good idea,' I said. 'I would prefer not to drive into Whitehawk in anything less than a Sherman tank.'

But nevertheless, we left what is known as civilisation behind and wove our way into the wastelands of Whitehawk. The burned-out cars and rubble on the roads did not inspire confidence.

'Can you drive any faster?' asked Mr Rune from the rear seats.

'I am pretty nifty at driving now,' I told him, 'but I would not care to chance my arm at anything too swift hereabouts, what with all these potholes in the road. And there are stingers out, too,' and I swerved around one.

'Well,' said Mr Rune. 'If you cannot. It's only that we *have* been followed ever since we left the station.'

I glanced into the rear-view mirror. Behind us travelled

---

[*] Well, I *had* had a very rough night with no sleep. And sixty guineas! He *was* asking for it.

an evil-looking car, all black including the windows, but with a lot of chrome upon its bumper parts.[*]

'Count Otto Black?' I said. And I shuddered when I said it.

'Or at least his minions. It would not have taken the brain of that overrated oaf Einstein to have drawn the obvious conclusion that we would return to Brighton by train. They were waiting for us at the station.'

'So what are we going to do?'

Mr Rune spread the map upon his great big knees. 'According to this, we are not far distant from our destination. Let them catch up a bit, then accelerate, signal left and take the first turning right.'

'As if *that* is going to work.'

Mr Rune made sighing sounds. 'I recall,' said he, 'chatting with JFK shortly before he was driven along Dealey Plaza. "It looks like rain," I said. "Best have the driver put the roof up on your convertible. You wouldn't want your wife to get her dress wet." But did he listen?'

'That is very tasteless,' I said. And I let the evil black car catch up, and then I accelerated, signalled left and took a sharp right turn.

'Lost them,' said Mr Rune. 'For a moment at least. Left again and then first right. You're doing very well.'

'I am falling asleep at the wheel,' I said.

'We'll soon be there.'

And very soon we were.

In a horrible houseless cul-de-sac, with high brick walls to either side of us and another one ahead.

'We have come the wrong way,' I said, with some degree of panic, 'and we are boxed in. There is no way out. This is not good. This is definitely not good.'

'Take deep breaths and steady yourself. It is just as I expected.'

'There is nothing here. Just walls.'

---

[*] It looked just like that one in the movie *The Car*. And isn't *that* a great movie?

'We are where we should be.'

'This cannot be right.'

Mr Rune passed the map to me and said, 'Study the map, young Rizla.'

I studied the map and looked back at him. 'We must have come the wrong way,' I said. 'This cul-de-sac is not on the map, as far as I can see. We came up this road,' and I pointed, 'along here, then turned right here, then left again, then first right. But first right is not on the map. We are lost.'

'We are *exactly* where we should be. This cul-de-sac is *not* on the map.'

'Why not?'

Mr Rune grinned at me. 'Because this cul-de-sac is within one of the Forbidden Zones,' said he. 'Surely you read of them in my masterwork *The Book of Ultimate Truths*. I clearly recall giving the tome to you to read and memorise. I impressed upon you the importance of what was written therein. Don't tell me that you never read it.'

'I did flick through it,' I said, 'but the newsagent's down the road from our rooms had all these Lazlo Woodbine thrillers that I had never read and—'

'Ah,' said Mr Rune. 'Well, this explains much, such as when on our previous cases you said that you couldn't have solved them because you lacked for my prior knowledge. I thought that you were simply being modest, or perhaps amusing, as the necessary details are all to be found within *The Book of Ultimate Truths*.'

'Yes, well perhaps I will read it later. For now I think I had better back us out of this death trap before the black car boxes us in.'

No, no, no,' and Hugo Rune shook his head. 'As you have never read my book,' he said, 'have you ever wondered why I have such a down upon cabbies?'

'It has crossed my mind,' I said. 'I just put it down to your dislike of paying for anything.'

'No, my dear boy. It is much more than that. It has to do with the *London A to Z*, a map book that purports to display to its buyer all the streets of London. In fact, it does anything but. "A to Z" stands for "Allocated Zones", those zones in which ordinary mortals are allowed to travel. But there are other zones in London hidden from the general public. London is far bigger than it appears to be on any map. In fact, the world is far larger than it appears to be on any map, which can be easily demonstrated if you have a rectangular map of the world and attempt to fold it around a sphere of a similar scale. You will find a lot of leftover map. The Forbidden Zones. London cabbies – in fact, *all* cabbies – know of these zones because they are members of a secret organisation known as BOLLOCK.'

'*Bollock?*' I said.

'Meaning the Black Order – London's Legion of Cab Knights. Taxi drivers learn "the Knowledge", but what they really learn is "the Secret Knowledge", handed on from generation to generation. Knowledge of the location of the Forbidden Zones.'

'But what is in these Forbidden Zones?' I asked.

'All that is missing. All that is lost. The ballpoint pens, the yellow-handled screwdrivers, that pair of glasses or whatever it was that you put down for a moment and can never find again. Although this can also have something to do with congregational instinct amongst inanimate objects, which explains why buses always come along three at a time. Or small-screw phenomena, which explains why there are always two small screws left over when you reassemble that broken toaster, which now appears to be mended. But we cannot go into those matters here. They are explained at length in *The Book of Ultimate Truths*. So, let me continue about all those things that unaccountably go missing. That postal order that should have arrived for your birthday. That job application that you sent off. Put this on a worldwide scale. What about the things that go missing from the corridors of power in Westminster? All these things go into the Forbidden Zones. Which is why, of course, I reinvented the ocarina.'

'What?' I said.

'My ocarina,' said Mr Rune, taking it from his pocket and tootling out a little trill.

'Your ocarina has something to do with the Forbidden Zones?'

'It is our means of entry to the secret labyrinth that lies within them. I have travelled into those regions before. In fact, I was trapped within them for a goodly spell before being released by a chap named Cornelius Murphy. But that is another story.'[*]

'And this is a cop-out,' I said. 'You cannot just spring all this on me out of the blue at the last minute to explain things. That is not the way it works.'

'Rizla,' said Mr Rune, 'every case that we have been involved in during the course of the last year has led towards this moment. Put them all together in your mind. See the connections. I confess that I did not know that the Chronovision was hidden in one of the Forbidden Zones. Did not know, in fact, until we drove into this cul-de-sac that was not on the map, guided here by the hole burned into the map.'

'So what has your ocarina to do with it?'

'My *reinvented* ocarina. The notes between notes, Rizla, the cracks between the piano keys, a series of notes that cannot be played upon any normal instrument open the portals into the inner labyrinths of the Forbidden Zones. We are here. The ocarina is here. I will play and you will drive.'

'Absurd,' said I.

'Everything is absurd, Rizla. Everything. Life is absurd; love is absurd; death, too, utterly absurd. Which is why we try not to think about the absurdity of everything. In fact, we don't really think very much about *anything*. We just go on doing what we're doing. And all things considered, and I *have* considered them all, it is probably better that way.'

'Well,' I said, 'I am really sorry that I did not do more than flick through your book. Although I do remember

---

[*] And a good 'n.

reading about how hedgehogs inhabit the Aquasphere, where rain comes from, where they float about, held aloft by the natural helium inside them, but sometimes get punctured during overexuberant rutting and plunge to Earth. Which is why you see them splatted on to country roads.' And then I yawned and fell asleep.

'Wake up!' cried Mr Rune.

'What?' I went. 'What?'

'Rear-view mirror.'

I blinked up at the rear-view mirror. It seemed mostly filled by a black and evil-looking car.

'Wah!' I went. 'Wah!' And had I had sufficient space I would have flapped my hands and taken to the turning in small circles.

Well, at least I had room to flap my hands.

'Stop doing that,' ordered Mr Rune. 'Put your foot down hard and drive.'

'But we will crash into the wall ahead.'

'No, we will not. Trust me . . .'

And I trusted Mr Rune.

I put the cab in gear and put my foot down hard and drove.

And Mr Rune wound down his window, stuck his big head out and played his ocarina.

And the evil-looking black car roared after us.

And the wall ahead grew nearer and nearer.

And suddenly it filled all of the world.

And there was a terrible . . .

Nothing. No sound apart from a kind of gulp. As in swallowing. As if we were being swallowed into blackness. And then into light. And I slammed on the brakes and the cab skidded around and we came to rest amongst more than a million ballpoint pens.

Which is where I might reasonably have ended this chapter.

But as you see, I did not.

★

'Where are we?' I asked. 'What *is* this place?' And I peered all around and about in a skulking and fearful fashion, for it seemed that we were in some vast chamber, walled with brick, with countless pillars and columns. And there was a roof some great distance above, but it was lost in shadows as there was really not much light.

'Magnificent,' said Mr Rune, gazing through his open window. 'This architecture predates all of the great cathedrals. It is the work of a hand older than Man's.'

'I do not find that encouraging,' I said.

'Well, you can always look on the bright side – our pursuers no longer pursue.'

'And do you know where we are?'

'Within the labyrinth.'

'And the Chronovision is here? *Somewhere?*'

'Undoubtedly. I kick myself for not having reasoned this out earlier. If it were hidden within the realm of Man, I would surely have found it already. It is all so obvious now.'

'Hm,' I said. 'I think you will find that you are all alone in that opinion. Are we safe here, by the way?'

'For now,' said Mr Rune.

'Then do you mind if I get my head down for a few hours? Eight will do, then I will be all perky again.'

'No time for sleep,' said Mr Rune. 'Drive on.'

'We are three-feet deep in Biros here. I do not think the cab will move.'

'Then we'll have to walk. Bring the torch.'

'What torch?'

'The one that cabbies always keep beneath the dashboard. Beside their pistols. Bring the pistol also.'

'Pistol?'

'Bring the pistol.'

It was a rather odd pistol of a design that I had never seen before. But as all this was so unlikely anyway, I did not care. I just brought the pistol, and felt more comforted bringing it.

Mr Rune and I struggled to open the cab doors, then we waded through Biros. We waded through Biros, and yellow-handled screwdrivers, and house keys and car keys and penknives and spanners and tickets. Tickets! There were thousands of tickets. Tens of thousands of tickets. Millions and billions and trillions of tickets. Cloakroom tickets, bus tickets, train tickets, concert tickets.

'Now you know where they all go to,' said Mr Rune.

'Yes,' I said. 'But *why*?'

'Control,' said Mr Rune. 'It is as simple as that. Or as complicated. A man's life appears to travel in a straight line from birth to death. He does this and that along the way, of his own free will, he thinks. But in truth, he is constantly thwarted, constantly made to do that which he does not wish to do, guided – pushed, more like – into other things. Free will? Plah!' went Hugo Rune. 'You will find that what a man does is not a product of his *own free will*. It is the product of *what he loses*.'

Mr Rune plucked up a single ticket from the countless numbers that lay in great swathes about us. 'What do we have here? Ah, a ticket to see The Who, a popular rhythm combo, at the Hanwell Community Centre, last February. Let us suppose this. The buyer of this ticket was really looking forward to the concert. He queued up, but when his time to enter came, he could not find his ticket and so was sent upon his way. Miffed and angry, he wandered into the nearest alehouse and there, as seeming chance would have it, he met the woman who would later become his wife. And bear him a child who would later invent a space-drive system based upon the transperambulation of pseudo-cosmic anti-matter. None of this would have occurred had his ticket to see The Who not gone unaccountably missing.'

'But surely that is a good thing. I thought the Forbidden Zones were run by baddies. Who is in charge of the Forbidden Zones, by the way? Or is anyone – or anything – actually in charge? Or does this stuff just happen?'

Mr Rune ignored my questions. 'Shortly,' he said, 'when all this is at an end, you will recover your memory and know once more who you really are. And when you do, *you* will recall that the only reason that you came to

Brighton was because something unaccountably went missing. This seemingly trivial event changed the course of your life.'

'I doubt that very much,' I said.

But I was wrong to doubt.

And I began to yawn once more, for I was really all in.

'Pacey-pacey, Rizla,' said Mr Rune. 'The man of destiny knows better than to linger long beneath the lifted leg of serendipity's spaniel.'

And of course I would not have argued with *that*!

And so we pressed on for a goodly way and then we came to the tellies. I shone my torch up at them and its light did not reach very much of the way up the pile. And my, oh my, oh my. They were the Great Pyramid of Televisions. There were so many of them, I did not dare to consider their number.

'You do not lose TVs,' I said. 'Not like Biros or car keys.'

'Or dry cleaning?' said Mr Rune. 'Or suitcases on air flights?' Or aeroplanes themselves – do you recall Amy Johnson? Or ships? Have you ever heard of the Bermuda Triangle? What now of Whitehawk's evil reputation? This is where all the "stolen" items really go.'

'I am scared now,' I said. 'And I want to go.'

'And we will, when we have acquired that which we have come here to find.'

'What does it look like?' I asked.

Mr Rune gazed up at the countless TVs. 'Like one of those,' he said.

We shared a special moment. And also the contents of Mr Rune's hip flask, for which I was grateful.

'You must scale the peak,' said Mr Rune, 'and find the Chronovision.'

'*I* must? But how will I know it, when I find it? So to speak.'

'Hm,' said Hugo Rune. 'Well, let us put ourselves in Father Ernetti's place. He is a Benedictine monk and he constructs a television set, which is a window into past events. What would it look like?'

'A bit gothic,' I said. 'About twenty feet high, all covered with carved cherubs and such like, with lots of gilded bits and bobs and a big crucifix on the top.'

'Perhaps you'd better wait here while *I* search,' said Mr Rune.

'Good idea,' I agreed. 'Then I could have a little sleep.'

'Settle yourself down, then, Rizla. I will search alone.'

'Oh no,' I said. 'That is not fair. We have come this far together. Let us both search.'

'You will know it, if you find it,' said Mr Rune. And he and I began our search.

Now I could, of course, drag this out for a bit, and possibly make it exciting. But there would not be much point, *and* it was *not* exciting.

Mr Rune had not climbed more than two levels up the pyramid of TVs before he cried, 'Eureka!'

'You have found it?' I said.

'I have,' said he. 'Pray give me a hand to get it down.'

I did as I was bid and we struggled it down together. And when we had done so, I gazed upon it.

'And *that* is *it*?' I said.

'It is,' said Hugo Rune. 'Father Ernetti's Chronovision.'

'But it looks just like a nineteen-fifties Bakelite TV.'

'There *are* subtle differences.'

'Well, they are lost upon me. But bravo to you, Mister Rune. Our search is over. Now let us smash it to bits.'

'Excuse me?' said Mr Rune and he raised one of those hairless eyebrows of his.

'Well, that is what we came here to do. That is what our quest has all been about – seek and destroy. Well, we did the seeking, now we have found it, so let us get on with the destroying.'

Mr Rune held the Chronovision in his great hands and clasped it to his great chest. 'Not as yet,' said he.

'Not as yet?' I said to him. 'But you told me that this is

the most dangerous device on all of God's Earth. That the man who has it within his control can view all of the past – the past of any living man. That the secrets of any living man can be shown upon the screen. And so the man who owns the Chronovision can become the most powerful man on Earth, because no man can have secrets, no matter how dark, from him. Am I correct?'

'You are,' said Mr Rune, 'which is why Count Otto seeks it.'

'And why it must be destroyed. Put it down and I will stamp upon it.'

'No,' said Mr Rune. 'This cannot be.'

'Oh no,' I said. 'Do not tell me this. You mean to keep the Chronovision for yourself. After all we have been through. You have tricked me throughout – you had no intention of destroying the thing. You just wanted to get your own hands upon it.'

Mr Rune put down the Chronovision and it floated there upon that sea of tickets. 'Do you trust me, Rizla?' he asked.

'I did,' I said. 'Absolutely. But now I am having my doubts.'

'Such a pity.'

And Mr Rune swung his stout stick.

And struck me down with it.

PART II

'Ow!' I went, when I regained consciousness. 'That hurt!'

'And it was meant to.' Mr Rune glared almost-daggers at me. 'Have a word with yourself, if you will. I am Hugo Artemis Solon Saturnicus Reginald Arthur Rune, the physical embodiment of the universal consciousness. I am *not* some self-seeking blackguard yearning for ultimate power.'

'I am sorry,' I said, 'but you did not need to bop me on the head.'

'You had a nice sleep though, didn't you?'

'*Very* nice, actually,' I said, rubbing at the bruise on my head. 'Where are we now? Is it safe?'

'Still in Whitehawk, in the domicile of an old friend of mine.'

'You have a friend in Whitehawk?'

'I have friends everywhere.'

I took in my surroundings. They were *not* altogether insalubrious. 'This does not look too rough,' I said. 'Where are we? Exactly?'

'Inside a tepee.'

'What?'

'The tepee of Chief Whitehawk.'

'Chief Whitehawk,' I said. 'Well, I will probably wake up in a minute.'

'You are not dreaming, Rizla. Now rouse yourself, breakfast awaits.'

And indeed breakfast awaited.

And it was the breakfast of the Gods.

I had never seen anything like it and I had dined upon some pretty nifty cuisine during my time with Hugo Rune.

I took it all in, in breaths and in gasps.

'I have died and gone to Heaven,' I said. 'You hit me too hard with your stick.'

'The chief always puts on a decent spread,' said Mr Rune, seating himself in an ornate chair and tucking a napkin into the collar of his shirt. 'But then there is a branch of Lidl on the border of Whitehawk.'

'Ah,' I said. 'That explains everything. You never get better value for money than at Lidl.'

'Quite so,' said Mr Rune. 'Tuck in.'

I seated myself in a similar chair.
There were two at the table and both rather nice.
And I dined upon viands and wondrous fare.
With wines that were mulled with a cinnamon spice.

And I nibbled at nubbins of newt in the raw
And fresh peccary that was done in a roast.

308

And caviar cheese that you sucked through a straw.
And something like butter to spread on your toast.

Which was not actually butter but a vegetable-oil derivative, which although low in soluble jobbies was high in polyunsaturates. Which was just the way I liked it.

I was ravenously hungry, ridiculously hungry. I felt as if I had not eaten for a month. I got stuck in and I munched on and glanced around the tepee. It was a considerable tepee, with a central dining area, an open-plan kitchen with a peninsular unit and an eye-level hob. The worktops in this kitchen were of grey slate and the doors of bird's eye maple. And there were many labour-saving devices of the kind that no doubt saved considerable labour on the part of those who knew what they were for.

There was also a sports and gymnasium area, with dartboard, billiard table and one of those machines where you run along on top of a conveyor belt, for reasons that must make some sense to those who have the wish to use such things. I was also impressed by the indoor garage facility and the chief's collection of automobiles. I spied an Aston Martin DB7, a Ferrari and the new R-Type Jaguar. Which led me to believe that not everything that got nicked in Brighton and entered Whitehawk ended up in the Forbidden Zone. Then there was the pool, the solarium, the sauna, the five-screen cinema complex and the private bar.

Then there was the shopping mall, the airport and . . .

'I think I have concussion,' I said to Mr Rune. 'I am sure I am hallucinating.'

'That would be the peyote flakes you sprinkled on your Rice Krispies.'

'That would be it, then. Where is Chief Whitehawk, by the way? I would like to thank him for breakfast.'

'He's out leading a hunting party of braves. The great herds of Sussex buffalo migrate towards Roedean at this time of year. They'll take a few head on the golf course, I shouldn't wonder, then be back later for the feastings and celebrations.'

'Are we safe here?' I asked. 'From Count Otto and his minions, I mean.' And I wolfed down another helping of wolf.

'Safe enough.'

'And the Chronovision?' I swallowed another portion of swallow.

'That is safe, too.'

'Then you have *not* broken it up.'

'Not as yet. There is much that I must learn from that remarkable device before it is destroyed for ever.'

'Hm,' I went. And then, 'Oh,' I said, 'I recall you telling me that the Chronovision can be tuned to any living individual and replay moments in their past.'

'That is correct,' said Mr Rune.

'Then I want you to tune it in to me. My work here is done. I want to know who I am.'

Mr Rune shook his head. 'Not yet,' said he. 'And your work here is not yet done – there are two more cases, two more figures in the Brightonomicon: the Coldean Cat and the Wiseman of Withdean.'

'Forget them,' I said. 'We have the Chronovision – that was the object of the exercise. I will miss all this mad stuff, I know, and I have really enjoyed myself with you, although it has nearly been the death of me on numerous occasions. But I think it is time that I found out who I really am.'

'No,' said Mr Rune. 'In a word, no. Everything must be brought to completion. The balance of equipoise must be maintained. You'll be on your way as your true self in a couple of months.'

'*A couple of months?*' And I made what must have been a very grumpy face. 'Perhaps I will just clear off on my own, then,' I said. 'My memory will eventually return. Probably.'

'Take your chances on your own, eh?'

'Yes,' I said.

Mr Rune pulled a copy of the *Leader* from somewhere and tossed it across the table at me. I almost caught it, but it went in my plover's egg. I plucked it up and cast an eye across the banner headline:

THREE DEAD IN LEWES
ROAD-RAGE SLAUGHTER

The text beneath told a tale of terror, of how a young man driving a stolen Morris Minor had mowed down three innocent ladies of the Chiswick Townswomen's Guild. There was even a police Identikit picture of the 'teenage psycho killer'.

'Oh, by Crimbo!' I went, and I cast the newssheet aside. 'It is me. I am a wanted killer. I am leaving a trail of corpses, as if I am Lazlo Woodbine.'

'Calm yourself, Rizla,' said Mr Rune, applying himself to the last of the locust lasagne. 'I'm sure I can square things with Inspector Hector, get you off the hook, as it were.'

'Yes, you must,' I said. 'You tell him. Explain that I only mowed those women down because they had killed you.'

'I might put it somewhat differently.'

'Well, whatever. Phone him now. There will be a phone somewhere. Oh yes – there is a row of phone boxes over there by the disco dance floor.'

'All in good time,' said Mr Rune.

'What?'

And then a distant tepee flap flew open and a group of what can only be described as Red Indians, in fringed-buckskin get-up and full war paint, came bustling in. The biggest of the bunch wore a magnificent war bonnet of eagle feathers, with decoratively beaded earflaps and matching tow bar. He flung down his bow and his quiver of arrows and, grinning, advanced upon Mr Hugo Rune.

'Greetings, He-That-Clouteth-Cabbies,' grinned this noble savage.

'Greetings, Chief.' And Mr Rune rose from his seat, tossed away his napkin and greeted the chief with a handshake that was not Masonic, but might have passed for one any day of the week, excluding Tuesday.

'What news?' asked Mr Rune.

'Much news,' said the chief, and he sat himself down in Mr Rune's chair. 'Many signs and portents in the Heavens.

Omens of the coming of Ragnarök. In Rottingdean, woman give birth to child in shape of hairdryer. And in Hove, masked walker arrested by police for illegal pamphleting. Him taken to cells at Sussex Nick, asked to take off scarf around face. Him refuse and officers take off scarf and anorak and trousers, too. And find no man inside. Only clothes.'

'Suggestive,' said Mr Rune.

'Police say it happen all time,' the chief continued. 'Say scientists know of it for years. New evolutionary leap forward, clothes becoming sentient. Explain all those single shoes you see on motorways, trying to meet up with other clothes, form manlike shapes. Have hands, see, gloves, opposable thumbs. And not just clothes. Fruit and veg and minerals, too. Many famous celebrities not men at all, say scientists, many just piles of fruit and veg and minerals, too.'

'Like "rock" musicians,' I suggested. 'The Strawberry Alarm Clock, or The Rolling Stones.'

The chief nodded approvingly. 'Have liking for young squaw here,' he said. 'Know how to talk the toot.'

'I have been practising,' I said. 'Hey, what do you mean, "squaw"?'

'What news of Count Otto Black?' asked Mr Rune.

'Him plenty mad. Scout report see him drive round and round Whitehawk each day 'til evil black car run out of petrol. Then rant and rave. Then storm off towards Kemptown. Scouts follow but then lose him each time. He enter timber house, then timber house sink into ground and he gone.'

'*The Bevendean Bathyscaphe*,' I said.

'Damn tootin',' said the chief. 'And now,' and he grinned up at Mr Rune, 'need help from Great White Brother, in exchange for satisfying Great White Brother's voracious appetite for almost a month now.'

'*Almost a month?*' I said.

'You did have a *very* long sleep,' said Mr Rune. 'You needed to get your energy back. It would have been a shame to wake you.'

'Ludicrous!' I said. 'And what of the headline in this morning's *Leader*?'

'All right,' said Mr Rune. 'I did it for the sake of continuity. We deal with one case a month. We had to get rid of the rest of November. And anyway, if you had bothered to look properly, you would have observed that that newspaper is almost a month old.

I rolled my eyes and shook my head.

'Young squaw been overdoing firewater?' asked the chief.

'I am still half-gone from the peyote flakes,' I said. 'I have to concentrate really hard to stop you changing into a spaniel. And stop calling me a squaw – I am a brave.'

'Enough toot for now,' said the chief. And to Mr Rune, 'Big mystery baffle chief and braves, even medicine man not know what to do. I call in on him where he work in pharmacy in Boots and he say him only able to prescribe aspirin. Aspirin not much help to battle demon.'

'Demon?' said Mr Rune. 'What of this?'

'Demon plague tepee of Chief,' said the chief. 'Not mention it to Great White Brother before because embarrassing, but as Great White Brother stuff face endlessly with Chief's grub, and always boast know every damn thing, Chief now request that Great White Brother put money where mouth is and trounce demon.'

'As indeed I will,' said Mr Rune. 'What is the nature of this demonic manifestation?'

'Man with head of bird.' The chief did beakish mimings. 'Big beak hooter and smell like buffalo's backside. Him ride upon motor scooter, wear parka with fun-fur trim on hood and word "VESPERADO" in studs on back. Many lights on front of scooter, many mirrors, too.'

'That is no demon,' I said. 'That is a Mod.'

'Young brave with girlie hair know this "Mod"?' asked the chief.

'I have not got girlie hair,' I said. Although I *had* slept for a month and my hair was getting pretty good at the back now. 'But I do not understand – why does a Mod on a scooter bother you so much? You could always just shoot his tyres with an arrow, or something.'

'You not understand,' said Chief Whitehawk. 'Arrows pass through demon and scooter, as if him moving inter-dimensionally, possibly employing some technology creating time/space interface, most likely through transperambu-lation of pseudo-cosmic anti-matter. Although that only supposition as Chief don't know jack about science.'

'Clearly not,' said I. 'So what does he get up to, then, this demonic Mod on his transperambulating Vespa?'

'Him come into tepee. Use Chief's kitchen. Use labour-saving devices and contents of Chief's Frigidaire 2000 Series fridge-freezer with built-in ice-cube dispenser. Also Chief's spice wheel, use up all fenugreek last week, preparing ragout of spaniel with Hollandaise sauce, a dish Chief never seen before. Chief take note and write down recipe. But that not the point.'

'Extraordinary,' I said. 'And have you ever tried to speak to him?'

'Why young brave with squaw-cut ask all questions?' asked the chief. 'Great White Brother should ask questions. Organ-grinder speak, not monkey.'

'Steady on,' I said.

'There, him speak again. Silence loquaciousness with tomahawk if say more.'

'But . . .' But I said no more.

'It's an interesting conundrum,' said Mr Rune, 'When he does the cooking, does he still wear his decorated parka?'

'No, him take off parka. And bird's head. Put on chef outfit. Oh, and him swear a lot. Swear all time, in fact. Many bad words which Chief no like.'

'This is bonkers,' I almost said. But I did not.

'One question,' said Mr Rune. 'Is he always alone?'

'Ah,' said the chief. 'Forget to mention: him never alone. Have kitchen staff with him. He swear at them. And diners, too. All this—' the chief made expansive gesturings '—all this change, become like restaurant. Many tables and chairs. Nice white tablecloths on tables. Irish linen. Only come from Harrods, such tablecloths. And diners dine and Chief stride amongst them, striking at them. But they not see or hear Chief, nor feel Chief's blows. As if Chief not exist. Most exasperating.'

'How have I never seen this?' asked Mr Rune.

'Great White Brother always turn in early after mighty feastings. That reason him no see. But Chief cheesed off with it now.'

'And well might you be, Chief. Now, Rizla,' Mr Rune said to me, 'your observations on this.'

'You will not let him hit me with his tomahawk?'

Mr Rune rolled his eyes. 'Your observations,' he said.

'Well,' I said, 'if the Chief can see these people, but he cannot touch them, they must be ghosts, surely. Was this tepee built upon an ancient restaurant mound or something?'

'Very good, Rizla, but about as far off the mark as it is possible to be.'

'Thank you very much,' I said. 'You have drawn some conclusion of your own, then?'

'Only the most very obvious. We shall sit up tonight and view this phenomenon for ourselves.'

'I think I am up for that,' I said. 'It might be weeks before I need another sleep.'

At seven of the evening clock, Mr Rune sent the chief and his braves off to the pub and he and I settled down to wait.

'You would not care to give me a clue, would you?' I said to Mr Rune. 'Or is it something that I should have read in *The Book of Ultimate Truths*, so you are not going to tell me out of spite?'

'Hugo Rune is never spiteful,' said he. 'Hugo Rune is a gentleman. And a gentleman puts kindness above all else.'

'So will you give me a clue?'

'No,' said Mr Rune, but kindly. 'Fear not. Observe and then present me with your own conclusions.'

I shrugged and we waited and presently we heard the

approaching engine noises of a Vespa motor scooter, which rather put the wind up me. And then its rider entered the tepee without first opening the flap. Which put the wind up me somewhat further. He took off his helmet and parka and entered the kitchen area. And others followed him and began worrying at saucepans and gratin dishes and labour-saving devices. And then the diners appeared and suddenly there were tables and chairs for them to sit at and on. And I viewed this and shivered a little and shook my head a lot. And feared that if this was indeed a ghost's restaurant, then there was always the chance that Norris Styver might have escaped from Lewes and might just turn up here in search of a snack.

Seemingly oblivious to all fear, Mr Rune played 'Eat Your Greens Up, Sonny Boy'* upon his reinvented ocarina.

When the ghostly diners were all seated, a ghostly waiter moved amongst them taking orders and conveying them to the kitchen area where the Vesperado chef shouted swearing words at his kitchen staff and the cooking began.

And the dishes that the staff prepared were wonderful. But the chef took exception to each and every one of them. He bawled abuse and stamped his feet and carried on in a most ungentlemanly manner.

If I had been working for him, I would have punched him. In fact, so disgusted was I by his behaviour that I got up from where I was sitting and took a swing at him on behalf of his staff. But my fist sailed through him as if he was not there. And he went on shouting and swearing, oblivious.

And the diners seemed little better than the chef. When their marvellous food was served up before them, they sniffed at it and pecked at it and raised their noses haughtily. A right snotty bunch were they.

'What a crowd of ingrates,' I said to Mr Rune.

'Do you recognise any of them?' he asked.

---

* A popular music-hall tune of the 1890s often performed by Little Tich, when not doing his famous Big-Boot Dance.

I gave them a good looking-over. 'I do,' I said. 'Surely that is that chap off *Blue Peter*, the one who was sacked because of the cocaine-fuelled lady-sheep incident. And that is the sports-commentator fellow who recently lost his job over a cocaine-fuelled lady-boy incident. And that is—'

'You *do* know these people?' said Mr Rune.

'I have read about them,' I said, 'in the society pages of the *Argus*. That's Brighton's mayor, Terry Caroghan. And that fellow there. And that woman with the preposterous breasts. They all live here in Brighton. They are all past-their-sell-by-date B-list celebrities. Except for Terry, he's okay. There is something about them that is not quite right, but they cannot be ghosts, because they are not dead.'

'And if not ghosts, then what?'

'You know, do you not?' I said.

'I fear that I do,' said Mr Rune, 'and I fear for what will shortly occur.'

'Is something going to happen? Should we run away?' My hands began to flap. And I tried very hard to control them.

'Remain calm,' said Mr Rune. And I tried very hard to do so.

A portly fellow now entered the ethereal restaurant. He was big and he was broad, with a most commanding presence. He apologised to the waiter for his late arrival, claiming that he had encountered transportation difficulties, and was escorted at once to his table. The best in the restaurant.

I looked on and my jaw hung slack.

I looked up at Mr Rune and his did, also.

'Mister Rune,' I said to him, when I could find my voice, 'do you see what I think I see? Do you see who has just entered this ghostly restaurant?'

Mr Hugo Rune nodded slowly. 'It is me,' he said.

PART III

The ghostly Mr Rune sat himself down and ordered a bottle of bubbly. His instructions were brief but explicit: 'The best you have,' said he.

I looked on and the real Mr Rune looked on also.

'It *is* you,' I said. 'Nice suit. Unusual style, though.'

'Cease, please, Rizla,' said Mr Rune.

The ghostly Mr Rune perused the menu. In the kitchen, the ghostly chef shouted at his staff.

'Let us take ourselves over,' said Mr Rune to me, 'to where *I* apparently am sitting. Let us overhear what there is to be overheard.'

The ghostly Mr Rune did further perusals of his ghostly menu. The waiter returned to him in the company of the champagne, which he uncorked and poured. The ghostly Mr Rune did tasting and said, 'It will have to do,' and then ordered everything upon the menu.

'What odds he finds a rat-bone in his dessert?' I asked the Mr Rune with whom I was standing.

This Mr Rune hushed me into silence and viewed his ghostly doppelgänger.

A curious buzzing came from this fellow and he reached into an inside pocket and drew out a small plastic something with buttons upon it, pressed one of these then pressed the plastic something to his ear. 'Rune,' said he.

'It is a phone,' I said. 'A tiny little phone without wires.'

'A *mobile* phone,' said the real Mr Rune.

'But they have not been invented yet.'

Mr Rune looked at me.

And I looked at Mr Rune.

'The future,' I said.

'Exactly. These apparitions are not ghosts from the past. We are witnessing a future event.'

'But how?' I asked, thoroughly puzzled.

Mr Rune raised his hand and we listened as the future Mr Rune spoke into his mobile phone. 'Count Otto,' said he.

'What news? Yes, I see, our contacts in Hollywood have taken up the film rights. That's splendid news. They don't like the name, though. Don't want to call it *The Brightonomicon*. Sorry, you're breaking up there. No, yes, I heard you. Call it what? Well, that's a very foolish name, but I suppose these fellows know their own business best. Although I do recall an evening I spent with Alfred Hitchcock. He was discussing this movie he had in mind, wanted to call it *The Cross-Dressing Mother-Loving Motel-Shower-Slasher*. I suggested something simpler.

'But, *what*? A twelve-movie deal based on the cases, with Elijah Wood playing Rizla and Ian McKellen playing me? And who will be playing you? Gary Oldman. Good choice. Well, go ahead and clinch the deal. I'll see you back here in a week. Call me, we'll do lunch at Groucho's.'

I looked at the real Mr Rune.

And he once more looked at me.

'One of the things I have liked about all this stuff,' I said, 'is that I have never been able to figure out what will happen next. And then when it does happen, it is never less than interesting.'

'This must not come to pass,' said Mr Rune. 'This must not be allowed to come to pass.'

'What year is it?' I asked. 'Who is the president?'

'Rizla, I will strike you with my stick.'

I became somewhat emboldened, although I know not why. 'If this *is* the future,' I said, 'then it is all your fault. I remember well enough that business at Eat Your Food Nude, all those rock stars who have to die aged twenty-seven. You showed me a glimpse of what would happen if they do not die at the appointed time. And now you are being shown a glimpse of your future. I will bet it is because you have not destroyed the Chronovision. This is what is going to happen because of that. You are going to end up as the partner of Count Otto Black.'

'This can never be allowed to happen,' said Mr Rune.

'Well, in my humble opinion, there is one way to stop it: smash up the Chronovision and all this will vanish away.

Chief Whitehawk will be impressed. He will probably lay on a big belly-buster for tomorrow's breakfast. Although whether it will be on the scale of *that*, I could not say.'

And I pointed towards the starter courses that the future Mr Rune was being served. There were many of them and they were big with it.

'I cannot destroy the Chronovision *yet*,' said the Mr Rune who was with me in the present. 'I wish that I could, but I cannot.'

'Listen,' I said, 'somehow, someone or something has afforded us this glimpse of the future. It is not some accident that it should happen here and now. It is to show *you* what is going to happen if you do not take the appropriate steps to stop it happening. Best heed it,' I said. 'Smash up the Chronovision.'

'I cannot,' said Mr Rune once again, 'not until all the cases have been solved. Two remain on the zodiac – the Wiseman of Withdean and the Coldean Cat.'

'That is ridiculous,' I said.

And the future Mr Rune got stuck into his starters.

'As Count Otto Black works on behalf of a God who moves between the seconds of time, so do I work on behalf of another. I cannot destroy the Chronovision until I have encountered the Earthly manifestation of my God. I must meet the Wiseman of Withdean, Rizla.'

'Which is why our quest is *not* yet at an end?'

'Quite so,' said Mr Rune.

'Well, I wish you would not keep springing stuff upon me. Oh, look, your future self is already finishing that bottle of champagne.'

Mr Rune glanced at the label on the bottle. 'I really do let my standards slip,' said he. 'The present myself would never drink that.'

'So, having seen this future self of yours, what do you intend to do *now*?'

'Leave,' said Mr Rune. 'Leave at once.'

And that is what we did.

11
The Wiseman of Withdean

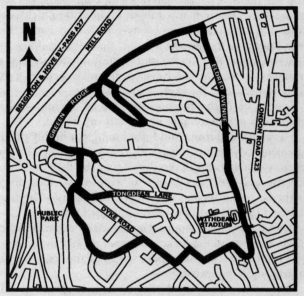

The Wiseman of Withdean

PART I

It was January and it was cold and it was not fun any more.

Mr Rune had acquired rooms for us in a street in Hove called St Aubyns. The rooms were those of a basement flat. An unfurnished basement flat. Exactly how Mr Rune acquired these rooms I am not certain. He had me take down the 'To Let' sign outside and 'dispose of it discreetly'. He also had me gain entry by means of a crowbar through the kitchen window at the rear, there being some talk of 'keys being lost' and 'locks that would have to be changed'.

I really hated those rooms in Hove. They were dark, dire and dank, and I tell you they stank, and the central heating was broken. I was all for us taking our chances back at forty-nine Grand Parade, but Mr Rune would have none of that. And one night, as by the light of a stuttering candle I stuffed crushed newspapers up my trousers for insulation, I chanced to discover the reason why: forty-nine Grand Parade had been burned to the ground.

It was arson, the police claimed, probably an attempt at insurance fraud. And there was an Identikit picture of the likely suspect. And the likely suspect was me.

I curled up in that position favoured by the soon-to-be-born, stuck my thumb into my mouth and fretted.

I was a wanted man. And I was hiding out in this ghastly basement. My spiffing coat with the Astrakhan collar was severely scuffed from all the sleeping on the floor and I was very hungry indeed. I began to wonder whether things might be better for me if I simply walked into Brighton nick and handed myself over to Inspector Hector.

'Don't even think about such an option,' came the voice of Mr Rune from the darkened corner nearest to the door. 'We must face such vicissitudes with stoicism. Matters will shortly adjust themselves.'

'To our favour?' I asked. 'For they surely cannot get any worse.'

'And it's rude to talk with your thumb in your mouth.'

I huddled down and made bitter grumblings.

Moonlight shone in through the uncurtained windows and lit upon the Chronovision standing by the fireplace, propped up on a beer crate and plugged into the wall.

I so dearly wanted to smash that thing to pieces. But of course, before I did so, tune it to myself. I had asked Mr Rune again and again concerning this, but his refusals had been absolute. He had, however, allowed me to view certain images on the screen.

At first, when I saw the crackling black and white

pictures, I felt certain that he had tuned to some television station that I had never heard of, which showed old newsreel footage all day, perhaps being beamed to us from the future, where there might be all manner of TV channels like that. In fact, there might even be channels that showed nudie films and Japanese game shows where contestants were tortured in the name of entertainment. Although such things as those were probably too much to hope for. But, I felt certain, I was *not* really viewing the past.

I watched footage of Hitler making speeches at Nuremberg, and I swear that as the camera panned across his cronies in the background, I spied Mr Rune chatting up Goebbels's wife.

And I watched the coronation of Edward VII in 1901. And there was Mr Rune also, in a front seat in Westminster Abbey, accompanying the organ on his reinvented ocarina.

But then, as the images became more distant in time, I knew that this Chronovision was the real McCoy.

And when I watched the opening of the Great Exhibition of 1851 with Mr Rune leading her Majesty Queen Victoria (Gawd bless Her) through the exhibits and introducing her to Charles Babbage, 'the Father of Computers', I was amazed beyond all reasonable amazement.

Mr Rune fiddled with the dials and I viewed Victorian London. And it was *not* how we were told it was in the history books. There was technology then that we do not possess now. Slim metal towers topped by spheres of steel rose to all points of the great metropolis, transmitting electricity upon radio waves. Electricity without wires. And there were flying hansom cabs and gentlemen's landaus. And great turbine-driven airships that carried thousands of British troops. And the British Empire ruled almost all of the world.

We watched the abortive launch of the 1891 Moonship, sabotaged, said Mr Rune, by Joseph Merrick, the Elephant Man, who was really a human/alien hybrid, the alien part being Martian.

I have to say that when I watched it all, I said to Mr Rune

that if someone put it all together, they would have the makings of a half-decent novel, possibly in a genre called 'far-fetched fiction'. Mr Rune replied that such a book would one day be written, but that *I* would not be its author.

And backwards through time Mr Rune tuned that Chronovision, that window on past events. And I watched Victorian music-hall performances, battles and coronations, the Great Fire of London, Shakespeare directing his plays, with a little help from Mr Rune. Columbus setting sail.

And upon the first Sunday in December, Mr Rune allowed me to watch the crucifixion of Christ.

I have never in my life seen anything so brutal. It made me weep to watch it, I can tell you, and the nobility of the man being tortured to death on that cross will stay in my mind for ever. Whether he was really the Son of God, I could not have said then. I had never given religion too much thought, apart from the Eastern Schools, that is, because I had always fancied becoming a lama and doing all that magical stuff – levitation and leaving your body and seeing folks' auras and suchlike.

I read a lot of *Doctor Strange* comics back in those days. When I was not reading Lazlo Woodbine.

I do not want to dwell much on the Crucifixion. It makes the hairs stand up on my arms just to think about it. And it makes my arms start to flap somewhat, too. Which is a habit I have long been trying to curtail.

And so I lay there in the light of the moon and the stuttering candle and hated and feared and was in awe of that Chronovision. And curled up in my soiled coat, my trousers stuffed with newssheets, I spent another uncomfortable night on the floor in our rooms in Hove.

And when daytime appeared, offering us sunlight but naught in the way of warmth, Mr Rune stretched and rose and straightened his cravat and said, 'Let us go and take breakfast.'

We took our breakfast, as ever we did of late, in

Georgio's Bistro in George Street. It was an ex-Wimpy bar, now in private hands, run by a family of Italians who were straight from Central Casting.

There was Mama and Papa and Mario and Luigi. And they all worked together in their Hellish kitchen, but unlike chefs of a future time they did not swear at all. They sang. Songs about pasta and Peroni beer, Ferraris and football, lino and loft insulation.

Now, it has to be said that I did not care at all for going out for breakfast. Do not get me wrong here – Georgio's put on a decent spread at a price that was fair and bunged in an extra cuppa for free. The reason I did not like going there was the reason I did not like going *anywhere*. And that reason, I regret to say, was because of my disguise.

Well, I could not just walk abroad upon the streets of Brighton, could I? There were 'wanted' posters up everywhere and my face was upon them. I had suggested to Mr Rune that I don a tweed jacket and a trilby hat, as Laz had done when he sought to disguise himself. With the trilby and tweeds, he always managed to pass for a newspaper reporter. In *Headless Dames Don't Give Any* (A Lazlo Woodbine Thriller), even his own mother failed to recognise him.

Mr Rune, however, pooh-poohed my suggestion. He had a better idea. And so I was dragged-up. And by this, I do *not* mean that I had a bad childhood. Make-up was applied to my face and, what with my 'girlie hair', Mr Rune felt convinced that I could pass for his daughter any day of the week. With the possible exception of Tuesday, of course.

And so I walked the streets of Hove in high heels and a mini-skirt – which is nippy in December, I can tell you, receiving many a curious glance and many a curious offer too from strange old men in raincoats who took me for a Bangkok lady-boy.

But, fair play to Mr Rune, the beat bobbies of Brighton nick did not recognise me, even when we passed them closely by. The 'first constable', whom we had encountered before the tea-weeping statue of Queen Victoria during the case of the Lansdowne Lioness, even chatted me up and offered to show me his truncheon.

'Oooh, Matron,' said a passing lady in a straw hat, whom I took for a moment to be a dragged-up Fangio. But sadly, was not.

'Two Big Boy's Breakfasts,' said Mr Rune to Mario. 'No, make that three, if you would be so kind. I have a hunger on me this morning that can only be quenched by a full English.'

Mario did not say, 'Oooh Matron,' but Mario rarely said anything. When he did say anything, it was to me and he whispered in words of Italian.

'We might be forced to take breakfast elsewhere quite soon,' said Mr Rune to me when Mario had departed, singing a song about Formica. 'I don't know how much longer I can put off the engagement.'

'Engagement?' I asked. 'What engagement?'

'Yours to Mario,' said Mr Rune. 'He asked me for your hand in marriage the first time we came here. Naturally I agreed, in return for free breakfasts.'

'You granted *him* my hand in marriage?' I said. 'I am appalled.'

Hugo Rune shrugged.

'I do not want to marry a waiter,' I said. 'I want to marry a doctor, or a solicitor, or an architect.'

'Most amusing,' said Mr Rune. 'Have you seen this?' And he cast me the morning edition of the *Leader*.

EARTHQUAKES IN BRIGHTON

ran the banner headline. And beneath this much purple prose regarding rumblings beneath the streets and houses tumbling down.

'Count Otto Black,' said I, 'and his nuclear-powered subterranean Ark.'

'Correct,' said Mr Rune, 'but I meant the article beneath it.'

So I read the article beneath it.

ROCK NIGHT
BRIGHTON ROCK
At Hove Town Hall
If heavy makes you happy, then
Hove Town Hall is the new rock
venue to be at.
Tonight 10 p.m. – 2 a.m.
Have hair? Be there. Rock on.

'Heavy?' I said to Mr Rune. 'What is this heavy that makes you happy?'

'Heavy metal—' said Hugo Rune, 'it's in its infancy. But when the bass line blasts from the Marshall stack and turns your guts to jelly, you just have to up and bang your head.'

'Bang your head?'

'It's a dance.' And Mr Rune demonstrated this dance, which appeared to consist of rhythmic duckings of the head accompanied by the playing of an imaginary guitar.

'Ah, yes,' I said. 'I recall now that I have read all about heavy metal in the *Leader*. Are you telling me that you actually *like* heavy metal?'

'Dear boy,' said Mr Rune, 'I *invented* heavy metal.'

I shook my head, but as breakfast arrived I smiled at Mario and fluttered my false eyelashes. Just for the Hell of it.

'I cooka yours justa da way you lika it,' said Mario, which is how Italians speak. 'I give you da-bigga-da-sausage. I give you da-bigga-da-sausage anya tima you please.'

I fluttered my lashes and rolled my eyes and Mario departed.

'*You* invented heavy metal?' I said once more to Mr Rune.

'Where do you *really* think that Robert Johnson got his chord sequences from? He *didn't* sell his soul to Satan, I told you that already.'

'*You* taught Robert Johnson how to play?'

327

'Forward planning,' said Mr Rune. 'For this evening.'

'I do not understand,' said I, tucking into the biggest sausage I had ever seen, 'but I do have to insist that you explain to me *now* and not later. It is always such a cop-out when you explain later.'

'We are nearly at the end of our quest,' said Mr Rune. 'Oh, look.' And he pointed beyond my shoulder with his fork. 'Zulus, thousands of them.'

I turned not my head, nor even batted an eyelash.

'This is *my* da-bigga-da-sausage,' I said, 'and *I* am going to eat it.'

Mr Rune's hovering fork returned to his own breakfasting plate. 'Forward planning,' he said once more. 'Forward planning will always hold the advantage over a hastily conceived stratagem. Allow me to offer you an example of this.' And Mr Rune leaned back in his chair and grinned at me.

I leaned back in mine and did likewise.

And the leg of my chair buckled and I fell heavily to the floor. And would you not know it, by the time I had managed to scramble up and find myself another chair, Mr Rune had eaten my da-bigga-da-sausage.

'Forward planning, you see,' said Mr Rune. 'I knew that chair had a dodgy leg, which is why I sat you there.'

'You thorough-going swine,' I said, but I did have to smile when I said it. 'So, all right, you won da-bigga-da-sausage, but please explain about this forward planning when it comes to the field of heavy metal.'

'I gave Robert Johnson the formula,' said Mr Rune, 'the chord sequences that later musicians would recognise to be *the* chord sequences. All rock music is based upon those chord sequences. This event—' And Mr Rune pointed to the Rock Night advert in the *Leader* '—could not have occurred had heavy-metal music not come to pass. It also required the invention of the Stratocaster and the Marshall stack. Naturally I had a hand in these also.'

'Naturally,' I said, shovelling egg down my throat.

'So that this event would come to pass, here in Hove tonight.'

'Why?' I asked. Which *was* a reasonable question.

'Because I have to meet and speak with Him. And He will be present at the event.'

'Why will this *He* be there?' I asked.

'Because *He* is a heavy-metal fan.'

'Oh, I see,' I said. 'But who *is* He?'

Mr Rune mopped up the grease from his plate with his toast and then downed the toast. '*He*,' said Mr Rune, 'is the Wiseman of Withdean. The last in His line. *He* is a direct descendant — the last direct descendant — of the man you saw upon the Chronovision.'

'Little Tich?' I said. 'I did like his Big-Boot Dance.'

'*Not* Little Tich,' said Mr Rune, and his non-food-stuffing hand moved to the stout stick that lay across his lap.

'Only joking,' I said. 'Then whom?'

'He is the last direct descendant of Jesus Christ.'

I was very glad that I did *not* have da-bigga-da-sausage in my mouth at that moment, for surely I would have coughed it all over Hugo Rune.

'The last direct descendant of Jesus Christ?' I managed to say.

'Christ did *not* die upon the cross,' said Hugo Rune. 'Me and the other disciples could not bear for that to happen. Matthew bribed Pilate to have Christ taken down before he died, although he feigned death and word was put about that he was dead. He was tended to and returned to health and smuggled out of the Holy Lands by Joseph of Aromatherapy. He was brought to England, to Brighton, in fact, and from thence to a London borough known as Brentford.'

'Brentford?' I said. 'That rings a bell somewhere.'

'Brentford is the site where the biblical Garden of Eden was located.'

'That I do *not* believe,' was my reply to *that*.

'Flutter your eyelids some more,' said Mr Rune, 'and enquire of Mario regarding that third breakfast.'

I did as I was bid and then returned to our conversation. 'The Garden of Eden was in England?' I said.

'Many believe that *all* biblical events occurred in England,' said Mr Rune, 'but they didn't, only those of the Old Testament. Christ married a Brentford lass. He eventually died and was buried there in the borough. I own a house on The Butts Estate in Brentford. The body of Christ lies in a catacomb beneath it, uncorrupted by the ages.'

'And Christ fathered children?' I said.

'Only one,' said Mr Rune. 'A boy. Colin.'

'Colin?' And I took the opportunity to roll my eyes once again.

'Who married and had a single son and so on and so forth to the present day.'

'And you seek this present-day descendant? This last in the line of Christ?'

'I do,' said Mr Rune.

'And why?'

'Because *I* cannot defeat Count Otto Black alone.'

'You have me,' I said.

'Dear boy.' And Hugo Rune smiled upon me. 'You remain faithful and for that I am grateful. But Black is allied to a powerful force – that God which exists between the seconds. I alone, or even with your inestimable assistance, would be insufficient to deal with this opponent.'

'And this chap, this last descendant of Christ's bloodline, does he know who he is? *What* he is?'

'No,' said Mr Rune, 'he does not, which is why we will have to convince him. Show him. And we will need to do this through the agency of the Chronovision. Which is why I cannot as yet destroy it.'

'It will be a bit of a shock for him when you tell him,' I said.

'No doubt, but that is what I must do.' Mr Rune's second breakfast arrived and he tucked into it.

'Woulda da loverly lady care for another da-bigga-da-sausage?' said Mario to me.

'The biggaist-bigga-da-sausage you have, big boy,' I

replied and did a bit more fluttering. Mario returned to the kitchen, limping curiously.

'What if he will not play?' I said to Mr Rune. 'Have you thought about that? What if he does not want to be what he is? And hang about here, if he is a heavy-metal fan, maybe he has already gone over to the dark side. I am sure I read that this heavy-metal lot eat their own young and sacrifice spaniels to Satan.'

'That's a popular myth put about by Christian Fundamentalists,' said Mr Rune, 'who are in fact in league with the Dark One themselves. Heavy metal is a force for good.'

I shrugged and snaffled away some bacon from Mr Rune's plate. 'Heavy metal is too loud for me,' I said. 'I prefer soul. Are you sure you have got this right? Would Christ's descendant not prefer soul music also? It is *soul*, after all, is it not?'

'No,' said Mr Rune. 'It is metal. I am Hugo Rune. I think, therefore I'm right.'

'And you know the identity of this chap? You can pick him out of a crowd? I think you will find that they all look the same. Long hair and black T-shirts. The girls look rather special, though. I've seen them.'

'I do *not* know his identity,' said Mr Rune. 'I have no way of gaining it from the Chronovision.'

'I tell you what,' I said. 'Being out together at the same time is not a good idea. One of us should always be at the flat, guarding the Chronovision, prepared to smash it to pieces should Count Otto appear through the floorboards in his bathyscaphe.'

'Which is why I never leave you alone there,' said Mr Rune, who, having finished his second breakfast, was now rising from his chair, 'in case a rat runs beneath the floorboards and you locate a hammer.'

'But he will find us eventually. I bet he has spies everywhere.'

'Have no doubt of that. But for now, follow me – we're going shopping.'

'For a new suit?' I said, as we left Georgio's Bistro once

more without paying the bill. 'I do miss my tweeds. Do you know a good tailor around here?'

'Our finances do not run to a tailor,' said Mr Rune, making good progress up George Street.

'But you never pay,' I said, mincing after him.

'We will find you something in one of these charity shops. Something short and in leather. We can't have you looking out of place at Rock Night.'

Now, I do have to say, I looked pretty damn good, and that I *am* saying myself. Mr Rune found me a remarkable ensemble, not leather but black PVC, bra, mini-skirt and matching stiletto thigh-high boots. And all for a fiver at the Sussex Beacon, a George Street charity shop. I wondered about those boots, though, very big for a girl. But Mr Rune actually *paid* for the outfit. Which somehow made it rather more special.

I posed in front of the crazed bathroom mirror, the only mirror in the flat. God, if I had not known that was *me*, I would have fancied me *myself*. Mr Rune had had me dye my hair black and whiten up my face somewhat and put on lots of eye make-up and lots and lots of lipstick. And we had stuffed the bra with scrunched-up *Leader* and I tottered up and down, getting the hang of my heels.

Now, do not get me wrong here, in case you were thinking that I was enjoying this, being tarted-up like a lady of the night. I was not getting some kind of vicarious thrill from this. I was being a professional. I was helping Mr Rune. And I was protecting myself from recognition.

But I *did* look *hot*.

'I reckon I will pull tonight,' I said. And then I rethought what I had said and did not say anything else for a while. But I continued to practise upon my heels.

And then I went to wait in the front room, because Mr Rune wanted to use the bathroom.

I tottered about in the front room, where the Chrono-vision stood on its crate in the corner. I really, truly wondered how it worked. It did not have an aerial, for one thing, and it looked just like a down-to-earth 1950s Bakelite television set.

Television sets have always puzzled me. Well, at least the invention of them has. According to history, a Scotsman named John Yogi Bear invented the television set. All on his own. He pieced it together and plugged it in and turned it on. But think about this: there was nothing for him to watch on it, was there? He had invented the first television set but there were no television stations broadcasting programmes. So how did he know that it worked? And even if he did know, somehow, what was the point of it when there were no programmes?

It must have been like inventing the first telephone and then discovering that there was no one you could call up on the phone to boast about it to.

It made no sense to me. And in all the truth that there is, it still makes no sense!

At length, Mr Rune appeared in the front room.

'Where did you get all *that*?' I asked, for he looked simply splendid.

He sported a broad-shouldered long black leather coat that reached almost to the ground, leather biker boots, leather trousers, a leather waistcoat and a leather hat.

'You do not need to know how I acquired these items,' said he. 'Just trust me: in the future, *all* heroes will dress like this.'

'I want to dress like that *too*,' I said. 'It looks, well, it looks . . . cool.'

'You look "cool" in your own special way,' said Mr Rune to me. 'Now let us away to Rock Night,' and he added, '*Bitch*.'

PART II

Mr Rune strode along Church Road, swinging his stout stick before him, and I took joy in this, although I am not certain why. He brought down a cleric who was riding past on his bike and I took some joy in this also. But Rock Night was not due to start until ten and it was only eight of the evening clock.

'We will stop in here to partake of alcoholic beverages,' said Mr Rune, pointing with his stick towards an alehouse we were approaching.

The alehouse was The Albion, and it was as rough as they come.

'In you go, bitch,' said Mr Rune. 'The first round is on you.'

'Stop calling me that,' I said as I pressed open the saloon-bar door of The Albion. 'It is not big and nor is it clever.'

There was a pre-Rock Night crowd taking ale in The Albion – a whole lot of men in black (who had nothing to do with aliens or the CIA) and a whole lot of girlies looking gorgeous. It was a fair old pre-Rock Night crowd, but I did not have to elbow my way to the counter. The crowd sort of parted before me.

Behind the counter stood a fellow clad head to toe in leather. He was all chains and straps and belts with one of those gimp headpieces with the zip-up eyeholes and the zip-up mouth hole, too.

'Gmmph mmph mmph,' he said to us.

'Perhaps you should unzip your mouth hole,' I suggested to him.

'Mmph?' said the gimpish barkeep.

'And your ear holes also.'

Zips were unzipped. 'Can I help you, sir and madam?' he said.

'I know that voice,' I said. And I did. 'Fangio, is it *you*?'

Fangio removed his gimp headpiece. 'I'm sweating like a *Blue Peter* presenter in this,' he said. 'And helloooo to you.'

'It is *me*, Fange,' I said.

'I don't think we've been introduced,' said Fangio. 'My name is Malcolm. Might I call you bitch?'

'No, you might *not*,' I said. 'Malcolm?' I said.

'It's a suave name, Malcolm,' said Fange. And he looked at me closely.

'Not *that* close,' I said, backing away.

'Are they your own bosoms?' said Fangio.

'No, I am wearing them in for a friend.'

'Rizla, is that *you*?'

'It *is*,' I said. 'I am in disguise.'

'I didn't notice,' said Fange. 'What are you supposed to be? Let me guess. A fireman, is it? Or a Presbyterian?'

'Two pints of your finest ale,' said I. 'And it is very good to see you again.'

'Two pints of Old Daughter-Slaughter coming up,' said Fangio. 'Is that your own navel, by the way?'

'Just pull the pints.'

'Great coat, Mister Rune,' said Fangio as he presented our pints to us. 'And it's very good to see you again. I no longer have my bar at Grand Parade – it burned down when the fire spread from your rooms – but happily I was able to save the accounts book. Would you care to settle up what you owe me? I think I might take an early retirement.'

Mr Rune sipped at his pint. 'Put this upon my *new* account,' said he, 'as this will now be my new local.'

Fangio made groaning sounds. 'Are those your *real* legs?' he asked me.

'I am in disguise, I told you. We are here on what must be our all-but-final case or conundrum. I am undercover, like Lazlo Woodbine.'

'He was in here earlier,' said Fangio, 'wearing a tweed jacket and a trilby hat. I didn't recognise him at first. Thought he was a newspaper reporter.'

'No,' I said, 'he was *not* in here earlier. Lazlo Woodbine does not exist – he is a fictional character.'

'He said that people are always saying that about him. He left me his business card.'

'Show it to me,' I said.

'I mislaid it,' said Fangio. 'But he *was* in. Said he was on a case, the biggest of his life.'

'Stuff and nonsense,' I said. 'Do you have any complimentary peanuts or chewing fat?'

'Only loaves and fishes,' said Fangio.

'Loaves and fishes?' I said. 'As in—'

Mr Rune shushed me to silence. 'Why only loaves and fishes?' he asked the leather-bound barkeep.

'Funny thing,' said Fangio. 'This fellow was in here earlier – heavy-metal fan, long hair, beard, black T-shirt – and he asked for something to eat. But the van didn't turn up today and the freezer and the fryer are empty. And there were all these other punters in here too and they all wanted something to eat. And they ate all my crisps and were still hungry. And then this other fellow came in, who was wearing a tweed jacket and a trilby hat and I thought he must be a newspaper reporter, but he wasn't, he was—'

'About the loaves and fishes,' I said.

'I'm coming to that. The fellow in the tweed jacket ordered a bottle of Bud and put down his bag of sandwiches on the bar – sardine sandwiches, they were. Then he went out to the toilet. And while he was out there, the other fellow, the one with the long hair, and the beard, and the black T-shirt, he took this bag of sandwiches and offered it around the bar, to everyone who was hungry. And they all took a sandwich. All of them. And that's dozens of sandwiches, right? But after that, the fellow with the long hair, and the beard, and the black T-shirt put the sandwich bag back on the bar. And damn me if the sardine sandwiches weren't still in it. And then he left the bar. How did he do that, eh?'

'Perhaps he just walked out of the door,' I said.

'I *mean*,' said Fangio, 'how did everyone eat sandwiches, but the sandwiches were still in the bag? Is it voodoo, do you think? Or was he Paul Daniels?'

'And then did this "Lazlo Woodbine" eat the sardine sandwiches?'

'Don't talk silly,' said Fangio. 'Lazlo Woodbine doesn't eat sardine sandwiches. He only eats hot pastrami on rye.'

'There is a degree of truth to this tale,' I said.

'I have the sardine sandwiches here in the bag to prove it,' said Fangio.

'I'd like to take a look at those sandwiches,' said Mr Rune.

And whilst Mr Rune dined upon sardines on bread, I gazed about the bar. Now, just how possible was *this*? I wondered. That not only the last man in the bloodline of Jesus Christ, *but also* Lazlo Woodbine had both been in this bar today?

I have to confess that it did not seem all *that* likely.

Well, at least not the Woodbine bit.

'Ah,' said Fangio. 'Here's his card. I knew I had it somewhere. It was in my codpiece all the time.'

'Just hold it up for me,' I said, 'and let me read it.'

Lazlo Woodbine

Private Eye

Well, you could not argue with *that*!

Presently we had done with our pints, so Mr Rune ordered more. And soon we were done with those, too.

'We are nearing the end of our quest,' said Mr Rune to me. 'Soon, I feel certain, all will be resolved. This Lazlo Woodbine development is interesting, however.'

'Fangio is pulling our legs,' said I. 'Lazlo Woodbine does not exist. He is only a fictional character.'

'Just someone you read about in books,' said Mr Rune.

'Exactly.'

'A little like Jesus, then?'

'Nothing like Jesus at all,' said I.

'But Lazlo Woodbine is real to you.'

'He is real inside the books, but not outside them.'

'And who is to say, then, who is real?' said Mr Rune. 'You and I might just be characters in a book.'

'That is absurd,' I said. 'And if it were true, who is reading about us now?'

'Perhaps a character in someone else's book. Who is in turn just a character in someone else's book. And so on, ad infinitum.'

'Stop,' I said. 'You are scaring me.'

'It was only a thought,' said Mr Rune. 'Such thoughts occasionally cross my mind.'

'What time is it?' I asked.

Mr Rune perused his wristlet watch. A Cartier, I felt certain, and one I had not seen before.

'It is ten,' said Hugo Rune. 'We must be away to the ball.' And he whispered words into Fangio's ear and we went off to the ball.

I really liked the inside of Hove Town Hall. It was architecture in the public-utility style. It was unpretentious. It did not make any bones. It said, 'I am a modern town-hall interior, love me, or love me not.'

Well, I did not *love* it, but I *liked* it, with its horrible carpets, the dreadful paintwork, the appalling lighting. The upstairs bar was amazing, though – there were twelve bar staff behind the jump, which made me think of the twelve-bar blues and also of Robert Johnson.

The Rock-Night crowd was a-swelling and a-swelling, but we had no problem getting served.

And there was something else that I think I should mention in passing. And this was the Rock-Night crowd's attitude to Mr Rune. When we entered the town hall we had to pay, although we got a laminated 'club card'. But it was there at the door that the whispering began. I heard the door supervisors whisper to the fellows on the desk. They whispered, 'It *is* him,' when we walked up the stairs and into the upstairs bar.

'What is all this whispering?' I said to Mr Rune. 'What is all this "It *is* him" stuff as you walk by?'

'I am revered,' said Mr Rune, modestly, 'These are *my* people.'

'*Your* people? How?'

'*The Book of Ultimate Truths*,' said Mr Rune, 'has thus far

338

only achieved what you might describe as "cult status".
Naturally it will go on in the future to become much more
than that. But here, Rizla, you are amongst my readers.'

'You mean *we're* characters in what *they* read?'

'That is *not* what I mean.' Mr Rune inclined his great
head towards what I can only describe as an absolute babe,
who approached him with a beer mat and a Biro.

'Might I have your autograph, Master?' she asked.

And Mr Rune obliged.

'Absurd,' I said. 'This is all absurd. And *I* say so.'

'You could always bathe in my reflected glory,' said Mr
Rune. 'As my acolyte, there'd be sex in it for you. That
young chap looks interested.'

'I do not want to have sex with chaps!' I declared.

'That young lesbian—'

'Now *there* is a thought,' I said.

But it was not really, truly a thought, for I have never
been a lady's man. I am a sensitive fellow, me. I want a
relationship. I know that sounds a bit wimpy, but that is
the way I am. I do *not* do casual sex. I do not think I *could* do
casual sex.

Although.

'Are you sure she is a lessa?' I asked Mr Rune.

'Trust me,' said Mr Rune. 'I'm—'

'I am going to the bar.'

I got served at once. Six young barmen were keen to oblige.

'Two pints of whatever you have that is best,' I said.

'That would be Old Back-Masker,' said the most eager
barman, but I did not hear him properly because beyond the
bar in the town hall's ballroom proper, the DJ who was
hosting the night put on the evening's first music.

It was what I now know to be the greatest rock record
ever made.

Motorhead's 'The Ace of Spades'.

Now, I know what you are thinking: you are thinking
that if this really was the 1960s, then there is no way we
could have heard 'The Ace of Spades' being played at a

disco. That is what you are thinking, right? Well, wrong to you, because I *did* hear it. *I* was there. And to be fair, I had already met Robert Johnson. And *he* died in 1938.

So there!

And let us not forget the Chevalier Effect. It all makes perfect sense really.

The DJ's name was Tim McGregor, an ample Scotsman, large of beard and hair. And as chance, coincidence or bloodlines would have it, Tim was a direct descendant of Rob Roy McGregor, the man who invented croquet. Small world, eh?

Tim cried words into his microphone and down upon the dance floor beneath the stage and his decks, head-banging was all the rage and there was certainly good rockin' that night.

'It's hard to believe that Lemmy once played with Hawk-wind,' said Mr Rune to me. 'And with Sam Gopal – he was lead singer on '*Escalator*', which was something of a garage-psych classic.'

'Stop it,' I said. 'Have a word with yourself, please.'

'Quite so,' said Mr Rune to me, as I handed him his pint of Old Back-Masker, which I hadn't had to pay for, as the barman fancied me. 'Although this may be God's own music, we are here upon God's own mission, and we must find His son's last descendant amongst this swarthy crew.'

'Perhaps if you shouted out that you were *really* hungry, he might turn up with a bottomless packet of crisps?'

'I do believe that you still harbour one or two doubts.'

'Only trying to defend my sanity. I know I will lose in the end.'

'That large Sapphist with the moustache over there has taken quite a shine to you.'

'Stop it!' I said. 'I am *your* bitch, do you not remember?'

And Mr Rune laughed, and I laughed, so something must have been funny somewhere.

'I will miss you,' said Mr Rune, 'when all this is over.' And he patted me upon the shoulder.

'You have very cold hands,' I said. 'I wish I had kept my coat on.'

'You look adorable,' said Mr Rune. 'But he is here somewhere, and we must find him.'

'They all look the same to me,' I said. 'How will we know which one is *him*?'

'We will know,' said Mr Rune. 'We will know.'

Tim McGregor put on 'Killers' by Iron Maiden.

'That wouldn't have been my second record,' said Mr Rune. 'I would have probably gone for "Mouth For War" by Pantera or "Heart of Darkness" by Arch Enemy.'

'Or you might have chosen Slayer's "Raining Blood". It is a classic. Or possibly even Widowmaker's "Eat Everybody",' I said, as if I knew what I was talking about. Which I did not.

'And if Fangio were here, you might well have got nearly two pages out of such a conversation. However.' And Mr Rune went off to the gents.

I stood at the bar and leaned upon it, too, and sipped at my pint of Old Back-Masker.

A fellow with a somewhat lived-in face sidled up to me. He had long black hair and a bit of a beard and a black and tatty T-shirt, too, so he fitted in quite well with the rest of the throng. There was a certain twang of the brewer's craft surrounding him and it was clear to me that here was a chap who was not unacquainted with the pleasures of the pot room. He introduced himself to me as being Tobes de Valois.

And this he did between great belchings and hiccups.

'Are you here on your own?' asked Tobes as he swayed about before me.

'I am looking for someone,' I said, 'but *you* it is not.'

'It might be,' said Tobes. And he tried hard to focus his eyes in my general direction.

'I am informed that I will know who it is when I see them,' I said.

'I'll bet that makes sense,' said Tobes, 'but not to me.'

'Please go away *now*,' I said. Politely.

'If you fancy a bunk-up, I'm sure I could almost manage it. And if I can't, well, look on the bright side – I won't even remember it in the morning.'

It must be *so* much fun being a woman, I told myself.

'Are those your own titties?' asked Tobes. 'Only they don't look too convincing.'

'What?' I said.

'Nothing wrong with transvestism,' said Tobes, 'as long as you keep your dignity.' And then he fell down and I stepped over him. And Mr Rune returned from the gents'.

'You'll never guess who I just met in there,' said Mr Rune. 'Captain Bartholomew Moulsecoomb – he's guest bog troll for the night. Something of a cult hero amongst the heavy-metal crowd.'

'I thought pirates were more a New Romantic thing,'* I said.

'He quit the employ of Count Otto Black. Said he got fed up with having to feed all those animals. Especially the spaniels. The rest of his mutinous crew stayed on, though.'

'Any sign of God's great-great-great-great-grandson?'

'None,' said Mr Rune. 'What of you?'

'Well, I have just had a very interesting conversation with a chap called Tobes, but other than that, nothing.'

'He will be here,' said Mr Rune. 'He *is* here, somewhere.'

'Then I hope we find him soon. This music is giving me a headache. What is the DJ playing now?'

'Carcass,' said Mr Rune. 'Track three from their *Reek of Putrification* album.'

'Let us go home,' I said to Mr Rune.

'No, no, no,' said Mr Rune, and he waggled a porky digit at me.

'We should have asked Fangio for a more precise description,' I said. 'Distinguishing marks and scars, tattoos and whatnots. A proper detective would have done that.'

'Are you implying that I am an *improper* detective?' Mr

---

* Don't even think about saying it!

Rune raised that hairless eyebrow which I had come to know so well.

'It could be anyone here,' I said. 'It could even be *him*.' And I pointed down at the prone form of Tobes de Valois.

Tobes de Valois belched in his slumbers.

'Or him,' and I pointed towards a tall, imposing fellow who was striding our way. He was dressed all in black, with long black hair and one of those natty goatee beards that I had so far failed to grow to any convincing degree – although it had been getting pretty good before Mr Rune made me shave it off to disguise myself as a girlie.

The crowd seemed to part before the onward stride of the tall, imposing figure. He raised his hand as if in benediction and smiled benignly, too.

'I bet *that's* him,' I said to Mr Rune. 'Should I complain of a bunion and see if he offers to heal me?'

'Most amusing.'

'I am sorry,' I said. 'It is probably nerves. I really need the toilet now and I am not too certain about whether I should go to the gents' or the ladies'.'

'Stay here,' said Mr Rune. And he stepped forward to bid a hello to the tall, imposing figure and engage him in conversation.

And I heard the imposing figure say, 'They call me the Wiseman of Withdean.'

I crossed my shapely legs and perused the bottom of my empty glass.

'Another of the same, gorgeous?' asked the nearest barman.

'Yes, indeed,' I said and I ran my tongue around my lips in a manner that I had once seen Marilyn Monroe do in a movie on TV. I was about to ask Mr Rune whether he would care for another beer, but I saw him being steered away through the crowd by the tall, imposing figure, stepping over Tobes as they went on their way. They were making, it seemed, towards the fire exit.

'And I do not get an invite,' I said. 'Typical.'

343

And then Tobes de Valois lurched to his feet. 'Whoa,' he went. 'That was horrible. Felt as if someone just walked over my grave.' And he dusted himself down and ordered a pint from the bar.

'I think you have had enough,' I said to him.

Tobes glanced me up and down, mostly down, and winked lewdly. 'I'll be fine,' he said. 'I can drink until I pass right out, then sleep for less than five minutes and I'm stone-cold sober again.'

'This is quite a talent,' I said 'I wish *I* could do that.'

'I'm sure you can do a lot of other things. Are you with the lady-boys of Bangkok?'

'Actually, I am in disguise,' I said, as I sipped at the new free pint that had been given to me. 'And yes, I *am* a chap, although so far *you* are the only person who has discovered this. *And* you did it while you were drunk. What gave me away? Is it the bosoms?'

'Nah,' and Tobes shook his head. His hair looked somewhat nitty. 'I just have a knack for that sort of thing. I can tell if people are telling the truth or not, and whether they are good or bad. I get feelings, you know what I mean?'

'Not really,' I said. 'Am I good or bad, by the way.'

Tobes stared me up and down once more. Mostly up, this time.

'Good,' said Tobes. 'But there's something odd, as if you don't know who you really are, or something.' And he applied himself to his pint.

'Remarkable,' I said. 'You should go on the stage, or something.'

Tobes shrugged and raised his glass once more.

And as he did so, the shadow of his arm passed across a girl with long dark hair and long white legs, who leaned upon the bar, sipping a mineral water.

Which she suddenly spat on the floor.

'Ow did *that* 'appen?' she went, and started to cough.

I patted her gently on the back – which you can do to a strange girl if you are a girl yourself. 'Are you ill?' I asked. 'Can I help?'

'I'm fine,' said the girl. 'It's just me water. It *was* water, then suddenly it wasn't. It tastes like wine now.'

I took the glass from her hand and sniffed at it.

And it certainly smelled like wine.

It smelled like that really expensive vintage Mulholland Chardonnay that Mr Rune had once ordered for us in a restaurant that we never went to again.

I looked at the glass. And then I looked at Tobes.

'Oh my god!' I went. 'I mean, oh my God, sir. It is you, it is you.'

'It's me,' said Tobes and he raised his glass, but finding it empty, ordered another beer.

'I mean that it is *you*.' And I got a real shake on. 'Water into wine. Knowing good people from bad. Becoming sober in five minutes flat. You are The One – the One that Mister Rune seeks.'

'Rune?' said Tobes. 'Hugo Rune? I've read his book.'

'He was just here,' I said. And I really *was* a-tremble. 'But he left with . . . *Oh no!*'

'Do you mean Yoko Ono – John Lennon's bird?' asked Tobes.

'No,' I cried. 'It is that "oh no!" feeling you just had, that felt like someone walking over your grave. Mister Rune is in danger. Come with me, quickly.'

'I'll just finish this new beer,' said Tobes. 'Ah, that's better. So where do you want me to go?'

'To the fire exit,' I shouted.

'How exciting.' And Tobes stumbled after me.

'You are drunk again,' I said as I dragged him through the crowd.

'It's this Old Back-Masker,' slurred Tobes. 'I'm fine with wine. I can drink bottles and bottles. Must be something in the blood.'

We reached the fire exit and I pushed open the door. Beyond it was an iron staircase leading down to an alley.

'Mister Rune!' I shouted. 'Mister Rune, where are you?'

And then I heard it. A terrible sound. The terrible sound of a gunshot. I raced down the stairs with Tobes a-bumbling after me. And there ahead I saw him, sprawled in the dirt. And I saw the other man, too – the tall imposing figure, lounging on the bonnet of an evil-looking black car and smiling down at the body of Mr Rune, a smoking pistol in his hand. And then he reached to his head and drew off a full-face mask and threw it aside. And it was him, of that there was no doubt at all. The evil Count Otto Black.

'Go back inside, young woman,' he shouted. 'There's nothing for you to see here. Just disposing of some rubbish.' And he turned away and got into the car, which tore off at great speed.

'Oh no!' I cried. 'Oh no no no.' And I rushed to the body of Mr Hugo Rune, which was not easy in heels.

He lay flat upon his back, his stout stick at his side. I put my ear to that big chest of his, but Hugo Rune breathed not.

'Come on,' I said. 'Do not do this to me again.' And I shook at his leather lapels. 'I know you are faking it. Wake up now, this is not funny.'

Tobes peered over my shoulder and pointed with a grubby mitt. 'I think he's dead,' said Tobes to me. 'I really think he's dead.'

'He cannot be,' and I shook once more at the lapels.

'He can,' said Tobes. 'And he is.'

I looked up at Tobes and made a bitter face. 'How can you be sure?' I asked.

'Because I know these things,' said Tobes, sadly, 'just as I know good people from bad. But even if I didn't have a natural intuition for such things, I can't help feeling that the big gunshot hole in Mister Rune's forehead might just give it away. God, I'm pissed.'

And Tobes passed out and fell in a heap by the corpse of Hugo Rune.

PART III

I stared at the corpse of Hugo Rune, and the big bullet hole in his forehead. And I went, 'Wah!' and my hands flapped, and I span around in small circles.

It was over. It was all over. He really was dead this time.

'Do something! Do something!' I stopped flapping and spinning. 'What can I do? What can I do?' I flapped some more and span some more. Then caught my head on something or other and fell on top of Tobes.

And, 'You!' I shouted. And struck at him. 'You do something! You can do something!'

'Oh!' went Tobes, returning to consciousness. 'Not here, love, let's go back to my place. Oh, it's *you* – get off me please.'

'You have to do something.' I scrambled up and gave Tobes a kick. 'You have to bring him back to life.'

'Do *what*? And stop kicking me.'

'Bring Mr Rune back from the dead.' I dragged Tobes to his feet. 'Go on, do it.'

'Have you gone completely insane?'

'No. You *can* do it. You *can*. You are Him, the One that Mister Rune sought, the last of your line. You have the powers.'

'Get off me,' said Tobes and he pushed me away. 'I'm really sorry about Mister Rune. I wanted to meet him – there are some things in his book that don't make a lot of sense to me – but *I* can't bring him back to life. Who do you think I am?'

'The last living descendant of Jesus Christ.'

Tobes looked at me.

And I looked at Tobes.

'Piss off!' said Tobes, which was not very Christ-like.

'You *are*,' I said. 'You turned that girlie's water into wine. You *can* do it. You *must* do it.'

'I can't and I won't. I have to return to the bar now – I have a real thirst on me.'

347

'Do it!' I said. 'Or I swear that you will never leave this alleyway alive.'

Now, looking back, that probably was not the best thing to say to the last man in the bloodline of Jesus.

'I know Dimac,' said Tobes, and he raised one of his hands and made foolish gestures.

'I know it, too,' I said. 'Mister Rune taught it to me.[*] Take one step towards the staircase and I will break your right hand off and ram it up your bum.'

'Couldn't we just talk about this?' said Tobes. 'Back at the bar?'

'Mister Rune is lying dead,' I said, 'and he will catch his death of cold if he lies there much longer. Bring him back to life and do it *now*.'

'I can't,' wailed Tobes and he wrung his hands.

'Then from this day forth the world will know you as "stumpy".'

And I reached forward.

And Tobes shrieked, 'No, all right. I'll try.'

I stood there. In that alleyway. In the bitter cold. I hugged at my naked arms and my thigh-high-booted knees knocked together.

Tobes knelt over the body of Mr Rune.

'Abracadabra,' he went. 'Come back to life. Shazam.'

'Do it properly.'

Tobes looked up at me with bitterness. 'And how *is* it done, *properly*?'

'Lay your hands on him. Pray or something.'

'This is ridiculous.'

'Do it!' I made knuckle-clicking sounds. Which hurt my knuckles somewhat. Tobes laid his hands on the body of Mr Rune and prayed.

'Now I lay me down to sleep. I pray the Lord my soul to keep,' prayed Tobes.

---

[*] Which he *did*. Although I have not mentioned it before. But I *am* mentioning it now.

I looked over his shoulder. But Mr Rune was still as dead as he could be.

'It doesn't work,' said Tobes. 'I'm not who you think I am. I'm just a bloke. I can't work miracles.'

I leaned down and whispered words into the ear of Tobes. These words described to Tobes in graphic detail *exactly* what I would do to him should he fail in his allotted task. So horrendous were these threatened tortures that crucifixion would have been little more than a Sunday-School picnic in comparison.

'Awake from the dead!' cried Tobes. 'Return to life.'

And there came a drumming-humming sound that caused my ears to pop. And then a light so pure and white that I had to shield my eyes.

And when the noise had died away and the brightness was all gone, I opened my eyes, and I looked down, and Tobes was there, but Hugo Rune had vanished.

'He has gone.' I pointed. 'What happened? Where has he gone?'

'Dunno,' said Tobes. 'Did you see a real bright light?'

'You did it wrong.' I kicked at Tobes. 'You sent him off to Heaven or something. You are in trouble now.'

And I prepared to beat the Holy bejaysus out of the great and many, many times great-great-grandson of God.

'I wouldn't do that,' said a voice that I knew. The voice of Mr Hugo Rune. And I turned and there he was, big and bald and breathing and hole-less in the forehead.

'Praise the Lord!' I cried. 'Oh, by Crimbo, praise the Lord.'

'I feel that we should both do that.' And Mr Rune sank to his knees.

12

The Concluding Chaotic
Conundrum Of
The Coldean Cat

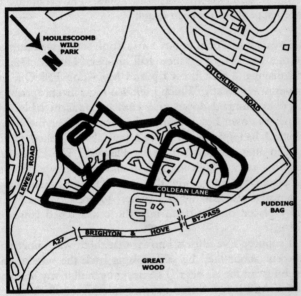

The Coldean Cat

PART I

We knelt in the icy alleyway and bowed our heads before
Tobes, the man who had brought Mr Rune back from the
dead. The last of the bloodline of Christ.

'Thank you,' I said and I raised my head. 'Thank you, sir,
for that.'

Tobes looked most embarrassed. He obviously did not

take too much to us kneeling there before him. Although I am reasonably sure he preferred it to me kicking him.

'Get up,' said Tobes. 'It wasn't *me*. Something weird just happened, but I didn't do it.'

'You did,' said Mr Rune, now raising *his* head, 'and my eternal thanks to you. And if you will return with us now to our rooms in St Aubyns, I will show you something that will explain everything.'

'I'm returning to the bar,' said Tobes. 'This would never have happened if I'd been drunk.'

We owed it to Tobes to buy him a drink and so we returned to the bar. In the dance hall proper, Tim McGregor was playing 'I Got the Clap and My Knob Fell Off' by Lawnmower Death. Which I felt was most inappropriate.

Tobes slumped down in a chair at a vacant table. Mr Rune sat down beside him and I brought over the beers, which I had gained for free. I must have looked pretty raddled after my sojourn to the alleyway. The knees had gone out of my thigh-high boots and my hair was all over the place. It is funny how that look really gets men going, is it not? I also had whisky chasers to go with our beers, and I placed one of these into the outstretched hands of Tobes.

'I suppose I've always known that there was something different about me,' he said, tossing back the whisky and reaching out for his beer. 'I've never been ill in my life, you know. And weird things happen around me all the time. Crips* leaping out of their wheelchairs in Lidl when I pass them by on my way to the off-licence section. Which is why I get drunk all the time – it drives me nuts.'

'And why you wake up sober five minutes later,' I said.

Tobes hung his head. He had finished his beer. I offered him mine and he took it. 'That man,' said Tobes, 'who stepped over me, who shot you in the alleyway – that man is pure evil.'

---

* I know. But if *He* says it – well, it must be okay, mustn't it?

'Count Otto Black,' said Hugo Rune. 'And I walked right into his trap.'

'How could he know,' I asked, 'that you would be searching for the Lord Tobes here?'

'Don't call me *that*,' said Tobes. And he downed Mr Rune's Scotch, which I found most amusing.

'I am sure he would have searched our rooms at forty-nine Grand Parade before he torched them,' said Mr Rune. 'He would have found the map of the Brightonomicon. He reasoned it out. I have to give him credit.'

'Perhaps then he has also located our present rooms and has taken the Chronovision.'

'I have no doubt of it,' said Mr Rune, 'for I gave him our address.'

'But you said to Lord Tobes in the alleyway—'

'He will have taken what he believes to be the Chronovision. I removed the real one this morning before you awoke and substituted a similar television that I'd purchased from the Sussex Beacon in George Street.'

'That sounds most unlikely,' I said.

'But nevertheless it is the case. And so I suggest that the three of us collect it now. And if it is convenient to you, Lord Tobes, might I ask that we return to your abode for the night?'

Lord Tobes did not answer this. For he was asleep once more.

I would have liked to have stayed a bit longer at Rock Night. I was rather warming to heavy metal. And all the free beers were not going amiss, either. But Mr Rune roused Lord Tobes and asked again if we might stay with him, and him being as nice a fellow as he was, he said yes.

After we had downed a few more drinks.

Which we did, so I did get to stay a bit longer, after all.

And I had a dance, too. Several dances, all of them the head-banging dance that involved the fingering of invisible guitars. I got really into that dance. And I must have been pretty good at it, too, because a most appreciative audience of young black-T-shirted fellow-me-lads formed about me as I danced and I got even more free drinks.

'I can see that being a good-looking woman really does have its benefits,' I said to Mr Rune when I returned to our table once more, somewhat sweaty.

'Beware the balance of equipoise,' said Mr Rune. 'For every favour offered, one is expected in return.'

A handsome young stud dressed in the de rigueur black, who had earlier identified himself to me as Matty and joined me in dancing to some of the more frenzied numbers, came over to our table.

'Can I buy you a drink, Yola?' he asked.

'Yola?' said Mr Rune.

I shushed at him. 'If you have no objection to buying for my granddad and my brother also,' I said.

'Your *granddad*?' said Mr Rune.

I shushed him once more.

Matty made away to the bar and shortly returned, as I had requested that he did, in the company of a bottle of the house champagne.

And four glasses.

'I shall uncork the bubbly,' said Matty, popping the bottle.

'What is zis?' asked another fellow, giving Matty a bit of a push.

I looked up at this interruptive fellow. It was Mario, the waiter from Georgio's Bistro.

'Hello, Mario,' I said. 'Sit down with us, have a drink.'

'I turna my back,' said Mario, 'anda my betrothed, she go outa on da town, taking drinks from this gigolo.'

'I'm not a gigolo,' said Matty. 'I'm a computer programmer.'

'You are a son of a bitch!' And Mario thumbed his teeth, which judging by all the Mafia movies I had seen was not a very good sign.

'It is not what you think,' I said to Mario. 'Matty is only a friend.'

'But you said—' said Matty.

'What *did* you say?' said Mr Rune.

'She's my girlfriend, anyway,' said a very tall fellow called Solo, who I had met earlier, and who had also bought me a drink.

'Whose girlfriend are we talking about?' said Tim McGregor, who I had met while I was dancing on the stage and who had promised to buy me a drink when he was taking his half-time break.

'My fiancée,' said Mario, pointing at me.

'I am *not* his fiancée,' I said.

'But my papa, he pay the dowry money to your papa here.' And he pointed to Mr Rune.

'*What?*' I said rather loudly. And my loud '*What?*' awoke Tobes, who had nodded off again at some point.

'Whose round is it?' asked the great-times-whatever grandson of Christ.

'Yours, I think,' I said.

Tobes looked around. 'And who are all these people?' he asked.

'Well . . .' By this time there were quite a lot of people gathered around our table. A lot of *male* people, all in black T-shirts. 'Well, that is Dave, and that is Marcus, and that one is Neil—'

'Chris,' said Chris.

'Sorry, that one is Chris. That one is Neil.'

'You have a lot of friends,' said Tobes.

'Ah,' I said. And I looked all around at my newfound friends. There *were* lots of them. The only ones who had not bought me drinks were the ones who were presently on their way to do so and had just popped by our table to enquire what my preference was.

'And this nutter here,' said Matty, nudging at Mario with the champagne bottle, 'seems to think that Yola here,' and he gestured at me with the bottle, 'is his fiancée.'

'And I am *not*!' I said.

'Well, of course you're not,' said Tobes. 'You're not any bloke's fiancée.'

'Thank you,' I said.

355

'Because how could you be, seeing as *you* are a *bloke*.'

Now, it must have been at this precise moment that the stand-in DJ chose to change records, because there was a sudden silence. And I do not know whether you have ever heard the term 'the silence was deafening', but *this* was one of those moments. The silence was also a *pregnant* silence.

Pregnant with the promise of the premature birth of something very violent indeed.

Now, I do not know who hit whom first. I think Mario hit Matty. And I will bet that Matty would have hit him back if he had not been coming at me with the champagne bottle. Mario must have brought Matty down, because Marcus, who was also coming at me with a bottle of his own, this one being full of Guinness, fell over Matty and crashed down hard on our table, spilling drinks.

A fact that did not please Tobes.

Tobes, I think, hit Neil, or it might have been Chris. But it was certainly Dave who hit Solo and Solo was a very big chap and he just started hitting everybody.

Funny how these things spread: what begins as a localised brawl soon becomes widespread mayhem.

And as to *who* had the petrol bomb, or *why* they had it with them, I cannot say. But at that moment Mr Rune rose, taking Tobes by the arm, and I followed on in their wake.

The Sussex constabulary had a busy night. The mayhem spilled from the burning town hall and many shop windows were broken.

At a little after three of the new morning clock, Inspector Hector read the Riot Act through a loud-hailer atop the Sherman tank.[*] And the first of the tear-gas grenades were launched.

We watched a lot of it on TV at Tobes's house in Withdean, which we journeyed to in a cab that Mr Rune hailed.

---

[*] The one the Sussex constabulary use for making patrols around Whitehawk.

I will not go into details here regarding the fate of the taxi driver, but there was a stout stick involved. The ongoing riot was broadcast live from a news helicopter that circled over the war-torn streets of Hove. It all looked very exciting.

'What are we drinking now?' I shouted to Lord Tobes.

'Calvados,' Tobes shouted back. 'And don't call me Lord.'

'I did not.'

'You were thinking it.'

'Oh, look,' hollered Mr Rune, 'the rioters have set The Albion ablaze.'

'That is a shame,' I bawled. 'I hope Fangio is okay. Oh, look, there he is. What is he doing with that axe?'

'Looting the dry cleaners across the road,' thundered Mr Rune. 'They do have exceedingly good cameras on those newsreel helicopters, don't they?'

'Almost unbelievably good,' I screamed. 'As is this Calvados.'

'Enjoyable as all this is,' boomed Mr Rune, 'I think we should get down to business.'

'Lord Tobes has fallen asleep,' I yelled. 'Perhaps we should do it in the morning.'

Mr Rune agreed that perhaps we should. So we finished the Calvados. And the brandy and the cans of beer in Tobes's fridge. And a bottle of banana liqueur I eventually located beneath the kitchen sink, because there is always one somewhere if you are desperate enough to search for it and prepared to search long enough.

Then Mr Rune and I fell fast asleep in Lord Tobes's sitting room. Which I must explain about, because the reader might be wondering why all the shouting and hollering and bawling and booming and yelling had been going on. Tobes's sitting room was approximately the size of a football pitch and the chairs and the TV were positioned on opposite sides of it. When asked to explain how he had such an impossibly huge room within what was indeed a very small house, Tobes adequately explained that the estate agent had told him that the living room was 'deceptively spacious'.

So, that explains that.

Morning sunlight came in through the distant windows, but we did not heed its arrival. We slept in late. But to be fair, it had been a stressful night.

I got to yawning and opening my eyes somewhere around three p.m. Lord Tobes still snored, but of Mr Rune there was no sign to be seen.

However, there was a certain smell, and that was of frying bacon. I dragged myself from the sitting-room floor and shambled the considerable distance to the kitchen.

A naked man was cooking food. I knew him at once to be Barry, the chef from Eat Your Food Nude who had served his time at Grand Parade before leaving over some trifling matter, which involved his wages.

'Hello, Barry,' I said. 'What are *you* doing here?'

'Mister Rune called me earlier,' said Barry, 'said it was an emergency. He had me call in at a secret place and bring him a Bakelite television. And call in at Lidl for supplies.'

'But I thought you—'

'An emergency is an emergency,' said Barry. 'And I *am* a professional.'

Mr Rune breezed into the kitchen, tapping the morning's *Argus* against his leg.

'Sunny-side up, those eggs,' he said to Barry, 'and French toast all around. Did you get those da-bigga-da-sausages?'

'All is under control, Mister Rune,' said Barry.

I shook my head and sat myself down at the kitchen table.

'You will need to eat a hearty breakfast,' said Mr Rune, seating himself also, 'for today is the day.'

'The day for what?' I asked.

'The final day,' said Mr Rune. 'The last that you and I will spend together.'

'Oh,' I said, then, 'No, I do not want that to happen.'

'But nevertheless it will be so. One final conundrum, and

for you, I feel, in the great tradition of your fictional hero Lazlo Woodbine, a final rooftop confrontation.'

'Not with *this* hangover,' I said. 'And certainly not in these clothes.'

'The hangover will shortly pass, but I agree that it would be better that you end our adventures in a manly fashion. Barry here will give you a haircut and there are clothes for you hanging on the door there.'

I glanced towards the door. And there clothes hung: a three-piece suit of tweed, in a dry cleaner's plastic sheath.

'Fangio picked carefully during his looting,' said Mr Rune. 'If you recall, I whispered certain words into his ear before we left his bar to go to Hove Town Hall. These words were to the effect that should the unlikely occur – to whit, a bit of a riot – he should slip across the road and loot the dry cleaners and pick you out a suit.'

'But how . . .' But I did not bother to go any further with that. Instead, I took the suit and myself to Tobes's bathroom, showered, washed the make-up from my face, dried all nice and put on the three-piece suit. A shirt and some shoes would have been lovely, but beggars cannot be choosers.

Mr Rune rapped on the bathroom door. 'I have a shirt and a pair of shoes here. Hurry now or I will have to eat your breakfast.'

Dressed in this spiffing attire, I returned to the kitchen and sat down once again. 'Thanks for this,' I said to Mr Rune.

'Well,' said the All-Knowing One, 'I think we've had sufficient mileage out of you being dressed as a woman. Best to have you well turned out now that the end is near.'

'And it will end *today*?' I asked.

'The fourteenth of February. One year to the day since we first met.'

'February?' I asked. 'I thought it was still January.'

'I let you sleep in again,' said Mr Rune. 'You needed to regain your strength.'

I shook my head and opened my mouth to protest. But

just then Barry served up breakfast, so I used my mouth to set about that instead.

And we were more than three breakfasts in, and Barry had finished my hair cut, before Tobes appeared in the kitchen. 'Who drank my banana liqueur?' he asked. 'I was saving that for a special occasion. Like *now*, when there's no more booze left.'

'Rizla drank it,' said Mr Rune. 'On the first night we came here. Pray sit down and join us for breakfast.'

'There is a naked chef here,' said Tobes, observing Barry. 'Is that not illegal?'

'Best eat,' said Mr Rune. 'There's a busy day ahead.'

Tobes unearthed a bottle of home-made sloe gin from within the apparently hollowed-out kitchen toaster.

'That can't be right,' said Barry. 'I just cooked toast in that. How—'

'Do not even ask,' I told him. And we enjoyed sloe gin with our breakfast.

'We must sit before the Chronovision now,' said Mr Rune. 'There is much that you must see, Lord Tobes.'

Our breakfast finally concluded, Mr Rune dismissed Barry and handed him a bundle of large-denomination money notes.

I raised my eyebrows at this and the hairs stood up on my arms.

Mr Rune took Lord Tobes and me to the sitting room, explained to Lord Tobes the workings of the Chronovision – to whit, what it did rather than *how* it did it – then fiddled with the knobs and we sat down to watch.

And we saw it all in a sort of fast-forward, starting with the life and eventual natural death of Jesus, then continuing with the history of his subsequent bloodline. And as event after event unfolded, I saw it – what history actually was. What human life actually was. This series of seemingly random and disparate incidents, the losing of something trifling, which led to someone meeting someone. The decisions of small folk that affected the great. And how it all fitted together to move Mankind forward. Towards what?

Well, I could not say then and still cannot. The Chrono-vision showed only the past. The future was still to occur.

But I did see the point and Lord Tobes saw the point, too. And the point was so simple that it was almost obscene. There *is* purpose to it all. Our little lives *are* part of a greater something, and that something is what Mankind might become – *should* become – if all things work to the good.

But all things rarely work to the good. At least, they have not so far, because there has always been someone who will seek to use the world to his or her advantage. They crop up in every age, like a cancer. And Mr Rune and his kind, and the ancestors of Lord Tobes, do battle with them, unseen and unknown to the rest of us.

It is the stuff of which movies are made.

And it is sad, but true.

Which was a track by Metallica that I had quite liked at Rock Night.

When Mr Rune finally switched off the Chronovision and pulled its plug from the wall, Lord Tobes and I did not have anything to say to each other.

Each of us was alone with his thoughts.

Which is how, I suppose, we always are.

'Well,' said Lord Tobes, breaking the silence, 'I suppose then that there is nothing for it other than for the three of us to engage in battle against Count Otto Black.'

'Thank you,' said Mr Rune, and he nodded. 'I only wish that we had some vintage champagne to toast the success of this remarkable alliance.'

'I'm sure I can find some somewhere,' said Tobes.

And he did.

PART II

'About this battle,' I said to Mr Rune as I chugged down the champagne of Tobes in his preposterously huge sitting room, with us all sitting very close together. 'It will be one of those fight-to-the-death sort of jobbies, I assume.'

Mr Rune raised his glass to me.

'No chance of a truce, I suppose?'

'*Truce?*' went Mr Rune, and he spluttered champagne. 'That blackguard shot me dead last month.'

'It is the killing bit that I am not too keen on,' I said. 'Could we not get him arrested and committed to jail for life?'

'Perhaps you would care to turn him in yourself,' said Mr Rune, 'what with your Identikit picture up on the "wanted" board.'

'Ah, *that's* where I knew you from,' said Tobes. 'Knew I recognised your face from somewhere. You're the Lewes Road-Rage Maniac and the Grand Parade Firestarter (twisted firestarter).'

'The road-rage thing was not my fault,' I protested. 'Well, it was, but it also was not. And I never burned down Grand Parade.'

'I understand,' said Tobes, raising his hand as if in benediction. 'I am not judging you.'

'*You* could absolve me of my sins,' I said. 'In fact, *you* could work a little miracle and remove my face from the wanted posters.'

'I absolve you of your sins,' said Tobes. 'Go and sin no more.'

'And the other bit?'

'I thought I told you to sin no more. Get thee behind me, Rizla.'

'Sorry,' I said and I chugged further champagne.

'It has to be life or death,' said Mr Rune. 'There is no choice. Recall if you will the vision of a possible future that we experienced in Chief Whitehawk's tepee.'

'With the swearing chef and all those B-list celebrities?'

'And myself in cahoots with Count Otto Black. That must not come to pass.'

'All that sounds very familiar,' said Tobes.

'It does?' asked Mr Rune.

'It does. You see, I have these dreams. Very vivid, they are, and I think that they might be premonitions. Like, I'll dream that someone's cat will get run over and the next week it does.'

'Have you warned people, then?' I asked.

'I've thought about that,' said Tobes, 'but it doesn't make any sense. You see, if I was to dream of someone dying in a car crash, and it was a premonition, and so warned them and they didn't go out in their car, then they wouldn't be killed in a crash. Well, how could I have had a premonition about a car crash if the car crash wasn't going to happen? I wouldn't have had the dream in the first place, would I?'

'He does have a point there,' I said to Mr Rune.

'A rather dodgy one,' said Hugo Rune.

Tobes shrugged and finished the champagne. 'But what you were saying about a restaurant with B-list celebrities and a shouting chef – I had a dream about that a month or so back. In fact, you were in it, Mister Rune, chatting on a portable phone and selling film rights to Hollywood.'

I looked at Mr Rune.

And Mr Rune looked at me.

'And it was inside a tepee?' I asked.

'Oh, *that's* what it was. I thought it was a circus tent.'

'I am doomed,' said Mr Rune. 'Your dream came to us also, Lord Tobes. We witnessed it all.'

'Don't despair,' said Tobes, who rose from his chair and rootled about beneath its cushions. 'My dreams are not always correct. And some of them are frankly absurd. Why, only ten minutes ago I dreamed—'

'Stop,' I said. And Tobes stopped.

'Why am I stopping?' he asked.

'Because,' I said, 'we are forgetting one precious detail. Well, Mister Rune and myself are anyway. The Chronovision. In the vision of the future, the Chronovision was still extant, was it not?'

'It was,' said Mr Rune.

'Then surely all we have to do is smash it up now, right

now. Which was what we were originally intending to do with it, if I recall.'

'Good thinking, Rizla,' said Mr Rune. 'Without the Chronovision, that particular future cannot exist. Do you have a hammer in this house, Lord Tobes?'

'Ah,' said Tobes, and he fished about beneath his cushions. 'By happy coincidence, yes.'

I took the hammer from Tobes and took the long hike across the living-room floor to where the Chronovision stood. I knew that it had to be done, but it *did* seem such a shame to destroy something so miraculous. It made me feel as if I was the ultimate vandal.

'I hate to do this,' I said, 'especially as I could have found out who I really am if Mister Rune had only twiddled the dials for me. But I realise that it must be done. Wondrous as this instrument is, it could mean the ruination of Mankind if it fell into the hands of Count Otto Black. And so it must be destroyed.' And I raised the hammer.

And then I paused.

'Go on, then,' shouted Mr Rune, viewing me through his telescope. 'You know you really want to.'

'I was just wondering,' I shouted back, 'what if it explodes when I hit it? Perhaps we should give it a rock 'n' roll send-off and throw it out of the window instead.'

Mr Rune stroked his chin.

'I don't want you breaking my windows,' shouted Tobes. 'And anyway, I clearly recall that you were going to hit it with the hammer.'

'Recall?' I shouted.

'In the dream I just had ten minutes ago. The one I was going to tell you about, but you made me stop.'

'Eh?' I shouted, which is not as easy as you might think. 'You just dreamed that I was going to smash the Chronovision with this hammer?'

'Yes, that's what you *were* going to do. But like I said, I'm sure that not all my dreams can be correct, because this one was frankly absurd.'

'Perhaps you should tell us about it,' said Mr Rune.

'No,' said Tobes. 'You'd only laugh.'

'I'm sure we wouldn't.'

'You would,' said Tobes. 'Go on now,' he yelled at me. 'Take a swing at the Chronovision, get it over with.'

I raised my hammer.

'Not yet,' said Mr Rune. 'I beg you, Lord Tobes, speak to us of your dream.'

'Oh, all right.' Tobes sat down in the armchair, but as he had not replaced the cushion after rooting for the hammer, he sort of sunk into it, pranging his bum on a spring. 'Ouch,' he said. 'I should have recalled *that*, because *that* happened in the dream also.'

'Will you *please* tell us?' And Mr Rune wrung his big fat hands.

Tobes rose from the armchair and rubbed at his bum. 'Well,' he said, 'like I was saying . . . Yes, that's right, I'd just hurt my bottom, and then there was some chitchat – I was speaking, I think. And then you shouted for Rizla to smash the Chronovision. Then the absurd bit happened.'

'And the absurd bit *was* . . . ?' And Mr Rune leaned forward in his chair.

'A house,' said Tobes, 'like the sort of house that a child would draw – this house appeared, came right up through the floorboards. Damn near demolished *this* house, I can tell you. Gave me such a start that it woke me up.'

Now, even though Lord Tobes had not shouted, I had heard every word. Which was probably a miracle, but I could not say for sure. But—

I looked at Mr Rune.

And Mr Rune, in the distance, looked back at me.

And then from beneath our feet there came a rumble.

'Smash the Chronovision!' shouted Mr Rune. 'Smash the Chronovision now!'

'Yes, that's what you said,' said Tobes. 'And what *is* that God-awful rumbling?'

Great vibrations shuddered through the room and rolled across the mighty floor. China ducks fell from the walls, along with a painting of a crying child. Ornaments tumbled from the mantelpiece as the mighty floor began to rise.

'Smash it, Rizla!' roared Mr Rune.

I raised the hammer above my head, but I did not have time to swing it because suddenly I was borne aloft upon the room's carpet and broken floorboards and the roof of the rising bathyscaphe. I glimpsed the distant Mr Rune falling back and taking grip on his stout stick. But I did not see Tobes, though he must have been there somewhere.

Floorboards shivered and shattered. The sounds of destruction pounded my ears and brick dust filled my nostrils and throat. I clung to the now rooftop carpet as it rose up and up. And above me, growing closer by the second, was the living-room ceiling.

I tried to jump from the rising rooftop, but would you not know it, but the sleeve of my tweed jacket was snagged upon a nail. I scrunched up my shoulders and ducked my head and prepared myself for oblivion.

And then with a kind of rocking, grinding, halting kind of motion, there was a rock and a grind and things became motionless.

And I was . . . well . . . phew . . . about a mere three inches from oblivion. But still all snagged like a fish on a hook and somewhat covered in dust.

And then I heard new sounds beneath me – the sounds of a door being opened and sounds of manic laughter, too.

'Ho, ho, ho,' went these sounds of manic laughter. 'Excellent navigation, Mister Mate. It would have been your 'nads on a plate if you'd harmed the Chronovision. Now hurry along, man, fetch it in. A lively evening's viewing awaits us. Get a move on, you oaf!'

The voice was that of Count Otto Black.

The mate's name was Phil. And he said, 'Aye aye, Captain.'

There was a fumbling and bumbling beneath me, and sounds as of broken floorboards and of mashed-up fixtures and fittings being shifted. And then the mate gave a cry of, 'I have it, Captain. And unharmed it is.'

Followed by more sounds of manic laughter from the mouth of Count Otto Black.

'Do you want me to fish their bodies from the wreckage, Captain,' asked the mate, 'so that you can defile them in an unspeakable fashion, as the fancy takes you?'

'Tempting though that is, Mister Mate,' crowed the Count, 'I now have what I want. And what my God has in store for Rune's soul far out-grosses anything that I could seek to do with his body.' And then he laughed once more for good measure.

'Blackguard!' I thought. And I tried once more to release myself from the nail that I was snagged on, up on the roof of Count Otto's subterranean ark.

'Take us below, Mister Mate!' called the Count. And the door slammed shut upon them.

'Take us below – oh by Crimbo,' I whispered. 'I will be ground to oblivion.' And I wrestled once more with my snagged-up sleeve and received no joy in return. And suddenly the rocking, grinding and halting motion jerked into reverse and *The Bevendean Bathyscaphe* submerged.

'Oh by Crimbo, by Crimbo! By Crimbo!' I scrabbled about at the now-sinking rooftop, trying to free myself. And over the apex of the roof, two faces grinned at me.

'Mr Rune!' I went. 'Lord Tobes!'

'We both snagged our sleeves upon rooftop nails of this here ark,' said Tobes, 'and so were saved from being crushed to our deaths. Was *that* a miracle or what?'

I would have said something in reply, but it suddenly became very dark and I became greatly afeared. And I would probably have voiced my fears, probably something to the effect of, 'Get us out of here, Lord Tobes!' had I been able to make myself heard. But the sudden sound of whirling blades cleaving through the earth would have drowned out what I might have said, and so I did not say it.

So to speak.

And it certainly moved at a fair old lick, that subterranean ark. And on its rooftop we did not get mashed, but we did have to cling on tight. I do not know how long we travelled for, nor how fast, nor how far, but it was very scary and it did not smell too nice.

But suddenly we came to a halt. And with the suddenness of halting came a suddenness of light. Bright light. Bright light and whiteness, too. I looked up fearfully into the bright-light whiteness and saw that it was all-over tiles. We were inside a great domed structure composed of what seemed to be millions of tiles. Many tunnels ran away from this place and although it looked rather wonderful, it also smelled very bad.

Stretching my snagged arm to its limit, I dragged myself to the apex of the roof and there was joined by Mr Rune and Tobes, who were still similarly snagged. 'Where are we?' I asked Mr Rune.

'The cathedral,' said himself.

'The *what*?'

'The main chamber of the Brighton sewerage system. I visited it on one of their popular sewer tours during the Brighton Festival.'

'You did not take *me*,' I said.

'It must have been the day you went to see The Lady-Boys of Bangkok.'

'I never *did*,' I said. But I had done. 'But why are we *here*?' I asked, as I fanned at my nose from the pong.

'Don't you ever go to the cinema?' Mr Rune asked, dusting earth from his leather coat. 'Supervillains always have mountain lairs or inhabit the innards of extinct volcanoes. And how fitting *this* is for a sewer rat like Count Otto Black.' And Mr Rune chuckled. And then I shushed *him* into silence. From beneath us came sounds of the door being opened, and Count Otto's voice once more.

'Home again, home again, jiggedy jig,' the Count cackled. 'Bring that Chronovision, Mister Mate. And all the rest of you, me hearties – you've earned your rum tonight.'

I peeped down and beneath me saw the Count doing his foolish dance as he pranced along, followed by the pirates who had once sailed under Captain Moulsecoomb on *The*

Saucy Spaniel. They presently vanished into one of the many tunnels of the great sewer system.[*]

'It would be nice if we could climb down now,' said Mr Rune.

And as if at a magic word, the nails came away and we all tumbled down from the rooftop.

'Ouch,' I said. And so did Mr Rune. Tobes did silent chucklings.

'And so what now?' I asked of Mr Rune when he and I were on our feet and rubbing at our bruised parts.

Mr Rune had a firm hold upon his stout stick. 'Follow the villains,' said he.

'Well, yes,' I said, in a hesitating fashion. 'But actually I *do* go to the cinema as often as I can. And I *do* notice all the plot holes in the movies. *Now* would be the time to disable Count Otto's ark, to be on the safe side.'

'Exemplary thinking,' said Mr Rune. 'Lead on.'

I led on and did so with caution, for there might still have been some pirates on board.

Now, you have to picture this really, or it makes little sense. Picture, if you will, Noah's Ark. Everyone knows what Noah's Ark looks like. It is a big ship with a house on the top. Myself, Mr Rune and Tobes had been snagged on the roof of this house, and when we dropped down, we did so on to the deck of the ark. From this deck ran a lowered gangplank, by which Count Otto and his pirate crew had most recently taken their leave.

The only truly noticeable differences between Noah's Ark and the Count's was that the actual ship parts of the Count's were constructed from riveted steel and there was a hefty great revolving blade arrangement on the front that enabled it to dig through the ground. And it was nuclear powered, of course. Though I do not actually know what powered Noah's.

---

[*] Built in 1840 by the renowned engineer and mystic Isambard King-dom-Come and still reckoned to be one of the finest in England. Another triumph for Brighton.

Oh, and there were these big caterpillar-tracks beneath Count Otto's. Oh, and some rather dangerous-looking guns mounted on the forward part of the deck. Oh, and—

'Pacey-pacey, Rizla,' said Mr Rune, 'for surely as the quixotic seagull of haste besmirches the tart's handbag of time, so too does the spaniel of hesitance foul the footpath of destiny.'

Which I took in the way it was meant, I suppose, and pacey-paceyed along. With care.

We found ourselves first in the bar, of course, which brought great joy to Tobes. He took himself straight behind the counter and helped himself to a bottle of gin. We followed him and then I led the way below, although I do not really know why *I* was leading. I had no idea of where I was going. Although of course, it *had* been *my* idea, so I suppose that I should have done the leading.

Below was lit by bulkhead lights and looked like the inside of an ocean liner. Animal noises came to us and we soon found ourselves moving stealthily between countless cages.

'Damn me,' said Tobes, stopping at one. 'That's my cat, Coldean – I wondered where he'd gone.'

'*The Coldean Cat!*' I said. 'What a cop-out. That has to be the most tenuous link to the Brightonomicon ever. And half of the others have been pretty duff.'

'Which reminds me,' said Mr Rune, 'it seems like months since I've given you a badge.'

'It matters not,' I said. 'I have lost all the others.'

'Then you'd better have the full set.' And Mr Rune dug into his leather-coat pocket and brought out a handful of badges. He counted them into my hand. 'You didn't have these,' he said, counting in several, including one of a Morris Minor, the Saltdean Stallion. One of the Chrono-vision. Another with a gaudy representation of Jesus – 'For Lord Tobes here, the Wiseman of Withdean,' Mr Rune explained. And a final one with the portrait of Count Otto Black. 'Something for you to remember him by.'

'Well, thank you very much,' I said and I stuffed the

badges into my pocket. 'But the point of these badges has always been lost upon me. And *now* is hardly the time for such trinkets, surely?'

'Their time will come,' said Mr Rune. 'Now let us proceed.'

And so we proceeded, until . . .

'I think we are in the engine room,' I said. 'Does that, or does that *not*, look like a nuclear reactor to you?'

'It looks like *three* nuclear reactors to me,' said Tobes, and he giggled foolishly.

'You are drunk again,' I said in horror. 'You have drunk that whole bottle of gin.'

'Drunk, but happy,' said Tobes. 'If a mite sleepy.'

'Oh . . . my . . . God!' I said.

'What can I do for you?' asked Tobes.

'What do we do?' I asked of Mr Rune. And my hands were starting to flap.

'Keep him conscious,' said Mr Rune, 'while I position the bomb.'

'What bomb?'

Mr Rune unbuttoned his coat and drew it widely open. Within were many sticks of dynamite. 'Forward planning' said the Lad Himself. 'One must be prepared at all times.'

'Plah!' I said, for I had always wanted to say it.

'I shall set the timer for, what shall we say, fifteen minutes?'

'That will be cutting it somewhat fine,' I replied. And, '*Wake Up, Lord Tobes!*' I continued.

'Fifteen minutes should be enough,' said Mr Rune, pulling sticks of dynamite from the lining of his coat and linking fuses together. 'Time enough to leave this vessel, confront Count Otto, destroy the Chronovision and kill the Count.'

'Fifteen minutes will not be long enough for all *that*. And hold on here,' for a terrible thought had just struck me terribly. 'This is a nuclear reactor. If we detonate it, will there not be a nuclear explosion? We could destroy all of Brighton.'

'Tempting, isn't it?' said Mr Rune.

'No, it is not. I love this town.'

'We will not destroy Brighton,' said Mr Rune. 'This sewerage system was built in the days when men knew *how* to build sewerage systems. It will absorb the blast. All will be well.'

'But not at all well for us if we do not get out in time.'

'Have faith,' said Mr Rune. 'Have I ever let you down?'

'Well . . .' I said. But nothing specific came to mind. '*Wake Up, Tobes!*' I shouted once more.

Mr Rune had linked up the dynamite sticks and primed a rather high-tech-looking timer. 'Digital,' he said to me. 'They'll soon be all the rage.'

'Tobes!' I shouted. 'Tobes, we have to be going!'

Tobes awoke with a sober start. 'My but I'm thirsty,' he said.

'We have fifteen minutes,' I told him, 'before the big bomb goes off. We really have to be going.'

'Big bomb?' said Tobes. 'What big bomb?'

'We are blowing up the ark so that Count Otto cannot escape in it. Forward planning, you see,' I said.

'Oh, very good,' said Tobes to me. 'But what about the animals? You're not telling me that you intend to blow up my pussy?'

I paused and waited, but there was no sound.

Not a single small 'Oooh, Matron.'

'The animals!' I cried. 'We cannot blow up the animals!'

'Casualties of war?' said Mr Rune.

'*No!*' I said. 'We have to free the animals.'

And we *did*. And can you imagine how long that took, releasing all those animals?

We must have used up, well, at least three minutes of our precious time.

'I'm having trouble getting these spaniels out of their cage,' said Tobes. 'There just seems to be more and more of them.'

'Out! Out!' cried Mr Rune, shaking his stick at scurrying ferrets and foxes and wolverines.

Getting those polar bears out was not easy, either, but I will not dwell on that.

'They are all out,' I said, 'and I think we should be following them.'

'You're so right,' said Tobes to me. 'What are we waiting for?'

So we left the ark at the hurry-up and hurried-up down the gangplank. Animals were fleeing down the many tunnels. I waved them a little goodbye.

'Now, which of the tunnels did Count Otto go down?' I asked.

'That one,' said Tobes.

'No, that one,' said Mr Rune.

'No, I think it was *that* one,' I said.

'Does it matter,' asked Tobes, 'if the big bomb is going to go off and everything? Does anyone want a sip of this whisky?'

'Where did you get *that*?' I asked.

'From behind the bar when we came up. I got this bottle of vodka, too.'

'I'll take some vodka, please,' said Mr Rune.

'Which damn tunnel is it?' I shouted.

'That one there,' said Tobes. 'I was only joking with you.'

'Are you sure?' I said.

'I'm sure.'

We made for the tunnel, entered and marched along it.

'Do you know,' said Mr Rune to me, 'it's a funny old business, isn't it?'

'I am sure it is,' I said, as I marched. 'What business would this be?'

'Our business here,' said Mr Rune to me. 'Above,' and he pointed upwards with his stick, 'is the rest of the world, folk at home or out at their entertainments, and they know nothing at all of this, of what we are engaged in. To them, the world is a straightforward affair. They know not of our noble deeds.'

'I think that our noble deeds, as you call them, might

have recently had some effect upon their lives,' I suggested, 'such as the West Pier burning down, and I *do* take responsibility for the rioting and mayhem in Hove last month.'

'Such things will soon be forgotten,' said Mr Rune. 'People will go about their daily business. When you publish the book of our deeds, well, then we shall see what we shall see. Will you use your own name on the cover, do you think, or assume a nom de plume?'

I halted my marching and turned upon Mr Rune. 'Sometimes I really do not believe you,' I said. 'Which is to say, you are incredible. For the most part you are completely unmoved by the madness you invoke.'

Mr Rune shrugged and smiled. 'I come from Highland stock,' said he. 'My earliest ancestors were the Rankins of Mainstray. If you do not choose to use your own name, then please use that of my noble ancestor Robert.'

'Quite mad,' said I. 'We have less than ten minutes left, by my reckoning.'

'And just remember,' Mr Rune continued, 'to spell my name correctly and lay great emphasis on my charisma. And if Hollywood does buy the film rights, I would like to be played by Gary Oldman, or Anthony Hopkins, at a push.'

'Can I be played by Sean Connery?' said Tobes. 'Or Ingrid Pitt at a push?'

I shook my head and rolled my eyes. And then I said, 'What is that?'

That lay ahead of us. And there was a lot of *that*.

We crept ourselves forward upon tippy-toes and gazed at the whole lot of *that*.

Before and beneath us lay a wondrous cavern, carved, it seemed, from the living rock, as such caverns so often are. And it was the lair of Count Otto Black and it looked just the way that it should.

There was a great round central plaza there,
With a mosaic floor patterned out as a pentagram,
Computer banks encircled this affair,
And pirates stood, drank rum and dined on Spam.

Floodlights flooded all and round and back,
And at the very centre of this all
Stood the evil one, Count Otto Black,
Lean and mean and long and dark and tall.

The Chronovision rested on a gothic altarpiece,
With lighted candles in a ring around it,
And one of the pirates looked like Charlie Peace,
And I had really stuffed the verse, confound it!

'Well, it was hardly the time for poetry,' said Mr Rune. 'But you gave it your best, although I do have to say that it was probably the worst piece of verse I have ever heard. I recall saying to Byron once, "If you just gave the opium a miss every once in a while, then——"'

I cut Mr Rune off short. 'It was probably just delaying tactics,' I said. 'I know that the end is really near now. I was just trying to put it off for a bit.'

'With the seconds ticking away on the bomb?' said Tobes, taking a big slug of something alcoholic.

'Quite so,' said I. 'So what do we do now?'

'Well.' Mr Rune stroked at one of his chins. 'There are certain traditions that must be observed upon occasions such as these. Certain traditions, or old charters, or somethings.'

'What do you mean?' I asked.

'Well,' said Mr Rune, once more, 'upon such occasions as these, when we look down on the villain beneath, tradition generally dictates that the villain's henchmen, who have crept up upon us unseen, stick guns into the smalls of our backs and make us put up our hands.'

'Yes,' I said. 'Perhaps. But I feel that upon this particular occasion, we might dispense with that. It is a bit of an old cliché, after all.'

I do so agree,' said Hugo Rune.

'Put up your hands!' said Count Otto's henchmen.

PART III

Count Otto Black did not look pleased to see us.

He ceased his ludicrous dance along with his manic laughter and stared at Mr Rune with a look that spoke of horror.

'No!' cried the Count, raising high his hands and composing fists from them. 'Oh no, no, no, this cannot be.'

'Wrong, as ever,' said Hugo Rune. 'Having a little party, are we?' And he glanced, and so did I and so did Tobes as well, towards the tables laden with cakes and sandwiches and lots and lots of booze.

'Hm,' went Tobes, gazing longingly at the latter.

'No!' shouted Count Otto. 'No, I mean, yes, I mean, what are you doing alive?'

'Just visiting,' said Hugo Rune. 'I am here in the cause of justice. Ultimate justice, that is.'

Count Otto Black made a very fierce face. 'Kill them all,' he told his pirate crew.

The pirate crew made menacing motions, but none pulled a trigger, nor got stuck in with a cutlass.

'They don't seem too keen,' said Mr Rune. 'Perhaps you would care to engage me in armed combat – one to one, as it were. Naturally, I will offer you the choice of weapons.'

'Give me your gun,' Count Otto told the nearest gun-totin' pirate. 'I will execute these dogs myself.'

'That ain't fair,' said the gun-totin' one. 'Admiral Hugo is a decent enough cove. A proper gentleman, he is. You should fight him like a man.'

'Bravo there,' said Mr Rune. 'And your name is?'

'Dave,' said the pirate. 'You remember me, I used to be a pop star but I fell upon hard times and was reduced to running a hot-dog van on the seafront.'

'Ah, yes,' said Mr Rune.

'Ahem,' said I and I made motions to where my wrist-watch would have been had I been wearing one, which I was not. So to speak.

'Ah, yes,' said Mr Rune. 'Quite so. I would urge, with some degree of urgency, that all present, with the exception of the Count, take at once to their heels and flee.'

'What is *this*?' cried Count Otto, struggling to wrest the pistol from the gun-totin' pirate, but without success.

'Mister Rune has placed a bomb on board your ark,' I explained. 'It will be going off with a very big bang indeed in a very short time from now.'

'My ark?' The Count ceased his fruitless wresting and gaped in further horror at Mr Rune. 'A bomb aboard my ark?'

Mr Rune nodded. 'A *big* bomb,' he said.

'But my animals. My spaniels.'

'We set them all free,' said Tobes. 'We set the squirrels free first. And you know what squirrels are, open locks with no trouble at all. Could I have a sip of that champagne, by the way? It's a Mulholland eighteen fifty-one, isn't it?'

'Bomb!' went Count Otto, rocking on his heels. 'Bomb!'

'Bomb?' went the pirates, looking towards each other before, as if at a silent command – which argued strongly for the existence of telepathy – taking to their collective boot-heels and fleeing away at speed.

'Well,' said Mr Rune, 'your crew have deserted you, Otto. Choice of weapons, or just fisticuffs?'

'I think we should be running also,' I said.

'Go ahead, then,' said Mr Rune. 'I will join you shortly.'

'But the bomb . . .'

And then there was a great big bang and a very big cloud of smoke.

I ducked and Tobes ducked, though Tobes ducked with a bottle in his hand.

But Mr Rune did not duck at all. Mr Rune just stood there defiantly.

Because the bang had not been the bomb. The bang had been Count Otto. And as the smoke cleared, it became clear that Count Otto Black had cleared off. Clearly.

'A neat trick,' said Mr Rune. 'I confess that I should have seen it coming.'

377

'He vanished,' I said, 'and he took the Chronovision.'

Tobes took a large quaff of champagne. 'We'd better vanish, too,' he said. 'By my calculations, which are based not, I hesitate to say, on chronological indicators, but what is in all probability divine intuition, I would say that we have less than thirty seconds in which to make our escape before the bomb goes off. No, make that twenty, no fifteen. I mean . . .'

I looked at Mr Rune.

And Mr Rune took out his reinvented ocarina.

'This is no time to play us a tune,' I said. 'The bomb is about to go . . .'

'. . . boom!' I said. And I said this in the dark. Which might have meant that I was dead. But happily it did not.

'Boom,' I said once more. 'Hello, where am I? Is anybody there?'

Flame suddenly welled from a cigar lighter and I viewed the smiling face of Hugo Rune. And also that of Tobes de Valois, but Tobes was not smiling at all.

'We are alive,' I observed. 'But where are we?'

'Upon the trail of Count Otto,' said Mr Rune, 'and once more within the Forbidden Zones.'

'Then his vanishing act—'

'Precisely.'

'Precisely what?' asked Tobes. 'I all but wet myself. Though I managed to hang on to this champagne.'

By the lighter's glow, Mr Rune took this bottle and emptied its contents down his throat. 'Forward, gentlemen,' said he, 'and follow me.'

'Precisely what?' said Tobes once more. 'Explain this to me, please.'

'Do you know where he is heading?' I asked Mr Rune.

'I have my suspicions,' said the All-Knowing One. 'I feel that what you are about to see might well surprise you.'

And Mr Rune snuffed out his lighter and we stood in the dark.

'And what precisely is *that*?' asked Tobes.

'I have seen many surprising things since I made my acquaintance with you,' I said to Mr Rune, 'but to be honest, I do not find darkness sufficiently surprising as to be worthy of any particular note.'

'Plah!' said Mr Rune. 'Look ahead there, in the distance.'

And so I looked and slowly beheld the light at the end of the tunnel. It was quite a dim light, but there was the promise of brightness about it.

'Move towards the light,' said Mr Rune, and Tobes and I did so, in his company.

We reached the end of the corridor and then we looked and further beheld. And what we looked at and further beheld was truly wonderful.

'It is a city,' I whispered to Mr Rune. 'A subterranean city.'

And such a city it was. A mighty city, a vast and awesome city. Seemingly, too, a Victorian city, but unlike any other on the face of the Earth. But then this city was *not* upon the face of the Earth; it was deep beneath it.

The buildings were of the style known as Victorian gothic, but they were vast, rising like countless cathedrals, all carved terracotta and gargoyles and fiddly bits. And between these incredible structures and rising above their lofty pinnacles rose slim metal towers topped by shining spheres, about which twinkled electrical sparks.

'Tesla Towers,' said Mr Rune. 'The lost technology of the Victorian age. They transmit electricity upon a radio wave – the wireless transmission of energy. And see there,' and he pointed upwards, 'electrical airships, flying hansom cabs.'

'People,' I said. 'There are people down here. An entire lost civilisation.'

'The lost civilisation of Atlantis,' said Mr Rune. 'Mister Isambard Kingdom-Come was not incorrect regarding its location.'

'Oh no!' I said. 'Look there,' and I pointed.

'That is a flying saucer,' said Tobes. 'I have surely died and gone to the bad place. Which is rather disappointing, really, considering who I am.'

'You are *not* dead,' said Mr Rune. 'And those *are* flying saucers. I told you, Rizla, Mankind has been commuting between the planets and communicating with other off-world civilisations for years.'

'But how?' I asked. 'How can all this be here? And how come no one above knows about it?'

'There are those who know,' said Mr Rune. 'Those at the Ministry of Serendipity. Those in the places of power.'

'Well,' I said. 'I am stunned. I do not know what to say. But we will never find Count Otto here – he could be anywhere.'

Mr Rune tapped at his nose. 'We'll find him,' he said and

he took something from his pocket. Something small and furry. 'We'll find him with the aid of this.'

'And what is *that*?' I asked.

'A spaniel,' said Tobes. 'It's a tiny spaniel.'

'Oh yes,' I said. 'So it is.'

'I kept it back when we freed all the other animals from Count Otto's ark,' Mr Rune explained. 'It's a homing spaniel. It will lead us to Count Otto.'

'Ludicrous,' I said.

'I'm so glad you approve.' Mr Rune placed the tiny spaniel on the ground before us. 'Go on, Nathaniel, go and find your master,' he said, and gave the tiny spaniel a little encouragement with the toe of his black leather boot.

'Hold on,' I said. 'Nathaniel the spaniel?'

'Let's be moving along, Rizla,' said Mr Rune. 'This is not the time for idle chitchat.'

And so we followed Nathaniel. We followed him on to a spiral staircase that measured our footsteps down and down to the city beneath. It was a long walk down and by the time we had reached the bottom I was very dizzy.

'Pacey-pacey, Rizla,' said Mr Rune, marching onwards. 'The knotted condom of self-congratulation may well be—'

'Please do not,' I said. 'I will pacey-pacey as best I can. Oh, look, Nathaniel seems to know the way.'

Now, if from our vantage point above the city had looked vast and tall, from below, where we now followed the spaniel across a broad marble plaza, it looked vaster and taller and very daunting indeed.

'Mister Rune,' I said, as I caught up with the Big Figure, marching along, 'Mister Rune, I am somewhat concerned. The folk of this city might not extend us a hearty welcome. In fact, they might see fit to arrest us as undesirable aliens. Even to shoot us on sight.'

'Fear not, Rizla,' said Mr Rune. 'Follow the spaniel, all will be well.'

'Are Atlanteans teetotal?' asked Tobes. 'Or is there likely to be a bar nearby?'

'A bar,' said Mr Rune. 'Or possibly a restaurant.' And his eyes sparkled as he said the word.

'Let us just find the Count,' I said, 'then go home to bed, eh?'

'Spirit of adventure deserted you?' Mr Rune asked.

'This is a lot to take in,' I said, 'and it has been a long and trying day.'

'And it is far from over. Aha, Nathaniel has stopped and is doing that annoying whining that dogs do at doors. This must be the building we seek.'

We stood before a building of formidable size and structure that had a certain Hollywood feel to me. But then, what did *I* know?

'Where *are* all the Atlanteans?' Tobes asked. 'The streets are deserted. Oh no – there's someone, a lady in a straw hat. And who's that there – surely it's the masked walker. And there—'

'This way,' said Mr Rune and he pushed upon a door, which opened before him.

I shrugged at Tobes and Tobes shrugged at me. Nathaniel scurried between our legs and rushed on ahead of us both.

Tobes took stock of our present location and made approving sounds. 'Oh yes indeed,' said he. 'We are in a bar.'

And yes indeed that is where we were. In a subterranean bar. It looked very much how a bar should look, which is not how most of them do. It was of the Victorian ilk, with Britannia pub tables, much etched glass, a really snazzily patterned carpet and lots of framed portraits of folk that I did not know.

Mr Rune approached the counter, which was all brass foot rails and mahogany top. There were copper spittoons as well, and I thought that I might just have a spit in one if the opportunity arose.

Behind the counter stood a barman all done up in Victorian garb. He wore a high starched collar with a blue silk cravat, a suit of dark stuff and much in the way of mutton-chop whiskers. And a smile.

'How might I serve you, gentlemen?' he asked.

'Fange,' I said, as I gaped at the barman. 'Fangio, it is you.'

'It *is*,' said the barlord. 'And it is you also.'

'But what are *you* doing *here*?'

'I saw this ad in a newspaper,' said Fange, 'the *Weekly World News* – "Experienced bar staff required to serve in alternative reality. Ability to talk toot essential." Well, I thought, I'll have *that*, because, after all, my bar in Hove *had* been destroyed in all the looting that went on last month. I wonder who started all that chaos, eh?'

I did clearings of the throat. 'Search me,' I said.

'Why?' asked Fange. 'What are you hiding?'

'I am not hiding anything.'

'I am,' said the barlord. 'Can you guess what it is?'

'I'll have to stop you there,' said Mr Rune. 'This, I regret, is not the time for toot.'

'Aw,' said Fange.

'Aw,' said I also.

'We'll just have some drinks, if we may,' said Mr Rune. Firmly.

A broad smile crossed Fangio's face. 'Right,' said he. 'Drinks, is it? Well, we have a number here upon the hand pumps that you might not have tried before. Would you care for me to recommend something?'

I winked at Fangio. 'Go for it, Fange,' I said.

'Three whiskies,' said Mr Rune, 'from that bottle there behind the bar.'

'Aw,' said Fange.

And, 'Aw,' said I also.

'And I'll have a large one,' said Tobes, who knew nothing of toot.

Fangio took up three glasses and placed them on the counter, took down the bottle and poured out the whiskies.

'This reminds me of a funny story I heard,' he said. 'Would you care for me to relate it to you?'

'Yes I would,' I said.

'No we wouldn't,' said Mr Rune.

'Aw, come on,' said Fangio, 'this might well be my last appearance in this epic adventure. At least let me talk the last bit of toot.'

'No,' said Mr Rune, and he took up his glass.

'Look out behind you!' cried Fange. 'Zulus, thousands of them.'

Mr Rune shook his head.

'I could call you a cab,' said Fangio.

Mr Rune shook his head once more.

'I know where Count Otto Black is,' said Fangio.

'There,' said Mr Rune. 'At last.'

'What a villain, that bloke,' said Fangio. 'Puts me in mind of that Brownfinger in the James Bond movie.'

I opened my mouth, but Mr Rune made me shut it again.

'No takers, then?' said Fangio. 'I can get at least two pages out of getting the names of supervillains wrong. Some are quite saucy and prompt the occasional, "Oooh, Matron."'

Mr Rune finished his whisky. '*Where* is Count Otto Black?' he asked.

'Upstairs,' said Fange, 'top floor – he has the penthouse suite.'

'Thank you,' said Mr Rune. 'Follow me, gentlemen.'

'Can I come, too?' asked Fange.

'No, you cannot. Which way to the lift?'

'Through that door, you spoilsport.'

The lift was Art Deco style, big and full of polished brass, with spreading fanshaped design work and tortoiseshell floor buttons. Mr Rune pressed the one marked 'Eagle's Nest' and the stylish lift sped upwards.

'We are now on the Count's home turf, as it were,' said Mr Rune. 'Be on your guard at all times and put your trust in me.'

'*I* could have waited in the bar,' said Tobes.

'You could have,' Mr Rune agreed, 'but I feel that your gifts may need to be called upon.'

'I don't have any gifts,' said Tobes. 'I was given a spaniel once, for Christmas, but it ran under a bus.'

'Was it a Brighton bus, with a local celebrity's name on the front?' I asked.

Mr Rune made tooth-grinding sounds.

The lift came suddenly to a halt and Mr Rune's podgy fingers took a firm grip upon the pommel of his stout stick.

The doors slowly opened and we peered out. At the penthouse suite of Count Otto Black.

It was a magnificent suite, extravagantly appointed with many an expensive-looking doodad. Leather-bound volumes bricked its walls and brass contraptions littered the horizontal surfaces of exquisite tables.

'*My* books,' said Mr Rune. '*My* scientific equipment. *My* tables.'

'It looks as if he helped himself before he burned down our rooms,' I observed.

'The pungent turd,' said Mr Rune. Which I found quite amusing.

'Where do you think he's hiding?' asked Tobes.

'I doubt if he is hiding at all,' I said. 'He will not be expecting us.'

Mr Rune shook his head slowly. 'He *will* be expecting us,' he said. 'He knows that I can gain entry to the Forbidden Zones. However, I remain puzzled on one matter: he has access to this realm, but he could not find the entrance point to the place where the Chronovision was hidden.'

'He is not the Reinventor of the Ocarina,' I said. 'Are you not Mister Hugo Rune, whose eye is before E, except after C? Rune, whose navel knows the secrets of the ancients? Rune, whose bum is the square of the hypotenuse? Rune, whose—'

'That is quite enough, thank you, Rizla,' said Mr Rune. 'Now be on your guard and follow me, this way.'

Before us hung a magnificent pair of doors, tall and wide and heavily laden with ornamentation. I liked not the look of those doors, though, for the carvings upon them were of tortured souls being bothered by horrible demons.

'Suggestive,' said Mr Rune.

'Plah!' was the best I could manage.

Mr Rune put his great hands to the doors and pushed the blighters open.

Beyond lay a wonderful room, black-carpeted and lit by massive *torchéres*. And there was a desk resembling a marble sarcophagus. And behind this desk was Count Otto Black.

He sat there on a gilded throne, stroking Nathaniel the spaniel.

And he smiled a wan smile in our direction.

And then all Hell broke loose.

PART IV

They came at us from everywhere and horrible they were. Nasty, spiny, evil things as black as the Bottomless Pit. They closed in about us and I closed my eyes and my hands began to flap. The smell of death was up my nose and Hell was in my ears. I tried to scream, but no sounds came, so I turned in small circles instead.

And then something smacked me right in the head.

'Rizla, stop doing *that*!'

I rubbed at my head and opened my eyes. The hideous things were gone.

'You will have to do better than that, Count Otto,' said Mr Rune. 'An elementary calling, voided by a simple counter-spell.'

The Count made a bitter face behind his desk.

'Magic,' I said to Mr Rune. 'And you—'

'I am a Master of the Mystic Arts,' said Mr Rune, 'and enough is enough.' And he strode to the desk of Count Otto and brought his stout stick down hard upon it. 'Return the Chronovision to me,' he demanded, 'and I will spare your life.'

The Count looked at Mr Rune and then the Count

laughed. 'Spare *my* life?' he said. 'You are in *my* world now, Mister Rune, it is *you* who must beg for *your* life.'

'Such histrionics,' said Mr Rune. 'Such bluff and bluster.'

The Count's hand strayed to a button that rose from his marble desk. It was a blood-red button. The Count's finger hovered above it.

'One little tap,' said Count Otto, 'and you will be despatched to your grave.'

'Hm,' went Mr Rune and in a flash, he had drawn from his stout stick a glittering blade that he held to Count Otto's throat. 'Then the two of us will die,' he said, 'and Rizla here will dispose of the Chronovision.'

The Count's finger continued its hovering. 'Thus and so,' said he. 'But why must we persist in this? Answer me truly, Hugo Rune, are we not made of special stuff, you and I? Are we not men above the faceless hordes of humankind? We are remarkable men, and together we could achieve remarkable things, extraordinary things.'

'What are you suggesting?' Mr Rune's blade twinkled at Count Otto's throat, its tip deep in amongst the great black beard.

'An alliance, plain and simple. We are men of learning, men of great esoteric knowledge. Each of us seeks recognition for our unique talent. You crave fame, I crave infamy. Together we could aspire to a middle ground that would benefit us both. Together we could have it all.'

'The world?' said Hugo Rune.

'Who could stand against us? With the aid of the Chronovision we could gain control of everything. We could create an Earthly paradise, a new Eden.'

'You and I?' said Mr Rune. 'You are suggesting that *I* should trust *you*?'

'We would swear an oath, a magical oath stating that neither would seek to deceive or destroy the other. Think of it, Hugo – you and I united, benign rulers of the world above. Better surely this than that we go on from age to age as antagonists?'

'Well,' said Mr Rune.

'No!' I shouted. 'No!'

'A noisy boy,' said Count Otto, 'but we could find a place for him. Perhaps he might like to be Prime Minister of England?'

'What?' I said.

'He *is* a good boy,' said Mr Rune. 'He'd make a good Prime Minister.'

'*What?*' I said again, but with greater emphasis.

'And the other chap,' said Count Otto, 'he is the One, I assume. Perhaps he would like to be Pope?'

'Is there a bar in the Vatican?' asked Tobes.

'Stop it,' I said. 'And you stop it, too, Mister Rune. You cannot side with this, this—'

'Pungent turd?' said Tobes.

'Pungent turd,' I said. 'Remember the vision we had in Chief Whitehawk's tepee. You do not want that to come true, surely?'

'As Lord Tobes said,' said Mr Rune, 'a premonition cannot be a premonition if that which occurs in it does not come to pass. Perhaps it would be for the best if the Count and I forgot our differences and worked together for the good of all.'

'No,' I said. 'Do not do it. You cannot trust him. You must not side with him.'

'Think of it, Hugo,' said the Count, 'think what you could do for Mankind if you were in control of it. You could end all wars, all suffering. And you know how to do it, don't you? You are the All-Knowing One. You wrote *The Book of Ultimate Truths.*'

'An alliance,' said Mr Rune. 'A magical oath. Complete and utter trust between us?'

'Absolutely,' said the Count. 'We will draw up a contract and sign it with our blood, and together we will set the world above to rights.'

Mr Rune nodded thoughtfully.

'No,' I said. 'Do not do it. Do not trust him. It is just a trick.'

'Silence, Rizla,' said Mr Rune. 'I cogitate, don't interrupt.'

'Tell him, Lord Tobes,' I said to Lord Tobes. 'Tell him, Lord Tobes – do something.'

'I'm for peace, me,' said Tobes. 'If these two fellows can make it up and be friends, well, I think that's very nice. And we should all have a drink to celebrate.'

'This is wrong,' I said. 'All wrong.'

'Perhaps it isn't,' said Tobes. 'It was in my vision, after all. Perhaps it was a good vision, not like all the others.'

'No,' I said. 'It is not right.'

'Imagine, Hugo,' the Count continued, 'your *Book of Ultimate Truths* upon every bedside table of every home in the world. The *Third Testament*, as it were. The recognition you so justly deserve. With myself at your side, what companionship we would enjoy, what amazing things might we achieve.'

'If trust were to exist between us,' said Mr Rune.

'Which it does,' said Count Otto. 'Does it not?'

Mr Rune eyed Count Otto Black. 'The button,' he said.

'The blade,' said Count Otto Black.

Mr Rune drew back his blade and sheathed it in his stick. 'Trust,' said he.

'You schmuck!' cried Black and his finger hit the button.

The floor beneath Mr Rune dropped away and the Perfect Master plunged down. Smoke and flames belched up from below and a terrible scream belched with them.

And Count Otto Black placed his spaniel down and clapped his hands together.

'No!' I shouted. 'No, no, no!'

'Yes, yes, yes,' said Count Otto. 'And now farewell to you.' And his fingers reached once more to the button and my hands started to flap.

'Do something!' I shouted at Tobes. 'And do it now, or he'll do for the both of us.'

But the Count laughed his laugh and his finger plunged down and the floor beneath us fell away.

★

But we did not fall. We hovered there. Hovered in thin air.

Smoke and flames roared round us. But the fire did not hurt and the smoke did not make me cough. I looked down in wonder at my floating feet and then across at the Count, who had suddenly ceased his laughing.

And then I saw him, Hugo Rune, rising from the flaming pit below. Up and up he came, like a leather-bound blimp, until he, too, did hovering above the marble desk of Count Otto Black.

And Mr Rune shook his head and said, 'You really are a very wicked man, Count Otto. I feel that there is no hope for you.'

And then Mr Rune drew the blade from his stick and cleaved off Count Otto's head.

'He never did?' said Fangio. 'In a single stroke, like a Samurai?'

We were back in the bar once more and we were drinking hugely.

'Swish,' I said. And I mimed swishing. 'And blood came shooting out of the Count's neck and everything.'

'Urgh!' said Fangio. 'I think that would have made me sick.'

'It made *me* sick,' I said, 'but it was a good kind of sick.'

'It didn't make me sick,' said Tobes. 'But then I never get sick. A waste of good drink, sick is.'

'So you really have mastered the art of levitation, Mister Rune,' said Fangio. 'Taught to you by your chum the Dalai Lama, I suppose.'

Mr Rune made a certain face and then he shook his head.

'No?' I said. 'Then how?'

'You'd better ask Lord Tobes.'

I looked towards the great-many-times-descendant of Lord Jesus Christ. 'Tobes?' I said. 'What is this?'

Tobes shrugged and tried to look humble. 'I could hear what Mister Rune was thinking,' he said, 'and Mister Rune knew that I could. He wasn't going along with Count Otto's nonsense; he was only waiting to make his move.

And he was praying that I would offer him my support when he did so. Which I suppose I did.'

'That was a great deal of trust on your part,' I said to Mr Rune. 'What if Tobes had not been able to help?'

'Naturally, I had a back-up plan.'

'Did you?' I asked.

'No,' said Mr Rune. 'I did not.'

'And what about this Chronovision thing?' asked Fangio. 'You said that your quest was all about that, all the cases and conundrums of the Brightonomicon.'

'Rizla smashed it to pieces,' said Mr Rune.

'I did,' I said. 'Count Otto had it under his desk. It was a bit gory, but I gave it the rock 'n' roll ending it deserved and threw it out of the window.'

'Then the world as we know it is saved,' said Fangio. 'The next round is on me.'

And we enjoyed the next round.

And the next.

Which I am sure was Hugo Rune's, but Hugo Rune did not pay.

PART V

At a little after ten-thirty of the Friday-evening clock, Mr Hugo Rune, Lord Tobes and I returned to the world above. We pushed open the manhole cover in the middle of the Pavilion lawns and struggled up through the opening.

We were a little gone with the drink and we each stood there a-swaying. I gulped in the Brighton breeze, clicked my joints and gazed all around and about myself. We were less than twenty yards from the front door of what had once been forty-nine Grand Parade, my home for almost a year, now nothing but a blackened, gutted shell. I shook my head and shrugged.

And, 'Well,' I said, when I could find sufficient breath. 'I can not believe it is all over. It seemed so sudden. And now it is done.'

'Did it lack for excitement?' asked Mr Rune. 'Would you have preferred more explosions? Or perhaps a final roof-top showdown involving a guest appearance from Lazlo Woodbine?'

'It did cross my mind,' I said, 'but the excitement was sufficient.'

'You will find,' said Mr Rune, 'and you may quote me on this, that truth is more of a stranger than fiction.'

'Right,' I said. 'But tell me this: I know I saw Count Otto die, and horrible it was to see, but, is he *really* dead?'

Hugo Rune grinned down upon me. 'He's dead for now,' he said.

'For *now*?' I took to dusting myself down. I was somewhat besmirched from all the sewer-pipe climbing.

'Time,' said Mr Rune, 'all this has been to do with time, as I have told you before. And for the time being, we can consider the Count to be no more.'

'For the time being?' I did further dustings down. And I was still rather wobbly on my pins.

'Consider it to be a game of chess,' said Mr Rune. Who did not seem at all besmirched, or even wobbly now, and was clearly in the very best of spirits. 'Checkmate and the game is over. But the players remain and so do the pieces, to be replaced upon the board for future games.'

'And that is how it is for you and Count Otto?'

'In a manner of speaking, yes. The Chronovision is destroyed. This game is over. But there will be other games in other times.'

'And will I play in these games?'

'No, young Rizla.' And Hugo Rune patted my shoulder. 'You have played your part, and loyally, too. But now you must return to your own life. You will have adventures of your own to engage in. Great adventures, be assured of that.'

'But I still do not know who I am. And if truth be told, I think I would rather just stay here with you.'

'That cannot be,' and Mr Rune shook his great bald head. 'Tonight you return to your own life. Oh, and in some far and distant future time, when the time is right and you take up your pen and record your adventures with me, do make sure that you spell my name correctly.'

'Yes,' I said. 'But no, I do not want to go.'

'But nevertheless you must.'

'And so must I,' said Lord Tobes, 'to that pub over there. Will either of you join me for a pint?'

'I will,' said Mr Rune, 'but later.'

'I will *now*,' said I.

'No.' Mr Rune held up his hand. The one with the stout stick in it. 'You have done enough. It is time to say farewell.'

'Well, if that's how it is,' said Tobes, 'I suppose it's farewell.' And he put out his hand to me and I shook it. 'And you certainly *do* have some adventures coming up,' he continued. 'I was just having a bit of a standing nap there, and you'll never believe what happens to you. You see, there's you and this Irish bloke and you walk into a pub and—'

'No,' said Mr Rune, and he waggled his stick at Lord Tobes.

'Then ta ta for now, then,' said Tobes. 'And I'll see you in the pub Mister Rune. If I'm sleeping, give me a wake up.'

And with that, Tobes departed into the Brighton night.

'Do I *really* have to go?' I whinged at Mr Rune.

'You do, my boy, you do. And see, here we are at the East Street cab rank. We will take a taxi to your point of departure.'

'I think I would rather walk,' I said.

'Not a bit of it.'

There was no queue for the cabs and ten stood all in a row awaiting fares. The cabbies leaned upon the foremost vehicle, smoking cigarettes and talking about football.

Mr Rune rapped his stout stick on the bonnet of this foremost cab. 'Shop!' cried he. 'Important persons requiring transportation.'

The cabbies looked up from their discussion, took

in Mr Rune and me and then looked back towards one another.

And then, 'It's 'im,' said a cabbie called Jonie, who favoured a team called Newcastle United. 'That's the blighter what struck me unconscious in Hangleton and nicked my cab.'

'Damn right!' said a cabbie that I recognised to be Dave, who was the Brighton Seagulls supporter whom Mr Rune had clubbed down during the Curious Case of the Centenary Centaur. 'I recognise that nutter and his stout stick.'

'And he done me and nicked my cab in Woodingdean,' said a cabbie called Colin, who was known for his love of West Bromwich Albion.

And I also noticed Darren, whom Mr Rune and I had encountered during the Sensational Affair of the Sackville Scavenger. He supported Hull, I recalled. And also Ralph, the Chelsea FC supporter.

'I think perhaps we *should* walk,' I said to Mr Rune. 'Or perhaps *run*, which might be quicker.'

'He didn't hit *me*,' said a cabbie called Salvador de Allende Fernandes Mal de Mer, an ardent supporter of the Benedictine Bears, if my memory served me well. 'But as I, like you, my brothers, am a member of BOLLOCK, the secret cabal of cabbies, I will join you in thrashing these scoundrels.'

Mr Rune sighed deeply. 'It pains me to say it,' he said, 'but running would perhaps be the best option.'

And off he went at the hurry-up.

And off went I in pursuit.

And after us came the cabbies, in the manner of a lynch mob of old. All they lacked for were burning torches.

Mr Rune's *lung-gom* leaping carried him at considerable speed along the length of East Street, across Grand Junction Road and on to the promenade. I rushed after him as best I could. The cabbies followed with vigour and in swelling numbers, too, it seemed, as I glanced over my shoulder.

I thought I saw Sean O'Reilly, the Arsenal supporter who had been struck down during the Baffling Business of the Bevendean Bat. And also Andy, who favoured Brentford United, who had 'got his', as it were, whilst Mr Rune and I were applying ourselves to the case of the Birdman of Whitehawk.

Mr Rune had by now reached the Palace Pier and was leaping his way along it. And I ran too with a spring in my step, as cabs on Grand Junction Road swerved to a halt and other cabbies sprang from them.

On to the pier and along it I ran.

And that thought came to me once again.

Piers only go from the land to the sea.

There is no escape to be had at the end of them.

Although in truth, there had been the last time, with *The Saucy Spaniel* and Captain Bartholomew Moulsecoomb. But *this* time? Well, it did not seem too likely.

I ran through the penny arcade and past the gypsy caravan, where a tarot reader named Freda turned cards on a gate-legged table. And on and on and panting now, and after Hugo Rune.

Until finally . . .

I was at the very end of the pier.

And there stood Hugo Rune.

I puffed and panted and gagged and gasped. 'We are trapped,' I managed to say.

'We're here,' said Mr Rune, without so much as a puff.

'I know,' I said. 'Now what are we going to do?'

I heard the cries of approaching cabbies. They had ceased to run, because they must have realised that we were trapped.

I glanced back and beheld them: a truly menacing crowd advancing at a slow and even pace.

'I said,' said Mr Rune, 'that we are here. At our destination. Your point of departure. And the exercise did us good and sobered us up and we saved ourselves the cost of a cab. In a manner of speaking.'

'We . . . are . . . trapped!' I cried between puffings.

'Never say die,' said Mr Rune. 'But now, I regret that we must say farewell.'

'What?' I went. 'What?'

'Farewell,' said Mr Rune, and he shook me by the hand. 'And thank you, Rizla, for everything.'

And with that said, and no more, he lifted me bodily with a single hand, swung me out over the railings and dropped me into the sea.

'No!' I went. 'Ooooooooh noooooooo!'

And then I hit the water. That cold, cold water.

And the last thing that I saw was Mr Rune saluting my departure and then setting about the cabbies with his stout stick.

And then the cold waters closed above my head.

And that was that for me.

PART VI

And then I awoke with a cough and a croak in a rather cosy bed.

I did blinkings and gaspings and gaggings and chokings, and then I did lookings around.

'Where am I?' I asked. 'And how did I get here?'

A smiling face smiled down upon me. It was a smiling face I knew. 'You are in Brentford Cottage Hospital,' it said.

'Omally,' I said to this smiling face, this bright and smiling teenaged face. 'John Omally, it is you.'

'And it's yourself, too, Jim Pooley, you silly bugger.'

'Yes,' I said. And I drew in breath. 'Jim Pooley, that is me. I am Jim.'

'You're Jim, all right,' said John and he patted me upon the shoulder. 'And I can't take my eyes off you for an evening, can I?'

'Can you not?' I asked. 'Can I have a glass of water?' I continued.

'I'd have thought you'd had enough of water.' John

decanted a glass from the jug upon the bedside table, helped me into a seated position, which involved some plumpings-up of pillows, and handed me the glass. 'If I hadn't misplaced those tickets to see The Who,' said John to me, 'that Enid Earles would never have gone down to Brighton with *you*.'

'Enid Earles,' I said. 'Yes, I remember.'

'And what happened to her?'

'She played me false, John,' I said. 'But no, wait. What of Mr Rune? Is Mr Rune all right?'

'Mister Rune? And who would this Mister Rune be?'

'Hugo Rune,' I said, 'the Perfect Master, the Cosmic Dick, the Hokus Bloke himself. He reinvented the ocarina, you know.'

'Never heard of the fellow,' said John. 'How is the water?'

'It tastes like—'

'It is,' said John. 'It's vodka.'

'Well, thank you very much.'

'You had me worried there.' John patted my shoulder once again. 'You're my bestest friend. I wouldn't want anything to happen to you. You need me to protect you. One night away and you're—'

'One *night*?' I said. 'Pour me another of these, if you will.'

'I will *not*,' said John. 'You are still clearly in your cups. Did you fall off the pier in your drunkenness? Was that it?'

'Er, yes,' said I. 'That was it. But that was a year ago, John, when it happened the first time. When I went down to Brighton with Enid Earles. You will not believe the adventures I have had since then. But they are all true, believe me.'

'Jim,' said John to me, 'Jim,' and there was a *certain tone* to his voice. 'Jim, you have been away for a single night. No more, no less. You left for Brighton yesterday, which was Friday, Saint Valentine's Day and you have been returned to Brentford in an ambulance *today*, which is *Saturday*. Not a *year*, Jim, a single day. That is all.'

'No,' I said. 'It cannot be. I was gone for a whole year.

Where are my clothes? You will see. Boleskine tweed – Mr Rune acquired them for me.'

'There is no Rune,' said John. 'And no tweeds, Boleskin or otherwise – you were in your undies when they pulled you ashore, the tidal currents had your kit off.'

'No,' I said. 'No.'

'Yes,' said John. 'Yes.'

'But I was there with him. I had adventures, incredible adventures, for an entire year. The Brighton Zodiac. The Brightonomicon. Count Otto Black.'

John Omally shook his head. 'Delirium, Jim. Dreams. You went yesterday, you're back today. Between you and me,' and John did 'talkings from behind his hand', 'I'd let this one drop if I were you, or you might end up in the psychiatric ward for a prolonged stay.'

'But I—'

John mimed the wearing of a straitjacket.

And very well he mimed it too.

And then he took my glass from me, poured further vodka into it and drank it himself.

'Just a single day?' I said.

'You can check the calendar if you want.'

'Just a single day, really?'

'And a single day was quite enough for you. Next time you plan a weekend in Brighton, I'm coming with you.'

'I will not go there again,' I said. 'Ever.'

'Good man,' said John. 'Now, do you think you can find your feet?'

'They are at the end of my legs.'

'Do you think you could persuade them to leave your bed and accompany me down to The Flying Swan for a lunchtime drink?'

'I am a sick man,' I said. 'I am not well.'

'The first round will be on me, to toast your safe return. And the second also – how's that?'

'I do not have any clothes,' I said.

'I've brought you some of mine,' said John. 'Well, not actually mine, they were the daddy's. And they're tweeds, as it happens. Get yourself togged up and I'll meet you out-side.'

And with that John departed.

And I lay back in my hospital bed.

'It was all a dream,' I said to myself. 'Well, *that* is an original end to an adventure, if ever there was one. You wake up and find that it was all a dream. Well, Mister Rune, my dreamtime companion, if I ever *do* write the book of our adventures together, I will know how to end it, with a twist in the tail that no one will be expecting – that it was all a dream.'

And with that I rose from my bed and got dressed and left the cottage hospital.

And made off with Omally to The Flying Swan.

PART VII

Well, almost. I was almost out of the door.

'And where do you think *you're* going?' asked a very stern voice indeed.

I turned to view the stern-looking face that had uttered these very stern words. It belonged to the matron and she stood with folded arms. A badge upon her breast spelled out her name, Ms Mavis Patron.

'Out for a healthy walk in the park?' I suggested. 'Thought I might have a bit of a jog, too. I am all well and cured now.'

'Oh, well and cured, is it? No more shouts of "Help, Mister Rune, save me"?'

'What?' I asked.

'In your hours of delirium.'

'Ah,' said I. 'Those. I am sorry, I was . . . er . . . delirious, I suppose.'

'And you're all better now then, are you?'

'Could not be better,' I said. 'It was all a dream, you see.'

'All a dream.' The matron said this slowly. Deliberately. 'You are certain of that, are you?'

'Absolutely certain,' I said.

'Absolutely certain?'

'Absolutely.'

The matron nodded, thoughtfully.

'So I will be off,' I said.

The matron nodded slowly and then she smiled. 'Go along, then,' she said. 'And I don't want to see you here again.'

'Nor me,' I said. 'Farewell.'

And I made once more for the door.

And then I paused and turned back to the matron. 'Just one thing, I said, 'before I go.'

'Yes?' said the matron.

'Well, two things, actually,' I said. 'Firstly, thank you for looking after me.'

'That is what we do,' said the matron. 'And secondly?'

'Well, secondly,' I said, 'if I was hauled from the sea, unconscious and wearing nothing but my underwear, how did anyone know who I was and where I lived, so that I could be brought back here to Brentford?'

'You have your uncle to thank for that,' said the matron.

'My uncle?' I said. 'What uncle?'

'I didn't catch his name,' said the matron. 'He was a very large, imposing gentleman, with a long leather coat and a shaven head. And, oh yes, I almost forgot – he said that I was to give you this.'

And the matron delved into her apron pocket and brought out a drawstring bag. She handed this to me and said, 'Just you be careful in the future, James,' and turned away and went about her business.

I weighed the drawstring bag upon my palm.

I gave the drawstring bag a little shake.

The drawstring bag's contents gave a little rattle.

And I knew just what they were.

And so I withdrew the drawstring and emptied the contents into my hand.

And there were twelve little badges.

And I went down to the pub.

Epilogue

And that is it. The end of my tale. I complete this final chapter with those twelve little badges before me on my desk. They are somewhat faded now and rusted, too, but I look upon them with fondness, with recollection of the adventures that I had with Hugo Rune.

I have had other adventures since that magical year. Many adventures. I am proud to say that it was I who helped defeat the reincarnation of Pope Alexander the Sixth who, like Count Otto, sought to rule the world. I also played my part in foiling the invasion plans of aliens from the lost planet Ceres. Oh, and it was me that took the Brentford United football team on to glory in the World Cup during the opening years of the twenty-first century. Yes, I have lived a long and adventurous life.

I never saw Hugo Rune again, nor Tobes de Valois, nor Count Otto Black. But I know they are out there somewhere, doing what they do, being what they are.

And the rest of the world goes on, unknowing, blind to the wonder and the magic.

But it is there, everywhere, every day, if you take a moment out from that world of the ordinary just to breathe it in, to dream a little, to feel that magic and that wonder.

And we go on. Myself, Jim Pooley, my bestest friend John Omally, and Norman Hartnell (not to be confused with the other Norman Hartnell, of course) and Neville the part-time barman. We are here, in Brentford, in our world, a world unchanged by time and unchanging.

Perhaps if you are ever down our way, you will call in at The Flying Swan and join us, down a pint of Large and talk a little toot.

And take time.
To wonder.
And to dream.

Take time.

Farewell.

'Nice work, Rizla.'
'Thank you, Mister Rune.'